Praise for *Castle to Castle*

"Céline's experiences have not mellowed him. Here, as in all his novels, . . . he hates everybody, regardless of race, creed or color. If anyone is singled out, it is his publishers, whose limousines, he says, grow ever longer, while their authors, in rags, cling behind like pitiful hitchhikers. . . . the translation is a masterpiece"—*New York Times Book Review*

"*Castle to Castle* [is] a literary event of the first order."
—*Newsweek*

"*Castle to Castle* proves how appallingly up to date its dead appalling author is. . . . Céline's style consists of outcries and exclamations, groans and curses, all in white heat, separated by dots which like machine-gun bullets mow down even the mitigating orderliness of grammar."—*Nation*

"Céline's mastery in creating one of the truly cathartic experiences of contemporary literature is indisputable."
—*Saturday Review*

"As a literary construction, *Castle to Castle* is . . . a hateful papier-mâché fun-fair castle inhabited by real monsters."
—*Time*

T0165830

**Books by Louis-Ferdinand Céline
in English Translation**

Journey to the End of the Night

Death on the Installment Plan

Mea Culpa *and* The Life and Work of Semmelweis

Guignol's Band

Conversations with Professor Y

Castle to Castle

North

Rigadoon

London Bridge

Castle to Castle

Louis-Ferdinand
Céline

translated by Ralph Manheim

 Dalkey Archive Press

First published in French under the title *D'un Château L'Autre* by Éditions Gallimard
© 1957 by Éditions Gallimard
First published in Ralph Manheim's English translation by Dell Publishing Company, Inc.
English translation © 1968 by Dell Publishing Company, Inc.
Reprinted by arrangement with Dell Publishing

First Dalkey Archive edition, 1997
Second printing, 2007
Third printing, 2011

Céline, Louis-Ferdinand, 1894-1961
  [D'un château l'autre. English]
  Castle to castle / Louis-Ferdinand Céline ; translated by Ralph
Manheim.
        p.   cm.
  I. Manheim, Ralph, 1907- . II. Title.
PQ2607.E834D213 1997 843'.912—dc21 96-51792
ISBN 1-56478-150-X

ISBN 13 978-1-56478-150-5

This publication is partially supported by grants from the Services du Conseiller Culturel,
the National Endowment for the Arts, a federal agency, the Illinois Arts Council, a state
agency, and by the University of Illinois, Urbana-Champaign

www.dalkeyarchive.com

Castle to
Castle

Frankly, just between you and me, I'm ending up even worse than I started . . . Yes, my beginnings weren't so hot . . . I was born, I repeat, in Courbevoie, Seine . . . I'm repeating it for the thousandth time . . . after a great many round trips I'm ending very badly . . . old age, you'll say . . . yes, old age, that's a fact . . . at sixty-three and then some, it's hard to break in again . . . to build up a new practice . . . no matter where . . . I forgot to tell you . . . I'm a doctor . . . A medical practice, confidentially, between you and me, isn't just a question of knowing your job and doing it properly . . . what really counts . . . more than anything else . . . is personal charm . . . personal charm after sixty? . . . there might still be a future for you in the wax works, or as an antique vase in a museum . . . a few old fogies in search of enigmas might still take an interest . . . but the ladies? Your dapper graybeard, painted, perfumed, and lacquered? Doctor or not, practice or no practice, the old scarecrow will stick in people's craw . . . If he's loaded? . . . well, maybe . . . hmm, hmm, . . . he'll be barely tolerated . . . but a white-haired pauper? . . . take him away. Just listen to the ladies, on any street corner, in any shop . . . talking about some young colleague . . . "Oh, Madame, oh, Madame, that doctor, what eyes . . . he understood my case at a glance . . . and those drops he prescribed . . . noon and night . . . those miraculous drops . . . why, that young doctor's a wonder . . ." Then wait and see what they have to say about you: "Crabby, toothless, ignorant, hunchbacked, always hawking and spitting . . ." you're cooked . . . the ladies' chit-chat rules the country . . . the men bat out laws, the ladies attend to the serious business: public opinion . . . or a medical practice is made by the ladies

. . . you haven't got them behind you? . . . go drown yourself . . . the ladies in your neighborhood are feebleminded, they're blithering idiots? . . . perfect! The stupider, the more bigoted, the more chronically asinine they are, the better they rule! . . . you can put your shingle away, and all the rest . . . The rest? Everything was stolen from me in Montmartre . . . everything . . . on the rue Girardon . . . I repeat . . . I can't repeat it enough . . . people pretend not to hear . . . the exact things they need to hear . . . though I've said it plainly enough . . . the works! . . . Somebody, liberators, avengers, broke into my place and carried everything off to the Flea Market . . . they sold it all . . . I'm not exaggerating, I've got proof, witnesses, names . . . all my books and instruments, my furniture, my manuscripts . . . the whole shebang . . . I didn't find one thing . . . not a handkerchief, not a chair . . . they'd sold even the walls . . . the apartment, everything . . . put it in all their pockets . . . and there you have it . . . Oh, I know what you think . . . it's only natural . . . I can hear you . . . that such things can never happen to you, that you've taken your precautions . . . that you're as good a Communist as any millionaire, as good a Poujadist as Poujade, as Russian as the dressing, more American than Buffalo . . . hand in glove with everything that counts, Lodge, Cell, Sacristy, the Law! . . . the champion new-style Vrenchman* . . . the historical trend runs straight through your asshole . . . honorary brother? . . . certainly! . . . executioner's helper? we'll see . . . guillotine licker? . . . Oh, well!

Meanwhile I haven't even got a "Pachon" * . . . I borrowed one to get rid of the pests, there's nothing like it . . . you sit them down, you take their blood pressure . . . They eat too much, drink too much, and smoke too much, so it's unusual when they don't run a maximum of 220 . . . or 230 . . . to them life is a tire . . . the only thing that worries them is their maximum . . . a blowout . . . death! . . . 250! . . . all of a sudden they're not so droll and sceptical anymore . . . you tell them about their 230 . . . and you never see them again! That

* See glossary

look they give you as they leave . . . what hatred! . . .
You're a murderer, a sadist! "Good-bye, good-bye!"

Okay . . . at any rate I take care of them with my Pachon
. . . they'd come to get a laugh out of my poverty . . . 220!
. . . 230! I never see them again . . . all in all, without going
into details, I'd be glad not to practice anymore . . . but I've
got to survive . . . it's hell . . . until the retirement age! Or
maybe . . . but there's no "maybe" about the need to econo-
mize! on everything! and right away! first the heat! . . . never
more than forty degrees all last winter. Of course we're used to
it . . . we've had our training all right . . . Norse training.
We stuck it out up there for four winters . . . nearly five . . .
at twenty below . . . in a wrecked stable . . . without heat,
absolutely without heat, pigs would have died of the cold . . .
take it from me! . . . we're trained! . . . the thatch blew
away . . . the snow and the wind danced in that place! . . .
Five years, five months of ice! . . . Lili sick, she'd been operated . . . and don't take it into your head that that icebox was
free . . . not at all! . . . make no mistake . . . I paid for everything . . . I've got the bills, signed by my lawyer . . . certified by the Consulate . . . which explains why I'm so flat
. . . it wasn't only the pirates of Montmartre . . . there were
the pirates of the Baltic, too . . . the pirates of Montmartre
wanted to bleed me till my guts ran down the rue Lepic . . .
the Baltic pirates thought they'd get me with scurvy . . . so
I'd leave my bones in their "Venstre" prison . . . it was touch
and go . . . two years in a pit . . . seven by ten . . . then
they thought of the cold . . . the blizzards of the Great Belt
. . . we stuck it out! for five years! Paid for, I repeat! my sav-
ings, you can imagine . . . all my royalties . . . blown away
by the blizzards . . . plus the court seizures . . . some joke!
Oh, I'd kind of foreseen it all . . . a faint suspicion! . . . my
suit, my one and only, dates from '34. That was my hunch! I'm
not the Poujade type, I don't discover catastrophes twenty-five
years later, when it's all over, dead and buried! . . . just for a
laugh I'll tell you about my premonition of '34 . . . that we
were headed for times that would be rough on coquetry . . . I
had a tailor on the Avenue de l'Opéra . . . "Make me a suit,

but take care, something really long-wearing . . . Poincaré, supergabardine . . . The Poincaré model!"

Poincaré had just launched the style, that tunic of his, a really special cut . . . I got my money's worth . . . I still have that suit . . . absolutely indestructible . . . as you can see . . . it survived Germany . . . the Germany of 1944 . . . the bombings, and what bombings! . . . and four years . . . when they were making goulash out of people . . . fires, tanks, bombs, and myriatons of wreckage! It's faded a little, that's all! and after that all the prisons . . . and the five years on the Baltic . . . and to begin with, I'd forgotten, the clandestine life in Bezons-la-Rochelle . . . and the shipwreck at Gibraltar! I already had it . . . Nowadays they boast about "nylon" suits, "Grévin" * outfits, atomic kimonos . . . I want to be shown . . . mine is right here, worn, I admit, worn to the weft . . . fourteen years of hard knocks . . . we're worn to the weft ourselves.

I don't try to look picturesque, it's not my way, I don't dress to attract attention . . . painter style . . . Van Dyck, Rembrandt . . . Vlaminck . . . not for me . . . inconspicuous, undistinguished . . . I'm a doctor . . . white smock, imitation nylon . . . neat and proper . . . indoors I look perfectly all right . . . but outside it's not so good with my Poincaré outfit . . . I could buy a new suit . . . of course . . . by scrimping a little more . . . on everything else . . . I hesitate . . . I'm just like my mother . . . thrifty, thrifty! but still I have certain weaknesses . . . My mother died of a heart attack, on a bench, and of hunger too, of privation, I was in prison, in the Vesterfangsel in Denmark . . . I wasn't here when she died, I was in the death house, Section K . . . I was there for eighteen months . . . Nobody's as deaf as the people who refuse to listen . . . don't be afraid of laying it on too thick.

I'll tell you about my mother. In spite of her heart ailment, her exhaustion and hunger and everything else, she died convinced that it was only a bad moment, but that with courage and frugality we'd see the end, that everything would be the same as before, that a sou would be a sou again and a quarter

of a pound of butter would be back at twenty-four centimes
. . . I'm pre-1914, I admit . . . wild spending horrifies me
. . . when I look at the prices, the price of a suit, for instance!
. . . I know it's not for me . . . I say, only a President, a
"Commissar," a Picasso, a Gallimard can afford to buy clothes!
. . . the price of a "Commissar suit" would give me enough
calories to subsist, to work, to look at the Seine, to visit two,
three museums, to pay the telephone bill, for say at least a year
. . . only crazy people buy clothes nowadays . . . potatoes,
carrots, sure . . . noodles, carrots . . . I'm not complaining,
we've seen worse . . . a lot worse . . . and paid for it . . .
don't forget it! . . . all my royalties, the whole *Journey!* . . .
and not only my furniture and my manuscripts . . . everything's been taken from me by main force! . . . not only in
Montmartre and Saint-Malo! . . . south . . . north . . . east
. . . west . . . pirates everywhere! . . . Côte d'Azur or Scan-
dinavia! . . . the same breed . . . No use trying to tell them
apart . . . All they want is to put Article 75* on your ass,
the master permit to skin you alive, to steal everything you've
got, and sell you for stew meat.

Back to my trifling affairs . . . I was talking about menus
. . . As far as I'm concerned, the less I eat, the better off I
am . . . okay . . . but with Lili it's different . . . she has to
eat . . . it gets me down . . . her line of work on our diet!
. . . true, we have certain luxuries: the dogs . . . our dogs
. . . they bark! . . . somebody at the gate? . . . some pest
or murderer? . . . You loose the pack! *Arf! Grrr!* He's
gone . . .

"But," you may ask, "where do you live, proud Artaban?"

"In Bellevue, Monsieur . . . half way up the hill, parish of
Bellevue . . . You get the lay of the land? . . . the Seine valley . . . just above that factory on the island . . . I was born
nearby . . . I'm repeating myself . . . You can never repeat
too much for the stubborn . . . Courbevoie, Seine, Rampe du
Pont . . . Some people can't stand the idea that there should
be people from Courbevoie . . . my age, too, I repeat my age
. . . 1894! . . . I'm repetitious? . . . doddering and repetitious? It's my right . . . People who date from the last century

have a right to repeat themselves . . . and hell, why not! . . . to complain . . . to think that everything is lousy and screwed-up . . . among other things, I don't mind saying, all that gluttonous, thirsty rabble that never stop talking about the Bastille and the Place du Tertre . . . All those people are from God knows where! . . . from Périgord! The Balkans! Corsica! . . . not from here! . . . You saw the great skedaddle as well as I did . . . and where did they run to, the devil take the hindmost? . . . by the millions they ran back home! And the army with them . . . back to their holes in the ground and their feed bags . . . My foster mother in Puteaux, on the Sentier des Bergères . . . but maybe I shouldn't talk about her? . . . Let it go!

Let's get back to Bellevue . . . to our Spartan diet . . . I wouldn't mind for myself . . . my trouble is my head . . . the less I eat, the better . . . true, I teeter . . . people might say: the man's drunk . . . they do . . . My advice to you . . . Get people to think you're a drunken no-good lush . . . slightly cracked . . . with a bit of the jailbird thrown in . . . You're despised? . . . You get used to it . . . Anyway, I'm getting on, the less I eat, the better off I am . . . but Lili isn't old, she has her dancing lessons to give . . . they don't bring in very much! . . . no heat . . . she does the best she can . . . so do I . . . well, let's not burst into tears, but it's no go . . . To be perfectly frank and honest about it . . . we have a much harder life than the poorest workman down below at Dreyfus's . . . When I think of what they've got . . . social security! Yes, Madame! insurance, vacations . . . a whole month of vacation . . . Maybe I should picket Dreyfus's? . . . tell them I'm mistreated? That I don't even get a sweeper's wages? they wouldn't understand . . . a sweeper at Dreyfus's! social security, vacation, insurance! If I were from Dreyfus's rock-pile,* I'd be respected . . . but Gaston's rock-pile,* they'd only laugh! . . . I've only got one privilege . . . because I crusaded for the Vrench, I'm entitled to posters all over the walls, calling me the king of traitors, accusing me of cutting Jews in little pieces, of selling the Maginot Line, Indochina, and Sicily . . . Oh, I have no illusions . . . they don't believe a word of their horror stories, but one thing is sure . . . they'll hound me to my dying day . . . I'll always be the whipping-boy of the left-wing racists! the raw material of propaganda . . .

But let's get back to serious things . . . I was talking about the winter in Bellevue . . . the cold . . . don't make me laugh . . . I hear people griping . . . I'd like to see them for two minutes under Scandinavian conditions . . . in the Baltic winds, with holes in the roof and the thatch blowing away . . . and twenty below . . . not for a weekend, for five years, Madame! partly in a cell . . . I'd like to see Loukoum cracking the Baltic pack ice . . . Or Achille, for instance, and his gang . . . oh, oh! . . . But first of all, give those birds two years of stir at the Venstre, and Article 75 on their ass . . . I can see the look on their faces . . . it would do them a world of good . . . you could stand to look at them and shake their hands . . . they'd finally get to know something else beside words . . .

I was talking about the island down below . . . there are certain things that need saying . . . things that interest old men . . . they haven't very many seventy-five percent disability cases down there, or men who enlisted in 1912 . . . I'm not finding fault, only saying what's what . . . If I'd been a bit of a drunk from the start, beginning in public school for instance, I'd never have had any trouble, I'd be a sweeper at Dreyfus's now . . . with fringe benefits, security, status . . .

Let's talk about medicine . . . a few patients still come around . . . I won't deny it . . . I can never boast of having no patients at all . . . no! they come around from time to time . . . fine . . . I examine them . . . no worse than other doctors . . . no better . . . I'm friendly, oh, very friendly! and extremely conscientious! . . . never a phony diagnosis . . . never a capricious treatment, in thirty-five years never a risky prescription . . . thirty-five years is a long time when you come to think of it . . . it's not that I don't keep abreast of developments . . . I do, I do . . . I read all the prospectuses from start to finish . . . five, six pounds a week . . . I throw them all in the fire . . . Nobody's going to accuse me of "irre-

sponsible medication" . . . once you stray from the old Pharmacopia . . . suffering catfish! . . . where do you think you'll
end up? . . . In the criminal courts . . . the Tenth Chamber?
. . . Buchenwald? Siberia? . . . No, thank you . . . nobody's
going to put me on trial as a cabalist, as a dangerous alchemist. I've got nothing on my conscience. Except one little
thing . . . that I never ask for money! I simply can't hold out
my hand . . . not even for the Social Security . . . not even
for my war pension . . . and I'll never change . . . idiotic
pride! And what about the grocer? . . . for noodles? for a
package of zwieback? . . . and the coal? . . . or even tap
water? . . . I've hurt my reputation more by never taking a
cent from my patients than Pétiot * did by cooking them in the
oven! . . . I'm an aristocrat, that's all . . . an aristocrat from
la Rampe du Pont . . . Mr. Schweitzer, Abbé Pierre,* Juanovici,* Latzareff* can afford grand gestures . . . mine just look
batty and shady . . . especially in a character that's just out
of stir, nobody knows exactly how.

These patients I've been telling you about, the ones that still
come around, they tell me all about the state of their health,
the ailments that beset them . . . I listen . . . it never stops!
. . . the details, the circumstances . . . compared to what
Lili and I have been through in the last twenty years . . .
they're amateurs, beginners . . . and the condition it's left us
in . . . tender rosebuds . . . give them a third . . . a tenth
of it . . . they'd be crawling under the furniture . . . all the
furniture . . . bellowing with horror the rest of their lives!
. . . Listening to their jeremiads, I can't help saying to myself, "You numbskull, how did you get yourself into such a
mess? What's wrong with you?" I give up. Ask the cat . . .
Thomine here that's purring away . . . *brrr* . . . *brrr* . . . on
my paper . . . she doesn't give a good goddamn about all my
headaches! *brrr! brrr!* the whole world is indifferent! animals!
men! they want a fat man! . . . that's right! . . . as fat as
Churchill, Claudel, Picasso, Bulganin all in one! posteri pos-
teras! and *brrr! brrr!* you'll make it too! . . . Communist-
capitalists! All champion belly builders! Coupon-clipping commissars! ghosts of 1900, but improved . . . try and tell my

patients for their own good! . . . it's always for their own good! . . . that they might try eating a little less meat . . . to go easy on their digestion! you'll see what hatred is . . . You've stepped on the toes of the gods . . . Food and Drink! no political passion can hold a candle . . . devotion, fervor! . . . an atheist of the beef-steak! an enemy of whiskey? Wipe him out.

For my part, as I was telling you, life . . . even a very ascetic life . . . is very expensive . . . considering that nobody helps us . . . neither the town hall nor the Social Security, nor any political party, nor the police. . . . far from it . . . all the people I see get help . . . they all pimp . . . one way or another . . . more or less . . . a fat envelope . . . free premises . . . like Abbé Pierre . . . like Boileau* . . . the Companions of this . . . the Companions of that . . . of the King or the Salvation Army! . . . like Schweitzer, Racine,* Loukoum . . . there's always some feed bag . . . the gravy brothers . . . a penny, if you please.

It would only be funny, and no more . . . I wouldn't gripe if I hadn't been bugged so much on the subject of racism! for ten years, I'm telling you . . . ten years! too crummy to believe! they gripe about their Suez Canal? . . . if they'd dug it with their hands . . . they'd have something to complain about! what they stole from me on the rue Girardon was the work of my hands! . . . will they take it with them to Paradise? . . . maybe . . . ten years of misery, two of them in a cell . . . while they, Racine, Loukoum, Tartre, and Schweitzer were passing the hat one place or another, picking up the dough and the Nobel prizes! . . . enormous sums! stuffed, bloated like Goering, Churchill, Buddha! Superstuffed, plethoric commissars! Ten years, I say! it sticks in my craw . . . including two in the clink . . . with Article 75 on my tail! Who gives a damn? writers of my asshole! . . . nobody bats an eyelash, I can talk myself hoarse, it's as if I'd been having a "unit party" up there, as if I'd given everything I owned to the alcoholics of Montmartre on purpose! . . . and they're not fixing to put up a plaque, with the neighborhood band and a reception at the town hall, saying: "This place was robbed." I know those customers, what doesn't touch them personally, them and their bowels, doesn't exist! never mind! . . . I haven't forgotten a thing . . . the petty thefts or the big ones . . . or the names either . . . not a thing. Like everybody who's a little soft in the head I make up for it by my memory . . . what a laugh! . . . taking advantage of my absence . . . in the clink with Article 75 on my ass . . . to walk off with everything I owned! I've had news of my looters, I keep informed, they're doing all right! Crime has agreed with them . . . the agent Tartre, for instance! . . . down on his knees to me while the Krauts . . . idol of the Youth, Grand Sar of Blah-Blah . . . flabby chin, flabby ass, glasses, smell and all! crossbreed of Mauriac and crab-louse . . . a little of Claudel Gnome et Rhône! * fragile hybrids . . . scavengers of the plague! crime pays! . . .

While we're on the subject of literature, let me tell you about Denoël * . . . Denoël, who was assassinated . . . oh, he had his nasty ways . . .! There's no denying it, he sold you down the river when necessary . . . given the right time and circumstances, he tied you hand and foot, and sold you out . . . after which he was perfectly capable of changing his mind and apologizing . . . like . . . like (a hundred names) . . . but he had one saving grace . . . his passion for literature . . . he really recognized good work, he had respect for writers . . . Brottin is a horse of a different color . . . Achille Brottin is your sordid grocer, an implacable idiot . . . the only thing he can think about is his dough! more dough! still more! the complete millionaire! More and more flunkeys around him . . . with their tongues hanging out and their pants down . . .

Denoël the assassinated read everything . . . Brottin is like Claudel, all he reads is the financial page . . . his reading is done by the "Pin-brain-Trust": Norbert Loukoum, president . . . ah! . . . their idea of reading is to smoke, wash their feet, and play the trumpet! they decide heads or tails . . . who cares? another author more or less . . . they've got thousands and thousands in the cellar . . . toss the whole mess in the garbage? . . . the garbage collectors won't read it! . . . what do I care? . . . garbage pail! what does that make me look like? Emptying garbage? Me with two garbage cans waiting for me . . . if I don't, who will? . . . not Brottin . . . it's my lookout . . . chin up, boy! not Loukoum! he'd sooner die . . . I've been taking the "chin up, boy" routine for going on sixty-four years . . . and it's time to do it again . . . the garbage can and "chin up, boy" . . . from my place to the road it's a good two hundred yards . . . downhill, I have to admit . . . I take them down in the dark so as not to be seen . . . I leave them on the road . . . but people walk off with them . . . I've had at least ten garbage cans swiped . . . It's not just the "Purges" * . . . but this constant robbery . . . everywhere and always! Besides, toting my own garbage cans doesn't help my reputation any . . . people have stopped calling me "Doctor" . . . just plain "Monsieur" . . . pretty soon they'll be calling me "you old bum!" I'm prepared . . . a doctor without a maid, without a housekeeper, without a car, who hauls his own garbage . . . and to top it off writes books . . . and who's been in prison . . . just think it over . . .

And in the meantime, while you're thinking it over, if you'd buy one or two of my books, it would be a help . . .

Never mind about that . . . what really burns me with hatred . . . especially on this road! is the cars! . . . they never stop! there you can see real madness . . . the rush to Versailles! the charge of the motorcars . . . weekdays! Sundays . . . as if gasoline were free . . . one-seaters . . . three-seaters . . . six-seaters! . . . All jam-packed, so help me! . . . where are they all going? . . . to eat, to drink, and worse! . . . more, more! . . . Businessmen's lunches . . . munch, munch . . . business trips . . . biz, biz . . . business belches, wrp, wrp, it's pitiful . . . and they've stolen three garbage cans from me! Millionaires in a fury because their engines won't burst! they splash me . . . and my garbage cans . . . all the while belching *canard aux navets!* plutocrats, Poujadists, Communists, belching and farting all over the freeway! the coalition of *canard aux navets.* Eighty miles an hour! belching and farting harder for the peace of the world than a hundred million pedestrians! Historical duck . . . historical inns! historical menus! . . . you're so drunk when you get up from

table (*Château Trompette 1900*) it's a pure miracle! . . . a
flick of the wheel . . . if you don't demolish the whole embankment, and the maple tree and the poplar with it! not to
mention your steering geer! bingo! two thousand poplars! wild
expedition! autopunitive! screeching stinking brakes! . . . the
whole freeway and the tunnel! . . . roaring drunk . . . passing, double-passing, plunging into the chasm! ah, the delirium,
the fervor of it! . . . ah, *Château Trompette 1900!* . . . new
life in your veins! . . . into the chasm! *Canard aux navets!* . . .
thirteen hundred cars bumper to bumper! Christ almighty
Jesus, flesh bursting with blood, ready to roast! step on the gas!
the oven opens! The Mass is ready! Not with holy water . . .
with hot blood, the whole tunnel full of blood and guts . . .
the rare bird who escapes will never really know whether he's
killed the others or not . . . Crusade! Off to the wars! pilgrims
of the accelerator! Seize the moment, crush the poplars! farting,
belching, furious, drunk as lords! *Château Trompette!* duckling
maison! The cops look on . . . grumble . . . wave their arms
. . . stir up the air! . . . From thirty miles around the faithful
have come . . . to see it all! to take it in! both embankments are
full of them . . . mamas, papas, aunties, babies! sadistic sheep!
the abyss at eighty miles an hour, the fire-balls, the cops in
despair . . . stirring the atmosphere! . . . smoking tunnel!
Château Trompette! . . . burning asphalt! . . .

Oh, if I were rich, I tell you, or if I even had Social Security,
I'd watch all this disorder, all this dilapidation of hydrocarbon,
lipides, and rubber, this crusade of gasoline, duck, and super-
booze, with Napoleonic calm! mamas, papas, jalopies . . . let
them all be swallowed up . . . why not? Three cheers! But the
trouble is . . . I haven't the wherewithal . . . can't afford it
. . . that's all . . . and you're taken with resentment, bitterness, hatred . . . being splattered by those swine . . . knowing that at every stopover, every Yquem, every spin of their
wheels they run through enough for us to live a month on! . . .
without even smashing up! uprooting a hedge! . . . Their
masochistic rage doesn't impress me! . . . hell no . . . or
Loukoum's corset! or Tartre's crummy tricks . . . or Achille's
googoo eyes . . . any more than Vaillant! * . . . what makes

him valiant, I'd like to know? . . . who tried to murder me . . . that's right . . . he went up there with exactly that in mind! so he runs around telling all and sundry . . . he even writes about it! . . . hell! I'm here! it's not too late! let him come, I'm waiting for him. I'm always here, I never go out, I stay in especially for the latecomers . . . another spring . . . two . . . or three . . . I won't be here any more . . . it'll be too late . . . I'll have died a natural death . . .

Drinking water? . . . sure, sure . . . taste it . . . tastes like chlorine, you say? . . . might go down with plenty of wine in it . . . but straight? . . . it's a joke, but it's not funny . . . this alleged drinking water saturated with chlorine . . . it's undrinkable, I say . . . oh, there are plenty of other things to complain about . . . my situation in general . . . and anyway I bore everybody with my lamentations . . . I have my nerve . . . Achille Brottin said exactly that the other night: "Make them laugh! You used to know how. Can't you do it any more? . . ." He was surprised. "Everybody has his little troubles! you're not the only one! . . . I've got mine too, don't worry . . . If you'd lost a hundred and thirty million on de Beers . . . forty-seven million on Suez! and listen . . . in two sessions! and fourteen million on the 'Croix'—that I had to take to Geneva myself . . . at my age! crosses* to the buyer . . . luckily my son helped me . . . fourteen million in 20-Swiss-franc pieces! . . . can you imagine?" I thought it over, I tried to imagine . . . Norbert imagined too . . . he was present . . . Norbert Loukoum, president of his "Pin-brain-Trust" . . . he said it was awful . . . the tears came to his eyes! . . . Achille, the poor dear old man, toting fourteen million crosses . . . conclusion: "Céline, you're washed up! . . . You owe us enormous sums of money, and you've got no more verve! . . . Aren't you ashamed of yourself?" When Loukoum says "verve" . . . his mouth is so thick and blubbery . . . what you hear is pretty funny . . . it's his age! besides, his words come out like marbles of shit . . ."cloaca diction" . . . in feeble spasms . . . Anyway, Norbert Loukoum crows in feeble spasms . . . that nobody reads my books anymore . . . he, president of the "Pin-brain-Trust"! nonentity triumphant!

Okay! . . . I know where I stand . . . they hate me . . .
nothing to be surprised at . . . but what about my friends?
. . . supposedly heartbroken that I can't manage to make up
for it with my medicine . . . as a practitioner . . . that I
ought . . . blah! . . . pure devotion . . . balls! with my intuition! my miraculous cures! . . . and blah! . . . the truth of
the matter is that my old friends are mostly waiting for me to
kick off . . . they all picked up a few manuscripts, papers,
dibs and dabs, at the time of the great pillage . . . on stairways . . . in garbage cans . . . in safekeeping, foreseeing
that once I kicked off it was all bound to be valuable . . . but
couldn't I kick off right away, Christ almighty! . . .

I know all that's been taken, I have the inventory in my head
. . . "Casse Pipe" . . . "Volonté du Roi Krogold" . . . plus
two or three rough drafts . . . not lost at all . . . not for everybody! Certainly not! And I know something else, but I don't
let on . . . I listen to my friends . . . sure . . . I'm waiting
for them to kick off too! Them first! They all eat a lot more than
I do! just let one little arteriole burst! hope! hope! . . . and I'll
meet them all in Charon's boat, enemies, friends, all with their
guts around their necks! . . . Charon smashing their faces in
. . . good! . . . ah, sadistic Norbert! he had it coming to him
. . . Brutal! He and Achille . . . they'll be torn open from
ear to ear . . . they'll have a kind of loudspeaker for their
nasty remarks! each one of them! *bingo!* and *wham!* atta boy,
Charon! . . . it's all set up! ah, Achille won't be thinking of his
Suez stock any more! or his de Beers! or his crosses! . . .
square in the face! bang! Ah, they'll look sweet in Charon's
bark! and the whole "Brain Trust" with them, don't forget!
. . . their mugs wide open and their eyes dangling . . .
That's how Charon treats his passengers . . . won't it be
comical! . . . much funnier than Renault in Fresnes! * . . .
When my old friends come to take a little look . . . to see if I
won't be passing on soon, I get a good laugh, I see them on the
Styx, and Charon tickling them! . . . *boom* . . . *bam!* that's
for their thieving ways! Those little faces! Oh, they're so clever!
. . . Loukoum's rosebud mouth is just right for it . . . so
blubbery and twisted the only sounds you can make out are

vuâââ! wâââ! . . . profuse bucal cloaca! . . . he'll look lovely
split from ear to ear! The whimsical Norbert . . . and Achille!
with his lascivious googoo eye hanging behind his ear! . . . I
can see it . . . or a charm on his watch chain . . . or around
his neck . . . Fetching! . . .

Confidentially, my friends don't know a thing . . . sure!
sure! . . . they rub their hands over the Renault business . . .
let them! But what about the Charon business? . . . hell . . .
they suspect nothing . . . they deny, they smoke, they fart
. . . smug . . . sardonic . . . practically sure of living a hundred years thanks to those little pills . . . and those Mira-
dor super-drops . . . I may be a sap, but never mind . . . one
thing I know . . . I know how Charon'll get to them . . .
Boy, will they look funny in his boat! . . . Split, that's right!
smash and *wham*, from ear to ear . . . meanwhile they give
me a pain in the ass . . . they hand me a line, they perorate,
they get drunk on hot air . . . and so sure of themselves . . .
their fifteen-shelf cabinets full of suppositories and drops . . .
not to mention the apéritifs! what a selection! . . . sweet
ones, bitter ones! total optimism! ah! ah! . . . a dab of foie
gras, a cigarette, two glasses of Mumm's . . . you wouldn't believe it . . . the roadside restaurant at home! . . . the freeway at home! . . . they think you look pale and worn! depressed, neurasthenic! and they gave *you* advice . . . those
diets you recommend are no good! in the first place! the living
proof! their wives keep telling them to stop seeing you! that
you're wrecking their stomachs, their livers, their spleens . . .
that you, singlehanded, are capable of darkening all the fireworks in the world . . . with your gloom . . . that you ought
to be forbidden to practice . . . because you've been in prison,
and why not put you back? . . . in a way they're right . . .
but I'm not wrong either . . . drooling and doddering, okay!
. . . but plenty of ardor and passion about one thing . . .
having them all croak before me . . . the whole lot of them!
Let them wallow in steaks . . . etcetera, etcetera! until they
burst . . . with all the trimmings!

I'm only thinking, anticipating . . . the two of them . . .
Achille and Loukoum . . . are still talking . . . I'd stopped

listening . . . they repeat themselves . . . "How funny you used to be!" I agree that I was rather droll, that maybe I'd be droll again . . . with a bit of a bank account . . . like Achille, for instance . . . that's right, like Achille . . . with his "hundredth" all tucked up in the bank . . . hallelujah! or like Loukoum, his grand castrator . . . punks if there ever were, both of them . . . but situated, glory be, where the manna falls . . . honors, dividends, security! . . . "Family, Work, Country"? * Shit! . . . It was a good idea to rub him out . . . Verdun, blah blah . . . I knew him with his sixteen "maps" in Siegmaringen, I know what I'm talking about.

But one fact remains . . . that my books don't sell any more . . . so they say . . . or not much . . . that I'm outmoded, senile! that's hogwash! a put-up job! . . . their idea is to buy it all up from my widow for a song! . . . sure . . . I admit it, I'm getting on! But what about Norbert? Doesn't he ever look at himself? And Achille . . . when you open the door, you've got to hold him . . . or the draft would blow him away . . . and his whole Pin-brain-Trust with him . . . they're all so doddering there's nothing else in the world . . . the only thing they understand is the way they go *mmm! pfwah! plop!* underneath! wet farts! . . . I could go *pfwah! plop!* too! Which reminds me of Christian IV, . . . another big farter Christian IV of Denmark! all his life! . . . all he did was to fart around . . . like Brottin . . . Brottin in publishing, Christian IV in royalty . . . his tricks were the death of him! . . . like Brottin! . . . I went up there to his kingdom . . . to have a look . . . to get the feel of his prisons . . . it wasn't him any more, it was his arch-descendant Christian X, a stupid rotten double-timing Boche . . . after we got out, we lived across the way from him, in a garret: Kronprinzesssgade* . . . go see if you've got the nerve to live in a street with a name like that! . . . which shows that we know something about him . . . Rosenborg Castle . . . I'll tell you about it . . . but meanwhile let's get back to my present . . . not so rosy . . . and more hard days to come . . . mostly on account of Brottin! Brottin the frantic spoiler! the stamp collecting slob! Brottin with his cellar full of Prix Goncourts . . . full of worthless novels . . . maybe he shits them . . . *flop! plop!* . . . if you find him quieter, even more googoo-eyed than usual, it means that he's pondering, cogitating, shitting his thousand and thirteenth author. The King of Publishing, so to speak!

Charon will wake him out of his reflections! with an oar, dear lady . . . *wham!* . . . *smash!* . . .

I apologize for talking about myself . . . I'm overdoing it . . . troubles? . . . you have your own! . . . these literary men are the limit . . . so afflicted with me-me-ism . . . and what about doctors? Just as bad! . . . and plumbers? . . . and barbers? . . . all the same . . . no modesty . . . and cabinet ministers? . . . and Abbé Pierre, the one-man movie? . . . I keep thinking of Charon . . . the way he'll knock the me-me-ism out of them! the whole crew! with his blessed oar full in the snout! *wham!* from ear to ear! . . . you get the picture . . . their heads practically off! their eyes dangling! . . . the ferry to the other world . . . that come-on for tourists! *bingo! zing!* . . . from ear to ear! crowds of the well-heeled rubbing shoulders with the riff-raff . . . extra-small pension holders . . . very languid *dames aux camélias,* bearded magistrates, Olympian sportsmen, all pell-mell, getting their faces split! *wham!* Why wouldn't I write about the Stygian Guignol instead of my own mawkish troubles? Maybe that would boost my sales? Kramp thinks so . . . Kramp who packs the bundles at Hirsch's . . . When it comes to flair and intelligence, Kramp is a little less of a dunce than Achille . . . not quite so intent on making a mess of everything . . . he has an occupation at least . . . he delivers . . . it's unusual to find a man who does something . . .

No doubt about it . . . if I belonged to a Cell, a Synagogue, a Lodge, a Party, a Church, a Police Force . . . no matter which . . . if I'd come out of the folds of some "Iron Curtain" —I'd do all right! sure as shit! . . . to some Circus . . . that's how Maurois, Mauriac, Thorez, Tartre, Claudel do it . . . and the rest of them! . . . Abbé Pierre . . . Schweitzer . . . Barnum . . . I'd have nothing to be ashamed of . . . and no question of age! Nobel Prize and Grand Cross guaranteed . . . Doddering, decrepit, pissy, no matter, you're an "honorary

this and that," a party standard bearer . . . Juanovicist? okay!
anything goes, you can do what you please as long as you're a
fully recognized clown! as long as it's perfectly clear that you
belong to a Circus . . . you don't? . . . that's bad! No tent?
The ax! . . . When I think of the "tent" I had! . . . When I
think that Altman* . . . who now calls me a sub-shit, an obscene mercenary monster, the disgrace of France, Montmartre,
the Colonies, and the Soviets . . . went sick with ecstasy from
reading the *Journey* . . . and not *in petto!* not at all! but in
Barbusse's "Le Monde" . . . in the days when Madame Triolette* and her gastritic Larengon* translated that excellent
work into Russian . . . which gave me an opportunity to take
a gander at their Russia! *at my expense!* and not at the expense
of the government like Gide and Malraux and all the rest, the
deputies and so on . . . you can see I was sitting pretty! I'm
putting the dots on the i's! . . . a little better than the agent
Tartre! crypto of my balls . . . that blind crab-louse! one look
at him is enough to send you to the hospital! I could have un-
seated Barbusse! . . . Palace hotels, Crimea, Security forever!
The U.S.S.R. opened its arms to me . . . I really have something to laugh about . . . What's done is done, I know . . .
History doesn't pass the platter twice . . . they settled for
what they could get . . . Zola three times diluted . . . leav-
ings of Bourget! unsalable crap! . . . Achille's cellars are full
of it! . . . tomorrow Latzareff! . . . Madame! . . . Tintin!
. . . tomorrow their servants . . . every last dishwasher . . .
will have his little idea!

The reception they'll get from Charon? *That's the question!*
. . . *Wham! Bam!* Take it from me!

But back to my story . . . now and then, I've got to admit,
some stubborn bastard manages to discover me in the sub-
basement of some storehouse under a pyramid of returns . . .
oh, I could easily get used to the idea of being the scribbler
that nobody reads any more . . . rejected by pure, purified
Vrance! the doctor more monstrous than Pétiot! more criminal
than Bougrat* . . . oh, I could be perfectly happy about it
. . . but there's the question of noodles . . . which defy dialectics . . . the question of cash! Loukoum, Achille, and com-

pany are secure on the noodle end . . . which accounts for their philosophical airs . . . take away their noodles, you'll hear them screech all right! With the noodles there's no reprieve. "And what about the other string to your bow?" I can hear you asking. "Medicine?" The patients shun me, that's all. I admit it . . . Out of fashion? . . . Definitely . . . I'm not up on the new drugs? . . . that's a lie . . . I get them all . . . I read all the prospectuses from A to Z . . . do my colleagues know any more? Not a thing. What more do they read? Nothing. Have I got the healer's instinct? I'm saturated with it! traversed by waves and fluids . . . with a quarter of the "new drugs" I get . . . a tenth . . . I could poison all Billancourt, Issy, etc. . . . and Vaugirard! Landru* hands me a laugh . . . all the trouble he went to! . . . when it comes to "doing good," nothing escapes me! the most shattering discoveries! . . . I wouldn't be like my colleagues who let penicillin molder and rot for fifty years! a stupidity more magnificent than Suez! While I watch and wake! I can rejuvenate any nonagenarian that comes around in five seconds . . . make him twenty . . . thirty years younger . . . I've got the serum right here on my desk . . . What healer can hold a candle to me? . . . serious, guaranteed, certified, reimbursed by the Social Security! an ampul before each meal . . . make you a super-Romeo! "Relativity" in ampuls! . . . I'll make you a present of it! you drink up Time, so to speak . . . the wrinkles, the melancholia . . . the acid stomach! the hot flashes . . . What can I go into? . . . the Comédie-Française, young lady! Arnolphe jumping rope . . . reinvigorated! Madeleine Renaud will be Minou, Achille will go to the Luxembourg! to the puppet show! And what about the Academy? . . . Mauriac at last a choir boy . . . not bothering us any more . . . all his inhibitions exposed . . . an ampul before every meal! guaranteed by the Social Security . . .

If I were a quack, I'd do all right . . . that would be a way . . . and not a bad one . . . I'd turn my office in semi-Bellevue into a refriskyment center! . . . a "new look" Lourdes . . . Lisieux on the Seine . . . see what I mean? . . . but the catch! . . . I'm just a plain little doctor . . . I could be a faith healer . . . I could get away with it . . . I can't . . . or a chiropracter? . . . no . . . it's no go!

I have time to meditate . . . . to mull over the pros and the cons . . . to wonder what does me the most harm . . . maybe my suit? . . . my shoes? . . . that I'm always wearing slippers? . . . my hair? The worst, I think, is not having a servant . . . and the last straw: "He writes books" . . . they don't read them, but they know . . .

I go out to meet my (rare) patients myself, I bring them in to the gate, I guide them so they won't slip (they'd sue me) in the mud, the slush . . . or the thistles . . . I run errands . . . those are the things that discredit you . . . I take out the garbage . . . myself . . . I tote the garbage can out to the road . . . you can imagine . . . how can anybody take me seriously? "Doctor, Doctor? for the child . . . tell me! Do you know about dried extract of cod heart fiber? . . . they say it's revolutionary . . . You've heard of it? and hibernation? what say? for mama's eyes."

I can say this, I can say that, who cares . . . they won't believe me anyway! Total distrust . . .

All that isn't so bad, you'll say . . . millions have died who weren't any guiltier than you . . . that's a fact! . . . believe me, I thought about it on those excursions through the city . . . escorted, super-escorted excursions . . . not once! twenty, thirty times! the whole of Copenhagen from East to West . . . in a bus with plenty of bars, full of cops with tommy guns . . . not talkative in the least . . . tourists of every kind, "common law," "politicals" . . . all on their best behavior . . . from the prison to their Court House and back, quite a ways . . . oh, I already knew the city very well, but in a bus full of cops you see the crowd with different eyes . . . That's what's lacking in Brottin, in Norbert, too . . . though they certainly have the "common law" look . . . *"homo deliquensis"* to a T . . . the perfect Lombrosos! . . . sight-seeing in handcuffs would do them a world of good . . . they'd finally see the faces of the cocktail party world . . . their true natures . . . not only the ones in the bus . . . the crowd . . . the street . . . their true faces . . . their horrible complexes . . . parakeets and jackals . . . Politiigaard, their Criminal Court . . . don't knock yourself out: . . . *Politii:* "Police" . . . *gaard:* "Court" . . . it's all from the French . . . What they wanted to know? . . . Whether I'd really sold the Maginot Line . . . the forts of Enghien . . . the harbor of Toulon . . . The Danes, who had me in the lockup not for a week, for six years, absolutely wanted to know why, why? the French people, the whole of France wanted to have me drawn and quartered . . . was it for this? or for something else? The Danes had no objection! hell, no! . . . but they wanted to have some idea . . . they don't torture in the dark, *à la Française* . . . oh no! . . . they reason . . . and while they rea-

22

son, while they ponder, all you can do is wait, they're slow . . .
they don't torture with their eyes closed . . . but take care
. . . the system has its drawbacks . . . while they investigate
. . . sagely, earnestly . . . they don't mind letting you rot in
their dungeons . . . they're worth seeing . . . I repeat the
address, Vesterfangsel, Pavilion K, Copenhagen . . . death
house . . . tourists, how about a little tour? . . . The Hotel
d'Angleterre isn't everything . . . or the "Little Mermaid" . . .

While they meditate about whether to hand you over or not,
you do a little thinking yourself . . . your problems . . .
you're no bother to them at the bottom of your hole! . . .
They're a gang of Tartuffes! ten times worse than ours! . . .
Protestant Tartuffes, hats off! you can rot while they're meditating . . . they don't mind . . . they're Puritans! . . . they'd
meditate for twenty years . . . until you've no body left . . .
nothing but rotten skin . . . scabs . . . lichen . . . pellagra
. . . and blind! . . . like all the prisons in the world, you'll
say . . . I won't argue . . . the Renault case isn't unique
. . . and once they've finished weighing the pros and cons
. . . they come and get you in the end . . . *crrreek, crrreek*
. . . in the middle of the night . . . the heavy door . . .
four bruisers in overalls! Remove the object! *Komm!* You hear
the pig-sticking! That *"pip-cell"* 11, 12! I know what I'm talking
about . . . The Tartuffe of the North is somebody! Molière's
Tartuffe is a baby . . . Plenty of times I've heard *Hjelp!*
Hjelp! Next day he's dead . . . you never see him again!

It happens in Fresnes? . . . naturally . . . everywhere!
. . . Renault? Tomorrow Cocteau . . . tomorrow Armide
. . . Abbé Fatso isn't exempt! . . . or Dr. Clyster! . . . even
Mauriac in his bikini, the "Express" as he calls himself . . .
they'll catch up with him! they catch up with everybody, at
midnight in the cage . . .

Hjelp! that means "help" . . . you've caught on! you arrive
in Copenhagen . . . "Taxi!" . . . Hotel d'Angleterre? . . .
Certainly not! Vesterfangsel! . . . don't back down! insist!
that's where you want to go! you want to see it! not the Little
Mermaid! You want to hear: *Komm! Hjelp!* . . . that's
all! . . .

When I think of the people I hear talking politics, I can see them in the bus . . . a real bus! with real gratings, jam-packed with criminals like you! . . . not criminals à la Charlie Chaplin! honest to God criminals with handcuffs and straitjackets! guarded by a dozen tommy guns . . . what a show! . . . the passersby weave and waver, cling to the shopfronts . . . for fear this might happen to them . . . their consciences quake! scared shitless! . . . memories . . . it's a rare passerby that hasn't got a little abortion tucked away . . . a little theft . . . nothing to be ashamed of! the only thing to be ashamed of is poverty! the one and only! Take me, for instance, no car, a doctor on foot! what do I look like? . . . The advantage of a doctor, even if he's a prize dope, is that with a telephone call . . . he gets there . . . often there's no ambulance available . . . taxis? . . . you can never find one . . . even the most idiotic of doctors has his car! . . . even with my ghastly reputation . . . the old jailbird . . . if I had a car, people wouldn't think me so crummy, so old . . . cars and more cars . . . what a laugh! . . . that one up there wasn't mine! nor any of these down here . . . I'm expecting Achille's . . . in case he wants to show me his horrible accounts . . . proving that I owe him enormous sums, so he says! *homo deliquensis,* as I've said . . . give him the whole bus to himself! and hell, why not? his whole Trust with him! . . . and Norbert trotting along behind! in handcuffs and corset! that's the way I see it!

When you got to Police Headquarters, you could wait at least five, six hours . . . for somebody to come and get you . . . five, six hours on your feet, each man in a vertical coffin, under lock and key . . . I can safely say that I've stood for hours and hours in the course of my life . . . on guard, cooling my heels,

in war as in peace . . . but in those vertical boxes at the Copenhagen *Politiigaard* . . . I've never felt like such a creep
. . . waiting to be questioned . . . by whom? about what? I
had plenty of time to think it over . . . here we go! . . . they
opened my box . . . they helped me up the stairs . . . they
had to! . . . two cops . . . the effects of beriberi and also of
waiting at the vertical . . . the office was on the fifth floor
. . . the cops helped me ever so gently . . . never any brutality . . . I tried everything to shake off my dizziness . . . to
keep from staggering . . . from crumpling . . . no use! . . .
I fold up . . . that's my pellagra! . . . You can read in any
medical treatise that it's easy to cure the scurvy . . . a few
slices of lemon . . . your health, sir! . . . all the same I'm a
wreck and always will be . . . they'll bury me this way . . .
okay, okay! So I'm on my last legs, but that's no excuse for
losing me in transit! I was telling you about the stairs . . .
Here we are on the fifth floor . . . an amusing little sidelight
on their *Politiigaard* . . . the way it's stacked . . . corridors
and corridors so twisty . . . hairpins and corkscrews . . . that
supposing you made a break . . . no matter when or where
. . . you always end up in a court where the "bruisers" are
waiting for you . . . special cops . . . you get a massage that
sends you to the hospital . . . so don't get any fancy ideas
. . . for me it was out of the question . . . not with my hundred years . . . all the "treatises" in the world can't change
it . . . what's done . . . is done . . . your Nordic prison is
built with that in mind! Those guys who are sticking their
necks out now in Budapest and Warsaw . . . some of them
are going to end up in the house of numbers . . . it's in the
cards . . . ask them in twenty years what they think about all
this . . . the tourist, as I said, doesn't see a thing, he follows
the guide . . . Hotel d'Angleterre, Nyehavn, the tattooed
babies, the Big Tower . . . the Mermaid . . . he's satisfied,
he goes back home, he talks a blue streak . . . He's seen . . .
two, three horses with the trademark of the Carlsberg brew-
ery, wearing their little summer hats! . . . that's what the tourist sees!

Back to my fifth floor! hoisted by cops on both sides . . .

here we are! they sit me down . . . three *Kriminalassistents*
are going to question me . . . by turns . . . oh, without the
slightest brutality . . . But so invariably boring . . . "Do you
admit handing over the plans of the Maginot Line to the Germans?" And myself just as invariably: *No!* and I signed! every
bit as serious as they were! all this went on in English . . .
that gives you an idea of the decline of our language . . . If
it had been under Louis XIV or even Fallières, they'd never
have dared . . . "*Do you admit? . . . Do you admit? . . .*"
My ass! *no!* non! signed . . . no comment! once I had said no
and signed, they put my handcuffs back on and took me down
to the bus . . . and off again . . . the whole city, from East to
West!

It went on like that for months and then one day I couldn't
move at all . . . the three *Kriminalassistents* came over to see
me . . . in my hole . . . to ask me the same question all over
again . . . and when I say a hole I mean a hole! go see for
yourself, ten by ten, twenty feet deep . . . a well . . . just
the thing for moss, beriberi and lichens! I who lived eighteen
years in the Passage Choiseul, I know something about dismal
abodes . . . but the Venstre takes the cake! a slight suspicion
that I'd die there? definitely . . . no scandal, no brutality . . .
"He couldn't take it!" Take Renault for instance . . . the way
they went about it! Stupid to be in such a hurry! two years at
the bottom of a well, they'd have had him! Nothing to worry
about! . . . for me, five, six months . . . I'd kick off . . . I
was supposed to! . . . seventy-five percent disability! . . . No
soap! . . . I stuck it out! Lousy luck!

Now, ten years later, here in Meudon-Bellevue, nobody asks
me anything . . . they tease me a bit . . . but not much . . .
I don't worry my head about them either . . . other troubles
. . . gas, electricity . . . coal! and carrots! The pirates who
walked off with everything I had . . . sold it all in the Flea
Market . . . they don't have to worry about hunger . . . or
anything else . . . crime pays . . . Olympic champions for
crust! arm-bands, ribbons . . . ten . . . twelve party cards! if
they'd cut off my head with a penknife, they'd have been on
the Arc de Triomphe! glory! and not "unknown"! . . . Oh no,
in neon lights.

But maybe it's wrong of me to complain . . . I'm alive after all . . . and I lose an enemy or two every day . . . cancer, apoplexy, gluttony . . . it's a pleasure the number that pass on! . . . I'm not hard to please . . . a name! . . . another! . . . there are good things in life . . .

Oh yes, I was telling you about Thomine . . . Thomine, my cat, I forgot! senility is no excuse . . . I was telling you about my patients too . . . my last few . . . in consideration of my kindness, my patience, and because they're all very old and I refuse to be paid! oh, absolutely! . . . these few very very old people still come around . . .

My way of life dates from the Second Empire . . . a practitioner of the "liberal arts" . . . supposedly . . . Once I've paid my taxes and my dues to the Medical Association, paid for my license and a bit of heat, and my burial insurance . . . I'm cleaned out . . . that's the truth! . . . flat! . . . liberal arts . . . a good joke . . . I know what you're going to say: "Bleed your Achille! all he has to do is sell a few of your books! . . ." Hell! that's one thing he's careful not to do . . . all he can do is scream that I'm ruining him . . . talk about monumental advances . . . oh, hypocritical Achille! . . . what people! . . . he does everything in his power, two-timing, three-timing, apocalyptic maneuvers! . . . to prevent people from buying my books . . . he keeps me in his cellar, he buries me . . . there'll be a new edition in a thousand years . . . but here and now in Bellevue . . . I can croak . . . "Ah yes, Céline! . . . he's in our cellar . . . he'll be out in a thousand years! . . ." In a thousand years nobody'll speak French! ah, jug-headed Achille! hell, it's like lace! . . . I saw lace dying out . . . with my own eyes . . . my mother in Père Lachaise hasn't even got her name on her grave . . . that's proof enough . . . I'll tell you about her . . . Marguerite Céline . . . on account of me, the shame of it . . . for fear people would spit on it . . .

Though I'd never claim to be a St. Vincent de Paul or an Axel Munthe, a lot of people say I make too much of animals . . . they're right . . . zwieback, bacon, hempseed, chickweed, hamburger . . . it all goes! . . . dogs, cats, titmice, sparrows, robins, hedgehogs . . . they eat us out of house and home! and the gulls from the Renault roofs . . . in the winter . . . from the factory down below . . . on the island . . . we're suckers, I have to admit! . . . especially as they all bring their friends . . . hedgehogs, robins, titmice . . . especially in the winter . . . from Upper Meudon . . . if it weren't for us, they'd have a pretty rough time in the winter . . . I say Upper Meudon . . . from further still! from Yveline! . . . we're at the end of the Forest of Yveline . . . the extreme tip . . . then comes the Bois de Boulogne, Billancourt . . .

All right, our animals are a drain . . . I admit it . . . in times like this we should watch our step . . . we do! we do! but then ten new birds turn up . . .

The scrawniest of my charges is spoiled compared to me . . . and I work harder . . . a lot harder! . . . and my protégé doesn't suspect it . . . brain work is invisible . . . I'm ending in total bankruptcy . . . it shames me . . . Last Sunday, for instance, a lady from Clichy, one of my earliest patients, a really distinguished lady, educated, intelligent, well-informed, came to see me . . . she'd crossed Paris from end to end in the Métro, on the bus . . . what courage! . . . I congratulate her . . . she isn't even out of breath! . . . she came to ask me a little advice . . . I've taken care of her whole family . . . in turn I ask her what's become of this one and that one, people I knew well . . . news about places too . . . Porte Pouchet, Square de Lorraine, rue Fanny . . . what

they've done with Rouguet's? . . . she knows . . . she knows
everything . . . some of them still remember me . . . they've
grown old . . . They send me their kind regards, their best
wishes . . . they all know what's happened to me . . . they
think it's terribly unjust . . . throwing me in the clink . . .
though if I'd stayed in Clichy they'd certainly have cut me to
pieces! . . . Let's talk about something else . . . about hospitals . . . about the enormous Bichat Hospital . . . and the
Town Hall . . . the officials . . . the Commies and the antis
. . . about Naile who committed suicide . . . he was a Pari-
sian like me . . . it's unusual in the Paris suburbs to find an
official who isn't from the Basses-Alpes or from Hainaut . . .
you don't feel at ease in the Paris suburbs unless you're from
the Drôme or Finistère or Périgord . . . at the Town Hall for
instance . . . "Where were you born?" Courbevoie, Seine . . .
the lady frowns . . . you've put your foot in it . . .

Anyway, à propos of Naile, we start talking about Aufray,
the former mayor . . . and then about Ichok . . . the phony
doctor, who committed suicide, too . . . it's amazing . . . you
never know what's going on . . . what's being hatched and
finagled in the corridors of a town hall! triple-padded doors,
offices "open day and night" . . . nobody ever there . . .
nowadays it's not in the sacristies that daggers are sharpened
. . . that prussic acid is sold! No, the mystery, the intrigue
have moved . . . you'll find plenty in the Welfare offices . . .
the biggest mystery to come my way in Clichy was the business with Roudière, a clerk in the Hygiene office . . . We'll
come back to it . . . This Monsieur Roudière died . . . of
cancer! yes, yes, but make no mistake! there was politics at the
bottom of it! . . . I know, I saw him . . . he was blackjacked!
. . . and how! . . . laid out cold . . . his ulcer bled for six
months . . . poor bastard, I won't bring him back to life . . .
there's no street named after him like so many other people
. . . if he'd done the blackjacking, there'd be a rue Roudière
. . . what a joke! Talking this way, about one thing and another . . . reminds me of the murder in the Maison Verte . . .
the stiff that disappeared . . . nothing unusual, a murder in a
bar, at the counter . . . the spice, the mystery . . . is that

they never found the corpse! They saw it happen . . . they saw the guy fold! with two knives in his back . . . he was through! By the time they'd notified the cops to come see . . . and gone for a stretcher . . . the stiff had blown . . . naturally somebody must have given him a hand . . . They arrest everybody . . . the owner, the witness, the maid, the whole shebang! an hour later the bulls come back! dirty work at the crossroads! the corpse was there, back again . . . the same one! with three knives in his back! . . . that was going too far! . . . they go back to Headquarters, spread the alarm . . . but by the time they'd got back to the bar the corpse had blown again! absolutely! hide-and-seek! . . . in the end they gave up . . . From one memory to another . . . Maison Verte . . . Porte Pouchet . . . I got to talking about St. Vincent de Paul . . .

"And how about St. Vincent de Paul?"

The famous old people's home . . . I've tended patients there too . . . sick inmates and nuns . . .

"How much does it cost now at St. Vincent de Paul?"

All old people worry about that . . . it's their obsession . . . the price of board at old people's homes . . . my mother and father collected the prospectuses of the Bonnaviat Foundation, the Garigari Foundation, the Petits Ménages at Euques-sur-Ourque . . . in my state, I must admit, the place for me would be St. Vincent de Paul . . .

"You know how much they ask?"

"Oh, in the old days it wasn't expensive . . . in the old days . . . but now . . . now, Doctor . . . it's 1,200 francs a day! . . ."

"A day?"

"Yes, yes . . . a day!"

"You think so? You really think so, Madame?"

That really wraps it up! . . . 1,200 francs at St. Vincent de Paul . . . might as well stay with Abbé Pierre . . . same racket . . . If you ask me, that takes the green banana . . . 1,200 francs a day . . . When I think of what Lili and I had to live on . . . a far cry from 1,200 smackers! . . . what things have come to . . . it takes a genius to keep alive . . .

For Brottin, of course, 1,200 francs is a joke . . with his two thousand authors in the cellar, two thousand frantic workers! . . . his Titans of the Lavender Series, turning them out with a crank . . . mimeographs, plagiographs . . . and so on . . . they'll give him a pension of ten million . . . Achille's as good as the Bank of France! with his authors in the cellar. . . turn the crank! and bingo! round and round! . . . he and his publishing house, his whole clique and family . . . they've all got so much bread they can't even count it . . . in thirty-six banks! all in the cellar! authors and money! . . . just go take a look at the pyramids, the impressive exterior is nothing, it's what's underneath that counts! deep down in the crypts! there sits the mummy with his gold! and his two thousand author-slaves! and sniveling Loukoum! . . . his Loukoum! . . . his private castrator! the gluttonous monster! slug mouth, hungry for shit, never leaves a scrap! the shit's in a drawing room? good! hoopla! there he slithers! dinner is served! . . . floods of slime . . . he sucks it in, he oozes it out! gulp, gulp! . . . that's him all right!

Okay, but meanwhile my patient, my old friend, had struck me a hard blow! I was aghast . . . 1,200 francs at St. Vincent de Paul! our future, mine and Lili's, looked grim . . .

Oh, you'll say, what about gas? You complain about the gas bills? . . . just give yourself the gas! . . . chin up! . . . read your favorite newspaper . . . people who can't take it any more give themselves the gas! . . . Not so good! After thirty-five years of practice I can tell you a thing or two . . . they don't always make it . . . far from it! they get revived . . . they don't die but they suffer plenty . . . on the way out, and on the way back . . . a thousand deaths, a thousand recoveries! and the smell! . . . the neighbors come running! . . . they wreck the joint! if they've stolen too much, fire's the answer! . . . they set fire to the curtains . . . a little more suffering for you . . . asphyxia and burns . . . to cap the climax . . . No, gas is bad business . . . the safest method, take it from me, I've been consulted a hundred times, is a hunting rifle in your mouth! stuck in deep! . . . and bang! . . . you blow your brains out . . . one drawback: the mess! . . . the furni-

ture, the ceiling! brains and blood clots . . . take it from me,
I've had ample experience of suicides . . . successful and un-
successful . . . Prison might help you! that's another way of
crossing out your existence! . . . Definitely! the dungeon that
annihilates time! . . . suicide little by little . . . but under
normal conditions everybody can't do time . . . in Bezons,
Sartrouville, or Clichy, for instance . . . ah, and don't forget
Siegmaringen! . . . there it was pretty urgent! . . . the lot of
them with Article 75 on their ass! . . . urgent, I repeat! they
all had good reason! the nabobs of the Castle just as much as
the small fry in the attics! . . . a general test of the nerves!
. . . the whole planet yapping and yelping . . . reviling
them as monsters and worse! . . . one kind of torture wouldn't
be enough . . . thousands and thousands . . . and then some
. . . for centuries! . . . even my patients at the *Fidelis* who
were practically dead, with the pus pouring out, eaten with
mange, spitting up their pancreas and their bowels, asked me
for a way to end like in a dream . . . Some dream! The politi-
cos in the Castle, I can tell you, were the most intent . . .
how to go about it? Did I know the best way? revolver? . . .
cyanide? . . . hanging? . . . Laval, of course, had his own
dodge . . . Laval was proud! he wouldn't deign to ask me
. . . and look what happened to him . . . cyanide spoiled by
moisture . . . he was so smart! how will de Gaulle end? and
Mollet? . . . they don't know . . . they go on chewing the fat
. . . as for me, I'll finish myself off in the garden . . . out
there . . . plenty of room . . . or maybe the cellar would be
better? . . . the cellar's a good place too . . . the cat goes
down to have her kittens . . . regularly . . . Lili helps her,
massages her . . . nobody will help me . . . They won't give
Lili any trouble . . . all neat and orderly . . . The police will
investigate . . . cause of suicide? . . . neurasthenia . . . I'll
leave a letter for the Public Prosecutor and a small sum of
money for Lili . . . when I go over the hill . . . Lili won't get
much . . . but all the same, enough to live on for two, three
years . . . after all the hurricanes, tornadoes, barbarian hordes,
looters of every camp, "warrants" and handcuffs . . . if we still
have a few cents left . . . it's a miracle! The whole world gone

haywire . . . I'd like to have seen Achille in that mess! him and his gang, his pantless Pin-brain-Trust!

Lili fighting the world? . . . I can't quite see it . . . Lili so generous . . . all generosity . . . like a fairy! . . . she'd give everything away . . . but what can I do about it? . . . I've done my best . . . ah . . . "Lavarède and his three sous!"*
. . . That was easy! Big deal! Going from one country to another through a thousand terrible adventures . . . my oh my, so he said . . . we say: hill of beans! . . . we went through four ferocious armies! thundering . . . from sky and rails!
. . . blasting everything! roasting everything! men, armored trains, babies, mothers-in-law . . . Flying fortresses . . . whole squadrons of them . . . ah, our kit and boodle! and the little money we had! and ourselves! . . . what we went through! deluge on deluge . . . a little worse than the Théâtre du Châtelet, I assure you! . . . real flames, real bombs, take it from me! Göttingen, Cassel, Osnabrück! volcanoes extinguished, revived, rephosphorized, remayonnaised . . . *bing!* and *boom* . . . the suburbs on top of the cathedrals . . . locomotives on belfries! . . . perched! Satanbamboula! seeing's believing! . . .

I come humbly back to my own case . . . Göttingen, Cassel, Osnabrück . . . who gives a damn . . . any more than about Trebizond or Nantes! . . . cities that might just as well have burned for two hundred years more . . . And Bayeux! and Baku! . . . and why not Naples? All burning . . . fire pots, *pot-au-feu* with all the punks in them! meat! guts! vegetables! . . . speeches, tremolos and statues, blablablah . . . roll the drums! Troubles, never see the end of them! we'll never get out . . . out of the muck . . . even if we never bought anything . . . what about the taxes? . . . gloomy bastard! . . . business demands optimism . . . defeatist punk! troubles? . . . troubles? . . . We've got too many to go worrying our heads over Hanover, Cassel, Göttingen . . . and what's become of their inhabitants . . . why not people from Billancourt . . . Montmartre? the Poirier family on the rue Duhem? . . . come, come, a little modesty! a little delicacy, if you please! . . . Lili's enough to worry about!

. . . Lili, I was telling you, has no sense of thrift . . . with me gone, will she have enough to get by for two years? . . . only two, no more . . . dancing lessons don't bring in anything! the ballerinas are always on tour . . . or on vacation, or pregnant . . . she won't have enough for two years . . . I'll have done my level best . . . nothing to reproach myself with . . . old, tired, and disabled: I'm taking a powder . . . it'll all run off smoothly . . . without a hitch . . . with a hunting rifle . . . no license required . . . Aftereffects of 1914 . . . I wouldn't want to break the law . . . never an outlaw . . . I've known what it means . . . thanks to the lunatic crumminess of my brothers! two-timing traitors the whole lot of them . . . take it from me . . . all raving feebleminded idiots, I've known plenty, or on the other side people like Achille, ferocious, vice-ridden bastards, loaded with bread, their pockets full of party cards . . . all the parties . . . who can poach and flout the law to their heart's content! Illusory immunity! Back to your pigsty! I know what I'm talking about . . . I hear boys who think they're pretty smart making light of the Code . . . oh oh! . . . where have they come from? . . . what office? . . . with what envelopes in their pockets? armbands? . . . fingerprints? I'm still waiting to see the ideal wise guy, the hep kid straight out of Carco, grabbing himself a thick slice at the expense of the Law . . . I'm waiting . . . in Criminal Court, for instance! calling the Judge a creep . . . sneering . . . and the Prosecutor a tongue-tied nitwit! and watch them all quaking! thumbing through the dictionary of argot . . . turning pages . . . begging his pardon . . . the Judge hiding under his Code . . . huddled up, white as a sheet! . . .

But the truth, alas, is different . . . the Law wins out . . . wherever you go! Uganda! Soviets! . . . Twelfth Chamber! No rapper . . . take it from me . . . will ever weaken . . . ever listen to your bright boy . . . no need of a closed session! . . . the bright boys haven't got a chance! . . . slickers from Neuilly, pimps from La Villette . . . Louis XV drawing-room or bar on the Avenue Zola . . . same difference! the wise guys clam up! once they get to the "Tenth," they forget everything they ever knew! . . . underneath the gibbet? . . . ditto

. . . at the guillotine? . . . in front of the firing squad? . . . the best you'll get out of them is historical sayings . . . Take Laval . . . "Vive la France!"

Oh yes, I admit it . . . "Suicide? . . . your suicide? . . .
it's a bore . . . Commit suicide . . . but shut up! . . . you
jackass! . . . it's monotonous!" I admit it . . . I blubber worse
than anybody . . . my panic at the thought of being an
outlaw . . . a shit-assed panicky conformist . . . that god-
awful fright freezes me! I hesitate . . . I start out strong, then
I weaken . . . I get muddled . . . and I'm not telling the
whole story . . . not by a long shot! . . .

When I think of all I missed . . . everything they had
cooked up for me . . . ah, my dear, it makes me sad! . . .
They came around and smashed my motorcycle . . . I was
gone . . . instead of me . . . to take out their disappointment
. . . the spokes! . . . and *bzing* . . . and *bzang* . . . frame
. . . lamp . . . gas tank! *bzing!* . . . drunk on vengeance
. . . kicks that would kill a mule . . . like it was my own
skull . . . What I missed . . . as if I'd sold Algeria . . . and
the Plaine Monceau . . . people never bother their heads
about who did what . . . all they want is for the victim to be
home . . . that's all! Just stay put! . . . To the lions! . . . if
he's taken a powder . . . it's unbelievable . . . cheated out of
the hunt, the kill . . . it drives them crazy! . . . the shouting,
the hubbub on the rue Girardon! . . . on the rue Lepic! . . .
ah, the bastard! the dirty crook! the skewer was ready for me!
give it to his motorcycle, at least! a commando! forty pairs of
clodhoppers . . . forty that weren't on the Meuse stopping the
Teuton tanks! Ah no! My IHP motorbike, that's the infernal
machine! . . . forty pairs of clodhoppers! . . . crushing,
smashing it into bits . . . that's what would have happened to
me if I'd stayed! square in the kisser! *bzing! bzang!* like to
Louis Renault . . . Renault was the factory and fifty billions!

. . . when the army does a cross-country with the green shits on its heels, you can expect anything . . . seven million deserters full of booze, you know what to expect! the Apocalypse . . . the world upside-down . . . everybody telling lies . . . kicks in the neck and motorcycle! . . . vengeance on objects and legless cripples! . . . assaults on the dying . . . so it was just as well for me to clear out of Montmartre! . . . without drums or trumpets . . . of course there will be more housecleaning . . . cutting people up in little pieces! any excuse will do! like fucking at the age of twenty . . . you're not particular . . . there are always heavenly excuses for murder! . . . but I'd like to be the audience myself . . . for a few minutes before I step down . . . "Just a minute, please, Mr. Executioner!" so's to watch the others first . . . wherever he says . . . Place de la Concorde . . . Champ de Mars . . . just to watch . . . I've paid for my place in the stands . . . seventy-five percent disability. I'm waiting! . . . they're getting the rolling mill ready? . . . okay . . . I, a son of the people, if ever there was one! eminently deserving of the job, I'm covered . . . Communist? . . . gracious, yes . . . a hundred times more than Bouchard, Thorez, Picasso . . . you won't find them doing their own housework . . . American? . . . more than Dulles! . . . accent and all! . . . do you realize whom you're talking to! . . . you pin-head! . . . I'll look at the winning mill . . . to see if it's *atomized?* . . . good! good! in line with the historic trend? splendid! . . . Imagine Mauriac reduced to foil . . . platitude, Girondin cries! . . . he'll go through like a postcard! . . . I'll encourage him . . . "Atta boy, François! Oil! Oil!" But then I calm down . . . My imagination is running away with me . . . Maybe I won't see a thing . . . too old! but all the same, when I look around me, I see signs of coming events! little appetizers . . . prostates, fibromas, tumors of the bronchial tubes . . . of the tongue . . . sweet little cases of myocarditis . . . pure joy! . . . Commies, bourgeois, housecleaners, the bugs will get them too! . . . the tiniest particle of a sub-atom, and out they go! . . . cancer of the throat? . . . they howl . . . they're not talking any more . . . furious on the rostrum, they leave it on

their knees . . . next stop the boneyard! . . . a bunch of kids!
. . . gangrenous wrecks! ah, martyrs? . . . Shit! . . . Ugh.

I content myself with little . . . I assure you . . . philosophical! . . . come around to Loukoum's door . . . no corset, no nylon will help him then! . . . or Achille either and his
billions . . . *knock, knock* . . . no Resistance, please . . .
ah, to make such a mess of my motorcycle . . . my little toy
. . . my motorbike from Bezons . . . my consultations have
always been free . . . not quite the same as Abbé Frime.

I've got an idea! . . . suppose they gave me the Nobel
Prize? . . . It would help me fine with the gas bill, my taxes,
my carrots . . . but those cocksuckers up there won't give it to
me! or their King! . . . they give it to every conceivable nance
. . . to the worst vaseline-asses on the planet . . . naturally!
It's all lined up . . . you've only got to see Mauriac in tails,
bowing like a hinge, delighted, ready and willing, on his little
platform . . . nothing troubles him . . . not even his glottis
. . . "Oh, how lovely and fat your Nobel Prize is!" . . . I was
talking about it with somebody yesterday . . . he protested:
"But come, come! Nimier has brought up your name! . . . Ingrate! . . . Haven't you read about it? A little pluck is all
you need! . . . Write another *Journey!*" People arrange everything so easily . . . Maybe I have my own opinion . . . The
Journey doesn't seem so terribly funny to me . . . Altman
didn't think it was funny either . . . or Daudet . . . and
what they want of me now is something irresistibly comical
. . . should I tell about the going over they gave Renault?
Sure! Not bad . . . or the wrecking of my motorcycle? . . .
pretty feeble . . . the great bonfire of my manuscripts? . . .
a paltry incident . . . but maybe people will go for it! maybe
it'll send them . . . ah, just supposing! okay, so I read the stuff
over, my pretty near 150 pages . . . it's not right . . . it
barely simmers . . . I'm handicapped by my respect for the
law . . . I've come down with gravity . . . What do I look
like with my gravity!

Another little story! . . . the head of the Editions Bérengères has been putting out "feelers" in my direction! yes, "feelers," as they say in the army . . . courting me, so to speak

. . . wants me to desert to him, white elephants and all . . . oh oh! why not? . . . so I reread the stuff . . . my masterpieces! obviously he hates Achille . . . and it didn't begin yesterday . . . he's always hated him! a rancid hatred! what he wouldn't give to see him attached, bankrupted, sold out! . . . bag and baggage at the Flea Market! and his case re-opened, his shady deals . . . justified on one ground or another . . . all reinvestigated . . . what ground? . . . blackmail most likely! . . . millions every month? So it seems . . . but still touchy . . . the kind of secret that's no secret to anybody! Gertrut is having a fine time! speculating! the look on Achille's face if I leave him! his mug! . . . Just let me say yes . . . sure . . . I'm going . . . me and my white elephants . . . My immortal works . . . to the Editions Bérengères! . . . but it shouldn't kill Achille right away! oh no! give him time to see his whole shack fold up! what a disaster! terrific! . . . my job is to open the breach . . . give his two thousand slaves a chance to escape! that'll be the time to trot out the records . . . the Law! . . . Won't that be the day! . . . Sensational! Sensational! Quite a guy Gertrut! Gertrut de Morny! . . . A bit of an anti-Semite, I suspect . . . couldn't it be on account of the Dreyfus case that they hate each other so? . . . maybe . . . they'll never tell me . . . they know so much about each other . . . you'd say they'd known each other a century . . . a thousand years of skulduggery! . . . Achille doesn't take me seriously any more . . . "You complain? . . . hell, there are plenty more! and they don't complain! you could have been shot? . . . couldn't you?" Gertrut is different, he knows how to handle me, he sympathizes . . . he reminds me of the risks I've run, the trouble I've been through . . . "Your furniture . . . your manuscripts . . . the little money you had . . . they've ruined you . . ." he practically weeps . . . Brottin is the hardhearted type . . . here I haven't been shot, and I come around complaining! . . . outrageous! . . . his arms drop limp at his sides . . . if I could only tell him what I think! . . . that what I'd like best is to see them fight . . . skin each other alive . . . to the finish . . . puncture each other's carotids! . . . if I resist the temptation to tell him . . . it's for the dogs, for the birds . . . if I go easy on him . . . for ourselves, too . . . people always talk too much . . . for the noodles . . . the noodles come first! and the coal and the gas! . . . if I'd told him what I thought of him, I'd never have seen him again! . . .

"Recapture your humor, Céline . . . if only you'd write the way you talk! what a masterpiece! . . ."

"You're very kind, Gertrut, but take a look at me! just take a look!"

I calm him down. "Look at the state I'm in . . . I can hardly hold a pen."

"No, no, Céline . . . you're full of vigor . . . the best age! . . . Take Cervantes! . . . I'm not telling you anything new."

"No, Gertrut . . . you're not telling me anything new! . . . the same age as Achille . . . eighty-one . . . Don Quix-ote! . . ."

That's the dodge all publishers pull when they want to stimu-late their old nags . . . they tell you Cervantes was a stripling . . . at eighty-one!

"And disabled worse than you, Céline!"

He goes on and on! . . . a flood of tonic words! . . . he presses his proposition!

Why did Achille and Gertrut fall out? . . . in the first place? . . . nobody remembered . . . it went back too far . . . over a horse? . . . an actress? Nobody knew . . . now it's over publishing . . . in the old days there were witnesses . . . and duels! . . . nowadays people fight over shops! . . . which would have more authors in his cellar? the foibles of two old fruitcakes! . . . I haven't told you about their looks . . . an antique vision, not much features left, it's the Period that counts! . . . do they date from before the Ferris wheel? or after? . . . Gertrut de Morny wore a monocle . . . a sky-blue monocle! . . . had he gone in for buggery? It's possible . . . in addition to women . . . rich? . . . plenty . . . but Achille had a certain expression you could recognize him by . . . his smile . . . the terribly embarrassed smile of an old chair-woman caught in the act, with her hand in the collection box . . . with Gertrut it was his monocle . . . the faces he made to keep it from falling off . . . to keep his wrinkled pouches from cutting off his eyesight . . . Achille's embarrassed smile had been his main charm around 1900 . . . "the Irresistible," they called him . . . Watteau! . . . Fantin Latour! . . . at the "Bazaar of Time" . . . on the bargain counter, all ancient articles look alike . . . monocles, grimaces, eyelids,   wigs . . . smiles . . . old   chair-women . . . old beaux . . .

But now it wasn't a question of ladies or the Dreyfus case!
. . . this concerned me . . . his idea of appropriating my
masterpieces . . . my immortal books that nobody reads any
more (according to Achille) . . . they're so hell-bent on doing
each other dirt they don't care what they say! . . . hell,
they've got whole cellars full of Giants of the Pen! . . . much
more breathtaking than me . . . alleged pederasts! alleged
common-law criminals . . . alleged collaborators . . . alleged
fellaghas* . . . alleged sadistic maniacs . . . alleged Muscovites! . . . geniuses galore! . . . baby geniuses! . . . doddering
geniuses! . . . female geniuses! . . . just plain geniuses! . . .
   Let's get back to the facts of history . . . nobody'll ever
convince me that Fred Bourdonnais, my first hustler, went out
all alone in the moonlight on purpose to get himself bumped
off on the Esplanade des Invalides . . . people were being
murdered there every day! that's right! . . . and he knew it
. . . that was the fashionable Esplanade . . . he had his
little vices? . . . of course! . . . but that was carrying vice too
far, all by himself at midnight on the Place des Invalides! . . .
what happened was bound to happen! . . . the funny part of
it was that once Bourdonnais had given up the ghost at midnight on the Place des Invalides, I was sold down the river . . .
like a slave . . . the Marquise Fualdès inherited me! . . .
inherited, no less! . . . bandit's booty! . . . and I was sold
again! . . . again! once more! . . . twice more . . . me and
my immortal masterpieces! . . . No misgivings marred their
pleasure! Male or female, the hustlers didn't leave me a thing
. . . "he's in prison, let him croak!" I ought to know a little
something about that . . . even in public school and later beyond "the blue line of the Vosges" . . . poetry was my down-

fall! and still is! Worse and more of it! Ah, sacrificial victim?
your ugly mug! . . . your blood! your furniture! . . . your
lyre! . . . your books! . . . off to the dungeon! bastard! the
whole works . . . we're waiting for you! . . .

Do you think Brottin, who's winking at me now . . . him or
Gertrut? what the hell do I care? . . . or the Marquise? . . .
ever pounded any sidewalks? Oh no, that's my job, the work is
all for me . . . to think up something amusing, something
. . . the pimps, male and female, who did their level best to
let me croak . . . they didn't succeed . . . are still there, with
their mouths wide open! waiting for a treat from me! . . . funnier! funnier! . . . demanding, stamping their feet!

Something funny? . . . that the day after the murder on the
Esplanade des Invalides, I was collared! at the other end of
Europe . . . and no punches pulled . . . for the count! . . .
six years! . . . a melo-comic arrest! over the roofs! . . . cav-
alcade between the chimneys! . . . a whole commando unit
of cops with revolvers drawn . . . Believe me, it was chilly on
the roofs of Copenhagen, Denmark, December 22! . . . Go
see for yourself . . . Tourists, take a look, nothing to fear . . .
Ved Stranden 20 (*tuve* in Danish) you'll find . . . past the
Bokelund grocery store . . . across the street, lit up day and
night, the *National Tidende* . . . the whole building . . . a
newspaper . . . you couldn't get lost if you wanted to . . .
well, anyway, at the end of December, the hunt for collaborators . . . the total house-cleaning frenzy was at its height . . .
the Circus of Europe . . . like right now in Budapest . . .
and here again tomorrow . . . like coitus, like lovemaking
. . . the Great Purge is here today and someplace else tomorrow . . . it's a necessity! . . . what a windfall I was! . . . my
carcass! . . . I really came in handy, me and Lili and Bébert
. . . from roof to roof! hunted beasts do wonders to escape
the butchers! here! . . . there! . . . everywhere . . . the
hunt is a sport! . . . okay, let's suppose you're avid tourists!
. . . you can hunt memories! . . . the hunt is up! I know,
everything gets forgotten . . . hasn't Verdun been forgotten?
. . . or pretty near . . . Ypres doesn't mean a thing any more
. . . but a little episode like our climb on *Ved Stranden*, Lili,

myself, and Bébert, the roofs, the drains . . . the bulls armed, aiming their wicked rods . . . hide-and-seek around the chimneys . . . Christmas 1945! . . . seems to me they ought to remember it a little . . . Copenhagen, Denmark, *Ved Stranden* . . . go take a look. I'd be surprised if people had forgotten all about it . . . but to tell the truth, it wasn't just the *National-Tidende* that stirred up the pack . . . and how! . . *Berlingske!* . . . *Land og Folk!* . . . *Politiken* . . . their jackal press . . . the whole lot of them! . . . the whole organizations of Israelites I'd sold . . . in addition to the forts of Verdun! . . . and the estuary of the Seine! As long as I was there, as long as they had me available . . . I could pay for the King, for his *Dronin* and the anti-Commintern pact! for the Frikorps! (their L.V.F.!*) . . . I was a gift from heaven! . . . I'd make up for it all! . . . Wipe out all the stains! . . . the blood on the keys! . . . anti-Macbeth! . . .

I'd be surprised if they didn't remember! have a look see . . . *Ved Stranden tuve* . . . ground floor: Bokelund's grocery store . . .

All their newspapers, headlines a mile high . . . their right-
wing plutocrats as windy as their Commies, Bopa and company! you'll say I was an easy mark! . . . Just the thing to ce-
ment their sacred union . . . conservatives and Muscovites!
. . . "do we impale him? . . . Christ, yes! . . . he's made to
order . . ." No compunctions over my corpse . . . nothing
but kisses! . . . I know how useful I am: the worst enemies
make peace! . . . magic! . . . magic! . . .

I have to laugh . . . Obviously I'd sold the plans of the
Maginot Line . . . That was taken for granted! But the question was . . . for how much? the exact figure? . . . there
were lots of suggestions . . . the widow Renault didn't sell a
thing . . . for billions? . . . come, come . . . let's be serious
. . . that's why there's so much talk about Louis, Emperor of
Billancourt! . . . and his vertebra! and his martyrdom! I'm
just as much a martyr, but no bread, you won't hear my widow
or son demanding explanations! . . . there won't be any X-
rays or embalming . . . hell, no . . . your penniless martyr
hasn't a leg to stand on! . . . the wells and furnaces are full of
bigger martyrs than Renault! and nobody X-rayed them or re-
corded their agony . . . no Brothers of Charity . . . and their
widows have remarried as quietly as can be . . . not a word
out of them . . . and their sons are off fighting somewhere!
. . . Dien-Pen-hu! . . . Oran! . . . and no fuss! So what do
I look like griping that they've done me every conceivable
wrong and that they're still persecuting me? it's an outrage,
etc . . . "You cur, it serves you right!" . . . They'd do better
to revive the flame . . . march up the Champs-Elysées! take
the rue de Châteaudun* by storm, oh, the beautiful bonfires
they're planning! oh, the terrific super-Budapests! . . . not to

mention all these irritations of the arteries! . . . these swollen little prostates! . . . howling tomorrows! . . . "a bottle of mineral water! . . . oh, oh, the blockheads! . . ."

Le Bourdonnais, who was murdered, was certainly a bad egg, a
hypocrite and a pimp . . . oh, no more nor less than Achille or
Gertrut . . . but snowed under as he was by debts, pending
accounts and bad checks! . . . I've told you how it ended . . .
if he'd been solvent, he'd still be alive, they wouldn't have
taken him for a ride . . . but insolvent? his number was up, it
was in the cards . . . Carbuccia,* a flower of innocence, a
tourist! . . . "According to who you are" . . . well, me and
my white elephants . . . you can imagine what happened to
me in all this! handed over . . . bag and baggage . . . to
those depraved grocers! . . . they'd never stuffed their bellies
so full! . . . pigs! . . . the worst thing about them is their
weight, heavy heavy! . . . their deceit . . . big fat layers,
their subtleties stick to your fingers . . . it takes you hours to
get your hands clean . . . sticky! . . . Le Bourdonnais was
washed up . . . young hippopotamus! three guesses whether
they saw him coming . . . with his clumsy tricks! . . . on the
Esplanade at night . . . a big hole in his back! . . . laid out
cold! . . . in the moonlight! the Fualdès dame inherits . . .
inherits me and sells me off . . . pass to Achille . . . that's
football for you, my treasures! my geniuses! . . . rugby! . . .
Fualdès receives, gets away! . . . Achille scores and wins!
. . . takes the whole pot . . . stows me away in his cellar!
. . . me and my white elephants! . . . I disappear from
view! the Marquise de Fualdès digests . . . Old stuff! . . .
The times have changed . . . Whoopee! Bagged and gagged
. . . A laugh! see you next year on the ice!

A buck private in all that . . . a square like me! . . .
spoiled darling! . . and, I repeat, it doesn't date from yesterday . . . ever since public school on the rue Louvois . . .

which doesn't make us any younger . . . takes you back to the Impressionists, to the Dreyfus case! public school is the keynote of the people . . . Mauriac can talk "Communist," he'll never know what he's talking about! He's a hundred per-cent *Chartron!** and will be to his dying day . . . *Chartron!* I flatter him!

So just then . . . when the cold feet were hanging out flags . . . when the tremblers were looting, when the deserters were triumphant, when the gollywobblers were coming up strong, when forty million yellow-bellies were taking their ven-geance, it wasn't exactly the time for me to show my face! It was as if Larengon the apostate or Triolette in her "double-duty bikini" were to cross the bridge in Pest . . . If I'd been at my mother's on the rue Marsolier, they'd have got me . . . like Le Bourdonnais! . . . *bam!* . . . like on the rue Girardon . . . "you stink" . . . that's reason enough! "He's got it com-ing to him . . . that's all . . . Bring him out!" Vaillant, who's boasted plenty and still regrets bitterly that he missed me, and by so little . . . there he wouldn't have missed me . . . if I'd been at my mother's aged seventy-four . . .

They left me nothing . . . not a handkerchief, not a chair, not a manuscript . . . if I'd been a stiff I would have stunk . . . I'd have inconvenienced them . . . like this I wasn't in the way, they were able to cart everything off and sell it at the Flea Market! at the Auction Rooms! . . . coming up hard with the joy of it! . . . Sold out . . . I'm like France . . . sold out, bag and baggage! . . . birth certificate and all! . . . sixty-three in a week! . . . Assassins, you've got him by the balls! . . . diving off the Budapest bridge? how many like me?

It'll be mighty amusing someday if a future Lenôtre digs up our tombs and our statues, our halos and our bank deposits . . . to see how much the "pure" took in . . . how many de Beers shares? How many Rhône shares? How many castles, whores, treasures, stables, embassies? . . . more than in '89? . . . less? . . . What debates! . . . at the Sorbonne! . . . at the Trois Magots! . . . in the *Annals!* . . . and if Hitler had won . . . Aragon joining the S.S.? Triolette a charming Walkyrie? . . . ah, those lectures! . . . an earful! . . . In the *Annals* for the year 2000 . . . the grand Communist marquises fighting for seats for fear of missing a single session! . . . a single one of their super-super Herriot's dazzling flights . . . with his rear end ten times as big as our Herriot's . . . not to mention the sensa-a-ational Abbé Pierre . . . ten revolvers!

To hell with the future . . . let's get back to our own affairs! that Gertrut should screw Brottin? . . . hell, why not? . . . that they should cut each other's throats! by all means! if you see him with his eyes hanging out, be sure to tell me about it for kicks . . . I'm speaking of Achille . . . let them skin each other alive . . . both of them . . . bright red, scarlet . . . peeled! . . . a good show! but before they fix each other up, listen to this! . . . it's funny! . . . in the days of the Hippodrome on the Place Clichy, Gertrut and Achille both had a hard-on for the same woman, one of those eaters of gold francs! a rival of the Bank of France! . . . anybody who remembers those "good old" days remembers Suzanne . . . what a screen artist! and her vaporous negligees against a background of "soft blue light!" of "moonlight" . . . what a sublime artist, absolutely silent, no talkies in those days . . . it's the word that kills! . . . a woman that talks softens your pecker, ah, they

49

came up hard at the silent pictures! . . . Take a look at the movie houses today! the trouble they have filling up! . . . blah-blah-blah . . . crushing, soporific . . . gloomy balls . . . soft cocks! . . . smiles, vaporous negligees! tender music! we'll be going back to all that! . . . and moonlight! I can safely say that you'll never find an idol who can hold a candle to Suzanne . . . not even with floods of money, tomtoms, and scandal . . . it's no use trying . . . I who had no time to spare, hell, no! . . . between deliveries . . . I still managed to gallop out past Bécon to see Suzanne in person on the set! . . . gives you an idea what an idol she was! . . . between La Garenne and Nanterre . . . whenever it stopped raining, they took advantage! . . . between the rubble heaps . . . hiring on the spot . . . we made up the crowd . . . I was a kid in the crowd . . . between showers, five francs! . . . two francs . . . a whistle blew! . . . everybody take shelter! . . . the first drop! under the bridge! save the equipment from the rain . . . and the dresses with their muslin trains! and the stars' makeup, carmine and oil and plaster of Paris! . . . beauties that had warmth . . . Did we help! . . . we husky extras weren't the only ones to help them to the shelters! the sightseers helped too! . . . the crowd! . . . when the whistle blew! and the first drop fell! everybody! and Suzanne!

What's become of all that? . . . I ask you . . . the stars and the extras? . . . and the crowd? . . . and the rain . . . what rain! . . . speaking of those far-off days I can say one thing: The real thing is dead! . . . I know . . . a fellow like me, still attentive to the real thing . . . looks like an ass! . . . For no reason at all . . . and they're proud of it . . . they crushed the whorehouses and street fairs . . . some jerk-off! . . . now the juice squirts all over the place! . . . the whole place is a whorehouse . . . and a street fair . . . from cradle to grave . . . all fucked up! The real thing is dead. Verdun killed it! Amen! . . .

Maybe I'm going to bore you . . . something funnier? . . . more titillating? . . . Maybe . . . ? All I care about . . . you know that . . . is giving you a laugh . . . Even before the days of Suzanne, I knew the Hippodrome with its horses

and wild animals! the big stable! and what mobs! . . . such
crowds that the omnibus gave up! . . . at La Trinité . . .
couldn't even get started! jam-packed with enthusiasts. And
what a show! men, lions, and horses, Marines, Boxers, the cap-
ture of Peking! Those are the things that give you the right
frame of mind! a sense of art! I don't know many writers of the
so-called left or right, holy-water addicts or Commies, con-
spirators of the cellar cafés or of the Lodges, who ever saw the
storming of Peking like I did on the Place Clichy . . . and the
bayonet charge of our little Marines! the storming of the
wooden ramparts . . . the clouds of powder smoke! . . . and
boom! . . . at least twenty cannon . . . all at once! . . . Sergeant Bobillot taking on a hundred Boxers singlehanded! . . .
grabbing their flag! . . . and planting ours, our tricolor! on
their pile of corpses . . . square in the middle! . . . Peking
was ours! And the fleet! coming down from the grid! the *Cour-
bet* on canvas! . . . the works . . . those were the shows!
Those shows formed the spirit!

Oh, wait . . . something even more terrific than Peking!
. . . the attack on the stagecoach . . . by three tribes of
mounted Indians . . . bareback . . . you need to have seen
those things! Where would you find two hundred Indians riding bareback today? . . . plus Buffalo Bill in person! . . .
shooting an egg in mid-air . . . in full gallop! you won't find
that in a hurry . . . no Hollywood hokum! . . . that egg in
mid-air . . . Buffalo Bill and his boys . . . the genuine article, spitting flames! . . . ah, and the best of all! . . . I forgot
to tell you . . . Louise Michel!* . . . Nowadays they talk
about sensations! suspense! what have they got? Nothing! . . .
there on the Place Clichy you didn't talk, you just looked and
trembled . . . look . . . the main attraction! Louise Michel
rising out of the darkness! deathly pale! all the spotlights con-
verging . . . for half a second! *"Bow-wow!"* . . . she seemed
to be climbing on a chair . . . *bow! wow!* . . . Angry! . . .
out with the lights! . . . my grandmother had lived through
the Commune on the rue Montorgueil, she knew . . . "That's
not Louise Michel, my boy . . . it's not her nose or her
mouth!" . . . you couldn't fool my grandmother . . .

Nowadays it's out of the question, you won't see Khrushchev, Picasso or Triolette climbing on a chair . . . the Desmoulins-Palais Royal effect! . . . not those pallid shouters . . . appearing under the spotlights *"bow! wow!"* . . . Thorez perhaps? Mauriac?

One thing is sure, nose or no nose, Louise had a perfect right! *"bow! wow!"* . . . and angry! . . . and how! . . . I say it and I'll say it again louder . . . later on! . . . when I have time to think about it . . .

"I've known him since the Dreyfus case! . . . he gets worse
every year! . . . every month! . . . the crustiest pirate of
them all! of the whole publishing trade! . . . him and his
whole gang . . . there's nothing lower . . . You're the laughing stock of his whole shop! . . . the whole buggering mob!
. . . the way they fleece you . . . champion sucker . . .
only too happy to be sabotaged, looted, and insulted! . . .
what a crew! . . . him and his head eunuch Loukoum!"

Gertrut of the sky-blue monocle, naturally he wasn't telling
me anything new . . . hell, no . . . Gertrut Bérengères, I
could have sold him some dirt . . . I knew Achille was crossing me up, I knew all about it! my, oh, my! When you come to
think that he . . . old Gertrut . . . had plenty of time to
spare and money coming in . . . he could afford to dig up
scandals that were of no interest to anybody, except maybe
himself . . . the bilious chit-chat of 1900.

To hell with all that! Gertrut! Achille! those crooks . . . I
only had one thing on my mind . . . cold cash and good-bye!
. . . what was I going to leave Lili? . . . *quid?* . . . how?
. . . what? . . . that little nest egg? . . . but there's the rub!
. . . nest egg, it's easy to say! . . . with me gone? my last
gasp? I could see the rush of "claimants"! . . . the mob! . . .
once the animal is dead, you see them swarming, stampeding
. . . those jaws! . . . all with claims . . . with papers, without papers . . . seals, stamps . . . or without! . . . pouring
out of every Métro station! . . . crocodiles with tears . . .
without! . . . those teeth! all with claims! Lili will be evicted
pronto . . . out on the street . . . I can see it as if I was there
. . . she's incapable of defending herself! . . . exactly the
same story as on the rue Girardon . . . or in Saint-Malo . . .

or Copenhagen, *Ved Stranden* 20 (*tuve*) . . . the same sect . . . the claimants . . . absolutely international . . . adapted to every climate . . . the same crooks . . . wherever you go . . . regardless of regime, philosophy, creed, or color . . . any pretext will do . . . they descend in swarms . . . like locusts . . . and you won't see Lili defending herself! . . . no! . . . the exact opposite . . . it's sad . . . romantic-sad . . . a dancer . . .

Why kid myself . . . Private worries, you'll say . . . but
even so . . . nobody . . . Gertrut, Brottin, or anyone else
. . . will advance me a plug nickel for a book like *Normance,*
and that's that . . . what the readers want is a laugh . . . in
the first place Paris was never bombed . . . not a single com-
memorative tablet, isn't that proof enough? . . . I'm the only
one who still remembers two, three families buried under the
ruins . . . as far as sales are concerned, *Normance* was a total
flop . . . for one reason or another . . . in addition to being
sabotaged . . . and then some! . . . by Achille, his clique, his
ferocious lackeys, and the hatchetmen of the press! . . . I was
expected to be provocative, to grind up some more Palestini-
ans, to run myself back into the cooler! and for good! . . .
"benefactors" they call themselves . . . chin up, boy . . . a
rap to end all raps! . . . twenty years, my dear sir . . . life
. . . oh oh, they've got the wrong slant! . . . I'm waiting to
see them all pulled in . . . thugs, all flirting with the guillotine, hard labor, and solitary! to see our beautiful Guyana re-
opened for them! Devil's Island restored . . . with a little
bonus thrown in, a little something on the tongue for each one
of them . . . an epithelioma or two . . . a whole assortment
. . . between the carotid and the pharynx . . .
   That's all very well . . . But in the meantime Brottin gives
me the lowdown: no soap! . . . "You sell less and less . . .
your *Normance?* . . . a disaster . . . nothing in it to put you
back in the clink . . . no pornography . . . no fascism . . .
poor bastard! . . . the critics, though . . . poison fangs! the
whole works! all ready! . . . it's impossible . . . they're dis-
gusted with you! . . . what about *their* hamburger? . . .
heartless! . . . their pay envelopes? . . . their families? . . ."

"Stop writing," you'll say . . . you're perfectly right . . . but what about Lili, the dogs and cats, the birds, and the snowdrops . . . we had some this winter . . . maybe you've got some idea?

In fact, I can assure you: even living at rock bottom . . . cutting down on everything . . . it's a hard fight with the elements, winds, drafts, humidity, coal bills! . . . cauliflower, smoked herring! the fight to go on living! . . . carrots! . . . or even crusts of bread!

But what about my style and my masterpieces? . . . cabala, boycott . . . naturally! I say string up all the plagiarists! and not only the plagiarists, the incompetents too! God knows! . . . at Achille's alone, thousands of them . . . for my money Dumel, Mauriac, Tartre, same noose! . . . the dozen Goncourt prize winners on the next tree! . . . oh, and I forgot the Archbishop of Paris! before the "due process" crowd . . . we wouldn't want that . . . start asking for his head at the Porte Brancion.

Talking about gas and such trifles, the bill's due tomorrow . . . I owe for two "readings" . . . I owe the tax collector, too . . . I owe for coal . . . I repeat myself? . . . hell . . . in the same situation . . . in the same mess . . . you'd be yelling so hard they could hear you in Enghien . . . they'd have to come and get you . . . with sedatives and straitjackets! Lili and I've been going on like this for fifteen years . . . with the pack at our heels . . . Fifteen years is a long time . . . the ferocious Teutonic occupation was only three years at most . . . think it over!

I see that I'm boring you . . . change the record! . . . string up the bourgeoisie? . . . the bourgeois of all parties . . . I'm all for it, posolutely! A bourgeois is a hundred percent stinker . . . I'm thinking of one in particular, Tartre! the cream of the sewer! the way he slandered me, moved heaven and earth to have me drawn and quartered, I vote him five . . . or six nice malignant tumors between the esophagus and the pancreas . . . top priority!

Tartre robbed me and slandered me . . . don't try to tell me different . . . but no worse than my relations . . . and he's

not amusing like my aunt! . . . far from it . . . my aunt's
shock . . . practically a stroke . . . at seeing me again! . . .
that I wasn't dead! . . . that they hadn't executed me! . . .
"You? You?" . . . she couldn't believe it . . . "You here?"

As you can imagine, she'd helped herself . . . walked off
with three pairs of curtains, six chairs, and all the enamel sauce-
pans . . . not that she needed any of it . . . hell no! . . . she
had two . . . three . . . of everything . . . but as long as everybody was helping himself and I was her nephew, why
shouldn't she too? . . . she, empty-handed? . . . when my
joint was being sacked . . . by total strangers . . . and she
was my aunt after all . . . In the first place I had no business
coming back . . . I was supposed to die in prison . . .
hanged . . . impaled . . . naturally she should inherit . . .
the most natural thing in the world . . . Tartre inherited
from me, too . . . and plenty of others! . . . "Hello, auntie"
. . . she jumps out of her bed in her nightgown to look at me!
me! "He murdered his mother! . . . arrest him! . . . arrest
him!" . . . Her first words . . . straight from the heart! so
overcome with emotion that she ran out screaming, denouncing
me: "Monsieur le Préfet! Help! Help! arrest him! He killed his
mother! Monsieur le Préfet! Help!" . . . down the Faubourg
Saint-Jacques and along the Quais . . . "Help! . . . help!"
The cops caught her on the run, beat her up at the police station . . . took her to a different station . . . released her . . .
beat her up again! "It's him, it's him! . . ." She started in
again . . . in the middle of the night on the Quai des Orfèvres
. . . she wanted the prefect of police to step in . . . to throw
me back in stir . . . so I'd never come around asking for
a chair . . . That was my aunt! . . . friends, relatives, all
the same! . . . scavengers when you're outlawed! . . . after
spending the rest of the night running around the Food Market, shouting that I had murdered my mother, galloping from
one stall to another, she finally collapsed in a pile of leeks! . . .
that time they trussed her up . . . took her to the hospital
. . . she was still yelling that I was this . . . that . . . any
damn thing . . .

Once they've stolen everything you own . . . your furniture, manuscripts, knicknacks, curtains . . . you can expect the worst . . . especially from relatives and friends . . . your vicious benefactors! . . . meaner than a sawed-off shotgun . . . the passion they put into tracking you down . . . my aunt in the bughouse . . . Tartre gone Commie . . . every last one of them ready to throw an epileptic fit if I even looked at them . . . As I said, Auntie wanted for nothing! Or Tartre! . . . well-heeled . . . everything in duplicate! in triplicate! . . . in town . . . in the country . . . frigidaires, automobiles, lackeys . . . the horn had been sounded for me . . . they were in on the hunt . . . that's all . . . Anything for me to be surprised about? . . . stupid bastard! . . .

I'm sidetracking you with trifles . . . I was telling you about Gertrut Morny . . . his keen interest in me . . . Tartuffe! . . . that I should leave Achille, that contemptible, scheming saboteur, for the Editions Bérengères . . . that Achille was my ruin . . . that Loukoum's greatest joy . . . him and his whole tribe . . . was reducing me to nothing . . . at the bottom of their cellar . . . me and my white elephants . . .

But what about Gertrut? . . . I've told you about his face . . . not an old chair-woman like Achille. More the musketeer type, with a musketeer's goatee . . . plus the big sky-blue monocle . . . sure . . . he handed me a line, promised me the moon . . . the sales I'd have . . . I'd recapture the "public favor"! It's true I hadn't much to lose! I couldn't have found a bigger crook than Brottin! . . . for eighty years and then some whole generations of authors had been trying to make a dent in his pocketbook, he'd never coughed up, not twenty francs! . . . in the battle for advances! . . . Achille put up the resistance of a Hercules! but maybe there was one little ruse that might work . . . get him to fork out ten thousand . . . twenty thousand . . . No harm in trying. "So long, Achille! I'm leaving . . . sick of your face . . ." He runs after you . . . with his sweetest smile . . . what hatred! Suits me! Let him hate me!

I didn't trust Gertrut around the corner . . . guess I've told you . . . but he was really rich, never a dull moment, when you got him started on Achille . . . the anecdotes, going back thirty! forty! years . . . the rottenness of that man . . .

showed me what I could expect of him! he cheated right
down the line . . . at everything . . . at cards, at the races, at
Enghien, at the Stock Exchange . . . he couldn't help it . . .
the way he hornswoggled his authors, his employees, his
maids . . . the bogus loans . . . that they never saw . . .
vouchers, contracts . . . flimflam . . . made them sign re-
leases . . . receipts! . . . how many had committed suicide,
fished out of the dam at Suresnes? . . . including giants of the
pen and ladies once famous who'd be a hundred and thirty
years old today!

Enough chit-chat . . . here comes the man to read the
water meter . . . I'd better be thinking about that kilo of noodles, that smoked herring . . . Hatred or not, Gertrut had the
faraway "don't-bother-me" look of the rich . . . he didn't understand about noodles . . . they were brutes of a feather
. . . the same exasperation . . . you, yes you, stupid, how
dare you mention noodles to them . . . rich people are only
interested in sport . . . the Stock Exchange, the paddock . . .
the sport of making their Suez stock go up . . . of swiping
each other's actresses, having them mounted by their jockeys
. . . the sport of passing red lights . . . every known sport
. . . they drool, they're coming apart at the seams, but never
a charity ball without them . . . and the little cocksuckers
. . . and kidnapping each other's authors . . . but there is
one sport they avoid like the plague . . . writing . . . they'd
sooner shit in bed . . . publishers aren't crazy! Writers die of
toil? What of it? . . . so do donkeys . . . what would Achille
do with a piece of paper? Just tell me that . . . what sport?
. . . what rotten thing would he make? Or Gertrut? . . .
paper dolls? . . .

If only, for instance, I could count on the critics . . . just a
little publicity . . . even insulting . . . not Mauriac's whole
circus, of course not . . . confessionals and playful urinals!
. . . or Trissotin Tartre . . . the united survivors of twenty
years of blah-blah-blah! . . . no . . . I'd be satisfied with a
few murmurs . . .

I can do without? Think so? . . . But don't say I didn't try.
Time to take action . . .

When it comes to action, I'm Napoleonic . . . Let's go. Arlette* on one arm . . . Simon* on the other . . . and forward march! Is that the studio up ahead? . . . we'll take it by storm . . . here we go . . . rejoice and take heart! . . .

Alas! . . . this cavern? The ruins and leftovers of three . . . maybe four Expositions! funereal bric-à-brac . . . and under that vaulting? higher than three . . . four Notre-Dames . . . all papier-mâché, stucco, giant canopies . . . This is it . . . this is the place . . . Oh, solemn moment . . . our voices . . . no good! we start all over . . . another recording . . . First Simon! . . . I've got to admit, I was moved. . . the phony vaulting resounds! . . . or if it's not the vaulting it's an amplifier! and myself, usually so soft-spoken, my voice is so horrendous it almost puts me to flight . . . what an effect! . . . I wouldn't have believed it . . .

Not at all, they say . . . you won't leave without singing something? . . . no false modesty if that's what they want . . . here we go . . . one! two! . . . vaulting or no vaulting . . . I ask the M.C., the one who speaks French a little . . . if the idea is to put them on sale? . . . my songs, my harmonies and false notes? . . . If maybe I could . . . ? Just a little record? . . .

"Oh no, Maître! No, later! . . . much later, I hope! . . . for our discothèque . . . your necrological recording!"

I saw what they were after! Later? later? . . . I disagree! . . . the prose, the readings . . . perhaps . . . but the songs, oh no, just as they are and right away . . . a bit of eternity on the wing.

I wasn't going to tell them that.

I won't go macabre on you and start in on waiters, undertakers, etc. . . . no! . . . I was talking about paupers' graves . . . not the local cemetery . . . further out . . . in Thiais . . . or even further . . . but once I'm gone . . . what about Lili? . . . the cats . . . the dogs . . . I can't see Lili taking care of herself . . . she's not made that way . . . all those "claimants" swooping down . . . friends, relatives, bailiffs, vultures of all kinds . . . oh, it's nothing new to us . . . we've seen pillage . . . here, there, everywhere . . . But Lili all by herself?

"He got everybody down on him . . . Lousy racist, we didn't loot him enough . . . let's massacre his widow!"

I protest too much? . . . not at all . . . my racist ideas haven't anything to do with it! Gang of Tartuffes! . . . The white race went out of existence long ago . . . look at Ben Youssef! . . . Mauriac! . . . Monnerville! . . . Jacob! * . . . tomorrow Coty . . . What's all the fuss about . . . It's the *Journey* that got me into all this . . . My most relentless persecutors date from the *Journey* . . . Nobody's forgiven me for the *Journey* . . . it was the *Journey* that cooked my goose . . . Maybe if my name had been *Vlazine* . . . Vlazine Progrogrof . . . If I'd been born in Tarnopol on the Don . . . but in Courbevoie, Seine . . . Born in Tarnopol on the Don they'd have given me the Nobel Prize years ago . . . but coming from right here, not even a Sephardim . . . they don't know where to put me . . . to blot me out . . . what dungeon to hide my shame in . . . what rats to invoke . . . Vrance for the Vrench!

If I were a naturalized Mongol . . . or a fellagha like Mauriac, I'd be driving a car, I could do what I pleased . . . secure in my old age . . . coddled and fussed over . . . my standard of living, boy oh boy! . . . I'd pontificate from my hilltop . . . I'd hand out enormous lessons in virtue, in intransigence . . . in mysticism! . . . I'd be on television every day, you'd see my icon all over the place . . . I'd be worshiped by all the Sorbonnes! . . . If I'd been born in Tarnopol on the Don, my old age would be one happy holiday, I'd average two-hundred thousand a month on the *Journeyski* alone! Altman won't say different . . . neither will Triolette or Larengon . . .

I'll try it one of these days . . . we'll see.

But born in Courbevoie-sur-Seine, you see, they don't let anything by . . . they never will . . . the only resister in the place! that's outrageous . . . can I prove it? the proof is that you won't find me in the dictionary . . . under doctor-authors . . . or at the stationery store . . . or anywhere else . . . same with the *Brottin Illustrated* . . . the "Punctual Review of Bromidics" . . . absolutely not . . . Norbert Loukoum wanted to put me in but ass backwards . . . that was his idea . . . words, text, pages, all upside-down . . . I called him a cocksucker and worse! told him he had an incestuous mouth, etc. . . . that he was one big lump of sadist-bite-me . . . we parted on those words . . . "My 'Excremental Review' is closed to you!" . . . which was what I expected . . . oh! the Bromidic Review! . . . not for me . . . there were other ways of fishing for noodles . . . other strings to my bow! Help me, Hippocrates . . . yes, the patients are few and far between . . . I've told you that . . . but you can never claim to have lost every single patient . . . the chiropractors, faith healers, nurses, masseurs, and so on always let a few slip through their nets . . . oh, not enough to pay for my license . . . or my dues to the Medical Association, or my life insurance . . . or to pay the plumber . . . or buy me a subscription to the Medical Review . . . which gives you an idea of our economic situation! my oh my! the poorest of the poor are spendthrifts by comparison . . .

But since this phony Bolshevism started up you can't say a word . . . Picasso! . . . Boussac! * Tartre! another Commie! . . . billions all over! . . . all prisoners of starvation! . . . no time for you . . . The fatter their belly, their ass . . .

their jowls, the bigger "prisoners of starvation" they are! Don't laugh! They'll cut off your head . . .

I'm suspicious of everybody! I don't laugh! . . . our dogs sniff and "*grrr!*" . . . drive everybody away . . . Bécart* said to me, must have been two days before he died: "You're stubborn, Ferdinand! . . . dogs are carnivorous, didn't you know that? . . . you're looking for trouble! . . ."

Let's get back to my difficulties . . . the long and the short of it . . . without exaggeration . . . the most unskilled laborer down there on the island, at Renault's, works less than I do, and eats and sleeps more . . . and in two days I'll be sixty-three . . . And respect? . . . I'm lucky if they don't chop me into little pieces! "Stinker! Stalinist! . . . Nazi . . . pornographer! . . . charlatan! . . . menace! . . ." and these kind words aren't whispered! . . . they're written in black and white! . . . all over the billboards! . . . And another capital crime: I give free consultations . . . does that make them hate me! . . . only garbage is free! "Ah, he wants to be forgiven! the lowest stinker of them all!"

I think it over . . . the amusing side . . . my fall from the heights . . . my dear old professor Etienne Bordas wrote me only the other day . . . "You, so distinguished a mind! born to the élite! . . . my best pupil!"

Hell! . . . lucky he's gone away! "Elite!" Ah, that's not the opinion of Lower Meudon . . . or of Upper Meudon either, for that matter . . . he'd have seen the posters! "Traitor, quack, Stalinist, pornographer, drunkard . . ." But maybe the worst of all for my reputation: "He hasn't got a car!"

The butcher, the grocer, the carpenter don't make their rounds on foot! A doctor on foot? . . . No wonder they talk . . . No car? The crust of that bum . . . dangerous charlatan, fit to be hanged . . . the sidewalk is for thugs . . . for whores . . . going to see a patient on foot? . . . an insult . . . naturally he throws you out! . . . and you complain!

Versailles isn't very far away, for instance . . . Can you conceive of a doctor . . . any doctor . . . going to Versailles on foot . . . Fagon* on foot? . . . and a patient conscious of his rights, Social Security, union card, subscriber to three, four, five newspapers, cousin to two, three hundred millionaires, thinks a damn sight more of himself than King Louis! XIV! . . . XV! . . . or XVI! . . .

On top of all this . . . the last straw! . . . the end of the world! . . . the shopping! they see me with my two shopping bags! . . . one for bones . . . the other for vegetables . . . mostly carrots!

In view of my age, my little tremor, my gray hair, I could pass for Professor Something or other in a pinch . . . Professor *Nimbus*, I'd hand people a laugh . . . they'd help me! but these posters! That's serious, inexpiable . . . and being born in Courbevoie . . . makes me feel like an adventurer . . . lower, much lower than a chiropractor . . . somewhere between a herborist and a condom . . . lower than Bovary . . . a coolie . . . coolie of the Occident . . . the future! . . . bearer of packages, crates, shopping bags . . . and garbage cans . . . bearer of crimes . . . of taxes . . . bearer of the *Médaille Militaire* . . . bearer of my seventy-five percent disability . . . the complete bearer . . .

Loukoum is certainly not going to help me . . . I don't argue . . . the impression is enough . . .

And there's more to it than my age and the wall inscriptions . . . the state of our house . . . "What keeps it standing?" . . . and my opening the gate in person . . . unlocking . . . locking up again . . . that's the end . . . it does look bad, I admit . . . and the location . . . I haven't told you? . . . in the middle of the hill . . . really an impossible place to live! the path! . . . the muck! . . . my poor patients in the winter . . . climbing, sloshing, breaking their necks . . . and I have the nerve to complain . . . naturally they don't come up . . . they never will . . . they follow the riverbank to Issy . . . everything in one place . . . baker, butcher, post office, drugstore, noodles, barber, wine . . . and the *Grand Rio*, 1,200 seats . . . triple-width screen . . . and God knows how many doctors! . . . what can I expect in the middle of my hill? the sick people up top stay up top, they're not crazy! the few chronic cases who risk it are questioned at the bar . . . am I really as crummy as people say? am I really the Pétiot type?

. . . did they see any pieces of victims? . . . ovens for tor-
turing the patients? . . . etc. etc. . . .

Now and then the rain sends me patients . . . not very
many . . . a few . . . who start up to the real Meudon . . .
and weaken half way . . . oh, only in winter . . . they're
making a big mistake, in the summer they'd enjoy the view
. . . it's unique . . . and the trees and the birds . . . not
just dogs . . . the way they sing! . . . you can see everything
. . . as far as Taverny at the far end of the department . . .
from my garden, from the path . . . yes, a garden . . . a little Eden three months out of twelve . . . what trees! . . .
and hawthorn and clematis . . . you'd never think it was
hardly a couple of miles from the Pont d'Auteuil! the woods,
the tail end of the Bois d'Yveline . . . then comes Renault
. . . right below us! you can't go wrong . . . where the bush
is thickest, that's us! the dogs will leap out at you, the pack!
. . . don't let yourself be intimidated . . . pretend not to
hear them . . . look at the view! the hills, Longchamp, the
grandstands, Suresnes, the loops of the Seine . . . two . . .
three loops . . . by the bridge, right next to Renault's island,
the last clump of pines, on the point . . .

Of course it was a lot more countrified when we came out
here delivering lace and fans . . . around 1900 . . . same
paths . . . oh, we had plenty of customers in Meudon . . . "it
will give him some air!" We breathed in the air . . . I
breathed in the air . . . we were suffocating in the Passage
Choiseul . . . three hundred gas jets . . . child-raising by
gas! . . . We started after the office . . . my father left his
Coccinelle Fire Insurance Co. on the run! And off we went
. . . the bus, we sat on top with our packages . . . we were
never back at the Passage before nine, ten o'clock at night . . .
the paths in Meudon haven't changed at all . . . serpentines,
corkscrews, precipices . . . it was something to find the customers in that tangle . . . very difficult ladies, and their difficult daughters . . . "it's not right . . . it's too expensive,"
etc. . . . anything they could dream up to make us take back
the bill but leave the merchandise! small repair job: ten francs
. . . anything to get out of paying . . . our customers in a

nutshell . . . what's become of those families? . . . the houses are still here, just about the same . . . and the paths . . . not too safe at night . . . it's all right for me, I never go out without my dogs . . . not one . . . three . . . four of them . . . and vicious! . . .

"And your patients?"

"No bargain . . . no easier to satisfy than the swellegant ladies of 1900! . . . our griping, cheating, thieving customers . . . enough to disillusion St. Vincent . . . If I'm the way I am, so poison hateful of all dealings with money, Communist at heart, a thousand percent, with sick people and well people, same difference, I believe it's my mother's customers who turned my stomach . . . the floozies and countesses of 1900 . . . the whole crew . . ."

But human nature doesn't change in the slightest . . . immutable gametes . . . the "changing" menopausal lady with a social security card can treat you to worse rages and tantrums than Madame de Maintenon . . . I've never been treated so brutally, called such names, and chased out with a broom except by a social-security "changer" whose feelings I was trying to spare . . . I didn't bring up the question of an operation . . . not yet . . . fibroma? . . . cancer . . . I didn't want to upset her . . . ah, my goddam delicacy . . . my tact . . . my menopause girl had no hesitation about unloading wagonloads of insults! . . . the neighbors heard it all . . . two or three of them stepped outside . . . I knew them by sight . . . "Oh, don't mind her, doctor! . . . she's highstrung! . . ." I think it was mostly my not having a car . . . if I'd had one as big as a house . . . with an enormous hood . . . she wouldn't have said a word . . . and turned it in once a year . . . I could do as I pleased . . . bigger and bigger . . . it's not a Communist world . . . hell no! but plenty materialistic . . . period! . . . disgustingly! Down to the last atom!

Drive a car, Suez or no Suez, and you exist . . . in Versailles it was how many carriages, today it's how much horse-power . . . Versailles, Kremlin, or White House . . . are you somebody? or aren't you? . . . Professor, Commissar, Minister . . . how much horse-power? . . . you a success? . . . yes or no?

. . . fibroma? . . . who cares? . . . cancer? . . . no, what type of body? that's what counts . . . what type of suspension? . . . Versailles . . . Windsor . . . White House . . . Cairo . . .

I'd like to see Louis XIV with a social security card-holder . . . he'd see if the State was him . . . think of the millions that the smallest subscriber represents . . . ah, Louis Drag-ass . . . think of it, Louis Soleil, scared even to change his surgeon! more dead than alive! . . . question of etiquette! . . . your social security slob thinks nothing of firing you . . . of calling you a putrid fish! . . . your recommendations? . . . don't make me laugh, you old clown . . . all I want out of you is "sick leave"! sign . . . affix your stamp and good-bye . . . you old parasite! "A week, see . . . a month . . . and step on it . . . damned old clown! your stamp! . . . your prescriptions? . . . ha ha! . . . I've got whole drawers and shithouses full of prescriptions . . . and better than yours . . . the greatest masters and professors and chiropractors of Neuilly, St. James, and Monceau! . . . you should see their waiting rooms . . . the carpets! the lawns! . . . the nurses . . . twenty dictaphones . . . well, even those demigods . . . we wipe our ass with their prescriptions . . . where does that leave *you*? . . . your stamp! . . . quick! don't look! . . . sign! . . . so long!"

I shouldn't mention it, but it's just too funny . . . most of the patients I see spend more on tobacco than we do on everything included . . . I mean Lili, myself, the dogs, and the cats . . .

One of my meanest drunks brandishes her bottle over my head . . . and under my nose . . . the red stuff . . . she defies me . . . I told her to stop drinking . . . "She might kill her little girl . . ." I ought to have her locked up . . . "You know, Doctor, she's dangerous, can't you do something? . . ." If I had her interned, she'd escape, she'd come back and do me in . . . that's how it is with drunks. "I was drunk. I didn't like him." And that's that . . . What Tartre and God knows how many others have been trying to do for years, knocking themselves out, jerking off, sweating blood and poison, turning heaven and earth and hell! But my drunken floozy was right there, all ready . . . my dogs were ready, too . . . especially the bitches . . . I only had to say the word . . .

Good Lord . . . leave her to the bottle? lock her up? I just didn't want to see her any more . . . I advised her to take another doctor . . . she was the only one who refused . . . she didn't want another doctor . . . only me . . . she didn't insult me, she only wanted to kill me . . . and for me to take care of her warts . . . burn them . . . every second time I refused . . . she always came back . . .

You've got to think of everything . . . what about my dogs?
. . . it's a miracle if they haven't eaten a patient . . . two patients . . . knock on wood . . . The garden is enormous and
on a slope . . . when the pack goes rushing down . . . howling . . . it's enough to chase away all the patients in the world
. . . not to mention the squawk from the neighbors . . . because when they start barking it's something . . . and the
harder I yell at them the louder they roar . . . they answer
back . . . when I'm expecting patients, you can imagine . . .
between two and four I take the whole pack up to the attic
. . . they bark from up there . . . louder!

Thinking it over, all in all, my pack doesn't help me in the
neighborhood . . . but they protect me against no-goods . . .
I'm suspicious of the people who pass . . . the ones I don't
know . . . and the ones I know . . . they hear the dogs barking . . . they were casing the joint . . . they turn tail . . .
murderers don't care for risks . . . they're more patient about
killing you than a bourgeois about buying Suez stock . . . I
know a thing or two about murderers . . . I've known them
here and there, all over, not just in prison . . . in life . . . five
. . . six . . . *arrgh! arrgh!* . . . they're gone! . . . I'm not
very long on confidence, I haven't any confidence in anything.
When I was in Pavilion K in the Vesterfangsel, the barking
. . . this is nothing by comparison . . . not just the prisoners
in the *pip-cell* . . . all the dogs in hell let loose until morning . . . mastiffs . . . how many? . . . a hundred . . . two
hundred . . . that prison was guarded all right . . . *intra
muros . . . extra muros!* two years . . . for two years . . . I
didn't sleep, I could hear them . . . The warden had no confi-
dence . . . Why should I? Prison is a school . . . you've

been? you haven't? . . . that's where you learn something
. . . People who haven't been in stir are a lot of drooling,
virgin ham actors . . . even if they're ninety and then some
. . . they don't know what they're talking about . . . you
hear them sounding off . . . what do they actually think? . . .
"Hell, if only my luck holds out to the end! if only I can steer
clear of it! . . ." Shitless . . . the big house . . . their obsession . . . Mauriac, Achille, Goebbels, Tartre! . . . that's why
you see them so nervous, so alcoholic, from one cocktail party
to the next, from one confession, one train, one lie to the next!
from one cell . . . one asininity to the next . . . will that warrant, those handcuffs, La Santé, catch up with them . . .
trembling . . . the one serious minute in their lives . . . the
only one . . . *finish* blah-blah-blah!

So why should I trust anybody? One patient I'm not suspicious of is Madame Niçois . . . maybe I'm making a mistake?
. . . no, with Madame Niçois . . . nothing to be afraid of
. . . really harmless . . . but her gestures! . . . those gestures! . . . worse than my boozie-floozie . . . she doesn't
threaten me, no . . . She doesn't brandish a bottle under my
nose . . . but she thrashes around for something to get hold
of . . . the gate . . . a bush . . . anything . . . she totters
. . . she doesn't remember . . . she's absent, so to speak
. . . weaker and weaker . . . she doesn't remember my path
. . . she gets lost . . . oh, my dogs don't bother her . . . she
doesn't hear them . . . she can't see much either . . . give
you an idea of the condition she's in . . . well, believe it or
not, what bothers her is that I don't make her pay . . .

As we were saying, Madame Niçois gets lost on the paths
. . . from Lower Meudon to my place . . . she's on her way
to Saint-Cloud, the neighbors catch her . . . she'd almost
reached the Bridge . . . looked funny to them . . . where
could she be going? . . . she lives on the former Place Faidherbe, parallel to the lower road, the extension of the rue de
Vaugirard . . . from her house you can see the water without
any trouble, the Seine . . . the shore road . . . which reminds me . . . about a hundred yards away, after the Virofles
highway, you'll see the famous old Restaurant, the Miraculous

Catch . . . it's in a sad state . . . not much more than a memory . . . but the balconies are still there, where the cream of the cream used to banquet in the cool river breeze . . . no more trees on the island out front . . . turned into a factory . . . but in the distance you can see Sacré-Coeur, the Arch of Triumph, the Eiffel Tower, and Mont Valérien . . . but the diners are gone . . . blotted out . . .

Oh, the river traffic is still there . . . all the movement . . . the tugs, and the strings of barges, high-riding, low-riding, coal, sand, junk . . . one after another . . . downstream, upstream . . . from Madame Niçois' place you can see it all . . . she's not interested . . . question of sensibility . . . the movement of rivers touches you or it doesn't . . . the barges passing through the arches . . . hide-and-seek . . . from Madame Niçois' window up there you can see them coming . . . almost to the Ile des Cygnes . . . and on the other side . . . past Saint-Cloud . . . what a stretch of river! from the Pont Mirabeau to Suresnes . . . the diners' view! . . .

They were more sensitive than we are, hadn't turned into hysterical niggers yet . . . I only have to look at Achille and Gertrut . . . oh, they turn my stomach . . . but all the same, under their folds and wrinkles and wattles, at the base, in the fiber, you can't help seeing a certain refinement . . .

The Miraculous Catch . . . those were the days when skiffs were in style and long striped jerseys, oarsmen with spike moustaches . . . I can see my father with spike moustaches . . . I can see Achille in a skiff . . . skull cap, jersey, and biceps . . . I see all the old-timers . . . ladies clucking as they rush for the boat . . . the circuit of "pigeon island" . . . rat-a-tat-tat! they're shooting . . . a rustling of silk, screams of joy and fright . . . silk stockings, flowers, fried fish, monocles, duels! . . . at the Catch, on those balconies over there, now fit to be chucked in the Seine! . . . a ruin . . .

I remember the pigeon-shooting as if I had taken part . . . the poplars in the wind! When I think of all the smacks I caught for misbehaving on the *bateau-mouche* . . . from Pont-Royal-Suresnes . . . that was a real *bateau-mouche!* none of your newfangled imitations . . . that whole boat was full of

smacks and wallops . . . the education of the day . . . clouts,
kicks in the ass . . . nowadays it's all so progressive . . .
modern children are "complex and cute" . . .

Yes, the fancy diners of the day had quite a view . . . not
only Mont Valérien and Sacré-Coeur on the other side, but the
whole valley of the Seine, the loops . . . I've got the same
from my window where I'm writing you, I can't complain . . .
and Longchamp too, the grandstands . . . directly opposite . . .

Ah, I can hear the old men talking . . . they talk as if they'd
been there . . . the liars! they weren't there at all . . . me?
. . . with drawn saber . . . the last July fourteenth review
. . . the whole garrison . . . plus the eleventh and twelfth
cuirassiers . . . charging . . . the last charge, you could say
. . . since then there hasn't been anything but parades, prom-
enades, rehearsals for Sacha . . . no more army . . . no more
Miraculous Catch . . . or real *bateau-mouche,* or children
who respect their fathers . . .

I'm getting sidetracked . . . maybe getting on your nerves?
. . . I was telling you about Madame Niçois . . . going
down to see her . . . I said the Catch was a ruin . . . but her
place . . . a miracle that it's still standing! an afternoon's work
for a bulldozer! . . . stairs, roof, windows! and my shanty? I
should talk . . . all that dates from before 1870 . . . long before . . . the landlord refuses to repair anything . . . he's
waiting for Madame Niçois to pass on, he'll sell the whole place
. . . no other grounds for "eviction" . . . she pays her rent
on the dot . . . sure, the landowner is a dog, a ferocious crook,
anything you like, but a receipted bill is a receipted bill!

Egotistically I've got to admit that it didn't suit me one bit to
go down to Madame Niçois' . . . and the dogs? I locked them
up in the attic and tied them . . . *crash!* I could see them
smashing the windows and flinging themselves on Madame
Niçois! . . . yes, from the fourth floor . . . absolutely . . .
they were raving wild to tear her to pieces! . . . couldn't
stand her gestures . . . clinging to everything . . . or nothing
. . . arms in the air . . . staggering . . . spinning . . . like
a leaf in the wind . . . she wasn't supposed to go out . . . I'd

told her often enough . . . I gave her my arm to take her home . . .

The sedatives befuddled her too . . . naturally! . . . I'm against drugs, but they're necessary in one case out of a hundred . . . Madame Niçois was that case . . . her disease developed very slowly . . . a form that strikes old people . . . not clearly definable . . . but spreading . . . with constant bleeding . . . oh, taking care of her, escorting her, so to speak, took infinite precaution . . . layer by layer of gauze separately . . . fine, delicate dressings . . . and as little morphine as possible . . . and never getting better, always bleeding a little . . . "Oh Doctor, doctor, take it out . . ." "Oh, Madame Niçois, come, come . . ." It's incredible, impossible the subtlety, the tact you need to treat cancer in old people . . . Alas, alas, I know all about diplomatic subtleties . . . I've been around the embassies . . . grotesque lumpishness compared to what it takes if you don't want your cancerous old woman to throw you out . . . you and your ointments . . . your hopes and your doodads and heat pads . . . The problem with Madame Niçois was to make her keep quiet, stay home, stop coming to see me . . . her condition wasn't improving . . . it couldn't . . . one day she'd fall down and never get up again . . . it wouldn't be long . . . Pétiot! Landru! Bonnot! Bougrat! . . . I was lucky if they didn't blame me for Dien-Penhu . . . for the fall of Maubeuge in 1914–15 . . . Naturally they'd say I'd finished off Madame Niçois . . . it was in the bag . . . didn't Tartre and a hundred well informed periodicals accuse me of selling the Straits of Calais? . . . I was used to it . . . But Madame Niçois on top of all that? Hell! if she passed out on the path? . . . no . . . I can still get around . . . sure . . . but down to the Seine? . . . no! . . . the people down there have read all about me . . . all the posters . . . the names they called me . . . consequence: "You see that old fogey? . . . etc. . . ."

Ah, it's not only my crimes . . . In addition, and maybe worst of all . . . there's the way I'm dressed . . . you can't expect me to have a new suit made for the critics of Lower Meudon . . . they don't think I look right? . . . if they could only see themselves the way I see them! . . . the explosion would be atomic . . . puffs of neutron . . . hideous horror . . . heads! souls! asses . . . absolutely . . . but what about Madame Niçois? . . .

So I went down to see Madame Niçois . . . but I repeat, I was on my guard . . . the people along the riverfront are hostile . . . plenty of reasons . . . this, that, and the other . . . one, the way I'm dressed . . . two, the posters . . . my not taking money, plus "no maid," "no car," the garbage pail, and the shopping . . . Obviously I could only go down there at night . . . I'd go down the "cowpath" with a dog, or rather two . . . on the cowpath after seven you seldom meet anybody . . . from the bottom of the path it's only a minute to the former Place Faidherbe . . . Madame Niçois, next to last house, third floor . . . I'd been there before . . . first I settle my mutt . . . I almost always take Agar . . . he waits for me, he sleeps . . . I'd never risk it without a dog . . . Agar's full of faults . . . he barks, he howls . . . and the way he tangles up his chain! . . . it's all over the place . . . he turns it into a snake . . . it's in front of you . . . it's twisted between your legs . . . it's behind you . . . you keep bellowing . . . "Agar! Agar! . . ." with him for a companion you're always on the verge of a nosedive . . . yes, yes, but Agar has one good quality . . . he doesn't make friends with people . . . he's not a social dog . . . he's not interested in anybody but me . . . for instance: at Madame Niçois', while I'm treating her, he's out on the landing, if there's anybody prowling around, I don't have to worry . . . even somebody on the sidewalk across the street . . . he'll throw a howling fit! . . . with all his faults, he's a real watchdog . . . no "supposedly" about him . . . Frieda, Lili's bitch up on the hill, is worse . . . she hardly knows me, won't go out with anybody but Lili . . . so I settle my mutt on the landing, on the doormat . . . Don't go thinking that I'm afraid, I'm not afraid of anything, but

76

after fifteen years of hot pursuit I wouldn't want to be bumped off . . . it's my sporting pride . . . by one of those pimply little hyenas, one of those jittering coke-heads with dreams of a marble tablet: "On this spot Lydoirzeff struck down . . ." and glory! Oh, it wouldn't surprise me . . . to have one . . . or two . . . or three of them waiting for me . . . down below . . . right there . . . and Madame Niçois in the know . . . to cap the climax! in cahoots . . . with her doped-up look and the cancer in her ass! . . . absolutely, I've known sicker people, nearer the end than she was, getting mixed up in crummier machinations than that . . . the moment I set foot out of doors, patients or no patients, I could look forward to trouble . . . if you're really devoted to your calling, you can expect the worst . . . especially on stairs, going up, going down . . . take my stairs on the rue Girardon, it was touch and go . . . the murderers were right there . . . they'd come to give me a *Prague* . . . a *Budapest* . . . they wrote me . . . they still can't forgive themselves . . . one good burst . . . no more jeremiads out of me . . . and no vague threats . . . oh no! . . . from a heavy-duty Stalinist . . . one Etienne Vaillant! . . . not the one in the Chamber . . . nobody's interested in the Chamber any more! History is made of caprices! whims! rages! scene 1: whoopie . . . hurrah . . . scene 2? . . . boo! dragass! shitass! look at Caesar . . . how many have tried it since? too many to count! from Louverture to Christine to Mollet! as many as there are writers who imitate me! . . . Caesar, Alexander . . . that's somebody! . . . but try to do the same! . . . like Vaillant No. 1! . . . and No. 2! . . .

But leave the past to the waxworks . . . Back to the present! to Madame Niçois! . . . I'm down at her place . . . as I was telling you . . . I check to make sure everything's all right . . . if Agar is behaving . . . he's asleep on the doormat . . . his ears twitch . . . stop twitching . . . I trust Agar more than Madame Niçois . . . the slightest suspicion on the stairway? . . . the slightest creaking of a door? . . . you'll hear from Agar . . . a revolution! "Wouldn't it be better for me to lie down, Doctor?" "Lie down, Madame Niçois . . ." I'd brought my instruments, syringes . . . compresses . . . forceps . . . "Am I still bleeding, Doctor? . . ." "Oh, no, Madame

. . . very little . . . less and less . . ." "And the smell, Doctor? . . ." "Less and less, Madame . . ."

Suppose I had Vaillant to take care of . . . Vaillant, my weak-kneed assassin . . . Tropmann or Landru . . . or Tartre in person . . . or the hundreds of thousands of bastards who've been hounding me for years, from prison to prison . . . straining at the leash . . . I wouldn't change my style . . . my methods . . . one iota . . . I'm the good Samaritan in person . . . the Samaritan of the cockroaches . . . I can't help helping them . . . Abbé Pierre is more like Gapon . . . Father Gapon . . . we'll see . . . but my case is already clear . . . I'm "Dr. Better and Better" . . . that's why, at the dispensary in the Vesterfangsel (lights on day and night) I was in charge of "lifting morale" . . . Suppose I saw Tartre there in his death agony . . . "bastard," I'd say, "get up, get better, you stinking shitass . . . make your getaway! recapture all your bile! don't be discouraged! . . . you're stupid as hell, but you're educated! . . ." Tartre or somebody else! . . . Obviously morale is everything . . . actually, the honest truth, I couldn't see Madame Niçois going on for more than five, six weeks at the most . . . and she didn't want to go to the hospital . . . oh, no, nothing doing . . . it's me she wanted . . . only me . . . my care . . . yes, she was in pain . . . but nothing terrible . . . cancer, yes . . . but the form that's more toxic than painful . . . luckily . . . yes, luckily . . . the form I wish you . . . the patient doesn't know what's going on . . . so befuddled . . . debilitated . . . what? . . . which? . . . he drools and trembles and sweats . . . Madame Niçois complained some . . . but not of a very acute pain . . . she was the kind that tries to get up . . . to talk to you . . . even to eat . . . and then she can't . . . she gives up . . . weaker and weaker . . . a look of death . . . That was Madame Niçois . . . as for me, I saw one thing . . . that I had at least two months ahead of me . . . of coming down here to fix her dressings . . . she couldn't possibly go out . . . the trek was for me . . . oh, but not in the daytime . . . oh no . . . only at night . . . Not that I'm so much afraid of being killed . . . no . . . but in the first place I didn't want to be seen . . . I wanted to be left alone . . . let them think what they like behind their windowpanes . . . okay . . . but I don't want to see them . . . that's all I ask.

Well then, Madame Niçois on her bed . . . I finished my dressing . . . I start talking to her about one thing and another . . . that the winter cold was over . . . soon there'd be lilacs . . . we'd frozen long enough . . . pretty soon the jonquils . . . lilies of the valley . . . this winter had been exceptional . . . broken all records . . . I pick up my cotton . . . she asks me for a roll . . . wants me to leave her one . . . ah, and the peach tree on the Route des Gardes . . . did it come through the cold all right? . . . I tell her . . . it's in blossom . . . the one that grows in the middle of the wall, between two blocks of granite . . . that tree was the spring itself . . . it was news to her . . . oh, I know how to buoy up people's spirits . . . give them a boost . . . in prison I saw hunger strikers, given up for lost . . . I got them to start eating again! . . . in a friendly kind of way . . . a little joke . . . and then another.

While we were chatting, I was putting my things away . . . oh, I almost forgot . . . the injections! . . . she needed one . . . two c.c.'s of morphine . . . she'd drop off to sleep . . . then I'd leave . . . I inject my two c.c.'s . . . I look out the window . . . I accuse other people of being voyeurs . . . but actually . . . I'm hopeless. . . . the complete peeper . . . I can't stand being looked at . . . but I myself, I admit . . . I'm terrible . . . wherever I am . . . well, there it was inevitable . . . the lights outside . . . I look into the distance . . . the Seine . . . Madame Niçois is dropping off . . . She's stopped talking . . . that window . . . I told you . . . looks out almost directly on the former Place Faidherbe . . . the riverfront . . . it's still pretty cold out . . . March . . . it's dark . . . you can see the water . . . I see it all right . . . naturally Madame Niçois doesn't . . . for one thing she's asleep . . . I even see people coming and going . . . men loading a barge? . . . I'll ask Madame Niçois . . . I wake her up a little . . .

"Say, Madame Niçois . . . have you seen those people down there?"

"Down where?"

"Loading the barges."

She doesn't know, she doesn't care . . . she turns over . . . she's asleep . . . I'll look all by myself . . . I've got to tell you that in addition to being a voyeur I'm a fanatic about the movement of harbors, about everything that goes on on the water . . . everything that sails or floats or docks . . . I was on the jetties with my father . . . a week's vacation in Le Tréport . . . Christ, the things we saw! . . . the fishing boats moving in and out . . . risking their lives for mackerel . . . the widows and their kids imploring the sea . . . the emotion on those jetties . . . the suspense! . . . make the Grand Guignol and the billion-dollar thrillers from Hollywood look like a kindergarten! . . . Well, down there the Seine . . . oh, I'm just as fascinated . . . just as nuts about everything connected with water and boats as when I was a kid . . . if you're nuts about boats, the way they move, their comings and goings, it's for life! . . . there aren't many fascinations that last a lifetime . . . whenever a barge comes along, I've got my spyglass . . . up in my attic . . . I keep my eye on it, I see the name, the number, the washing hung out to dry, the man at the wheel . . . I keep looking . . . the way it takes the arch at Issy, the bridge . . . either you've got the bug . . . or you haven't . . . if you've got an eye for those things, harbors, barges, docks, and dams . . . the movement . . . a measly little yawl puts into shore and down I go . . . on the run . . . I used to run . . . I don't any more . . . nowadays I'm satisfied with the spyglass . . .

Any old moldy, knock-kneed barge working its way through a canal . . . I'd follow it to the next lock . . . oh, I've followed girls all right . . . lots of them . . . but I've spent a good many more hours fascinated with the movement on the water . . . the hide-and-seek of the arches . . . the next arch . . . the big tank barge . . . another . . . a little yacht . . . a gull . . . two gulls . . . the magic of the bubbles in the current . . . the lapping of the water . . . you feel it or you don't . . . the procession of barges . . .

Through Madame Niçois' window I saw that the waterfront was busy . . . I could tell . . . men . . . I saw it was a barge

. . . either you've got an eye for those things . . . or you're a stupid landlubber . . . a different animal . . . okay . . . crazy about buses, for instance . . . okay . . . well, after staring hard at the waterfront I saw that this movement wasn't at all what I'd thought . . . no sign of a barge . . . no shipment of junk . . . or coal . . . this was something entirely different . . . absolutely . . . I wouldn't have believed it . . . my excuse is that the riverfront at the former Place Faidherbe is never lighted . . . the township can't afford it . . . in the first place there aren't enough people . . . in the second place the kids smash all the lamps . . . their greatest joy! . . . *bang* . . . it takes skill! . . . the township gave up long ago! result: total darkness! . . . makes you think of Suez! . . . besides, the street is all jagged cracks . . . enormous holes . . . needs a complete repair job . . . so does our path . . . what doesn't? . . . and what prevents them from fixing the road? . . . the big factory is spreading out . . . Still through the window I'm looking at this movement . . . they're not loading sand or coal . . . I tell Madame Niçois, lying there . . . I wake her up . . . the riverfront doesn't interest her in the least . . . she was back at what we were talking about before . . . the late vegetation, the spring . . . she won't talk about anything but the spring . . . I listen . . . we're not on the same wave length . . . me, it's the riverfront . . . and I can tell you . . . what I see in the blackness isn't normal and it's not a barge! . . . ah, those piercing eyes of mine! . . . damned if it isn't a *bateau-mouche* . . . I can even see the name . . . in enormous red letters: *La Publique* and the number: 114 . . . how do I see it? . . . Maybe a feeble glow from a light bulb? . . . from a shop window? . . . no . . . all the store fronts are locked up tight . . . but I'm positive! I look, I can see the whole square . . . and there it is: *La Publique* . . . pulled up by the dock . . . and the comings and goings on board . . . the people in twos . . . in threes . . . mostly in threes . . . they've come from up top . . . same path as we use . . . I imagine . . . they get into the boat . . . they talk to somebody . . . and they get off again . . . did I say: they talk? . . . well, that's what it looks like, I can't hear them . . . I

can only see them . . . groups of three . . . coming and going on the gangplank . . . I can see their faces some . . . well
no, not exactly . . . rather their silhouettes . . . yes, of
course, dim, muddled silhouettes . . . unclear . . . I'm muddled myself . . . who wouldn't be? . . . I was a little shaken
. . . in fact, I'd had a rotten shock! . . . that's right, a shock
. . . the whole of Europe on my ass . . . yes, the whole of
Europe . . . plus my friends . . . my family . . . all competing to see who could grab more away from me . . . not leaving me time to say boo . . . my eyes! . . . my nose! . . . my
fountain pen . . . the ferocity of Europe! . . . the Nazis were
no lovebirds, but don't tell me about the sweet gentleness of
Europe . . . I'm not exaggerating . . . that little warrant
. . . and all those public prosecutors . . . I admit it's left me
kind of groggy . . . for instance, I'm not quite sure about seeing these comings and goings on the shore . . .

Damn . . . I'm digressing . . . I'm getting you mixed up
. . . this *bateau-mouche* is really pulled up alongside . . . I
see it . . . nobody can tell me different . . . I can even make
out groups of people . . . coming and going . . . trailing
through the darkness of the landing . . . over the gangplank
. . . going aboard . . . they can't be excursionists . . . impossible . . . it's not that kind of place . . . besides it's the
end of March . . . a glacial wind . . . sure, we've seen worse
. . . Korsör up there! Baltavia, the Belt! . . . on the subject
of ice, I'll have a few things to tell you . . . but this right here
is no slouch . . . a mean shivery wind . . . you'd want to be
out strolling around . . . and this *bateau-mouche, La Publique* . . . it wasn't a dream . . . no, I could see it . . . but
like everything else, all misty . . . my own weakened state?
. . . anemia? . . . or from staring so hard? . . . Madame
Niçois had stopped listening to me . . . she was dozing . . . I
couldn't expect her to help me untangle the pros from the cons
. . . whether it was a real *bateau-mouche*? . . . in the first
place, even when she was awake, Madame Niçois had lost most
of her bearings . . . you only had to see her on the way to my
place . . . catching hold of branches . . . catching this and
that and the other . . . it wasn't drunkenness that made her

stagger . . . She just wasn't what she used to be . . . she couldn't have done six feet on the landing . . . ploof! . . . she'd have been in the drink! . . . six feet . . . it was up to me to go see . . . not to her . . . I'm not the hesitant type . . . was I cockeyed or not? . . . brass tacks! . . . either it's *La Publique*, or I'm screwy drunk! . . . on what! my senses off kilter? . . . facts are facts . . . Agar's even more rationally positivistic than I am . . . the least thing unusual in the air? . . . *grrr* . . . *grrr*! . . . a cyclone . . . you can't hold him . . . he'll make hash out of the former Place Faidherbe and all those people . . . people? . . . that are coming and going . . . and the shops . . . he'll make them open up . . . I've just got to say: Agar! . . . he's the loudest of the pack . . . the neighbors, for instance . . . their nerves . . . "Give him a shot, Doctor . . . put him out of his misery . . . he's making our lives unlivable . . ." suburban neighbors . . . it doesn't take much to make their lives unlivable! fatigue, the wear and tear of commuting, their nerves are on edge . . . your mutt is the last straw . . . plus the aggravations of life . . . exasperated wives, the housekeeping . . . being too near the department stores . . . you and your wolf pack are all they need . . .

Meanwhile Agar would put me straight . . . ghosts or not ghosts? illusion? or what? some effect of the water? "I'll be right back, Madame Niçois!" The stairs . . . there we are on the sidewalk . . . me and the dog . . . people coming . . . going . . . crossing the former Place Faidherbe . . . absolutely . . . Agar sniffs at them . . . he doesn't bark . . . I can't see their faces . . . they're wearing hoods . . . not real hoods, rags . . . ragged hats . . . kind of turbans pulled way down, anyway their faces are hidden . . . to give you an idea that this wasn't normal . . . besides it was dark . . . or pretty near . . . it's never completely dark . . . Agar doesn't bark . . . I approach the landing . . . I see it . . . positive . . . the *bateau-mouche* . . . a real one . . . and the number: 114 . . . and the name . . . I go still closer . . . it's an old one . . . none of the phony *bateaux-mouche* you see today . . . showcases for tourists . . . all glass! . . . that I see

passing when I look down from my window . . . this was a
genuine old one . . . obsolete . . . older than myself . . .
with an enormous anchor . . . up front . . . life preservers
all around . . . chaplets of life preservers . . . garlands of life
preservers, yellow, pink, green . . . life boats . . . and the big
collapsible smokestack . . . and the captain's bridge . . .
even the paint was period . . . coal tar and lilac . . . the
name plate must be new, *La Publique* . . . I'm not talking
through my hat . . . I know my *bateaux-mouche,* I'm not
making anything up . . . every Sunday when I was little, for
my complexion, we took one at the Pont-Royal, the nearest
landing . . . twenty-five centimes round trip to Suresnes . . .
every Sunday from April on . . . rain or shine . . . airing
the goddam kids . . . all the kids of central Paris . . . I
wasn't the only pale and pasty kid . . . and our families . . .
out for the "cure" . . . that's what they called it, the "cure"
. . . Suresnes and back . . . a bowl of air . . . full in the
wind! . . . twenty-five centimes . . . it wasn't exactly the
quiet type of cruise . . . you could hear the mothers . . .
"Stop picking your nose! . . . Arthur! Arthur! . . . breathe
deeply! . . ." The fresh air made the kids caper in all directions! climb all over . . . from the engines to the shithouse
. . . picking their noses, fiddling with their flies . . . and
especially over the propeller . . . watching the big whirlpools
. . . the eddies of bubbles . . . There were always fifteen
. . . twenty . . . thirty of them . . . hypnotizing themselves
. . . and their mothers and fathers with them! . . . and the
clouts! . . . hey, Pierrette! . . . hey, Léonce . . . we were all
there . . . howls! . . . tears! . . . *smack* . . . *wham!* . . .
breathe that air! . . . you weren't going to lay out twenty-five
centimes apiece for nothing! . . . "You little roughneck, you'll
end up in jail! . . ." children, the family plague! . . .
"breathe, breathe, damn it! . . ." *Bingo!* . . . *Zing!* "Breathe,
I tell you!" Childhood in those days meant clouts! "Breathe
deeply, you little thug!" *Whack!* "Leave your nose alone, you
hoodlum! You stink, you didn't wipe your ass, pig! . . ." Illusions about good instincts hit our families later, much later,
complexes, inhibitions, etcetera . . . "You stink, you didn't
wipe yourself! stop poking in your pants!" was enough in 1900,

and tornadoes of whacks . . . for emphasis and punctuation
. . . an unswatted kid would grow up to be a convict . . . a
criminal . . . a murderer . . . God knows what . . . and
you'd be to blame . . .

Result: the *bateaux-mouche* were noisy . . . punitive and
educational . . . deep breathing, uninterrupted clouts . . .
all over . . . on the anchor in the bow . . . in the stern over
the propeller! *Smack! wham!* "Jeannette . . . Léopold! . . ."
"Denise! . . ." "you've done it in your pants again!" Something
to remember their Sunday by! . . . pasty-faced, snot-nosed,
disobedient brats . . . the trouble the parents went to to make
them get the benefit of the fresh air! which they were absolutely determined not to breathe! . . . Pont-Royal-Suresnes
and back!

When everybody went over to one side, the whole boat listed
. . . naturally . . . the parents too! . . . The mothers started
up again! "You little thug, you do it on purpose!" And *wham!
bam!* . . . "Breathe! Breathe!" The captain yelled from his
shack . . . they should control themselves! . . . "Not all at
once!" . . . through his megaphone . . . No use! . . . they
knotted up worse and worse! . . . kids and parents and grandmothers . . . and clouts! and counterclouts! . . . and peepee
here and peepee there . . . everybody at the same rail! . . .
Going to capsize! . . . Can there be joy without disorder?
. . . *biff! bang!* Clotilde! . . . *boo hoo! bang!* clouts for all!
Gaston! . . . your pocket! . . . you're touching yourself! . . .
bam! . . . pig!

There were a lot of us taking the air . . . a cruise like that
was just the thing for our little asthmas, whooping coughs,
bronchitises . . . Pont-Royal-Suresnes . . . the shops, the
streets of central Paris . . . Gaillon, Vivienne, Palais-Royal
. . . were all full of pasty-faced kids who breathed only on
Sunday . . . Opéra . . . Petits-Champs, Saint-Augustin, Louvois! . . . all aboard for the cure! . . . pour out of those
back rooms! . . . And get the full benefit! . . . Breathe!
Breathe! Pont-Royal-Suresnes.

When it comes to asphyxia, our Passage Choiseul was the
worst of the lot, the unhealthiest: the biggest gas chamber in
the whole City of Light . . . three hundred gas jets working

around the clock . . . child-raising by asphyxia . . . the Seine was better, you've got to admit . . . the cure! . . . cruise or back room, the clouts were the same . . . in those days the "program" wasn't revised every week! oh no! . . . but clouts or not, the air, the foam, the propeller, the swell, the great seething eddy of bubbles, it was a paradise! . . . and "the gulls, mama!" *bang!* . . . "don't lean over!" especially when we got to Boulogne, the kids couldn't keep still! the Bois! . . . the air was too heady! . . . the mothers couldn't keep up with them . . . you'd see them weeping . . . sobbing . . . all over . . . on every bench . . . "Clémence! Clémence! . . . Jules, where are you? . . ." A certain amount of order was restored after the Point du Jour . . . the kids calmed down some . . . there were no more trees . . . only houses . . . the return trip . . . the Paris air . . . the Pont de l'Alma . . .

But say, I'd better go easy, I'm forgetting about you . . . telling you stories of childhood . . . I didn't go down there to get you mixed up . . . I'd better watch my step . . . as I was telling you, my sight's a little blurred . . . the former Place Faidherbe and the riverfront . . . but all the same, I see people . . . some kind of people . . . and the *bateau-mouche* . . . oh, the *bateau-mouche* much more clearly . . . no illusion about that! . . . and all these characters coming and going . . . crossing the square . . . and coming back . . . I may be fuzzy, but I can still see the boat's name: *La Publique* . . . and its number: 114 . . . those are the facts . . . While I'm about it, I look around . . . all around the former Place Faidherbe . . . the shops . . . not a single one open . . . or lit . . . not a showcase . . . but I see distinctly that this *bateau-mouche, La Publique,* isn't the present model . . . far from it! . . . like the ones I see from my window up there, crammed with tourists . . . I've told you about that, haven't I? . . . or even the 1900 model . . . this one's a real antique, practically all wood . . . and another thing that puzzled me . . . the way I could see these people coming and going . . . it was dark . . . it was black night . . . not a lamp lit . . . neither on the square nor on the road . . . and the shops . . . no neon lights . . . I'd better watch myself . . . and not get

everything balled up like Madame Niçois . . . neon, shop
windows, gas jets! how can I expect you to keep track? . . .
anyway, this coming and going . . . by twos . . . and threes
. . . no doubt about it . . . the feel of the air? . . . it was
almost cold . . . the visibility? I could see the other side . . .
yes, the opposite bank! . . . the island! . . . and the factory!
. . . the whole factory . . . while I'm about it, as long as I've
come down here, I look at everything . . . and up in the air
. . . the sky . . . I try to see . . . nothing . . . stars? . . .
I'm not sure . . . blinking lights? . . . maybe planes . . .
no! it was just plain dark! The kids had smashed them all . . .
so if there was a certain glow, it didn't come from the moon or
the lamps on the riverfront or the reflections in the water . . .
my bug is reason! . . . I've got to find an explanation . . .
I'm a doctor . . . I take it seriously . . . I can't stomach the
abnormal . . . a fact is a fact . . . either it is or it isn't! . . .
vide latus . . . well, maybe a certain phosphorescence if you
want to call it that? . . . a very subtle phenomenon! The few
times in my life that such subtleties . . . anomalies! . . . have
come my way . . . they still give me the creeps . . . I'm posi-
tivism personified . . . a fact is a fact . . . This *bateau-
mouche?* A mystery? . . . To hell with that! I'll turn it over
. . . keel up . . . I'll examine the bottom . . . and all these
people . . . phantoms or not! . . . and the island across the
way . . . and the factory on it . . . I'll sink it to see if it floats!
the factory! ah! ah, the world wants to laugh! I'll give you
something to laugh about! . . . but the opposite bank? I see it
more clearly than this one! better than in broad daylight . . . I
even saw the *Heraclitus* on the opposite shore . . . a real
barge, no hocuspocus . . . with washing hung out to dry . . .
and food being cooked . . .

Ah, and that wasn't all I could see over there . . . the beach
with the little poplars too, Billancourt . . .

Well anyway, strange as it may seem, I'd come down here to
see if it was a dream or not a dream . . . hot air, people, bubbles, or Christopher Columbus? Cortez? . . . ectoplasm or
nothing? . . . I had to make sure . . . I'd brought my Agar
down . . . if he barked . . . it was people . . . he didn't go

in for mirages! . . . hey! he was sniffing . . . he kept sniffing
at them . . . what does that make me look like? . . . I tried
to stir him up: *ksst!* Agar! . . . Agar! . . . *ksst!* . . . nothing
doing . . . him, the accomplished noisemaker . . . the neighbors' scourge! . . . "He's making our life unlivable . . ." All
right, I've had enough of this! I barked myself to get him
started . . . *bow wow!* to make him answer me! Go lay an
egg! . . . he sniffed at these passersby, that's all . . . if he
were willing to bark, Lili would hear him . . . that would give
her some news of me . . . we'd been gone for quite some time
. . . you could hear the sounds of the Seine and the riverfront
very nicely up there . . . if Agar barked, all the other dogs
would answer him . . . you hear everything fine up at our
place . . . sound rises! . . . the factory whistles, the bells, the
kids yelling, the clanking of the dump trucks . . . everything
. . . but Agar just doesn't feel like barking . . . he makes as
much noise as a tugboat . . . when he feels like it . . . But
now . . . nothing! he sniffs . . . at all these people, one by
one . . . and the gravel . . . and then he pisses . . . and
goes back to sniff . . . If that's the way it is, I'll shout up at
Lili myself . . . up in the direction of Bellevue . . . "Ho,
Lili . . ." I've got a bit of voice myself . . . take my word for
it . . . a rifle-range voice . . . the voice of the Twelfth Cuirassiers . . . "Ho, Lili!" . . . it carries at least to the Pont
d'Auteuil . . . I can hear myself . . . the echo . . . At that
exact moment, a hand! a hand touches my arm . . . I don't
turn around . . . Agar sniffs hard . . . harder . . . I turn
around . . . somebody . . . a kind of a clown-gaucho-boy-
scout, well, somebody in disguise . . . enormous fringed
pants . . . felt hat with more fringes . . . hat, pants, short
shirt . . . colored . . . all colors . . . a cockatoo . . . And
those spurs! . . . an enormous hat, yellow, blue, green and
pink, pulled down almost to the beard . . . that's right . . . a
white curly beard . . . Santa Claus . . . this character was
hiding his face . . . you couldn't see it . . . he was hiding
. . . between his beard and the umbrella of his hat . . .
What would you have done in my place?

"Who are you?" I ask him . . .

But all of a sudden I knew . . . Christ Almighty! . . . I hugged him! It's him all right! We hug each other . . .

"Ah, it's you! It's you!"

We hug each other some more . . . It's Le Vigan! * Christ, am I happy! Le Vigan! Here!

"It's you . . . it's you! . . ."

Honest to God, it's him . . . talking of surprises . . . right here, in this clown's rig . . . Le Vigan?

"Where have you been?"

"What about you?"

It's a fact, we hadn't seen each other in a long time . . . since Siegmaringen . . . a long time . . .

We'd both been hunted down . . . full time . . . and in court . . . he'd been heroic . . . the way he stood up to them . . . in handcuffs! . . . and defended me! . . . you won't find many like him . . . nobody, in fact . . . and the pack of jackals in the hall! . . . and they had to listen to him! . . . couldn't help themselves! . . . saying I was the only patriot! . . . the only real patriot! . . . and they were a lot of driveling, griping, poisonous hyenas!

Running into him there on the Quai Faidherbe! . . . Le Vigan! . . . Le Vigan . . .

"Well? . . . Well, Le Vigan, how about it?"

"Not so loud!"

I whisper: "You from the *bateau-mouche*?"

I want to know all about it . . .

"Yes . . . yes . . . Anita too! . . . careful . . . not too loud . . . Anita, my wife . . . she's inside . . ."

Usually I catch on quick, but this was too much all at once . . . *La Publique*, Le Vigan . . . Le Vigan done up like a gaucho! . . . with a white beard, when I thought he was in Buenos Aires . . . and with some Anita . . . Anita? . . . I couldn't quite figure it . . .

"She's inside . . . she's the fireman's helper . . . you don't know the fireman either?"

"No." Why would I know the fireman?

"You know him all right . . . of course, you know him . . . it's Emile! Emile of the L.V.F. . . . from the little

Francoeur Garage . . . where you kept your motorbike."

That stirred up my thoughts . . . why yes . . . yes . . .
the Francoeur Garage . . . in the alley . . . yes . . . that's
it! Emile . . . the L.V.F. . . . my motorcycle . . . I almost remembered . . . sure, that's it . . . sure enough! who'd gone
off to Versailles . . . and then to Moscow! . . . certainly!
. . . we'd heard about it . . . and then he'd come back
from Moscow . . . must have, or he wouldn't be here! . . .
but how'd he get to be a fireman? here on the former Quai
Faidherbe? . . . *La Publique?* . . . fireman? . . . and Anita?
and the admirable Le Vigan? . . . ah, good old Le Vigan . . .
he's the cashier, he shakes his money pouch, he pokes it, what
a pouch! . . . hanging down over his stomach . . . and clink-
ing . . . he shows me . . . he opens it . . . full of gold coins
. . . kind of like a game bag! . . .

"So you take the money?"

"I'll say . . . but hard coin . . . nothing else . . . no paper
. . . Charon's bark! . . . what did you expect! . . ."

I didn't want to seem surprised . . . anyway it was all perfectly natural . . .

"Yes, yes . . . of course . . ."

"Charon's bark . . . you know . . ."

"Yes . . . yes . . . naturally . . ."

"Well, you see, this is it now . . ."

Naturally . . . why not? . . . *La Publique* was Charon's
bark . . . It's all right with me . . . They call it *La Publique?*
. . . Fine . . . fine . . . I have no objection . . .

"Then these are all dead people?" Just trying to get things
straight . . . "All those people getting in?"

"What else would they be?"

So they were dead people . . . fine! . . . I wouldn't ask any
more questions . . . he was there, that was the main thing
. . . and not dead! . . . not dead! . . . in this screwy getup! . . . masquerading . . . with a beard! . . . and what a
beard! . . . hanging down over his game bag . . .

"Where's your lasso?"

Why not, while he was about it? I'm tactless . . .

"Let's not talk about lassos! *mazuma first*, son!"

The way he talks! and in English!

"Shekels, son! . . . and only sunbeams! . . . get that through your skull . . . and make it fast! Take it from me, Charon knows his business . . . hang around and you'll see . . ."

Friendly, isn't he?

"But just tell me this. How is it I can see you? . . . and the boat? . . . there's no light on the shore . . . look!"

A last shred of doubt after all . . .

"It's because you're just the one to see us . . . it's special . . . you wouldn't understand . . ."

A convenient explanation.

"And besides, I'm not allowed."

"You're not allowed? . . . and say, Agar not barking, is that special too?"

"Maybe . . . maybe . . ."

"You can't tell me that either?"

"No, damn it!"

Agar, the horrible blusterer, all of a sudden mute . . . discreet . . . special . . . am I supposed to believe that? . . . magic? . . . Agar . . . the boat . . . Le Vigan . . . all magic? . . . all dead? . . . sure . . . sure . . . why not? . . . even dead people are something . . .

I had to keep up the pretense: "Why'd you come back? . . . Couldn't make a go of it over there?" I knew his situation . . . It was still mighty dangerous for him around here . . .

"I couldn't take it any more . . . that's all . . . See?"

"Bored?"

"Yes."

"I understand . . ."

That's a fact. I understood . . . you know if you've been through it . . . you can't stand it any more . . . one fine day you're ready to risk everything . . . to have been born somewhere else . . . death, okay, but back home! that attraction . . . you can't reason about it . . . not the least bit . . . you just crawl . . . that animal magnet . . .

"Okay! Okay! . . . if that's how it is . . . but those people over there . . . coming and going . . . never stopping . . .

crossing the square . . . getting on . . . getting off . . . what are they doing?" Maybe he could tell me that at least! . . .

"They're going home . . . to get the fare."

I'm getting on his nerves . . .

Going home to get something? . . . those stiffs seem to be pretty innocent . . . Hell! . . . I've been thought dead . . . reported dead . . . suppose I'd have gone home and asked for a handkerchief . . . or a pin! . . . my heirs took over quick! wiped me out! . . . what did I find? . . . . thin air and threats! . . .

"That's a good one," I say . . . "You expect to find something if you go home? . . ."

"Home? Where?" He's flabbergasted.

"Where you hung out . . . On the Avenue Junot . . ."

"Hell, no."

"Then those people aren't dead?"

"Can't you tell? . . . Don't you catch the aroma?"

He was right . . . I smelled it . . . Agar sniffed at them . . . but I couldn't make him bark . . . Agar who barked at any damn thing . . . at a leaf in the wind . . . he's given up barking . . .

"He doesn't bark at you either . . . this place has got him down . . . it's not just the dead people . . . what about you? Are you alive? . . ."

A last vestige of doubt . . .

"But tell me, how'd you get here? . . . how'd you get away?" He should explain.

It was complicated . . . I listen . . . he was working in the Argentine . . . He'd found . . . a stroke of luck . . . some extra work with his wife, Anita . . . on location . . .

"You see the spurs? . . . take a look . . . 'gaucho' . . . picture was supposed to take two months . . . give me a part right away . . . I didn't ask, hell! . . . they practically forced me . . . ask Anita . . . historical picture . . . first a gaucho . . . then a bandit . . . and then a rebel general . . . a picture about their history . . . okay by me . . . just then Perón falls . . . and he was paying the subsidy! I say: good-bye, I'm clearing out, let's go . . . I wasn't going to hang around . . .

me and Anita . . . no soap! . . . Lebrun! Pétain! Hitler! I'd
had enough fun! . . . Perón . . . count me out! . . . all the
ports closed . . . guarded . . . lovely! . . . only place you
could get a freighter to France was Santiago, Chile . . . put
that in your pipe . . . the whole of South America . . . the
whole pampas . . . three months in the grass . . . grass this
high . . ."

He shows me . . .

"You don't know the pampas? . . . three months . . . Anita
in espadrilles . . . me, I had boots . . . I made new soles for
Anita . . . for myself, too . . . out of bark . . . not so easy
. . . if you find a truck tire, okay . . . but trees! . . . in the
Cordilleras you find everything . . . everything . . . a whole
camp full of trucks . . . kitchens . . . everything . . . it was
high time! get a load of this! . . . a train! . . . a real train!
. . . a city of gauchos! . . . and espadrilles! whole barns full
of espadrilles! and boots! . . . Did we outfit ourselves! . . .
you should have seen it . . . they gave us everything . . .
that's right . . . and dough . . . I didn't want to take it,
they forced me, they got sore . . . they'd seen me, they had a
movie house, they knew me . . . sound and all . . . they'd
seen me in *Goupil* . . ."

"You were terrific!"

He wouldn't let me go on . . . how unforgettable he was,
etc. etc. Not just in *Goupil,* in a raft of other pictures . . . he's
got to do all the talking . . . I've got to button up . . . and
make it fast . . . there wouldn't be time . . .

"Time? What do you mean?"

"Charon, see?"

He's got the terrors again . . . Charon . . . the alleged
Charon . . . But there was one thing . . .

"How'd you find the *bateau-mouche?*"

"Through Emile . . . through Emile . . ."

He calls him . . .

Emile's working . . . he walks down the gangplank . . .
rolls, I should say . . . Le Vigan introduces me. "It's Ferdinand!"

Emile doesn't know me . . . not at all . . . and I don't rec-

ognize him, either . . . I don't remember him . . . of course
I've changed . . . maybe he has too? . . . I look back . . .

Le Vigan tells me all about it . . . the tribulations . . . the
things that had happened to Emile . . . no joke . . . he'd
come from the cemetery . . . Emile! Yes, Emile! . . . I had a
right not to recognize him . . . straight out of the cemetery
. . . the mass ditch . . . here's the way it happened: as he
was coming out of the post office, the cops grabbed him . . .
they'd been tailing him . . . handcuffs . . . two seconds flat
. . . "This way!" They take him away . . . they try to . . .
the crowd won't let them . . . they pull him away from the
cops! "Stinking L.V.F." The whole crowd rushes him . . .
They lynch him! tear him to pieces! right then and there!
every bone in his body! femurs! head! pelvis! . . . they gouge
out one eye! that's why he was wearing a bandage . . . and
walking so funny, under himself you might say, like a spider,
revolving . . . I saw him coming down the gangplank, unrecognizable, like a monstrous insect . . . dumb, you've got to
admit, showing himself on that particular day . . . and at the
Post Office . . . the main one . . . the cops were nothing
. . . but the crowd . . . they didn't even give him time to
get to the police station . . . on the rue du Bouloi . . they'd
made hash out of him . . . hash and chunks of bone . . .
on the sidewalk outside of the Post Office . . . the main one
. . . a cart came by from the Food Market . . ."Take him for
meat!" they yell! The butcher didn't want him . . . "to Thiais!"
To the mass ditch . . . direct! . . . hell, it was bound to happen . . . he fell on a glorious day of Vengeance . . . Emile
wasn't the only one . . . thousands were lynched that day
. . . that same day . . . recognized for L.V.F.'s . . . or
something else . . . all over . . . in the provinces . . . in
Paris . . .

Okay . . . Emile in the ditch . . . Well about five, six days
later . . . the dead started moving . . . sort of wriggling . . .
under him . . . the stiffs . . . under and over him . . . disentangling themselves . . . absolutely! . . . hoisting themselves out of the ditch! . . . Emile, who'd come from the siege
of Moscow, who'd been through three Russian winters, had

seen plenty of guys buried a damn sight worse than that . . .
pull themselves out of a lot bigger holes! . . . craters, crevices, regular upside-down Pantheons . . . so he said . . . he
wasn't going to let a little thing like this surprise him . . .
heaps of every kind of wreckage . . . whole cities . . . suburbs, factories, locomotives! . . . and tanks! whole armies of
tanks in ravines so deep that the Champs-Elysées, the Arch of
Triumph, and the Obelisk would have disappeared . . . easy!
. . . just to show you that Emile was ready . . . on the spot!
. . . wedged in under the stiffs in Thiais . . . he hung on
. . . to scraps of flesh . . . scraps of clothing . . . and
heave! he hoists himself! right along with them! . . . moving?
. . . good . . . he moves too . . . golden opportunity! . . .
he lets them hoist him! that's right! . . . up and out! . . . he
hurt all over . . . but he didn't let go . . . if they were leaving, he was leaving too . . . he went down the hill with them
. . . to the Seine . . . to the riverbank . . . latched onto them
. . . like a pilgrimage . . . in twos and threes . . . like they
were saying their prayers . . . down to *La Publique* . . . okay
. . . dead-quiet pilgrimage . . . Emile didn't make a sound
either . . . nobody said a word . . . Emile's obsession: no
noise . . . not to be massacred all over again . . . not to be
noticed . . . he knew . . . that's all . . . he knew the main
thing was to steer clear of living people . . . he'd found that
out at the Post Office! he'd seen enough . . . cops or no cops!
. . . if he got caught again, he was through . . . Emile
wasn't dumb . . . he knew how lucky he'd been . . . thrown
into a ditch with people who just happened to be on their way
out . . . he wasn't going to leave them . . . "Going that way?
. . . Good, I'm tagging along . . ." He tagged . . . the path
. . . the zigzags . . . down the hill . . . and the gangplank
. . . but then! . . . the minute they got there . . . one foot
on deck . . . a voice! . . . Stentorian! "What do you think
you're doing? . . ." And to him personally: "Where the hell
have you come from? Who the hell are you?" Emile couldn't
see him . . . this being was behind him . . . he didn't turn
around . . .

"Out of the ditch . . . I'm with them . . ."

"Oh, so you're with them, you stinker! bastard! oh . . . so you're with them!"

And *wham! slam!* . . . his skull again . . . square in the skull . . . *bam!* . . . what's he packing? . . . a hammer? *wham!* . . . he passes out . . . he hasn't seen the monster . . . hasn't had time . . . who is it?

"I'm Charon, see!"

He comes to . . . he sees the being! . . . a giant! really something: at least three . . . four times my size! . . . built like a barrel . . . with a face . . . that face! . . . like an ape . . . part tiger . . . part ape . . . part tiger . . . and heavy! . . . the whole boat listed . . . wearing . . . he's still telling me his story . . . some kind of frock coat . . . but a uniform frock coat . . . embroidered with silver tears . . . but the most terrific: his cap . . . as big as he was . . . an admiral's cap! . . . tall! . . . and wide! embroidered with gold!

Emile handed me a laugh . . .

"There's nothing to laugh about . . . you'll see . . . at least three four times bigger than you . . . take it from me . . . when he gets to work on your face!"

Me and my giggles . . . Le Vigan wasn't saying a thing . . .

"You'll see him . . . his oar in your face . . . you'll see him!" A promise . . .

"He splits their skulls with an oar . . ."

"Oh?" I act surprised. Charon's oar he's talking about . . .

"Everybody that comes on board . . . he fixes them . . . am I right, Le Vigan . . . rows right into them . . . square in the head . . . I'm telling you . . . that oar . . . Am I right, Le Vigan?"

"Right! . . . Right!" says Le Vigan.

"That's how he does it . . . nobody sneaks through . . . it's the law . . . the law . . . and let them pay up! . . . take it from me . . . If I'd said the same as I did: present! Emile! . . . but how about the dough? if I'd had any dough, he'd have taken me! no question! . . . he'd have finished me off! let me go aboard . . . if I'd said: 'Here's the gold, sir!' . . . okay with

anybody else! not with him: cash! cash! . . . you'll see how
he fixes them . . . got some? . . . haven't? *Wham!* . . . *bam!*
ghosts or ghostesses! simper and sigh? Won't get you anywhere! . . . *Bam* . . . the brass, Admiral . . . absolutely ferocious! . . . no time to lose! . . . the brass! got some?
haven't? . . . mothers . . . kids . . . same difference . . .
wham! massacre! . . . pay up! and cash! . . . 'No brass?
go back where you came from!' . . . Can you imagine? . . .
they went back . . . Am I right, Le Vigan . . . What do you
say? . . ."

"Right . . . right . . ."

"It's him they pay . . . am I right, Robert?"

"Yes . . . yes . . . right . . ."

I've only got to look at the enormous pouch! . . . ah, and
the oar too! . . . the famous oar! . . . he wasn't lying . . .
what an oar! with an oar like that you could deliver! . . . and
I know oars . . . I can see it standing there . . . from the
dock to the top of the smokestack . . . the length of it! longer
than the gangplank . . . no man could lift that . . . only a
monster . . . no human strength . . . a skull smashes . . . I
could see that . . . But maybe they were pulling my leg? All
three of them? . . . Le Vigan . . . Emile . . . and the girl?
. . . Skulls or no skulls . . . let's get one thing straight . . .
how'd they get there? How had they met? . . . Le Vigan,
spurs and sombrero . . . Emile of the Cemetery . . . and
Miss Anita? . . . I was too old and tired to think anything was
impossible . . . all the same, one thing was sure, I was going
to make myself scarce! . . . oar or no oar . . . Charon or no
Charon! . . . all that was pretty screwy! . . . weird . . . curious! . . . let's say I was curious . . . born curious, you'll always be curious . . . but Emile here, Le Vigan, and the doll
. . . were a little more than weird . . . and this boat of theirs!
. . . *La Publique!* . . . On my way out one last question!

"Where'd you meet?" I asked them.

"At the Argentine Embassy!" and he adds: "On the rue
Christophe-Colomb."

"But you'd just come back from the Argentine."

"So what? We met, that's all. Anita and I wanted to go back

. . . Emile, well, Charon had fired him! Don't you see? . . . He wanted to take a look. He'd never been in the Argentine."

He and Anita had no regular papers . . . they'd shipped out of Santiago on the q.t. . . . or someplace else . . . they were all liars . . . but one thing is sure, if Le Vigan had got picked up even after all they'd said about pardon and so on . . . the rap wouldn't be soft . . . ten years! . . . twenty years! . . .

Blasted Gaucho Mardi-Gras . . . it was no joke . . . no question of movies . . . he and his doll had to blow . . . and quick . . . but what about the other guy? Bozo of the Cemeteries, what was he doing at the Embassy? sightseeing? . . . Emile of the L.V.F.? . . . he wasn't from the Argentine . . . Oh, just an idea . . . going over there . . . starting a new life . . . so he said . . . virgin continent . . . Did they get rid of him! . . . . "Don't you read the papers? Don't you know what's going on? Or maybe you're a Peronist?" They were going to question him some more . . . him . . . a bundle of rags and scraps and strings . . . if he'd opened his mouth . . . *boom!* . . . the bum's rush . . . that's how they met . . . on the sidewalk . . . "Hello, hello, how's it going? . . . You here? . . . You?" They weren't the only ones on the sidewalk . . . a whole crowd . . . interested in the New World . . . what bothered Le Vigan the most, he told me, was his costume . . . especially the spurs! . . . those people, in the line, asked where he came from . . . "From the Argentine!" . . . they wouldn't believe it . . .

It's a fact, I knew about spurs, they'd have gone half-way through a horse!

"You're so clever," I said.

That made him sore . . . he explained:

"I was historical . . . see . . . an episode . . . you can't take these spurs off . . . sewn right on . . . they don't wear them any more! a period picture . . . haven't you ever heard of period pictures?"

I was the nitwit.

And the other one? . . . Emile . . . Maybe he was period too . . . could be . . . and the *bateau-mouche?* . . . and all these people coming and going? in threes . . . and fours . . . the procession? all going to see Charon? . . . bringing their

bones? . . . to be welcomed with the oar . . . *wha-a-am!* . . .
a shower of brains . . . plausible enough . . . and all this
happening on the former Place Faidherbe . . . under Madame Niçois' window . . . on the riverfront . . . and Agar
sniffing at them . . . I could go ksst! ksst! till I was blue in the
face, he refused to bark! that loudmouth! . . . that lion!

Well, let's see . . . I'd come down here for Madame Niçois
. . . to fix her dressing, and here I was mixed up in this
screwy business . . . what was all this? . . . was it all imagination? Anita, the brunette in the work clothes? . . . Emile,
L.V.F.'s fireman's helper? . . . and those people, supposedly
dead, that I could clearly see parading . . . never stopping
. . . crossing the former Place Faidherbe . . . and going up
to get their dough? . . . and all that . . . without light . . .

Not a street lamp . . . not a shop window . . . I've told you
. . . was it me? . . . a dream? . . . I've had brutal treatment . . . sure . . . I know . . . certain shocks have left
their mark . . . I'm the emotional type . . . introspective
. . . yes . . . it's my privilege . . . but such hallucinations?
auditive? well, yes in a pinch . . . but visual? Baloney! . . .
visual hallucinations . . . very, very unusual . . .

But it wouldn't be any dream if that Charon of theirs showed
. . . their monster with the oar . . . and asked me what the
hell I was doing . . .

"Say, Emile, how come he took you on as a fireman?"

"Fireman and mechanic."

He pulls me up just like that. "Mechanic."

"You weren't a mechanic."

"Oh yes I was . . . hell, you came around often enough!
. . . don't you remember? your motorcycle . . ."

"Yes, yes, of course . . ."

He was sore that I didn't remember . . . his shop on rue
Caulaincourt . . . yes . . . it was dim . . . rue Caulaincourt
. . . far away . . . motorbike . . . rue Girardon, rue Francoeur, and so on . . . talking about it, he made me remember
. . . the whole thing . . . what in God's name had got into
me . . . in the end I'd only saved Bébert . . . what confused
me about this Emile was that he'd got so little . . . shrunk
. . . broken and twisted in fifteen, twenty different places

. . . kind of revolving under himself . . . the "Avenger Commandos" . . . or Charon . . . had messed him up . . . he
walked by twists . . . one twist . . . two twists . . . in the
opposite direction . . . like a spider . . .

"Say, Emile . . . you say the passengers pay?" I was thinking of myself . . .

"Sure . . . but Le Vigan takes the money . . . Look."

I look some more . . . Le Vigan's the cashier . . . he
doesn't hit anybody . . . Charon does that . . . before Le
Vigan there were others . . . lots of them . . . They all ran
out! bums! yes, the whole lot of them . . . he tells me all about
it . . . the whole lot . . . Charon had had his troubles . . .
They'd made off with twenty! a hundred money bags! . . .
the bums he'd taken on . . . any old tramp from under the
bridges . . . "Interpols and Co." . . . now he only wanted reliable men who'd be sure to stay on . . . He could count
on Emile . . . Le Vigan too and Anita . . . he'd massacred
Emile, he hired him half dead . . . and devoted heart and soul
to his machine . . . They never saw the daylight . . . never,
not any of them . . . *La Publique* cast off exactly at dawn
. . . that was the busy time . . . terrible . . . the time when
Charon showed up . . . handing out clouts in all directions
. . . everybody . . . first the ones who hadn't paid . . . then
the others . . . payers . . . non-payers . . . everybody got
his . . . jellied mugs! . . . oar massacre! . . .

Talking of costumes, I must say, only Le Vigan was funny
. . . the two others, Emile and Anita, could have showed
themselves anywhere.

"So you say he doesn't lie down on the job? . . . he's terrible?"

My obsession now was the brass . . . I'd never given
enough thought to brass . . . my whole trouble all my life,
that I'd thought about entirely different things . . . when I
think of Achille and the other billionaires . . . they never
thought of anything else . . . they're lucky . . . in the Purge,
for instance, if you had brass you were okay . . .

"I'll say . . . and he splits their face besides . . . he doesn't
care whose . . ."

"Not the ones that pay?" I make him repeat . . .

"Ho! ho! . . . as if he cared . . . you'll hear them . . . just stick around . . ."

I'd seen such things, but this was pretty fancy . . .

"The rich with the poor?"

"Hell, yes . . . *wham!* . . . *smash!* rich! . . . poor! mothers! the kids in their arms! *wham!* he bashes their heads in! brains all over . . . and *bam!* . . . you see the oar? . . . there! . . . that's his oar!"

I'd seen it . . . from the pier to the top of the smokestack . . . standing there! . . . something! . . . longer than the gangplank . . . much longer . . .

"First he smashes their skulls . . . then he rows around in their heads . . . square in the brains . . . that's right . . . 'Waking them up,' that's what he calls it . . . he'll do the same to you . . . he skims off their thoughts . . ."

"And then what?"

"Then what? . . . no more doubletalk . . . they go back home . . . or they pay up! You'll hear them bellowing!"

"Here? . . . there? . . . "

"You're crazy . . . not here . . . past Albon! . . . at Ville-neuve-Saint-Georges! . . ."

I didn't want to ask too many questions . . . so where was the "passage beyond"? . . . after Choisy? . . . All this was pretty fabulous . . . the massacre . . . and the rest . . . and Emile's story . . . but what about the smell? . . . that certain aroma? . . . I couldn't contradict that . . . that smell, no mistake . . . especially not me . . . after twenty-five years of "certificates"! . . . Agar sniffed . . . sniffed at all these beings . . . one by one . . . but not a murmur out of him! not so much as a *grrr!* . . . him that barks at a leaf . . . up there on the hill . . . if it falls . . . now, nothing . . . a hundred percent mute . . . so there must be something fishy about these people . . . and certainly an odor . . . and the oar? . . . I looked at it again . . . the bulk . . . Charon or no Charon, you'd need some strength to grab hold of it . . . and to lift it! . . . a monster . . . supernatural strength . . .

I still had questions . . . hanging around there, my curiosity

would get me in trouble . . . lots of questions! . . . just then
the factory whistle blew . . . change of shifts . . . one o'clock
in the morning . . . another whistle . . . longer . . . that was
a tugboat . . . calling Suresnes . . . reporting how many
barges . . . the locks . . .

All this was fine and dandy, but suppose this monster with
the oar caught me here? hanging around? . . . what would
happen . . . crazy to stand here laughing with these zebras
. . . and have him give me a dose of his methods? . . . send
me home like a bedbug . . . a half-spider . . . like Emile?
. . . all squashed and fractured! . . .

Oh, it was no time to fall asleep . . . think . . . sure . . .
meditate . . . but get out of there . . . even reduced as I was
. . . a wreck . . . practically out on my feet, I realized this
was no place to be hanging around . . . in the first place . . .
this *bateau-mouche, La Publique,* right at the bottom of our
hill? and all these pilgrims with their smell? . . . and Le Vigan
and the two others? . . . especially Le Vigan! . . . the admirable Le Vigan! . . . "Don't drag Ferdinand in the muck! . . .
he's a bigger patriot than any of you!" . . . and him in handcuffs . . . standing right up front . . . not in the wings, not in
a bistro, not in a milk bar, or at the Bal des Quatzarts! . . . he
all alone . . . before the Council of the Inquisition . . . when
they were trying to make him confess, to proclaim in a loud
voice . . . that he accused me, that I had brought him to this
. . . I and nobody else! . . . the rottenest mercenary traitor
he'd ever known! . . . the lousiest stinker of the whole Propa-
gandastaffel . . . the radio, the newspapers . . . clandestine
killers . . . me!

I'm telling you what happened . . . the historical events
. . . okay, but down there on the waterfront this was no time
to take root . . . hell no! . . . ravings? extravaganzas? . . .
good-bye!

"Oh, Le Vigan . . . listen . . . I'll be back in a minute!
. . . Got to take care of my patient . . ."

It was true . . . I'd come down there for Madame Niçois
. . . She must be awake by now . . .

"You see her window?"

I show him . . . you could see it clearly from the pier . . . the open shutters . . . the only one with the shutters open . . .

I'm not much afraid of anything, but I didn't feel like hanging around . . . maybe this character they called Charon was a hoax? . . . cock-and-bull? . . . but that oar? . . . I could see the oar! maybe the whole business was a trap . . . set for me? that would be going to a lot of trouble . . . I got to thinking . . . turning things over in my mind . . . and these people coming and going? . . . Another gag? . . .

"You see the window? . . . the first on the corner . . . the brown house . . . I'll be right back . . . I'll wave to you . . . go on, I won't talk . . . I won't tell anybody . . ."

Trying to set their minds at rest! some laugh! they split a gut . . . my song-and-dance . . . all three of them . . . they're doubled up . . . in addition they give me hell!

"Lousy fink! rube! beat it, you slob! . . . take a powder! don't let that lion loose . . . nitwit!"

Me and Agar both . . . sore at us for not hanging around . . .

"Stinker! Eel! No-good! . . . Go on and talk! go on! Traitor! Traitor!"

So I was a traitor too. I wasn't going to leave them the last word: "Clowns! extras! . . . chancres! . . . stinkpots!"

I threw it right back at them.

All of a sudden they were really smoking . . . that I should be leaving . . . they wouldn't have it . . . Le Vigan wouldn't take it either . . . ah, that got me! . . . offend Le Vigan! . . . the others okay . . . but Le Vigan! . . . I was almost going to turn back . . . to go on board their *bateau-mouche* . . . to explain . . . who was the biggest hero of the three! hell no! they're going too far . . . taking advantage of the circumstances . . . for a second I blew my top . . . Even Le Vigan . . . the nicest of the three . . . he should realize! . . . I'll make him eat his words! . . . that won't go down, sombrero . . . caballero! I'd make him respect me! . . . that's the way I am . . . dauntless! . . . I'd make him swallow his spurs! . . . even if he was Le Vigan . . . one time in Siegmaringen we'd had a little argument like this! Ladies and gentlemen! . . . I gave him a going-over . . . in the snow! . . . in the middle of the snow! . . . why? I don't remember . . . I'll tell you some time . . . Siegmaringen . . . another time . . . good idea to explain before the lies crop up . . . lies and pox and bedbugs . . . gossip spread by people who never set foot there . . . okay . . . it's a promise . . .

But now . . . here on the riverfront . . . he called me . . . they all called me . . . and not just me, Agar, too . . . poodles! finks! centipedes! . . . especially Le Vigan! and screwball! . . . by what right? I'd show them . . . Le Vigan . . . all three of them! I'd show them all three.

"Stool pigeons . . . corpse lickers! . . ."

I start up . . . I'd show them! . . . I'd show them! . . . I'd step up and show them what for . . . but one flip . . . they'd have me in the water . . . where would that get me? . . . I was wobbling on my pins . . . better riposte from a distance . . . in reverse actually . . .

"Assholes! dandelions!"

My voice was all right! . . . I could hear . . . one echo after another . . . as far as the Pont d'Auteuil . . . sound carries on the water . . . it was better to be going . . . you can't make such people understand . . . and Lili must be plenty worried . . . I'd been gone for hours . . .

So I give those zebras the go-by! "So long, you bastards!" I climb in reverse . . . I'm afraid they'll throw a big javelin after me . . . or the oar! . . . running backwards up the whole Cowpath . . . suppose they shoot . . . I keep an eye on them . . . they call me everything they can think of . . . I do the same . . . it's a two-way barrage on the Cowpath! And you know how I hate scenes!

"Geraniums! Morning Glories! Nasturtiums!"

"Nasturtiums!" . . . that gets them . . . they don't know what to say . . . All of a sudden they come back with "Excrement!" they start up again . . . you could have heard us in Bellevue . . . in the forest . . . Saint-Cloud . . . the whole valley . . . can you imagine? . . . I'm still climbing in reverse . . . suddenly I stop climbing . . . *Grrr! grrr!* a growl to end all growls! right there beside me! not an echo! an angry dog!

. . . oh no, not Agar . . . no . . . a different dog . . . I take a look: it's Frieda . . . Frieda on the prowl . . . Lili's dog . . . that dog was really nosey and vicious . . . she was after something in the thicket . . .

"Ah, there you are!"

Lili had been looking for me.

"Say, is that dog growling at me?"

She doesn't answer. She's got a question of her own.

"Where have you been?"

"To see Madame Niçois . . . you knew that."

"Such a long time?"

I stop retreating . . . we're almost at the house . . . but all the same I shout again . . .

"Greasers! Humming-birds! . . . Warblers!"

Down toward the shore . . . I want the last word . . . but that damn Frieda keeps growling . . . won't stop! . . .

"What's she growling at?"

"At Dodard! . . ."

"Dodard! . . . Dodard!"

"You think she'll find him?"

Dodard is our hedgehog . . . really a nice little animal . . . but always on the move . . . can't stay put . . . always trotting around . . . like it had a thousand feet . . . all over the place . . . in a hole . . . under a branch . . . under some other branch . . . Frieda's the one that finds everything . . . Dodard must be under a root . . . Frieda's going to dig up the whole garden!

Those characters down there, that sinister crew, won't accept defeat! they're stubborn!

"Peony!"

They're yelling . . . they're calling me . . .

"Make Frieda shut up . . . she won't find him . . ."

Frieda is rummaging and digging under a thornbush . . .

"Why are you shouting?"

"Le Vigan is down there . . . that's him shooting off his mouth . . . that's right . . . him and Emile . . . 'carrion!' that's what they're calling me . . . what do they think they are? . . . and their doll . . . Anita!"

I thought I'd let her in on it. She contradicts me . . .

"Forget about Le Vigan . . . you know he's in Amer-ica . . ."

Lili has always been skeptical, even when I have proof . . . Especially since Denmark . . . she says Denmark didn't do me any good . . . I couldn't very well tell her there was a boat down there . . . a *bateau-mouche* full of phantoms . . . and that our bozos were on it . . .

I'm shaken out of my perplexity . . . a bark! what a bark! *arrgh! arrgh!* ah, that's Agar . . . Now Agar starts in! And Frieda with him . . . both together . . .

"They've found him! There he is!"

Lili's overjoyed! Dodard has been found.

"You'll look some more tomorrow."

But she sticks to her guns. "No, no. He's here . . . look . . . they've got him . . ."

It's Dodard all right, she picks him up . . . he doesn't ruffle his quills, he knows us . . . Lili takes him . . . fine . . . we go up to the house, we take him with us . . .

"You should have seen Le Vigan done up like a gaucho!"

She lets me say what I please . . . "Sure! sure!" I can say what I like . . . as far as she's concerned, Le Vigan is over there . . . at the end of the world . . . and that's that! . . . she's being reasonable . . . of course . . . and I'm raving . . . once and for all! I'm in bad shape? Sure, I know it . . . and not just since Denmark! I know . . . my head, my heart, those dizzy spells . . . they're bad . . . the chills aren't as bad as they were . . . but the dizzy spells . . . they make the walls rock! I don't say anything . . . the main point is this: if I were to leave Lili . . . she doesn't realize . . . all alone against all these people as I know them . . . the wolf pack . . . she wouldn't go far . . . the claimants, heirs, relatives, publishers! . . . there you've got champion scavengers! worse than those clowns down there . . . with their rotten moth-eaten scow . . . those scarecrows! . . . tax collectors, heirs, publishers . . . my, oh, my! . . . no, Lili wouldn't go far . . . she and Dodard and the hounds . . .

"Take 'em to the pound!"

Well, I wasn't dreaming at all . . . it's freezing . . . I'm trembling . . . what have I got to tremble about? . . . fatigue? . . . that business on the water front? . . . I'd talked too much . . . had I? . . . what's making me shiver this way? . . . slowly we climb back up . . . Lili is carrying Dodard . . . I attend to the dogs . . .

I'm sorry . . . let's get down to brass tacks . . . these things . . . I've got to tell them . . . with my pen . . . not just any old story . . . at random . . . This story by my own hand . . . the document!

It didn't seem like anything much . . . a little river fantasy
. . . a crazy boat . . . the people on it . . . but hell . . .
the cold shivers . . . They really got me . . . I had to lie
down . . . shivering and sweating like a damn fool . . .
worse than Madame Niçois . . . I caught on right away . . .
an attack . . . it was an attack! No doubt about it! At the
beginning of an attack you know what's going on, later you just
rave . . . I'd been all right for at least twenty years . . . it
was the cold down there, the waterfront . . . I'd been afraid
of this . . . well, now I was in for it . . . the river wind . . .

Lili asks me what she should do . . . nothing, damn it . . .
leave me alone . . . a doctor, unless his patients have turned
him into a complete idiot, has only one idea . . . to be left in
peace . . . he knows what malaria is . . . you've got it all
your life and that's that . . . You get the "solemn shivers" . . .
and you shake your bed till it creaks and cracks! . . . one fit
after another . . . as regular as clockwork . . . you know exactly what to expect . . . first the shivers . . . and then right
away . . . you start raving . . . you rave and rave . . . I
could imagine the kind of crap . . . twenty years without an
attack!

"Don't pay attention, Lili!"

I warn her . . . Sure, but tomorrow? And Madame Niçois?
. . . of course . . . her dressing! . . . no . . . the day after
tomorrow . . . no . . . in three days . . . I'd go back down,
of course I would . . . I'd see *La Publique* again and her cargo
of harlequins . . . of course I would . . . and I'd give their
Charon a good working over! I'd make a floor mat out of that
so-called Charon—half-panther, half-monkey! . . . He won't
argue . . . he won't say boo . . . he'll get down on his knees

and beg . . . that phony . . . I'll smash his oar over his face
. . . One! . . . *bam!* I'll smash his enormous . . . *ouch!*
ouch! . . . oar into a thousand splinters . . . like a straw . . .
that enormous thing! . . . a straw? . . . no! . . . two! three! four!
at last I can feel my strength . . . the whole bed is rattling,
pitching, groaning, rolling with it . . . I know . . . I know
. . . it's nothing new . . . doesn't date from yesterday . . .
with twenty or thirty percent more I'd be a little better off than
with just my wounds! I'd be one hundred and thirty percent
disabled at least . . . I wouldn't be working to make you
laugh! to please Achille and his clique of half-assed queens
. . . ah, the shame of it! ah, Volga boatmen! . . . but the
boatmen have won out! . . . just take a look at the asses on
the lowest of the commissars . . . asses like archbishops . . .
every last one of them . . . When the fellaghas of the Nile
have archbishops' asses like that, you can say we're getting
somewhere . . . that's the dream of nations . . . of the whole
earth . . . archbishops' asses! commissars' bellies! . . . Picasso! Boussac! . . . Mrs. Roosevelt! . . . tits and all . . .
brassieres! the whole lot of them!

I get to wondering . . . even in my present state, clammy
and shivering, what Achille can do with his hundred million a
year? . . . *cash!* does he stick it up the asses . . . of his little
floozies? or his coffin? . . . He can have that supercoffin of his
decorated pretty nice, embossed, inlaid . . . padded with sky-
blue silk, with festoons and lattice-work and silver tears . . .
and for his head? the pillow of Eternity! . . . golden feathers
and fairy roses! . . . he'll be cute in the funeral parlor . . .
the eternal Achille! his mean eye closed at last . . . his horrible smile sandblasted . . . He won't be so bad to look at
when he's dead.

I'm talking big . . . trying to cheer myself up . . . hell, I'm
kidding myself! I'll pass on before he does . . . I work, that
hastens the end . . . he takes it easy . . . that's the ultimate
secret of gerontotechnics: don't work, let other people! . . .
that's the whole idea of being a pimp . . . and I, like it or
not, I bring the grist to his mill . . . for his tarts . . . for his
coffin . . . and I turn the millstone. "And gee-up, you don-

key!" I sweat, I knock myself out . . . he looks on . . . he takes care of himself . . . naturally he'll last longer . . .

Take B! or K! . . . or Maurice . . . some Communists they'd be in my place . . . turning Brottin's mill . . . their rear ends would shrink! They'd be a little more appetizing to look at! their asses and jowls! . . . no more nylon girdles . . . no more brassieres! . . . oh, dear Archbishop Commissars! . . . ye wretched of the asshole! . . . fine and dandy! you've forced them to sit down? At the table of the people or of the Holy Ghost? and you see them multiplied! . . . prize-winning swine, that's their nature, at any kind of table! . . . what a sadist you are! . . . no remorse? no tears? . . . aren't you sorry for them? . . . those tragic destinies? those colossal martyrs? Doomed to put on blubber? more and more of it! . . .

There, there . . . I'm playing around . . . looking for effects . . . I'm going to lose you . . . and Madame Niçois' dressing? . . . where's my head? what have I been thinking? . . . fever . . . yes, of course . . . but Madame Niçois' dressing? the night! . . . everything's black! . . . shiver, shake! Let the damn bed collapse! I've been shaking it enough! Crack . . . I'm shaking it with my fever . . . a real attack . . . and my anger . . . the things they yelled at me from down there . . . "Peony!" . . . from their lousy pirate ship . . . they dared! . . . "Coward!" and "come and get it! . . ." Don't worry, I'll go . . . not once, but ten times . . . and all alone . . . they'll see me again . . . I'm boiling with indignation! . . . I'm in fusion . . . I'll burn the bed . . . I caught this "fusion" in Cameroon in 1917 . . . they'll see what they'll see! . . . I feel my pulse . . . my temperature is still going up! 104° it feels like . . . that's when you get ideas . . . wacky ideas? . . . maybe . . . I'm all balled up . . . Lower Meudon, Siegmaringen, all jumbled . . . But what about Pétain? . . . oh, he was sitting pretty . . . he had the status of a Chief of State . . . like Bogomolev or Tito . . . or Gaugaule or Nasser! . . . sixteen food cards! . . . Laval . . . Bichelonne* . . . Brinon* . . . Darnan* . . . had fewer . . . only six each . . . or eight . . . not in the same class . . . and the rest of us, imagine! . . . only one . . . hell! Ministers, Chiefs

of State, nobodies! Injustice is dead! . . . all conked out! died
of Injustice! and not in beauty . . . no frills, no protocol! . . .
I make you laugh . . . always going on about the defunct . . .
whichever way I look . . . the defunct . . . Nobody's left
but Achille . . . waiting . . .

Just a minute . . . I'm pretty far gone, I'm not through yet
. . . I wish the bed would cave in . . . If I could only open a
gash in it . . . a watercourse . . . and me and my bed would
sink! I'm sweating . . . dripping . . .

"Do you want something?"

"No, no . . . darling."

I never want anything . . . I refuse everything . . . I don't
want a kiss . . . and I don't want a napkin . . . I want to
reminisce . . . I want to be left alone . . . that's it . . . my
memories . . . all the circumstances . . . that's all I ask . . .
I live more on hatred than on noodles . . . but genuine hatred
. . . no cheap imitation . . . and gratitude? . . . never mind
. . . I'm chock-full of that . . . Nordling* who saved Paris
wanted to get me out of the clink . . . History, take note! . . .
either you're a memorialist or not . . . Let's see now . . .
down there? . . . on the riverfront? . . . Le Vigan? . . . Was
he really dressed like a gaucho? . . . down there? Gaucho and
fare collector? . . . Was Le Vigan taking the fares? . . . I've
got to know . . . got to remember exactly . . . fever or no
fever . . . exactitude is what counts! . . . Achille and Gertrut
reject my work . . . they say I'm lying. That's right! . . . Let
them try to tell me it wasn't like that in Siegarmingen! So
what? . . . Short circuit? . . . I didn't see anything at all
down on the riverfront . . . no *La Publique* . . . no ghosts!
. . . Le Vigan wasn't dressed like a gaucho . . . no sombrero
. . . no, he was wearing an enormous turban! hell, that's right,
an enormous turban . . . I tore it off him in the fight . . . in
the snow . . . but say, what did we fight about? . . . his turban was a bandage . . . he had an earache . . .

Your memory is precise, faithful . . . and then all of a sudden . . . nothing . . . it's gone . . . old age, you say . . .
no! . . . I've got to get Le Vigan back! and Siegmaringen! . . .
and Pétain with his eighteen food cards! . . . I've got them

all . . . and Laval and his Ménétrel . . . I never leave them . . . and the Black Forest and the big eagle! . . . you'll see what I mean! that Hohenzollern Castle! . . . just wait! . . .

I can't make up my mind with this fever . . . Achille? . . . Gertrut? . . . one's as crummy as the other . . . But suppose they both run out on me . . . it's possible . . .

Oh, I'd made up my mind not to write any more . . . the very word "writing" has always struck me as indecent! . . . pretentious, narcissistic, "have-you-read-me?" . . . that was my reason, the only one . . . I'm just no candidate for the Pantheon . . . highest priced worms in the world! . . . Soufflot's* gluttons . . . no! . . . it's not vanity that prods me . . . it's the gas, the carrots, the zwieback . . . But I risked it, I stuck my neck out . . . for the gas and the carrots . . . and for the dogs . . . they've got to eat, too . . . I haven't written much . . . but look at the hatred . . . the fury people were in . . . and still are . . . I was never so well aware of the loathing people had for me as during the months when they put me in Sonbye Hospital in Denmark . . . between two spells of solitary . . . in the cancer ward . . . I'm still trembling, but I know what I'm saying . . . nothing doubtful, nothing imaginary about it . . . in the cancer ward at the Sonbye Hospital in Copenhagen, Denmark . . . and I can tell you there was screaming . . . all advanced cases . . . it was a kind of favor to put me there . . . after all it was better than the Venstre . . . besides, I was supposed to make myself useful . . . listen for the last gasps . . . ring for the nurse . . . help her to pack up the corpse . . . so she only had to roll it to the door . . . and into the corridor . . .

Everything is supposed to be so perfected, so amazingly hallucino-sanitary in Copenhagen, Denmark, enough to hit your head against the wall . . . don't believe a word of it! . . . it's just like any place else . . . I mean, it's the cleaning women who do everything and run everything . . . in the ministries, the restaurants, the political parties, the hospitals! it's the cleaning women who have the say . . . they're the ones who sweep away records, laws, state secrets, and the dying . . . the world sleeps . . . not the cleaning woman . . . termites! . . . termites! in the morning you don't find a thing . . . your moribund friend is packed away . . . Yorick, and no alas! . . . let them scream! let them wait! . . . morphine . . . injections . . . to hell with that! . . . I was the "watcher" on duty . . . the Samaritan with the bell . . . The last sigh? tinkle! tinkle! Ship him out! one the less! . . . Erna . . . Ingrid . . . came in yawning . . . rolled the guy out . . . I know what I'm saying, I'm not making it up . . . Sonbye Hospital; department head, Professor Gram . . . excellent clinician . . . subtle, sensitive . . . oh, he never said a word to me . . . you don't talk to the prisoners . . . I was undergoing treatment, too . . . I was falling apart . . . not from cancer, not yet . . . only from the effects of the hole, the cage, Vesterfangsel . . . I'm not making up the hole either . . . it was really a hole, extra-damp, pitch dark, only a little slit near the ceiling . . . get them to show you Pavilion K in the Vesterfangsel, Copenhagen . . . travel is educational . . . Nyehavn, Tivoli, the Hotel d'Angleterre aren't the whole story . . . you won't be risking anything as a tourist . . . The advantage of the cancer ward over the prison was that there were no bars or ventilation slits . . . The windows were high and wide and looked out on a sort of meadow . . . the meadows in the north are pale . . . pale as their sky and their Baltic . . . men, clouds, sea, meadows . . . all one . . . treacherous in a way . . . easy to see sprites . . . No sprites in the cancer ward . . . I wasn't there to dream . . . but to listen for death rattles . . . to wake up Erna . . . or Ingrid . . . too soon . . . too late . . . There was one good thing about Gram, he trusted me not to take advantage of being there without handcuffs . . . all those long nights . . . to make a getaway . . . it might have been easy enough . . . but . . . Lili would have been left alone . . . and Bébert . . . and where would I have gone? . . . the police had my description everywhere . . . they'd have picked me up . . . there's fuzz all over . . . every country in the world . . . fuzz . . . men are sex-fiends, thieves, murderers, but most of all they're fuzz . . . Sweden? . . . Malmö? . . . don't make me laugh . . . I wouldn't go a hundred yards . . . I'd be chained up worse than ever . . . tossed in the hold . . . and off to the F.F.I. . . . Delivery . . . that's the Swedish speciality! You don't believe me? . . . I'll give you the names of people who committed suicide . . . right in the ambulance . . . there . . . before my eyes . . . under the lantern . . . ah, the "right of asylum!" . . . I'd have liked to see Montherlant, or Morand, or Carbuccia try it . . . and see if they'd still be sipping cocktails with the best . . . if they'd still have their fancy apartments . . .

One advantage of this bell-ringing routine was that I had plenty of time to think . . . dying people in general are pretty noisy . . . and especially in my ward the people with cancer of the throat . . . but when you're condemned to death yourself . . . practically nothing fazes you . . . There's nothing like it . . . I didn't bat an eyelash, I just thought, I thought very clearly . . . not in a fever like now . . . pellagra interferes with your vision, you see a blur, but your head stays clear . . . you keep cool . . . all these dying people around me, two whole wards . . . it was simple to figure what would happen to me if I went back to Montmartre . . . they'd put me between two planks and saw me in half . . . caught red-handed? . . . no nonsense . . . the saw! . . . I'd heard they were taking everything! my apartment! selling everything at auction . . . and at the Flea Market . . . having a hell of a good time . . . burning the beds for firewood . . . so where could I go? the great slaking of vengeance! . . . Oh, those rabid assassins aren't as crazy as people think . . . They're sly . . . farsighted . . . even at the height of their delirium they hitch their wagon to a bank account . . . Laetitia! . . . the motto of the most frantic righters of wrongs, torture-masters, eye-putter-outers, and ball-cutters is: *"Pourvou qué ça douré!"*

I wasn't going to leave the Sonbye as long as they were willing to keep me for treatment . . . vitamins . . . porridge . . . "If only ittalasta!" That was my motto, too. I'd lost all my teeth . . . and about a hundred pounds . . . I've been kind of thin ever since . . . solitary doesn't do a man any good . . .

We can't take it . . . I wouldn't want you to think I'm soft
. . . that I need people to talk to . . . no, not at all! Silence
is fine with me . . . but those Danish coolers are really rough
. . . even the toughest experts—Norwegians, Finns, Swedes
—agree that they're just too horrible . . . I'd like to see Mauriac, Morand, Aragon, Vaillant, and *tutti*, them and their pipes
of Pan . . . after six months in one of them! ah, Nobel and
Goncourt prizewinners! and *frutti!* What a revelation! . . . the
heavenly shits! Their crumminess coming out underneath! As
for myself, I'm proud to say, my morale never cracked! my
body gave way, I admit . . . piece by piece . . . red ribbons
. . . gnawed away . . . the effect of the darkness and con-
finement . . . my being in the cancer ward didn't surprise
anybody . . . pellagra? . . . cancer? . . . the nurses didn't
care . . . they expected to roll me out in the corridor one fine
day . . . meanwhile, I could make myself useful . . . listen
carefully for that last gasp . . . ring neither too soon . . . nor
too late . . . load the corpse on the truck . . . after washing
it . . . and, most important, silently . . . never a word! either
to the nurse when I woke her up, or to my colleagues next
day . . . all in all, my presence there was very fragile . . .
barely tolerated . . . useful, but no tenure . . . a trifle . . .
a word . . . and out I'd go . . .

One morning I don't see a soul . . . no more nurse . . . the
doctors . . . ordinarily so regular . . . haven't come through
. . . In two seconds flat I say to myself: this is it! . . . under
certain conditions you get a total sensation of your life . . .
not some other time, but right now . . . you've got a direct
intuition, you know, before anything happens, that it's for you
and not somebody else . . . you've got an animal certainty
. . . it's human goofiness that dialectifies everything, muddles
everything up . . .

Another night and day pass . . . nobody says a word to me
. . . not a nurse in the ward . . . somebody dies . . . and
there he stays on his side, all yellow, with his mouth wide open
. . . not an intern in sight . . . nobody but me and the
croakers . . . I keep ringing my bell, but nothing happens . . .

Ah, someone's there! . . . not a nurse . . . a driver . . . in the big double door . . . wide open . . . I know that man . . . the same driver that brought me . . . no, not a brute . . . strong but quiet . . . not a prison guard . . . he's in civilian clothes, a gabardine jacket . . . same material as my Poincaré suit . . . a slight detail, irrelevant you may think . . . No, don't say that . . . the circumstances . . . both of us on our good behavior! nobody in the two wards but him and me and the croakers . . . not a nurse, not an assistant, not an interne . . . *"Komm!"* he says to me . . . he could have saved his breath . . . I knew . . . He was taking me back to the hole . . .

I can say that I've lots of memories in my crummy life . . . not the picturesque kind that don't cost anything . . . but paid for! . . . and at a very steep price . . . well, here between you and me, these circumstances mean a lot to me . . . this driver saying *"Komm"* in the doorway . . . not brutal or anything . . . standing there motionless . . . ready to take me back to the hole . . . on the other side of town . . . without an escort . . . without handcuffs . . . all perfectly trusting . . . in a limousine . . . and I'd be stuck there for months . . . that impression stays with me . . .

A few months in the hole means nothing to you . . . why would it . . .

It turned out to be quite a few months . . . while they were deciding whether to hand me over . . . or to keep me . . . with Article 75 on my ass . . . and every newspaper in Copenhagen dead sure that I'd sold, they didn't know exactly what, but at least the defenses of the Alps . . . Article 75 was an article of faith . . . their top-level reflections went on for years . . . should they hand me over? . . . should they let me die in prison? . . . at the hospital? . . . or someplace else?

As long as you haven't seen a civilian prison driver in the doorway, you haven't seen a thing . . .

Oh, it's no better now . . . not much better . . . to hell with the two of them! the ten! . . . the twenty! . . . the lousy skinflints! . . . Anyone who wants to work for people like that . . . can split a gut!

I talk to Norbert Loukoum about the hole . . . I do it on purpose, it gets him down . . . he's never been in . . . hell, no! . . . neither he . . . nor Achille! . . . nor Malraux! . . . nor Mauriac! . . . nor the foetus Tartre . . . nor Larengon . . . nor Triolette of the toyolette . . . the whole oily clique . . . the turncoat élite . . . who never get sick of playing the dangerous revolutionary . . . the iron men of the Iron Curtain . . . the superbazookas . . . the East-West bombshells . . . thunder on the left . . . and they're all mollycoddles . . . pensioned at birth . . . weaned from the bottle, slightly languid nurse, the dear old *lycée*, the little boy-friend, a cushy job . . . nothing to it! . . . ten, twelve changes of skin and sweaters, and it's in the bag: that big fat chameleon pension . . . and the Promenade des Anglais! . . . a little fun in the urinals . . . distinction . . . the Academy! . . . Richelieu! . . . the old bastards! . . . never paying! . . . always paid! Terminus at the "Quai of the Slippery Eels!" . . . Under the dome of the rectums and prostates . . . "Oh, so you're one too, my dear sir . . . gentler, more sensitive, a deeper licker! . . . Apotheon! . . ."

Richelieu foresaw it all! . . . Mauriac, Bourget, and Aspirine . . . At a certain stage of decadence the worst drones get to be the biggest kings! . . . Louis XIV couldn't have held a candle to Juanovici . . .

Don't get nervous if I jump around . . . if I zigzag and come back . . . that whacky business with *La Publique* . . . suppose you'd been there in my place!

"Still trembling?"

"No . . . no."

At a certain age . . . sixty-three . . . all you can do is say

no . . . no . . . and clear out . . . courtesy demands it . . .
you're one too many . . . how many times have people
wished you dead in the last sixty-three years? . . . too many to
count . . . you'd like them to put up with you for another few
months? . . . one spring? . . . two? . . . yes, yes, but then
first of all you've got to be loaded! rich! . . . rich! that's the
main thing! . . . and well disposed toward your heirs . . . a
living Santa Claus . . . and assure them in your will . . .
holographic certainty, notarized, sealed, and registered . . .
that everything will go to them . . . everything to Lucien
. . . nothing to Camille . . . and that you're really feeling
terrible! and that you'll never make another . . . because
you're on your last legs . . . last gasp . . . last everything!
that it won't be long . . . that your tongue is hanging out . . .
coated with black and yellow plaster . . . well, maybe in that
case . . . maybe? . . . they won't think you're such an abject
horrible rapacious tyrant . . . though it's the unanimous opinion . . . but watch your step . . . remember you're living on
borrowed time . . . puff and blow! . . . spit yellow! . . .
limp! . . . if they make you get up . . . stumble . . . collapse! . . . send for the priest . . . extreme unction does
wonders for the people who set all their hopes in you . . . in
your last breath! . . . it's amazing the way a dying man can
shatter a family's nerves . . . the cruelty of it! . . . can't he
get it over with? . . . the sadism of the "last moments" . . .
extreme unction, rain check . . . ah, you moribund slow-
pokes, you drive everybody crazy!

I've seen people dying all over the world, in the tropics, in
the ice fields, in indigence and wealth, in the pen, in power,
laden with honors, leprous convicts, in revolutions, in peacetime, in artillery barrages, in showers of confetti, every stop of
the *de profundis* organ . . . the most harrowing, I think, is
dogs . . . and cats . . . or the hedgehog . . . oh, that's my
experience . . . for what it's worth . . . I haven't gone out of
my way . . . believe me . . . I take no pleasure in it . . . if
one night I found Madeleine Jacob . . . let's say in the last
stages of cancer of the womb . . . I wouldn't be like Charon
. . . not at all! . . . I wouldn't disembowel her, I wouldn't

draw and quarter her, or hang her up on a hook by her tumor
. . . to drain like a putrid rabbit . . . no, without any whor-
ish coquetry à la Schweitzer or . . . Abbé Pierre . . . no, I
can say . . . I can prove it . . . that I'm the good Samaritan
in person! even with the most ferocious hater . . . the most
furunculous spasmodic . . . that you wouldn't touch with a ten-
foot pole . . . Madeleine, for instance . . . makes you puke
that she should even exist . . . a syncope of ugliness! As I live
and breathe, you'd see me down my feelings! I'd pat and cod-
dle Madeleine! play the ardent lover . . . like Abbé Pierre
. . . or the apostle of the *"Tropic Harmonica Digest!"*

"Last moments?" . . . Not so fast . . . I'm feverish . . .
Madeleine, Schweitzer . . . the Abbé . . .

I can see them coming . . . naturally . . . they exist! Madeleine, Schweitzer, and the Abbé . . . and I receive them . . .
oh, not with Charon's methods . . . I wouldn't smash their
skulls in a second time . . . make them die again . . . no
. . . the exact opposite . . . all gentleness . . . thebaic tenderness . . . two c.c.'s of morphine . . . why not? . . . Sy-
denham said long ago (1650) that he could cure anything he
pleased, any ailment whatever, with four or five ounces of
opium . . . that's why I tell my colleagues: don't waste your
opium . . . maybe there'll be a war . . . restrictions . . .
they promise this . . . they promise that . . . but your death
agony? . . . you can't expect Blablablah, to help you . . .
later! . . . oh, of course! . . . as late as possible . . . when
your time's up . . . your own little private supply . . .
everything in its time . . . moderation in all things . . .

There's nothing moderate about my memory . . . not by a
damn sight . . . it thrashes and shakes like my bed . . . and
that Madame Niçois . . . look at this fit she's got me into . . .
with her riverfront! . . . the chills! . . . the draft! . . . I've
caught my death! . . . and all these tormented souls . . . and
La Publique? . . . *La Publique* . . . I had plenty to hold
against her . . . that capricious old bag with her cancer . . .
all that gas-blowing on the riverfront with that gang of hoods
. . . those insulting stinkers! "Peony" they called me . . .
peony! . . . they dared! . . . the shameless bastards!

Ambassador Carbougniat,* as Vichyssois as Brisson, as much

a Doriotist as Robert . . . you should have seen his tantrums
. . . His Excellency! . . . don't send me to Vincennes! . . .
boy, did he shake his Embassy bed, sixty-nine fits in a row,
chewing whole mouthfuls out of his gobelins . . . it was really
alarming! . . . looked like he was going to eat the whole Embassy . . . the furniture and the files . . . everything . . .
They had to promise him a "super-class" job in the other hemi-
sphere . . . he was getting sicker than me . . . having me
there so near to him, in the Vesterfangsel . . . suffering agonies . . . because they didn't impale me . . . he claimed I'd
insulted Montgomery . . . and the Führer . . . and Prince
Bernadotte . . . you should have seen the letters he wrote to
the Baltavian ministers . . . regular ultimatums! I've seen
copies . . .

Lying here now in my fever, I tremble as much as he did . . .
I wet the bedclothes . . . oh, but I'm not goofy enough to
forget what I was . . . the prize package . . . the gilt-edged
quarry of the chase . . . Glory! Bravery! Supreme Flunkey-
dom! even here like this, worn to a frazzle, a tottering wreck, I
still get the same effects . . . Line up on the line . . . no de-
viations . . . The living proof is that they throw me out of
everywhere . . . invariably . . . like forty-five chancres . . .
everywhere . . . everything . . . the one and only genuine
shithead: Ferdinand!

And I've seen them all at work . . . with their asses . . . all
smeared with vaseline . . . licking everybody's balls . . . I
know their names and addresses . . . same as the addresses of
my moving-men and would-be assassins! I'm still here, only one
foot in the grave . . . and I know their ages . . . their birthdates, every last one of them . . . I say them over to myself
. . . their birthdates . . . I see their big moments of happiness . . . kick! trample! . . . in a vision! . . . they'll be a
thousand times worse . . . a thousand times luckier next time
. . . they've said as much . . . they've taken their positions
. . . some positions! . . . I see them . . . I see them . . .
over 102° you see everything . . . fever must be good for
something! . . . I never forget a thing! . . . never! . . . it's
my nature . . .

Yes, of course . . . after eight months in the hole . . . I
was falling apart . . . but I've told you that over and over
. . . hell! . . . I'm boring you . . . Anyway, I've got other
worries! my respect . . . my courtesy . . . go out to different
people . . . Achille, for instance . . . him and his surplus
profits . . . ninety million a year . . . not bad! . . . and already a billionaire! the superstinker! an army of flunkeys and
flunkettes sticking their tongues in all his holes, but does that
keep him from sighing and screaming and yelling? Torture!
Bloody murder! It's not enough! the tongues aren't juicy
enough! not enough gold nuggets in the books! they're burning him alive . . . his scribbler galley-slaves are leading him a
dog's life! . . .

The fever's dropping . . . I'm really not raving any more
. . . delirium? . . . delirium? . . . no, reflection! . . . "Destiny is Politics!" . . . that's right. That's Bonaparte's opinion . . . okay! Communists? . . . Good, let's commune . . .
Achille, for instance . . . tiller to the left . . . how much will
he give next time? . . . everything and then some! . . . the
Pontoise bridge and the Arch of Triumph! . . . and Mgr.
Feltin, Lacretelle*, and all the choir boys! Lacretelle and Monsieur Robert if you like, with Article 75 on their asses, would
they let so much as a fart or find anything better to do?
. . . well? . . . I can see Loukoum, a prelate if ever there
was one . . . the feebleminded are all for him! . . . his flabby
vagina-shaped puss . . . so prehensile! . . . so sticky! . . .

I'm still hot . . . I'm slinging balloon juice . . . I'm sorry
. . . No! Loukoum would be even more unbearable than all
the stinkers from *La Publique!* If Charon saw him, he'd give
up! No violence . . . he'd go soft . . . he wouldn't stir up his

skull with his oar . . . Make him recite the divine Sade back-wards? . . . Maybe . . .

I know . . . I know . . . I missed Charon! . . . If I'd stayed a minute longer, I'd have seen him! . . . Le Vigan and the others must have seen him . . . My excuse is . . . I felt the fever coming on . . . and I had another excuse . . . I'll tell you about it . . .

To hell with all that! . . . I can take you on an excursion with different people . . . delirium or not . . . a prettier place! . . . fever or no fever . . . really a very picturesque place . . . a tourist's paradise . . . dreamy, historical, and salubrious . . . ideal for the lungs and the nerves . . . perhaps a little damp near the river . . . the Danube . . . the shore . . . the rushes . . .

Maybe I shouldn't talk Siegmaringen up . . . but what a picturesque spot! . . . you'd think you were at an operetta . . .
a perfect setting . . . you're waiting for the sopranos, the
lyric tenors . . . for echoes you've got the whole forest . . .
ten, twenty mountains of trees! Black Forest, descending pine
trees . . . waterfalls . . . your stage is the city, so pretty-
pretty, pink and green, semi-pistachio, assorted pastry, caba-
rets, hotels, shops, all lopsided for the effect . . . all in the
"Baroque boche" and "White Horse Inn" style . . . you can
already hear the orchestra . . . the most amazing is the Castle
. . . stucco and papier-mâché . . . like a wedding cake on
top of the town . . . And yet . . . if you'd take the whole business . . . the Castle, the town, the Danube to the Place Pig-
alle! . . . the crowd you'd draw! . . . the Ciel, the Néant
and the Lapin à Gill wouldn't hold a candle to it . . .
Christ, the tourist busses you'd need . . . the brigades of police . . . the crowd! . . . and all ready to pay!

   In our time, I've got to admit, the place was gloomy . . .
tourists, sure . . . but a special kind . . . too much scabies,
too little bread, and too much R.A.F. overhead . . . and Leclerc's army right near . . . coming closer . . . the Senegalese
with their chop-chops . . . for our heads . . . nobody else's
. . . right now I'm reading the paper . . . they're weeping
over the fate of those poor Hungarians . . . if we'd been welcomed like them . . . if anybody'd spilled so many tears over
our misfortunes, we'd have been very happy, I can tell you!
we'd have danced the polka. If those poor Hungarian refugees
had had Article 75 on their asses, Coty wouldn't have kept
them for dinner . . . hell no! . . . if they'd been plain Frenchmen from France, he'd have cut them in two on the spot

. . . in ten if they'd been war cripples . . . especially with the *Médaille Militaire!* French sensibility is stirred by anything that's against France . . . the heart of France goes out to its professed enemies! masochistic to the death!

For us there in the attics, cellars, and broom closets, starving, I can assure you there was no operetta . . . our stage was full of men condemned to death . . . 1,142 of us . . . I knew the exact number . . .

I'll have more to say about this picturesque spot! it wasn't just a watering place and a tourist haven . . . tremendously historical! . . . A Shrine! . . . take a bite out of that castle . . . stucco, bric-a-brac, gingerbread in every style, turrets, chimneys, gargoyles . . . unbelievable . . . super-Hollywood . . . every period from the melting of the icecap, the narrowing of the Danube, the slaying of the Dragon, the victory of St. Fidelis down to William II and Goering.

Bichelonne had the biggest head of us all . . . not only a champion of Polytechnique and the École des Mines . . . History! Geotechnics! . . . He was an electronic brain! He had to tell us the which and the why! explain the crotchets of the Castle! every last one! did he know why it leaned south rather than north? . . . why those ramshackle chimneys, those wormeaten battlements and drawbridges leaned more to the west? . . . that goddam cradle of the Hohenzollerns! perched on its rock . . . out of kilter! lopsided all over . . . inside, outside! every room and passageway . . . the whole business! all ready to topple into the water for the last fourteen centuries! . . . go see for yourself . . . cradle and den of the worst pack of rapacious wolves in Europe! some Shrine! and believe me it wobbled under the squadrons, the thousands and thousands of Flying Fortresses bound for Dresden, Munich, Augsburg . . . by day and by night . . . all the little stained-glass windows cracked and fell in the river . . . you'll see!

All the same, this castle of Siegmaringen, this whole fantastic lopsided chunk of trompe-l'oeil managed to hold out for thirteen . . . fourteen centuries . . . Bichelonne didn't hold out at all . . . graduate of Polytechnique, minister, amazing mind . . . he died at Hohenlychen in East Prussia . . . pure coquetry . . . lunacy . . . went up there to be operated, have a fracture fixed . . He had visions of himself going back to Paris on the double beside Laval, triumphant . . . Arch of Triumph, Champs-Elysées, the Unknown Soldier . . . he was obsessed by his leg . . . it doesn't bother him anymore . . . the way they operated on him up there at Hohenlychen, I'll tell you about it . . . the witnesses have gone out of existence . . . so has the surgeon . . . Gebhardt, war criminal, hanged! . . . not for the way he operated on Bichelonne! . . . for all sorts of genocides, little intimate Hiroshimas . . . oh, not that Hiroshima makes me flip! . . . look at Truman, how happy he is, pleased with himself, playing the harpsichord . . . the idol of millions of voters! . . . the widower of millions of widows' dreams! . . . Cosmic Landru! . . . playing Amadeus' harpsichord . . . just wait a while . . . kill a lot of people and wait . . . that does it . . . not just Denoël! . . . Marion . . . Bichelonne . . . Beria . . . tomorrow B. . . . K. . . . H! The line forms to the right . . . shaking, stamping . . . yelling to get in . . . to be hanged quicker and shorter . . . roasted to a crisp . . . the whole National Assembly, the six hundred . . . listen to them, the state they're in, their impatience to be fed to the lions!

We 1,142 had other things to do beside looking at the landscape . . . we had to find our daily bread . . . myself, I've got to admit, I can get along on very little, but there, same as later

in the north, we were really starving, not temporarily for the
diet, no, this was serious . . .

All pretty miscellaneous! I read it over . . . How can I expect you to understand all this . . . not to lose the thread
. . . my humblest apologies! . . . If my voice wavers, if I
jibber-jabber, I'm no worse than most guides . . . you'll forgive me when you know the whole story . . . definitely! . . .
so bear with me . . . I'm lying here . . . making my bed
quake . . . all for you . . . getting my memories together
. . . I need the fever to boil me up . . . to put the details in
place . . . and the dates . . . I don't want to mislead
you . . .

In that teetering lopsided barn . . . twenty manor houses
one on top of the other . . . there was a library . . . that was
really something . . . a treasure . . . amazing . . . we'll
come back to that, I'll tell you . . .

For a while the 1,142 . . . Leclerc's army is coming closer
. . . closer . . . were shaken with worry . . . with a desire
to know more . . . more and more especially the intellectuals . . . and we had our quota of intellectuals in Siegmaringen . . . real cerebral types, serious . . . like Gaxotte
could almost have been . . . none of your sad sacks from the
café terraces, ambitious alcoholics, mental defectives with an
idea now and then, squinting from charm to charm, from urinal
to urinal, Slavs, Hungarians, Yankees, Mings, from commitment to commitment, from one Mauriaco-Tarterie to the next,
from cross to sickle, from pernod to pernod, from coat to coat,
from envelope to envelope . . . no, nothing in common! . . .
all really serious intellectuals! . . . not the gratuitous, verbal
kind . . . but ready to pay and paying . . . with Article 75 on
their ass! . . . real lamppost fodder . . . flawless intellectuals
. . . dying of hunger, cold, and scabies . . . Well, they were
anxious to know if ever, down through the ages . . . there
had ever been a clique, a caste, a gang as hated, as cursed as us,
as furiously expected and searched for by hordes of cops (ah,
lily-livered Hungarians!) to stick banderillas in us, fry us, or
impale us . . .

It took a lot of research . . . and I can assure you that our intellectuals investigated . . . all the lousy stinking bastards that had been tortured in one place or another . . . Spartacists . . . Girondins . . . Templars . . . Communes . . . We examined all the Chronicles, Codes, Libels . . . we weighed and sifted . . . we compared . . . were we . . . could we be . . . as stinking . . . as fit to throw on the dump, to spit on pitchforks, as Napoleon's friends? . . . after they'd shipped him to St. Helena . . . were we? . . . Especially his Spanish friends . . . the hidalgo collaborationists! . . . the *Josefins!* Good name to remember! . . . that's what we were . . . *Adolfins!* . . . the *Josefins* got theirs all right . . . all the Javerts* of the day on their ass! Practically the same hue and cry . . . as us, the 1,142 . . . with Leclerc's army in Strasbourg . . . and its chop-chop Senegalese! . . . (and the Hungarians complaining about the Tartars . . . Christ!)

Which shows you that that imperial library was rich, rich in everything . . . amazing what you could find there . . . fertilize your mind in every field . . . manuscripts, memoirs, incunabula . . . you should have seen our intellectuals climbing up ladders, Ph.D.'s, Academicians, graduates of the École Normale, all ages, expelled Immortals, rummaging through all that . . . ardent! feverish! . . . Latin, Greek, French . . . that was culture . . . and scratching their itch at the same time . . . on top of every ladder . . . and each one wanting to be right . . . each standing by his manuscript . . . his chronicle . . . that we were more hated or less than Joseph's collaborators . . . that the price on our heads was higher . . . or lower? . . . in francs . . . or in the escudos of the period . . . a Dean of the Faculty of Law inclined to "more" . . . an Immortal to "less" . . . We voted: fifty-fifty! The future is in the hands of God! Hell! The Immortal was way off! The events have proved that . . . the calvary of the *Adolfins* was infinitely more ferocious than all the other vengeances end to end! as sensational as the H-bomb! . . . a hundred thousand times more powerful than our piddling shells of '14! Super-hunt! sensational kill! and forever . . . none of us will ever see the end of it! . . . Saint Louis, the bum . . . it's for him we're expiating . . . the brute! the torturer! . . . and they made him a saint . . .

who baptized a round million Israelis by force . . . in the beloved south of our beloved France—that guy was worse than
Adolf! . . . which shows you what you can learn on the top
of a ladder . . . ah, Saint Louis! . . . canonized in 1297 . . .
We'll come back to him!

As long as we're here as tourists, I might as well tell you something about the treasures, the tapestries, the woodwork, the plate, the armories—trophies, armor, banners . . . every floor was a museum . . . not to mention the bunkers under the Danube, the fortified tunnels . . . How many holes, hiding places, dungeons had those princes, dukes, and gangsters dug? . . . in the muck, in the sand, in the rock? fourteen centuries of Hohenzollerns! secretive diggers! . . . their whole history was under the Castle, the doubloons, the slain, hanged, strangled, and mummified rivals . . . the top, the visible part, all phony, trompe-l'oeil, turrets, belfries, bells . . . for the birds! a mirror for skylarks! . . . the real thing was underneath: the family fortune . . . the skeletons of the kidnapped, the caravans of the Danube gorges, the treasures of Florentine merchants, adventurers from Switzerland, Germany . . . that's where their adventures had landed them, in the dungeons under the Danube . . . fourteen centuries of dungeons . . . oh, they were far from useless . . . a hundred times! . . . a hundred air-raid alarms! they saved our lives . . . you should have seen the swarming and scurrying! the crowd under the Danube in those pluricentenary weasel holes . . . families, babies, papas, dogs . . . Kraut soldiers and guards of honor, ministers, admirals, *Landsturm* men, and the wrecks of the *Fidelis* and the P.P.F.* and the screwballs from all over . . . and Darnand's men, groping their way from catacomb to catacomb . . . looking for a tunnel that wouldn't cave in . . .

So familiar with the Castle? . . . you must think I was in good with the Court . . . oh, not at all . . . I wasn't a guest . . . don't get me wrong . . . I didn't have sixteen food cards . . . or eight . . . just one . . . That's what situates a man:

the Card . . . I was admitted to the Castle, yes . . . but not to eat . . . to keep tabs . . . how many cases of flu? how many pregnant women? new cases of scabies? . . . and how much morphine had I left? . . . how much camphorated oil . . . ether? . . . and the state of my infants . . . on that point Brinon had to listen to me . . . I went to town . . . the way they were dying on us! . . . six a week! . . . they were killing off our babies on purpose . . . absolutely . . . with raw carrot soup . . . I mean it . . . all children of collaborators . . . infanticide . . . absolutely intentional . . . the real hatred of the Germans, I might say in passing, was directed against the "collaborators" . . . not so much against the Jews, who were so powerful in London and New York . . . or against the Fifis, who were supposed to be "the Vrance of tomorrow" . . . pure and sure . . . but against the *"collabos,"* the dregs of the universe, who were there at their mercy, really weak and helpless, and their kids who were even weaker . . . let me tell you: the Nuremberg trials need doing over! . . . they did plenty of talking, but all lies, nothing to do with the case, beside the point . . . Tartuffes! . . .

This children's camp in Cissen was a morgue operated on raw carrot soup, a Grand Guignol nursery run by phony doctors, Tartar charlatans, sadistic maniacs . . .

Naturally Brinon knew all that, I wasn't telling him anything new . . . but there was nothing he could do about it.

"I'm sorry, doctor, I'm sorry."

Brinon, "animal of darkness, secretive, very taciturn and very dangerous . . ."

"Watch your step, doctor . . . Watch your step."

Bonnard warned me . . . Abel Bonnard* knew him well . . . I have to admit that with me, in our work together, Brinon was always correct, regular . . . and he could perfectly well have reported some of the wisecracks that were attributed to me . . . in public and in private . . . that Germany was through . . . Adolf on the skids . . . it would have been easy for Brinon to have me sent someplace . . . "animal of darkness" . . . or not . . . he didn't . . . the Parties were suspicious of me, too . . . Bucard, Sabiani,* etc. . . . the *Mil-*

ice* . . . because I wasn't a member of anything . . . that I
ought to be in a camp . . . far away . . .

Public opinion is always right, especially when it's really idiotic . . .

Oh, of course I had reason to distrust Brinon, that "animal of
darkness" . . .

After we had exchanged our reports, complaints, and counter-
complaints, I went to see the patients . . . in the Castle . . .
from floor to floor, three or four every morning . . . I knew
the place well . . . the corridors and the hangings, the real
doors and false doors . . . the corkscrew stairways, cutting
across wainscoating and beams . . . enough dark corners to
be knifed in a thousand times over . . . and be left there to
dry for centuries . . . the Hohenzollerns didn't deprive themselves . . . experts in traps and tipping corridors . . . and
down into the void! . . . plunging into the Danube! . . . the
Dynasty . . . mother of Europe. . . more than a thousand
murders a day! . . . what did you think? . . . for eleven centuries! . . . Bluebeard's a piker with his six floozies in a closet!
What could he ever expect to found? . . . And what did that
make me look like, griping about their killing off my children with carrots . . . Brignon certainly agreed with me . . .
but a lord vassal like him . . . he found it healthier to keep
quiet . . . "Graf von Brinon" . . . said the sign on his
door . . .

A funny thing was the orderlies, all of the regular French
army, élite regiments . . . decorated . . . they must have had
orderlies like that in London . . . the same? . . .

Laval's floor . . . I attended Laval now and then . . . I
never came near Pétain . . . Brinon had suggested me, Ménétrel had just been arrested . . . "I'd rather die right away!"
. . . that was the impression I made on Pétain, same as the
people around here in Lower Meudon . . . or in Sèvres . . .
or Boulogne . . . or my mother-in-law . . . hell, I don't
mind . . . you get used to having nobody like you . . . good
riddance! good riddance! actually it's ideal . . . but how are

you going to eat? . . . total isolation is all very well if you can afford it . . . to be disliked and grow old on your income! . . . that's true happiness! . . . to never never be pestered! . . . a dream! Easy for rich people, Achille for instance . . . yes, Achille . . . but he's not so dumb . . .

So I knew that Castle very well, every nook and cranny, but nothing like Lili . . . she was really at home . . . all the hiding places and labyrinths! the trick tapestries with exits through goddesses; the apartments, boudoirs, cupboards with triple bottoms, corkscrew stairways . . . all the false exits, all the zigzags and interlocked landings . . . riddles . . . should you go up? or down? . . . really a castle to get lost in . . . the lost corners . . . the work of centuries of Hohenzollerns. . . in every known style . . . Barbarossa, Renaissance, Baroque, 1900 . . . From one door to the next I could get lost . . . I was fascinated by the portraits . . . the mugs on that lousy family . . . prolific! . . . corridors and statues . . . equestrian and recumbent . . . every which way . . . Uglier and uglier Hohenzollerns . . . with arbalasts . . . in helmets, breastplates . . . court dress . . . Louis XV-style . . . and their bishops! . . . and their executioners! with axes this big! . . . in the darkest corridors . . . The painters didn't knock themselves out in those days, they put all the same profiles on them . . .

Me complaining to Brinon that the doctors were liquidating our kids! a look at the profiles of those princes was all I needed . . . those boys must have been rough liquidators: hunchbacks, beer bellies, soldiers, bowlegs . . . and not just children . . . What were we doing in Siegmaringen anyway? . . . kids or no kids! . . . running away from our destiny, which was to have our bowels stewed, our cocks cut in little pieces, our skins turned inside out . . . And where had it got us? I did quite a lot of meditating in the Hohenzollern corridors . . . from one portrait to the next . . . I can say that those princes attracted me . . . especially the ones from the distant past . . . heads three, four times bigger than Dullin's,* faces without shame, horribly ferocious . . . one look at them and you knew: those were creators of Dynasties! . . . Bonaparte seems

more like a young lady—fine features, delicate hands à
la Fragonard . . . but these Hohenzollerns, especially the
early ones, when you see them you say: "What a bunch of Landrus!" . . . Another . . . even worse . . . Tropman!* . . .
The spit and image of Deibler!* . . . a whole string . . .
more and more treacherous . . . more and more cruel . . .
grasping . . . monstrous! . . . hundreds of thoroughbred
Landrus! . . . three . . . four stories of Landrus! Landru
cousins . . . And down below . . . maces . . . scythes . . .
spurs . . . slings . . . more and more sadistic! . . . Landru
dauphins! not the timid Landru of Gambais! . . . puny, fur-
tive, with a ramshackle stove picked up at the auction rooms
. . . no! . . . these Landrus were sure of themselves! . . .
the genuine article . . . *nom de Gott* . . . lances, breastplates,
the whole works! coats-of-arms *mit uns* . . . whole floors of
portraits! . . . the boot of *Gott* . . . no little rippers-up of
fiancées . . . oh no! . . . all imperial torture masters! . . .
the whole line! . . . fryers of duchies! . . . towns, fortresses,
cloisters . . . roast 'em on the spit! like it or not! kettles! . . .
kettles! . . .

Those mugs . . . whole processions of them . . . fascinat-
ing . . . between patients, between doors, I went to see them
. . . especially the ones of the twelfth, thirteenth century
. . . wait till you see them! all monsters! really? . . . that's
easily said . . . but when you take a good look at them and
think it over . . . more like devils . . . cloven hoofed! . . .
with lances! . . . horns! . . . founders of dynasties! that family resemblance! demons! . . . it was when they stopped being
devils that their family collapsed! . . . same with all Empires
. . . I can see the Russkis slipping . . . B and K and M . . .
look Luciferian enough . . . but they're not so sure of themselves . . . they put on airs, they wag their tanks, they dialec-
talize . . . they'll see . . . Lenin! . . . Stalin! . . . that was
the real article! Satans a thousand-percent! . . . that's what
the faces were like in the Hohenzollern galleries! five stories of
them! plus the turrets! . . . founders with no nonsense about
them! dynasties that last!

I'm a bit of an alchemist . . . you've probably noticed . . .

but serious! . . . I'm not telling you any fairy tales . . . I weigh the pros and cons . . . I've shown you *La Publique,* now we're touring in the thick of History . . . diversity is my law! . . . Siegmaringen Hohenzollern! . . . you've got a good laugh coming to you . . . and the fascination of those portraits, busts, statues . . .

From one turn to the next, I got lost . . . I'm telling you, I admit it . . . Lili or Bébert found me . . . women have an instinct for labyrinths, for ins and outs . . . they find their way . . . animal instinct . . . it's order that stymies them! . . . the absurd is their dish . . . to them the whacky is normal . . . Fashion! . . . for cats: attics, mazes, old barns . . . they're drawn irresistibly by Gothic manses . . . that we'd better stay out of . . . they're funny that way . . . that's embryogeny, the pirouettes and somersaults of the gametes . . . the perversity of the atoms . . . animals are the same way . . . take Bébert! . . . he'd peekaboo me through the transoms . . . *brrt!* . . . *brrt!* . . . big joke! . . . I couldn't see him. . . teasing me . . . cats, children, ladies have a world of their own . . . Lili went where she pleased all over the castle of the Hohenzollerns . . . from one maze of corridors to the next . . . from the bell-tower way up in the air to the armory on a level with the river . . . by sheer instinct! . . . reason'll only mix you up . . . wood or stone spirals, ladders . . . bends . . . up or down? . . . hangings, tapestries, false exits . . . all traps . . . even with a map you're lost . . . assassins in every corner . . . troubadours, bats, vagrant sprites . . . there's nothing you won't run into, I'm telling you, from one false exit, one false drapery to the next . . . on my way from Brinon's, or Marion's . . . or Y's . . . or Z's . . . I'm only giving you the names of dead people . . . I'll leave the survivors alone . . . the dead will do! . . . the ones who died in Spain . . . and the ones who ended up somewhere else . . . leave the gossip to the new Tacitus . . . I hear he's already been born . . . good! about the Castle he'll have to consult me . . . by that time it'll have toppled! . . . that worm-eaten wreck . . . equilibrium isn't eternal . . . fallen into the Danube . . . the *Schloss* and its library! laby-

rinths! . . . woodwork! porcelain and dungeons! . . . into the
drink! with its memories! . . . and all its thousands of princes
and kings! down into the delta! . . . ah, crashing, impetuous
Danube! the river will carry it all away! . . . ah *Donau blau!*
. . . my ass! . . . crashing fury, carrying off the Castle and
its bells . . . and all its demons! . . . Don't be bashful! Do
your stuff! and the trophies and the armor and the banners, and
the trumpets loud enough to shake the whole Black Forest, so
vibrant that the pine trees can't take it! . . . they totter and
fall . . . in avalanches . . . and that's the end of enchanted
castle, ghosts, triple cellars and potteries! Apothecaries and
pots! . . . porphyry Apollos! . . . ebony Venuses! all carried
away by the torrent! and the Huntress Dianas! whole floors of
Huntress Dianas! . . . Apollos! . . . Neptunes! . . the loot of
demons in breastplates, ten centuries of pillage! 'the work of
seven dynasties! you'll see when you get there, the warehouse
of superloot . . . I won't try to outdo Tacitus, but you can imagine that ten centuries of demon gangsters is something! . . .
and kings to boot! and that the Rome-Prussia traffic was nothing to sneeze at, those caravans of fat merchants! . . . ah,
Dianas! . . . Venuses! . . . Apollos! . . . antiques! . . . Cu-
pids! . . . traveling merchants! You can imagine whether the
princes helped themselves! . . . the Hohenzollerns! . . . the
gangsters of the Danube! . . . whether they furnished their
barn! . . . with really very nice things! . . . I'm a good judge
. . . I saw Pétain's apartment . . . his seven drawing rooms
on the seventh floor . . . and Gabold's* on the fourth . . . all
Dresden . . . floors of rosewood marquetry . . . marvelous
workmanship . . . you couldn't duplicate it for billions today
. . . the skills are gone . . . or those little tea services! . . .
oh no! . . . or Laval's place on the third floor . . . First Empire . . . bees, eagles . . . perfection . . . the velvets . . .
authentic Lyons . . . they don't make them anymore . . .

That's the way dynasties furnish their houses . . . pell-mell
. . . the draperies, the ornaments . . . fantastic monstrous
barn, a little overgrown, I've got to admit, three times the size
of Notre-Dame! . . . and the whole thing balanced on a rock
. . . and leaning! . . . anybody who goes to see it will tell

you . . . innocent tourists, they won't glom anything, too flabbergasted, knocked cold! . . . from what? . . . from seeing!
. . . the chests, the thousands of thingumajigs, the souvenirs,
the bric-à-brac . . .

I'm telling you all this ass backwards . . . according to the
tremors of my bed . . . I don't know what's shaking me like
this . . . my fever? . . . the spring collapsing? . . . I'm not
trembling quite so much . . . I think . . . That business
down on the riverfront didn't do me any good at all . . . *La
Publique* . . . and that crummy crowd of tightrope walkers
. . . and their insults! . . . and my malaria coming back . . .
and the wind of the Seine! . . . everything's twisting and
turning . . . that's how it is . . . I'm not up to it any more
. . . He's obscene, you'll say . . .

"Do you feel better? How do you feel?"

"Oh, you know . . . not so bad . . ."

I thought of this and that . . . I'm boring you again . . .
Yes, I thought of the way she was at home in that castle . . .
never lost . . . the way she'd find me in some corridor . . .
fascinated, looking at one more Hohenzollern . . . Hjalmar
. . . Kurt . . . Hans . . . another . . . a hunchback . . .
yes . . . yes . . I didn't tell you . . . they were all hunchbacked! Burchard . . . Wenceslas . . . Conrad . . . they're
driving me nuts . . . twelfth . . . thirteenth . . . fifteenth of
the name! Centuries . . . centuries! . . . centuries! . . .
hunchbacked and no legs! . . . cloven goat's hoofs . . . all
of them . . . Landru Devils! . . . ah, I see them! I see them
all! their warts too! . . . that family wart! . . . on the ends of
their noses : . . .

The head is a kind of factory that doesn't run exactly the way you'd like . . . imagine . . . two thousand billion neurons . . . all a complete mystery . . . where does that get you? . . . neurons left to their own resources! the slightest attack, your head goes haywire, you can't pin down a single idea . . . you're ashamed of yourself . . . Here on my ass like this, I'd like to tell you some more . . . about pictures, coats-of-arms, secret passageways, draperies . . . but I'm lost . . . I can't find anything . . . my head's turning . . . yes, but wait. . . I'll get back to you . . . and my Castle . . and my head! . . . later . . . later . . . I remember a word! . . . animal instinct, I said . . . Bébert . . . I've got the thread back . . . Bébert was at home in that Castle from the top of the turrets to the cellars . . . he and Lili would meet in one corridor or another . . . they didn't talk to each other . . . they behaved as if they'd never seen each other before . . . each for himself . . . the animal waves are like that, a quarter of a millimeter off and you're not yourself . . . you don't exist . . . a different world! . . . same mystery with Bessy, my dog, later in the woods in Denmark . . . she'd run away . . . I'd call her . . . blue in the face . . . she didn't hear me . . . off on a binge . . . she'd pass, she'd brush against us . . . ten times! . . . twenty times! . . . like an arrow! . . . and away she'd go around the trees so fast you couldn't see her legs! bat out of hell! . . . I could call her! I'd gone out of existence . . . Yet I loved that dog . . . and I think she loved me too . . . but her animal life came first . . . for two, three hours . . . I didn't count . . . this was one of her escapades . . . wild in the animal world . . . woods, meadows, rabbits, deer, ducks . . . she came back with bleeding paws, affectionate . . . she

138

died here in Meudon, she's buried over there, right next to the house, in the garden, I can see the mound . . . a painful death . . . cancer, I think . . . she wanted to die there outside . . . I held her head . . . I held her in my arms up to the end . . . really a splendid animal . . . a joy to look at her . . . a vibrant joy . . . she was so beautiful! . . . not a flaw . . . coat, build, stance . . . nothing like it in the dog shows! . . .

It's a fact, I still think of her, even now in this fever . . . in the first place I can't tear myself away from anything, a memory, a person, so how would I tear myself away from a dog? . . . I'm a virtuoso of fidelity . . . fidelity and responsibility . . . responsible for everything . . . a disease . . . anti-ungrateful . . . the world is good to you! . . . animals are innocent, even when they run wild like Bessy . . . in a pack they shoot them . . .

I really loved her with her crazy escapades, I wouldn't have parted with her for all the gold in the world . . . any more than with Bébert, though he was the meanest ripper of them all . . . a tiger! . . . but very affectionate at times . . . and terribly attached! from end to end of Germany . . . animal fidelity . . .

In Meudon, I could see, Bessy missed Denmark . . . nothing to hunt in Meudon . . . no deer . . . maybe a rabbit? . . . maybe . . . I took her to the Bois de Saint-Cloud . . . for a bit of a run . . . she sniffed . . . zigzagged . . . and came back in no time . . . two minutes . . . nothing to track in the Bois de Saint-Cloud . . . she walked along with us . . . but she was sad . . . she was a robust animal . . . she'd had a bad time of it up there . . . the cold . . . ten below . . . and no kennel . . . and not just for days! . . . for months . . . years . . . the Baltic frozen over . . .

All of a sudden up there with us . . . never mind, we forgave her everything . . . she'd take a powder . . . she'd come back . . . never a word of reproach . . . she ate out of our plates, so to speak . . . the worse the world treated us, the more we spoiled her . . . she's dead . . . but she had a bad time dying . . . I didn't want to give her an injection . . . not even a little morphine . . . the syringe would have frightened

her . . . I'd never frightened her . . . she was very low for a
good two weeks . . . oh, she didn't complain, but I could tell
. . . strength all gone . . . she slept beside my bed . . . one
morning she wanted to go out . . . I wanted to lay her down
in the straw . . . right after daybreak . . . she didn't like the
place I put her . . . she wanted a different place . . . on the
cold side of the house, on the pebbles . . . she lay down very
prettily . . . she began to rattle . . . that was the end . . .
they'd told me, I didn't believe it . . . but it was true . . .
she was pointed in the direction of her memory . . . the place
she had come from, the North, Denmark, her muzzle turned
toward the north. . . a faithful dog in a way, faithful to the
woods of her escapades, Korsör up there . . . faithful too to
the awful life . . . she didn't care for the woods of Meudon
. . . she died with two, three little rattles . . . oh, very discreet . . . practically no complaining . . . and in a beautiful
position, as though in mid-leap . . . but on her side, felled,
finished . . . her nose toward the forests of the chase, up there
where she came from, where she'd suffered . . . God
knows! . . .

Oh, I've seen plenty of death agonies . . . here . . . there
. . . everywhere . . . but none by far so beautiful, so discreet . . . so faithful . . . the trouble with men's death agonies is the song and dance . . . a man is always on the stage
. . . even the simplest of them . . .

I don't have to tell you that I absolutely wanted to get better
. . . to get up . . . for this to be only a slight attack . . .
hell! . . . a week! . . . a whole month! . . . and what a
summer, what weather! . . . it seems that never in the last
hundred years . . . it almost snowed! . . . fever doesn't prevent you from working as long as you're careful not to catch
cold again . . . consequently no riverfront! . . . and what
about Madame Niçois? . . . she could wait a week . . . ten
days . . . if I couldn't make it, Tailhefer would go . . . he
could go in his car . . . I'd give him a ring . . . he wouldn't
refuse me . . . I thought of everything, as best I could! . . .
Tailhefer was a Prince of Science . . . he wouldn't have any
trouble finding the former Quai Faidherbe . . . he couldn't
say no . . . he'd get a look at *La Publique* . . . we'd known
each other a long time, Tailhefer and me . . . he'd gone up
. . . a Master . . . as far as I'd gone down . . . to give you
an idea! . . . My only hope of paying the coal bill was my
books . . . that didn't sell! . . . shit creek! . . . the hope that
this one would sell? . . . rash! . . . that it might interest certain people . . . don't make me laugh! I often take my temperature . . . silly distraction! a briefcase to lean on . . . that's it
. . . and I scribble . . . I get ahead . . . rich people have
doubts . . . they can afford it . . . but poor bastards . . . no
youth . . . no health . . . barge right ahead . . . I'm boy-
cotted? . . . what of it? . . . "He hasn't committed suicide
yet? . . ." That's what amazes them . . . "Out of date, decrepit!" . . . Well, here's what I think of them . . . rotten,
stinking corpses! rejects from the wax works! . . . scrapings of
the dump! . . . each man to his idea! . . . need rewriting
. . . to the core! to the bone! to the atom! . . . worse, worse

than 1900! . . . ragouts of vanity! phrases, false bosoms! . . .
Madame Emery on the rue Royale . . . Paris . . . and
Trouville in the summer . . . could make you dresses a damn
sight better than their novels . . . the painstaking care! the
flounces and embroidery! . . . really fine workmanship! . . .
I don't see it anymore . . . everybody's entitled to his own
idea . . . I, who have seen Empires ground to hash, if I live
long enough (coal and carrots), I'll witness the hash of our "up-
to-date" writers . . . thickheaded yokels . . . fakers . . .
that's it! . . . coal! . . . carrots . . . tailor-made, that's the
main thing . . . and hand-sewn . . . a little appliqué of
memories! one here . . . one there . . . a historical incident
. . . hand-sewn . . . another . . . I owe you a "revolt of the
hungry . . ." Oh, a harmless little revolt . . . it may amuse
you . . .

I won't get up . . . I don't feel like getting up . . . Tailhefer will go . . . I'll give him a ring . . .

Revolt . . . not in Lower Meudon! No, in Siegmaringen
. . . I'm wandering, taking you for a ride . . . never mind!
. . . I'm collecting my historical memories . . . I don't want
to go wrong . . . here we are . . . Siegmaringen . . . the
morale . . . not so good . . . despite the appeals to the "com-
bative spirit" of "United Europe" . . . flabby! . . . as flabby
as right now despite the appeals of Dulles, Coty, Lazare, Youssef, the Pope . . . soft, soft, the morale was soft . . . the "certainty of victory" . . . just around the corner, and so on . . .
didn't cheer anybody up! . . . They didn't say anything, but
they thought what they thought . . . though God knows they
had a stake in victory . . . this elite of collaborators, 1,142 of
them all condemned to death, with Article 75 on their ass . . .
they began, the nerve of them! . . . to complain that the
food was no good, that the "*Stamgericht*" and even the "*Haus-
gericht*" was absolutely for the birds . . . starvation! That's
what they grumbled and pretty soon they were shouting . . .
and that the guests at the Castle, the pontiffs, ministers and so
on, "active" and "on ice," and their wives and mistresses, bodyguards, nursemaids and babies, were doing fine . . . and the
generals, admirals, and ambassadors from God knows where

. . . that all those people were superstuffed, fat and full of blood, with eight, sixteen food cards each . . . and it was time for them to cough up!

Naturally all this was passed on: the mentality of those people . . . born cops . . . a stool-pigeon or two in every garret . . . the Castle had its ears open! . . . you'll understand the whole Middle Ages if you've lived a while in Siegmaringen . . . the envy, the hatred of the villeins all around you, dying of rot and starvation, cold and fever . . . and the lords of the Castle had their special ways of keeping the rabble down . . . first the rumors! . . . spreading glad news . . . the rumor they circulated was that they were going to eat with the villeins . . . in person . . . without ceremony . . . by the drawbridge . . . with the 1,142 . . . the muttering rabble . . . the mob from the attics . . . first, bread would be distributed! . . . plenty of bread . . . to all the refugees . . . Thursday at twelve noon . . . on the dot of twelve! . . . we only had to be present! all of us!

You can imagine that rumors like that don't fall on deaf ears . . . that there was some crowd at the drawbridge . . . a mob . . . on the day set . . . they came at daybreak . . . you think the stomach hasn't got ears? . . . the *collabos* were all there by the drawbridge . . . all except the sick and dying of the *Fidelis,* who really couldn't get up, and the ones who had escaped into the Black Forest . . . Anyway, it's safe to say, out of the 1,142 at least 1000 were there, waiting to get something . . . and the talk, the discussions! . . . the reflections of the gastric juices! . . . black bread? . . . whole-meal bread? . . . rolls? . . . and all remarkably well informed . . . or lousy stool-pigeons? . . . Morale up-lifters? . . . who knew exactly what there was going to be! . . . for the children: croissants! brioches! . . . oh, not a doubt! . . . but I, knowing what it was like in Cissen, I said to myself: this is going to be a raid, a roundup of the hungry . . . this assembly is a hoax! . . .

While waiting for the brioches they exchanged fleas, lice, crabs, and itches . . . convulsive . . . you never saw anything like it . . . a little crowd of epileptics . . . that's what

hunger does! hunger worse than anything else . . . Were they
going to put it away! my, oh, my! . . . shifting from foot to
foot . . . scratching, plowing furrows in their scabs . . . all in
a kind of semicircle around the drawbridge . . . rolling their
eyes . . . fascinated . . . watching for the feed that was
going to come out . . . not just bread . . . ham, too . . .
sandwiches . . . with lard . . . but I'm not romantic about
food . . . I was quietly on the watch, looking out toward a
hole in the catacombs to the right of the bridge . . . a rockpile
. . . a kind of crater . . . I was expecting a kidney punch
. . . a raid of shuppos . . . something . . . a commando
from the cellars . . . a frameup . . . S.S.? S.A.? . . . *Sicher-
heit?* I could see that the Krauts were fed up . . . seeing us
there shifting from foot to foot, from doormat to doormat,
scratching, coughing, evil-minded, waiting for what?. . . the
child Jesus? . . . a revolution in Valhalla? . . . the Knights of
Siegfried and the Grail? . . . with rolls thrown in? and the
idea of our wanting more to eat! Not satisfied with our turnip
"Stams". . . our delicious margarine soups! . . . They had
reason to be fed up . . . especially as their affairs weren't
prospering . . . disaster in sight . . . their armies all in a
heap . . . we with our skeptical ways . . . and our spying
. . . we were fouling up their morale! . . . they'd already
lost their sky . . . you had only to look . . . behind every
cloud twenty . . . thirty planes . . . R.A.F. . . . a merry-go-
round . . . and the Americans! . . . three, four squadrons of
Fortresses . . . permanent . . . day and night . . . London
. . . Munich . . . Vienna . . . not a Kraut in the sky against
them . . . to give you an idea that we weren't very popular
. . . we and our cynical remarks . . . especially when you
remember that they themselves . . . Kraut to Kraut . . .
were out to get each other . . . Anyway, there around the
drawbridge . . . we kept debating . . . would it be plain K-
bread?* . . . or army loaves? . . . or brioche? . . . the
handout was supposed to be at twelve . . . at one we were
still waiting . . . scratching to pass the time, that's right . . .
I knew . . . this was going to end badly . . . quarter past
one . . . the whole bell-tower explodes . . . all at once . . .

a volley of bells! Magnificent bell-tower . . . you'll hear it if you go there . . . I kept looking at my hole . . . the crater . . . like I was sure that something . . . And sure enough . . . I see somebody coming out . . . looks like two big rats . . . two people, all muffled up! . . . women . . . two women . . . I see them, they're coming closer . . . I'd never seen them before . . . they come up from the bottom of the crater . . . they must live in the catacombs . . . nobody had ever gone down to the bottom of the catacombs . . . they went under the Danube . . . as far as Basel! . . . and on the other side as far as the Brenner . . . so it seems! . . . nobody had ever looked . . . Maybe these women had? . . . Anyway, these two . . . I knew the Castle well and I'd never seen them . . . nor Lili either . . . I ask her . . . one looked pretty young . . . oh, not the other . . . an ancient hag . . . twisted . . . both of them had parasols! . . . oh yes! . . . pink parasols . . . I could see the old bag close up . . . her nose . . . all covered with warts . . . she kept blinking . . . the other too . . . the light! . . . they must have lived in the dark . . . they were used to the darkness . . . but why? . . . and why the parasols? they didn't talk to each other . . . oh, yes . . . now they're talking . . . the old bag asks what's going on . . . they're talking Boche . . . that old woman is a rough customer!

"What's that? What's that?"

"*Franzosen!*"

"What do they want?"

"*Brot!*"

"Then go ahead. Go ahead!"

She sees me there looking, too . . . me and Lili and Bébert the cat! the younger one comes over and speaks to me in French: "I beg your pardon, Monsieur, are you waiting for bread too?" "Yes, I have the honor! it won't be long now . . . haven't you heard the bells? . . ." "Oui, oui, Monsieur! . . ." Our beggars were howling now . . . and kicking the drawbridge . . . sick of waiting . . . "Bastards! profiteers! traitors! There's bread in there! . . ." *Bzing. Boom!* "Hang Laval! stinker! bread! . . . shit! . . . Brinon! . . . cocksucker!

bread! . . ." The anger was rising . . . There were at least three hundred of them howling for bread! . . . climbing, crossing the moat . . . *Bzing zoom* against the drawbridge! . . . you can imagine, that drawbridge was massive, there could have been three thousand of them . . . quite a chunk of furniture . . . a whole army could have passed over it, artillery and all! the itching villains could bat their brains out! the more they hammered the less it moved! in my opinion this whole bread routine was a sweet little trap laid by Raumnitz to nab the malcontents . . . load all those troublemakers in a box car bound for some camp . . . "this way, my petulant friends!" The Krauts are slippery, slimy . . . you can expect anything! take the music halls, all the prestidigitators are Boche! . . . that proves it . . . and Göbbels is the champion! . . . you can't trust them around the corner! . . . "Little soldier boy! Gare de l'Est! . . . nothing to fear! pile right in!" . . . two million dead!

I could see it was a trap . . . a provocation . . . I kept my eye on that crevasse . . . at the bottom of the rockpile . . . where the two women had come from . . . sneaky-looking . . . and why the two pink parasols? . . . and those green and gray peplums covered with spiderwebs? . . . what cellar had they come out of? . . . search me . . . Better ask the one who speaks French . . . "You live there? . . . in the basement? Madame?" She had spoken to me, there was no impertinence in asking her where she'd come from . . .

"Yes, Monsieur . . . yes . . . and you? are you from Paris?"

"But to whom have I the honor, Madame?"

"Companion to the Princess."

The Princess wasn't very outgoing . . . she doesn't like us . . . she looks the other way . . . her nose tells me . . . I try to get a better look . . . three, four warts . . .

"Princess who?" I ask.

"Hermilie of Hohenzollern . . ."

That set me straight . . . she must have been telling the truth . . . the nose was right . . . I'd seen enough Hohenzollern phizzes in the last few months, their portraits in all the corridors of the Castle . . . on all the walls . . . eagle beak with a bud on the end . . . all with one, two . . . three lavender warts! yes, even the very old portraits . . . from the tenth . . . or eleventh century . . . noses like hers, hooked, with lavender warts at the end . . . like this princess . . . Seemed funny we'd never met her in her own Castle . . . believe me, there were lots of people in the Castle . . . every floor . . . fourteen ministers, plus Brinon . . . fifteen generals . . . seven admirals . . . and a Chief of State . . . with their staffs and retinues! . . . but her, we'd never seen her . . . hidden away sulking . . . neither Lili nor myself . . . especially Lili who went all over . . . they must have been living at the bottom of a tunnel . . . and they'd come out just on time for bread . . . for the big banquet . . . when the rebels were out of control . . . *Gzing! boom!*. . . and the curses . . . Hermilie all dignity with her parasol, paying no attention to the riffraff . . . speaking only to her companion . . . say, she wanted her bread bad . . . *nun! nun!* prodding her timid companion! . . . *nun! nun!* she should pound too! and not let these 1,142 howlers take her turn! *bzing! bam!* as if the bread was owing to them! pounding! pounding! the insolent horde! Just then the clarion . . . yes, at that exact moment . . . on the other side of the rampart . . . sounds the general salute . . . the Castle guard . . . not Boche clarions, Boche clarions are like bugles . . . no . . . real ones . . . you'd have thought you were at Lunéville . . . or La Pépinière barracks . . . the drawbridge jolts . . . the chains, the pulleys . . . it moves . . . downward . . . very slowly . . . it drops . . . *Bam!* . . . there it is . . . flat on the ground . . . This was it! We expected a troop of flunkeys loaded with baskets full of loaves, brioches, sausages and petitfours. . . a beautiful handout . . .

Hell, no! . . . it's cops that come out . . . first three or four . . . then at least fifty shuppos in a big wood-burning truck . . . and then another crowd of cops . . . the French police . . . and after them . . . the Marshal! . . . yes, the Marshal! . . . to the left and behind him, Debeney . . . General Debeney, the one who was amputated . . . but no more bread than butter up your ass . . . the Marshal . . . out for an out-

ing . . . that's what the 1,142 zebras had been waiting for!
. . . you might have expected . . . not at all! . . . that
they'd chew him out something terrible . . . that it was a
shame! a disgrace! him and his sixteen food cards . . . not at
all! . . . everybody knew! . . . and knew he ate them all up!
that he didn't leave a crumb for anybody! that his appetite was
remarkable . . . not to mention the total comfort . . . housed
like a king! . . . him who was responsible for everything! Verdun! Vichy! and all the rest! and all our misery! all the fault of
Pétain! Pétain up there, housed like a dream! . . . a whole
floor to himself! . . . heated! . . . with four meals a day! . . .
sixteen cards plus presents from the Führer, coffee, cologne,
silk shirts . . . a regiment of cops at his beck and call . . . a
staff general . . . four cars . . .

You would have expected that crowd of roughnecks to do
something . . . to jump him . . . to disembowel him . . .
not at all . . . just a few sighs . . . they step aside . . . they
watch him start on his outing . . . his cane out ahead . . .
and off we go . . . and dignified . . . he answers their greet-
ings . . . men and women . . . little girls: curtseys . . . the
Marshal's walk . . . but no bread, no sausage . . . Hermilie
of Hohenzollern doesn't greet him though . . . thornier, more
forbidding than ever . . . *Komm! Komm!* . . . to her lady-in-
waiting . . . they disappear . . . they don't even say goodby
. . . into the hole they had come by . . . the slit in the rock-
pile . . . she and her companion . . . no more Hermilie! no
more lady-in-waiting . . . they were gone under the Castle
. . . ah, they hadn't got any bread either! . . . hell! . . .
neither had we . . . damn! . . . Lili and Bébert and I . . .
we'd sort of come for that . . . we hadn't time to be sad . . .
I see Marion! I catch sight of him . . . Marion, the only one
who had any heart . . . who never forgot us . . . who always
came to the *Löwen,* bringing whatever he could . . . not
much . . . a few leftovers . . . mostly rolls . . . there were
rolls in the Castle . . . not very many, but say three four to
each minister . . . sometimes it's not so bad being a minister
. . . Marion always thought of us . . . and Bébert . . . his
big joke was when Bébert played Lucien . . . Lucien Des-

caves* . . . I put my muffler on Bébert . . . with his bristling moustaches he looked just like Lucien Descaves . . . that was our little joke . . . ah, it's far away . . . no more Lucien . . . no more Marion . . . no more Bébert! all gone! . . . with our memories! slowly, slowly . . .

As I was telling you . . . I see Marion . . . He was on the outing, too . . . but far from Pétain . . . they weren't on speaking terms anymore . . . far from it! . . in all regimes at all times, the ministers hate each other. . . and worst when everything is falling apart . . . absolute hostility! . . . a frenzy of rancor . . . they'd got to the point where they couldn't even look at each other . . . it rankled so bad they'd have massacred each other at the table . . . at meals . . . they sharpened their knives during the cheese course so menacingly that all the wives stood up! "Come! Come!" . . . and made their ministers, generals, admirals leave the table . . . they were on the point of drawing their swords! boiling! oh, it's the same all over . . . Berchtadgaden, Vichy, the Kremlin, the White House, no places to be during the cheese course . . . not with the Hanover-Windsors either . . . which explains why on this walk distances were kept . . . Protocol! . . . no question of arm in arm . . . far apart . . . all very far apart . . . way in the lead the Marshal Chief of State, all alone! his one-armed chief of staff Debeney three steps behind to the left . . . further on a minister . . . further still another . . . strung out at least a hundred yards . . . and then the cops . . . the whole procession at least two miles long . . . Say what you like . . . I can speak freely because he detested me . . . Pétain was our last King of France. "Philip the Last! . . ." the stature, the majesty, the works . . . and he believed in it . . . first as victor at Verdun . . . then, at the age of seventy and then some promoted to Sovereign! Who could have resisted? . . . A pushover! "Oh, Monsieur le Maréchal, how you incarnate France!" That incarnation jazz is magic . . . if somebody said to me: "Céline, damn it all, how you incarnate the *Passage!* the *Passage* is you! all you!"—I'd go out of my mind! take any old hick, tell him to his face that he incarnates something . . . you'll see, he'll go crazy . . .

you've pierced his heart! . . . he won't know which way is up . . . Once Pétain incarnated France, he didn't care if it was fish or flesh, gibbet, Paradise or High Court, Douaumont, Hell, or Thorez . . . he was the incarnation! . . . that's the only real genuine happiness: incarnation . . . you could cut his head off . . . he'd go right on incarnating . . . his head would run along all by itself, perfectly happy, seventh heaven! Charlot shooting Brasillach!* he was in seventh heaven too! another incarnator! both in seventh heaven, both incarnations! . . . And Laval?

Even under much more modest circumstances . . . more practical, too . . . this incarnation racket performs little miracles! in the food department, for instance! . . . suppose tomorrow they start rationing us again . . . that you're short in everything . . . don't beat your brains out . . . the incarnation trick will save you . . . you take any old hayseed, any provincial writer, and you go up to him! you grab hold of him, you petrify him right there in front of you . . . And you bellow at him: "Man alive, you're the one and only . . . the living incarnation of Poitou! . . . Those precious thirty-two pages of yours! The whole of Poitou!" That does it! You'll never want for anything after that! packages from the farm! . . . You do it again in Normandy! . . . Deux-Sèvres! and Finistère! You'll have enough for five, six wars and twelve famines! . . . you won't know where to store your ten, twelve tons of packages! Incarnators are tireless givers . . . they keep piling it on . . . you've only got to keep telling them that they've got the whole Drôme in their work! . . . the Jura! . . . Mayenne! . . . Roquefort if you like cheese! . . . I'm not seeing things . . . take Denoël! . . . Denoël the assassinated . . . a slimy two-timer if ever there was one, but very Belgian and practical . . . all in all, now he's a corpse, if I compare him to what came after him, it's really a shame! . . . Two days before he was murdered I wrote him from Copenhagen: "Clear out . . . damn it! . . . make tracks . . . the rue Amélie is no place for you . . ." He didn't split, people never do what I say . . . they think they're guaranteed . . . amulets rubbed with onion . . . okay . . . if that's how they feel about it . . .

anyway, the fact remains, that up to the time he was murdered he had all the butter he wanted, cheese, chicken, truffles . . . a sumptuous table . . . absolutely no trouble with his food supply! . . . he really lived well! . . . thanks to the Incarnationism of his authors . . . the revelation of their Mission . . . the Annunciation . . . but watch out . . . I'm warning you! . . . the thing is magic! . . . it can easily be fatal! . . . don't get intoxicated! . . . Witness Pétain! Witness Laval! Witness Louis XVI! Witness Stalin! . . . you go all out, nothing you can't get away with? . . . Goodby! . . . Playing the magician from province to province, unearthing incarnations of this one and that one . . . he lost his head . . . "Bravo! Charmed life! Nothing can touch me! . . ." But at midnight on the Place des Invalides, the charm broke! a cloud, the moon! the magic was gone . . . What finished Denoël, what put the quietus on his clowning, was his collection of provinces, the folklore addicts, the ecstatic incarnators of countrysides . . . the competing rat-racers: I! I! I! I'm Cornouailles! I'm Léon! . . . I'm Charente! . . . the epileptics of incarnation!

Nothing so unusual about it . . . "Kindly send Jeanne d'Arc!" I'll find you a dozen in every department . . . with packages thrown in . . . bologna . . . butter . . . whole carloads of cereals . . . turkeys . . . shepherd girls! . . .

"You have been entered in the Competition! . . . oh, how excellently you incarnate Cameroon! . . ." the bananas start coming! . . . dates, pineapples! the whole Empire was coming to table . . . to his table! . . . believe you me . . . nothing was lacking . . . poor Denoël had really solved the problem of food supply . . .

Pétain was another . . . the Incarnation, it's me . . . Imperial! . . . Did he believe it? . . . He believed it all right . . . that's what he died of . . . total Incarnation!

All this blarney . . . I'm forgetting you . . . we were talking about the outing . . . well, the beginning . . . the Marshal on the drawbridge . . . Hermilie of Hohenzollern disappearing into the cellars with her lady-in-waiting . . . Pétain and Debeney step lively, they follow the Danube . . . the bank . . . the ritual walk . . . all alone up front . . . the

ministers far behind . . . strung out . . . sulking, it looked like
. . . And the little crowd of grumblers, waiting, their gastric
juices ready for anything . . . nothing left for them but to vacate . . . They protested . . . but not too much . . . and
went back to the stables, the attics, the *Fidelis*, the woods . . .
what could they say? . . . all they could do was scratch . . .
rip off their scabs . . . well, they'd scratch somewhere
else . . .

Up above the clouds the snake dance goes on . . . squadrons on squadrons of R.A.F. . . . some diving in the direction
of the Castle . . . the Castle was their landmark . . . the loop
in the river . . . that's where they turn from north to east
. . . Munich, Vienna . . . squadrons on squadrons . . . We
wouldn't be blown up . . . that was the rumor . . . because
the Castle was being reserved for Leclerc's army . . . he was
already in Strasbourg with his Fifis* and his coons . . . you
could tell by the people coming our way . . . refugees with
their eyes popping out . . . the things they'd seen . . . the
wholesale decapitations . . . with the chop-chop . . . Leclerc's Senegalese . . . rivers of blood . . . the gutters full of
it . . . what we could expect from one minute to the next . . .
something for the scratchers to think about . . . for the 1,142
"wanted" to talk about in their attics!

When you come right down to it, Pétain and Debeney were
through . . . their act was washed up! . . . the "French Empire" act! . . . curtain! . . . the next act would be the Senegalese! . . . Pétain was through incarnating! . . . France was
fed up . . . send him home so we can kill him . . . turn the
page! . . . here he still cuts a figure . . . with Debeney . . .
and his straggling processional . . . and all spiffed out, the
stinkers! . . . those resplendent shoes! . . . stepping lively
. . . along the Danube, that little river so violent, so gay and
splashing, throwing its foam into the treetops . . . optimistic
river . . . great future! . . . yes yes, but Leclerc's army isn't
far off . . . and his chop-chop Senegalese . . . people hardly
ever know that it's time for the next act . . . that they're in the
way, time to come down off the stage . . . oh no! . . . they're
stubborn . . . they've got nice parts and they want to hold on

to them! . . . forever . . . the Marshal and Debeney on their
daily outing . . . banks of the Allier . . . banks of the Danube . . . outing and Chief of State, that's the whole picture
. . . What interested us, Lili and me and Bébert . . . was
Marion* . . . Marion and the scrapings of their tables, the
rolls . . . anyway it was better if Pétain didn't notice . . .
Marion . . . the Minister of Information . . . was almost
last in line . . . that's the protocol . . . first comes the sword!
that's Pétain! . . . and then Justice! . . . and then Finance!
. . . and then the rest . . . the scroungers, the so-called recent ministries . . . no more than three, four centuries old!
. . . to be a real minister, to "carry weight," you've got to go
back to Dagobert . . . Justice! . . . St. Eloi, there was a minister for you . . . Marion with his *Information?* . . . not even
fifty years . . . not presentable . . . but for the three of us,
including Bébert, the only one who counted . . . no two ways
. . . we had to join the outing . . . on the q.t. . . . so he
could slip us his rolls and scrapings while no one was looking
. . . Mattey wasn't very high in the outing order . . . his
place was after Sully . . . two hundred yards after the Navy,
the admirals, François I . . . in a black topcoat, Mattey, the
gravity of an administrator, black felt hat, a hundred yards
ahead of us . . . "I call on you, Monsieur Mattey, to feed the
French nation!" . . . That's how black-clad Mattey had been
recruited . . . "Mattey! fields and pastures!" . . . And he'd
dived right in! . . . Same as Bichelonne in the railroads . . .
"Bichelonne, you will transport all France!" And now . . .
they could only tag along . . . a hundred yards ahead of *Information* and me and Lili and Bébert . . . oh, I forgot . . .
the Danube is very sinuous and choppy . . . then suddenly it
gets wide . . . very wide . . . no more breakers and froth
. . . a broad surface of quiet water . . . right after the railroad bridge . . . there the ducks were waiting for us . . . or
rather they were waiting for Bébert . . a good hundred of
them, sticking right by us . . . paddling hard, swimming right
next to the shore to get a good look at our Bébert . . . ah, and
another animal too! . . . I forgot! . . . the eagle . . . we had
one of those, too . . . he came to the same place, but kept his

distance . . . not like the ducks at all . . . very distant . . .
in the fields on top of a high pole, all alone . . . you couldn't
get close to him . . . oh no! . . . not the Hohenzollern eagle!
. . . he saw us . . . we saw him . . . he didn't fly away!
. . . he moved a little according as we moved, far away . . .
he pivoted on his pole . . . slowly . . . I think he was looking mostly at Bébert . . . Bébert knew it . . . and Bébert,
that independent cat, world's record for disobedience, the way
he stuck to us! . . . he could see himself in the eagle's clutches
. . . What's wonderful in the animal world is the way they
know everything without telling each other . . . and far far
away! at the speed of light! . . . we with our heads full of
words, it's terrifying the way we knock ourselves out fuddling
and muddling . . . till we don't know a damn thing! . . . or
understand! . . . the way we stuff our big noodles! . . . full
up . . . busting . . . no room for more . . . not the slightest
mini-wave . . . everything slips by . . . we don't catch
it . . .

That royal Hohenzollern eagle was master of the fields and
forests all the way to Switzerland . . . he did exactly as he
pleased . . . nobody could intimidate him . . . commander
of the Black Forest . . . flocks and rabbits and deer . . . and
the fairies . . . every outing, he was there . . . same field,
same pole . . . I'm sure he didn't like us . . .

After about a mile and a half up the Danube bank, a silhouette . . . it never failed: a silhouette with gestures . . . meaning to advance . . . or go back . . . that Pétain should keep
going . . . or turn around and go home . . . we knew that
silhouette . . . it was Admiral Corpechot* . . . guarding the
Danube, commander of all the flotillas as far as the Drava . . .
he was expecting a Russian offensive . . . in the middle of
the Marshal's outing! . . . The Russian river fleet would come
sailing up the Danube! . . . he was dead sure . . . he had appointed himself Admiral of the Estuaries of Europe and Commander of Both Banks . . . he expected the Russian fleet from
Vienna . . . cutting across Bavaria to take Württemberg in the
rear . . . and Siegmaringen! . . . naturally! with all the collaborators . . . especially Pétain! . . . he could see Pétain

kidnapped! . . . trussed up in the hold of one of those sub-
mersible devices he'd seen coming out of the water! . . . oh,
he'd seen them all right! amphibian vehicles . . . past Budapest the river was crawling with them! . . . Corpechot told me
all about it . . . I was treating his emphysema . . . he knew
all the Russian plans! their material! their strategy! he even
knew the ins and outs of their aero-aqua-terrestrial device, cat-
apulted by hydrolysis, the Ader* system in reverse, subnautical
. . . give you an idea what we could expect . . . I was never
surprised to see Corpechot popping out by the riverbank, making signs that the outing was over, that the Russians had been
sighted! . . . it was no surprise to Pétain either . . . he about-
faced . . . the ministers, too . . . you can imagine, this Corpechot . . . they'd arrested him ten times . . . twenty times
. . . and released him twenty times . . . no more room in
the asylums . . . actually no more room anywhere for anybody . . . crazy or not! . . . you took what you could find
. . . crazy . . . not crazy . . . attics . . . backrooms! . . . stables . . . bunkers . . . station waiting rooms . . . absolute
frenzy! whole villages under the trains . . . huddled up . . .
in the woods . . . caves . . . if you found one, you stayed
there . . . people from every corner of Europe . . . I told you
Corpechot had made himself an admiral . . . he felt he was
entitled to it, a damn sight more than the admirals of the Castle,
the office admirals of Darlan's general staff! . . . in the first
place Article 75 . . . decorated with Article 75! . . . he hadn't
made that one up . . . warrant and all! absolutely genuine!
really hunted! . . . the circumstances of his departure proved
it . . . skin of his teeth! . . . last train! from the Gare de l'Est
. . . they'd only nabbed his son, his wife and sister-in-law . . .
all sent to Drancy! . . . another minute they'd have had him
. . . It was true! . . . I'd read the report in Brinon's office
. . . and his detailed biography . . . he'd been a gossip col-
umnist and later editor-in-chief of a big yachting weekly, the
Jib-boom! you could speak of him in Bremen, Enghien, or the
Isle of Wight . . . people listened with respect . . . he was in
every regatta . . . "Corpechot says!" . . . that was enough
. . . he was the authority! Naturally he was an easy mark for

Doenitz! . . . "Corpechot, you are the Navy! *über alles!* . . .
you will avenge France and Dunkirk!" Then they embraced
. . . "Trafalgar! Trafalgar . . ." and that's why he was here
with Article 75 on his ass . . . and his whole family in Drancy
. . . but he'd lost his bearings! . . . "Corpechot-you-are-the-
Navy" had had to deliver, earn his stripes . . . first in Ham-
burg . . . then in Kiel . . . then in Warnemünde . . . for
Doenitz . . . *Kriegsmarine!* . . . from camp to camp! . . .
and now with his promotion! . . . "Commander of the Forces
of the Danube!" . . . every body of water in Württemberg-
Switzerland! . . . and consequently the mission of guarding
Pétain, telling him how far he could go . . . not far! no further! . . . about-face! . . .

Oh yes, up in the sky we were doing all right . . . the English were dragging their wings! . . . it was pitiful to watch
those poor planes that didn't even dare to bomb us! intimidated
by the Castle! fucked! . . . but the Russians? . . . their amphibian submarines? Corpechot kept his eyes on the river . . .
the slightest ripple: the treacherous Danube! the Russian
peril! he'd made himself little mounds . . . at every bend . . .
kind of little semaphores . . . crow's nests . . . You could
talk to him up there, tell him about the R.A.F. . . . he'd
double up, laugh himself sick . . . childish, preposterous . . .
bombs? . . . he did the exploding! . . . "Good Lord, man
. . . Good Lord . . . you too! always looking at the sky!
stargazing! . . . grotesque . . . unbelievable! can't you see
that they'll come by the river? Come, come! Take a look! See
for yourself!" And he'd pass you his binoculars . . . his big
Licca . . . no time to joke! . . . "You're right, Admiral! . . ."
nobody contradicted him! . . . the second Pétain caught sight
of him, about-face!

That's the way it is at the end of a régime . . . nobody contradicts anybody . . . the looniest are king . . . one gesture
from Corpechot and Pétain and Debeney obeyed him . . .
Corpechot slept on the ground in the middle of a thicket . . .
any thicket . . . but he kept up appearances . . . absolutely
impeccable . . . admiral's uniform, tall cap . . . and patent-
leather shoes! . . . he'd had himself fitted out like that up

there at the Depot between two bombardments . . . rosy
complexion, big nose, big belly . . . double cape! . . .
"Stormy weather" outfit for seafarers . . . his Licca jiggling
on his belly . . . if you'd run into him on the rue Royale,
you'd have said right away: "No doubt about it . . . the Admiral is the Navy . . . the incarnation! . . ." The genuine article and the nuts . . . it's perfectly simple . . . the only
difference is where you meet them . . . the rue Royale or the
banks of the Danube . . . Twenty times . . . a hundred
times . . . Pétain had written to Abetz that Corpechot was in
the way! admiral or not! that he had enough with his own people . . . on every floor . . . ministers and higher echelons!
. . . that he was spied on when he went out walking . . .
Abetz couldn't do a thing! when everything's going to pot,
there's nothing you can do but observe and shut up . . .
Vichy, the papal nuncio . . . Corpechot-Danube . . . don't
contradict! . . . delay the change of scene, keep the stage a
little while longer . . . before the page turns . . . Deloncle? *
. . . Swoboda? . . . or Brinon? or Navachine?* with or
without a tommy gun . . . or Juanovici? . . . Stalin? or Pétain? . . . or Gourion? Nothing counts . . . only Corpechot's
command . . . all about-face! . . . the whole military estab-
lishment . . . and the string of ministers . . . and the rest of
the V.I.P.'s . . . and the four of us, Marion, Lili, me, and Bébert . . . so the fleet wouldn't catch us before the big bridge!
. . . the three-track suspension bridge . . . the outing is over
. . . back to the Castle . . . the big bridge . . . same bank in
reverse . . . the last get to be first! about-face! about-face! . . .
the party chiefs in the lead! . . . Bucard and his men . . .
Sabiani and his men . . . Bout de l'An* and his men . . . I
note in passing that Herold Paqui,* as shameless a liar as Tartre,
never set foot in Siegmaringen . . . he stayed fifty miles away
on his island, eating canned goods . . . he never saw anything
at all . . . except his police record . . . Doriot* never came
either . . . we never saw anything but his car, riddled, gutted
. . . he should have stayed in Constance! . . . a good life,
except for the itch . . . same as ours only worse . . . Déat*
never came along on these outings . . . that giant of political

thought preferred to stroll in the woods by himself . . . he didn't mix much . . . he preferred . . . he was working on a program for a "Burgundian and French Europe" with primo-majoro-pluri-deferred elections . . . he was meditating . . .

Meditating like this, I get to thinking about Noguarès* . . . Where does he come off, writing about Siegmaringen? he could have gone there at least, the lousy pompous bastard! he'd sooner have shat in bed! any more than you ever saw Charlot in the trenches with a bazooka, fighting off the Kraut tanks! . . . slippery bastards! . . . all free gratis! never paying! . . . whores of the galas! I can see them all, those men of pure steel, on the terrace of the Trois Magots . . . signing their photographs in the blood of their admirers . . . the sucker billions! . . .

All this meditating makes me delirious . . . What's become of Philip? . . . I was telling you . . . about-face . . . the return to the Castle . . . so there we were in the lead with Marion Information . . . well, practically in the lead, behind the party chiefs . . . this about-face gave us a good laugh one day . . . I haven't had much chance to make you laugh . . . we come to the railroad bridge . . . the whole caravan stops short . . . under the first arch . . . oh, not on account of the air-raid warnings! they were permanent . . . the sirens never stopped blowing . . . but the R.A.F. was looking for the bridge . . . at that precise moment . . . no razzledazzle! . . . dropping their strings of bombs over the bridge . . . straight down . . . every which way . . . three, four planes at a time. . . how did they manage to miss it? . . . their bombs sent up geysers! the Danube was boiling! and the muck splashing all over . . . and in the fields . . . two, three miles away . . . We were squeezed under the arch, pressed against the enormous granite abutment . . . a good chance to piss, the ministers and the party chiefs and the Marshal . . . I knew all their prostates . . . some had big business . . . for that the bushes were more convenient . . . so there they go into the bush . . . just then, I remember exactly, a detachment of prisoners come up in the opposite direction . . . with their *Landsturm* guards . . . prisoners and "territorials" . . . not very

worried any of them . . . Russian prisoners and old Boches
. . . so tired! . . . so tired! . . . all skin and bones the
whole lot of them, dragging their feet . . . and all in rags . . .
the Krauts with guns, the others without . . . where were
they going? . . . Someplace . . . we asked them . . . they
didn't understand . . . they didn't even hear the bombs . . .
how could you expect them to hear our questions? . . . They
were going along the same bank, that's all . . . in the opposite
direction . . .

Bridou* finished pissing . . . he shook it . . . thoroughly!
and then he said: "Gentlemen, we must act!" Act how? He
came out with his idea . . . "We must scatter!" . . . the cavalry principle . . . "dispersed order" . . . how many of us
were there under the arch, piled up against the abutment? . . .
about thirty . . . I saw that Bridou was right . . . the bombs
were coming closer . . . and closer . . . they'd be hitting
the bridge pretty soon . . . after all . . . such incompetence
was too good to last . . . but the whole group was very
hesitant . . . ministers, party chiefs, Franco-Boche cops . . .
no enthusiasm about "dispersed order" . . . of course, we
could follow the Russians . . . the dragass prisoners . . .
sure! they must be going someplace . . . must have some
idea? . . . they hadn't said a word . . . across the fields . . .
follow the prisoners . . . Here there's one little detail . . .
Madame Rémusat and her daughter were lying in the muck,
flat on their bellies in the muck . . . along the shore . . . a
bomb crater . . . they'd come to pick dandelions . . . they
were all covered with mud! . . . a thick layer . . . they must
have been scared, scared . . . they didn't move . . . dead or
not? . . . maybe. Anyway, they were flat on their bellies . . .
I never heard of them again . . . they lived at the other end
of town . . . I've told you, the Russian prisoners and their
Landsturm guards were moving away through the fields . . .
they hadn't even looked at us . . . the bombs were falling not
far from them . . . so tired, sleepwalking, they look as if they
couldn't stop . . . the bombs were falling all around them, almost on top of them . . . and us! hell! . . . a merry-go-round
in the air! . . . you didn't have to be a magician to know what

they were after . . . the bridge . . . that carried the whole Ulm-Rumania traffic . . . to bash it in . . . with us underneath . . . Pétain and his procession! Lovely! They'd aim right in the end . . . the whole bridge on our noodles, oh, the junk and guts of it, Madame! . . . stubborn bunglers! . . . waterspouts! . . . I looked at Madame Rémusat and her daughter, come to pick dandelions . . . flat on their bellies . . . the ministers pulled up their pants . . . they all talked at once . . . some were pro . . . some were con . . . to keep on? together? . . . to take the other bank . . . the generals and admirals were for dispersing . . . or single file? catch up with the Russian prisoners? through the alfalfa? if we stayed there, one thing was sure, we'd get the bridge on our heads! the whole thing! their bombs were practically bursting on top of us! the whole Danube was full of them . . . upstream . . . downstream . . . they rectified . . . geysers of muck! coming down by the carload in front of us . . . enormous craters in the bank! . . . *wham! plop!* . . . the blast squeezed us against the abutment . . . ministers, generals and guards . . . and me and Lili and Bébert . . . At that really dramatic moment Pétain, who hadn't said anything yet, spoke up . . . "Forward!" We should all get out from under that arch and follow him! "Forward!" . . . They should all button their pants and "Forward!" . . . himself and Debeney emerged! oh, without haste . . . very very dignified! direction: the Castle . . . so there we were strung out again . . . all the ministers and the party chiefs . . . the bombs kept attacking the bridge . . . we, the rest of us, tagged along . . . and all the way to the Castle . . . one burst after another . . . machine-gun fire . . . they were firing at us all right . . . but wild . . . I could see the bullets ricocheting . . . in the grass . . . in the water . . . I could see the grass tumbling . . . cropped short . . . they were lousy shots . . . the proof is that nobody was hit . . . and they were skimming the river . . . Pétain was talking with Debeney . . . both striding along, no hurry at all . . . same with the ministers . . . at least a mile and a half . . . the line hadn't deviated an inch . . . I can still see Bichelonne ahead of us . . . limping badly . . . that was be-

fore his operation, he insisted on being operated in Hohenlychen, up there in East Prussia, I'll tell you about it . . . right
now I'm on Pétain . . . the return to the Castle . . . the
Chief in the lead . . . under the bursts of machine-gun fire
. . . and the whole straggling line of ministers, generals, admirals . . . pants buttoned, clothes in order . . . all very dignified . . . and keeping their distances . . . If I seem to be
going on about Pétain, it's because of the story that he'd gone
so gaga he couldn't hear the bombs or the sirens, that he
couldn't tell the Kraut soldiers from his own guards from Vichy
. . . and mistook Brinon for the nuncio . . . I want to set
things straight . . . I can be fair, because he really hated my
guts . . . and you can take it from me that if he hadn't taken
command there at the bridge, if he hadn't got that procession
started, nobody would have come out alive! there would never
have been any High Court! . . . or Noguarès either! I can say
that I saw the Marshal save the High Court! . . . if not for
him and his cool head, nobody would have got out from under
that arch! . . . not one minister, not one general! or the people
in the bushes! it would have been all over! no indictment! no
verdict! absolute hash! no need for the Ile d'Yeu either! . . . it
was Pétain's firmness that made everybody come out from
under that arch! . . . same as it was Pétain's character that got
the army to the front in '17 . . . I can speak without prejudice,
he detested me . . . I can still see the bullets all around us
. . . the bank, the towpath riddled . . . especially around Pétain . . . and he could see if he couldn't hear! . . . all the
way to the drawbridge! . . . burst after burst! . . . ah, and
not a word out of him! . . . or Debeney either . . . perfectly
dignified! . . . and the funniest part of it, nobody hit! . . .
neither Lili, nor myself, nor Bébert, nor Marion! . . . at the
drawbridge, halt! good-bye! . . . everybody on his own! nobody waited! everybody went home! . . . the R.A.F. had
stopped shooting . . . gone back upstairs . . . we . . . Lili,
Bébert, and I . . . said good-bye to Marion . . . but I had
four rolls in my pocket! . . .

My consultation! . . . it was time! . . . on the second floor
of the *Löwen*, No. 11, our hovel . . . and when I say hovel, I

don't mean palace! two beds . . . some beds! . . . though
I've seen worse . . . a lot worse . . . We give Marion another
good-bye . . . we embrace . . . we weren't sure we'd ever see
him again . . . he had his room on the fourth floor . . . the
smallest of the lot! . . . I've told you . . . Information was
rock bottom in the protocol . . . with Dagobert at Clichy-sur-
Seine, for instance, Marion wouldn't even have rated a chair
. . . if you don't want to go wrong, always remember St.
Eloi! . . . imposture began in the year 1000! that's when the
flimflam began to take over . . . Excellencies right and left
. . . puppets! No real hierarchy! . . . well, to get back to serious things, there was no flimflam about my consultation . . .
that was serious! . . . I'll tell you about our setup . . . you
can go and see for yourself . . . I've read a lot of stories about
Siegmaringen . . . all balloon juice or ax grinding . . . pho-
nies, all frauds and fakers . . . Christ! . . . they weren't there
. . . not a one of them . . . at the time they should have
been . . . If I have a lot to say about toilets . . . especially in
the *Löwen* . . . it's because we were on the same landing,
across the hall, and it was always full! the whole population of
Siegmaringen, the beer hall, the hotels, ended up there,
couldn't help it . . . across from us . . . the whole upstairs
lobby and the stairs were jam-packed, day and night, with people who couldn't hold it any more, cursing, griping that it was a
disgrace . . . that they'd suffered enough . . . and they were
going to do it right there! . . . which was God's truth . . .
the whole staircase was a river . . . and naturally our corridor! . . . and our room! You can't conceive of anything more
laxative than the *Stamgericht,* kohlrabi and red cabbage . . .
the *Stamgericht* plus the sour beer . . . to keep you in the
toilet for life! . . . so you can imagine our lobby . . . the
cursing and farting of the people who couldn't hold it in . . .
and the smell . . . the bowl overflowed! . . . what can you
expect! it was always plugged . . . people went in three . . .
four at a time . . . men, women, children . . . every which
way . . . they had to be dragged out by the feet, by
main force . . . hogging the crapper . . . "They're dreaming!
They're dreaming!" the outsiders bellowed . . . in the corri-

dor, in the beer hall, in the street . . . and everybody scratching in addition . . . exchanging their scabies and crabs! . . .
and my patients! . . . mixed in . . . naturally they went out
and pissed on the others . . . and all over . . . Our corridor
was really alive! . . . I haven't mentioned the people that
came to see von Raumnitz . . . I'll tell you about von Raumnitz . . . another mob, headed for his office, one of his offices,
on the floor above . . . they went to the crapper across the
hall, too . . . the most bewitching moment every day was
when the crapper really couldn't hold any more . . . about
eight o'clock at night . . . full to bursting . . . a shit bomb!
. . . the great overflow from the bottom of the bottom! . . .
the whole beer hall relieving itself . . . the hallway was a
geyser! . . . and our room! . . . a waterfall down the stairs!
. . . the devil take the hindmost! . . . catch-as-catch-can in
shit! . . . that was when Herr Frucht arrived! the manager of
the *Löwen!* Herr Frucht and his bamboo pole! . . . he'd really
done everything in his power to save his shit-can . . . but actually he was responsible . . . he ran the joint . . . the kohlrabi stew . . . the beer hall, the restaurant . . . five thousand
Stamgerichts a day! . . . no wonder the thing overflowed! So
Herr Frucht came up with his bamboo pole! he poked and
stirred! . . . got the thing working again! . . . and put on a
fresh padlock . . . tightened the screws! . . . to keep everybody out! and that's that! Two minutes after he'd gone his
crapper was full again! people fighting to get in . . . all over
the lobby! . . . Herr Frucht wasn't Sisyphus . . . he could
swear his fool head off: *"Teufel! Donner! Maria!"* His *Stamgericht* customers would have flooded his joint, submerged it in
torrents of kohlrabi! if he'd really closed his crapper, if he'd really kept everybody out! and cemented the hole! . . . he
threatened to, but he didn't dare . . .

Anyway, we in No. 11 were wading! Enough said . . . you
get used to it, we had to . . . what was more to be feared,
worse than this little inconvenience, was that we'd be put out!
. . . thrown out . . . Boche style . . . the mealymouthed,
reasonable way . . . "in the interest of the general welfare!"
. . . better for my patients if I moved . . . give my consulta-

tions somewhere else . . . etc. etc. . . . too much confusion
. . . all sorts of reasons why I should vacate . . . rumors? rumors? . . . worse things have happened to me! . . . take my
word for it!

Let me explain about this big lobby (the ceiling, I should
add, was very low) . . . There wasn't just my office . . . and
the candidates for the shithouse . . . but also the people who
came to see von Raumnitz . . . Baron Major von Raumnitz
. . . the room directly over ours . . . No. 26 . . . I'll come
back to this von Raumnitz . . . I'm digressing again . . .
dragging you around like this I'll lose you . . . I want to
show you too much at once . . . I've got an excuse . . . I'm in
kind of a hurry . . . So we left the Marshal . . . the drawbridge came down . . . we went up to the *Löwen* . . . . I'll
clear the way for you! . . . got to! . . . first the mob on the
sidewalk . . . then in the lobby . . . the crowd of people
wanting to pee . . . they're all over the place . . . I push
them aside . . . and I knock on our door! No. 11, our pad . . .

It takes a lot to surprise me, but this time I really look twice!
. . . on my own bed, the one on the right, a man stretched
out, all disheveled and unbuttoned, puking and gasping . . .
and on top of him, straddling him . . . a surgeon! . . . well
anyway a man in a white smock getting ready to operate on
him . . . forcibly! . . . three, four scalpels in his hand . . .
head-mirror, compresses, forceps! . . . no possible doubt!
Behind him, up to her ankles in sludge and urine, his nurse
. . . in a white smock, too . . . with big white metal boxes
under her arm . . .

"What are you doing?"

I ask them . . . it's my right! And besides the guy underneath is bellowing.

"Doctor, doctor, save me!"

"From what? From what?"

"It's you I came to see, Doctor! The Senegalese! The Senegalese!"

"What about them?"

"They've cut everybody's head off."

"But he's not a Senegalese."

"He's starting with the ear! . . . it's you I wanted to see, Doctor!"

"But he's not a Senegalese, is he?"

"No . . . no . . . he's a lunatic!"

"And where do you come from?"

"From Strasbourg, Doctor. I've got a garage in Strasbourg! They cut everybody's head off . . . they're coming . . . they're coming! I've got a garage! I'm thirsty, Doctor! . . . make him get off, Doctor! he's choking me! . . . he's going to stick his knife in my eye! . . . make him get off, Doctor!"

Quite a situation . . . this character with his scalpels, crazy or not, it would really be best if the police came and asked him for his papers right away . . . and threw everybody out of here! . . . all the people from the street were pouring into my room! into the corridor and the crapper, and here this nut and his nurse! . . . I'd never be able to put them all out by myself! . . . the room was cramped enough just with you and the washbasin and the two sacks . . . you couldn't move . . . and now this crowd!

In questions of order, Brinon was the man . . . I was responsible to him . . . he was the one to go to . . . it was up to him to notify the police! one of the police forces . . . tell them there was a riot in the *Löwen*, the crapper and the corridor! In rough situations, I don't let the grass grow under my feet . . . the insane surgeon, this fellow under him . . . bellowing! . . . no time to shillyshally! Lili had already put Bébert in her bag . . . she never went out without him . . . she'd wait for me at Madame Mitre's . . . I'd go see Brinon alone . . . Madame Mitre directed the administration . . . really a big-hearted woman and full of tact . . . you could talk to her . . . it was she who was supposed to answer the questions of the ten thousand . . . this and that . . . a hundred thousand complaints a day! . . . you can imagine if these 1,142 "wanted" complained! and the women and the children! about everything! and the "workers in Germany" and the forty-six varieties of spies! and the wholesale denunciations! . . . that this one . . . and that one . . . should be arrested! . . . and Laval! . . . and Bridoux! . . . quick! . . . and Brinon! . . .

and myself! and Bébert! ah, exile, cauldron of denunciation!
bubble bubble! . . . What it must have been like in London!
. . . ten years in London, and not a single one of them would
have come back . . . all hanged . . . millions of denunciations! . . . especially the ones condemned to death! the meas-
liest little candle blinking at you from an attic! . . . don't beat
your brains out! . . . it's So-and-so, condemned to death, sweating and trembling and scribbling a thousand thousand horrors
about some other stinking pariah candidate for the torture
chamber! denouncing him to the Krauts! to Bibici! to Hitler! to
the Devil! ah, Tartre is nothing but a puerile snotnose failure!
. . . these were real, deep-dyed informers! their heads practically under the blade! the conditions you find once in a century! . . . hats off! . . . plots? whole shovelfuls! the *Milice*
. . . the *Fidelis* . . . full of them! . . . the Intelligence Service everywhere! four transmitting sets reporting everything
that went on night and day . . . you could hear them perfectly
right there at the *Prinzenbau* (our town hall)! . . . our last
names . . . first names . . . actions . . . gestures . . . intentions . . . minute by minute . . . twelve-dozen dyed-in-the-
wool concierges, yack-boxes, laundresses latching on to our balls
wouldn't have done a better job, spread worse gossip . . . We
knew! . . . but life is impulse, you've got to pretend to believe
in it . . . as if nothing were wrong . . . carry on! carry on!
Myself now at No. 11, I had to see my twenty-five . . . fifty
patients . . . give them what I couldn't . . . sulphur ointment
that never came . . . gonacrine, the penicillin that Richter
was supposed to be getting a shipment of . . . and never did!
life is impulse! . . . and keeping your mouth shut! . . . one
time later, I practiced medicine in Rostock on the Baltic with
a colleague, Dr. Proséidon, who had just come back from the
Paradise of the East . . . he'd built up the habit . . . the
face you need in states that really mean business . . . the
expression of a man who'll never think again . . . or anything
else! . . . "Even if you don't say a word, they can see! . . .
Get in the habit of not thinking anything!" My admirable
colleague! What's become of him? . . . he saw Paradise everywhere! "If Hitler falls, you won't escape it!" Those were the

words of a big intellectual: "Europe will be republican or Cossack!" . . . Hell, it will be both! and Chinese!

I know you haven't asked me . . . I'm just telling you what I think! . . . Turn Gazier* into a Cossack . . . you'll have silent doctors! silent nurses! . . . my colleague Proséidon was there for fifteen years . . . in Paradise! . . . "For fifteen years I 'prescribed' . . . for fifteen years my patients took my prescriptions to the druggist . . . they always came back empty-handed . . . he didn't have any! . . . oh, he didn't protest . . . not a word . . . neither did my patients . . . not a word . . . neither did I . . . not a word! . . ." When Monsieur Gazier, the Cossack, really knows his job, there won't be a word left to say . . . we there in Siegmaringen hadn't got to that point yet . . . we still had ideas . . . pretensions . . . I protested about the scabies, the sulphur I was supposed to get . . . same as Herr Frucht protested about his toilet . . . he'd have liked it to work . . . My training wasn't nearly complete! Herr Frucht died insane, later . . . later . . .

Damn! back to my room! . . . the screwball surgeon and his victim bellowing under him . . . calling out to me: help! I had to do something, get that room cleared out! I say to Lili: "This has been going on long enough! We're going to the Castle! . . . I take Lili . . . Lili-Bébert . . . I had a permanent card . . . "Priority at all hours" . . . I've got to admit it . . . priority . . . Through the postern gate under the vault . . . the ramp dug out of the rock . . . you should have seen that vault! . . . that magnificent equestrian ramp . . . leading to the Upper Court! . . . the Trophy Room! . . . the vault was high enough for lances to pass through! . . . three, four squadrons could have climbed up easy, boot to boot! the spaciousness of a period . . . Crusades! Off the Upper Court, first door on the right, Brinon's antechamber . . . I leave Lili with Madame Mitre and I shake hands with the orderly, a soldier of France! a real one! oh yes! . . . decorated regiment and all . . . even the *Médaille Militaire* . . . like myself . . . *Tap . . . tap* . . . he knocks . . . he announces me . . . to speak with Monsieur Brinon! . . . he receives me right away . . . He's sitting there as I knew him on the Place Beauvau

. . . and practically the same office . . . maybe not quite so
big . . . minus the telephones . . . but the same face, the
same expression, the same profile . . . I speak to him, I tell
him very respectfully that he might perhaps? . . . etcetera,
Christ! he knew all about . . . and a lot else besides! . . .
those people read so many reports! and see at least a hundred
cops a day! You can't teach them anything! . . . Sartine!*
Louis XIV! Brinon knew everything people were saying about
him . . . that he was really Monsieur Cohen . . . that his
name wasn't Brinon any more than the cat's grandmother . . .
any more than Nasser is Nasser! . . . little riddles for dinner
plates . . . that his wife Sarah dictated all his policies . . .
over the phone . . . ten times a day from Constance! . . .
the croakers at the *Fidelis* were all laughing . . . and the listening devices in the bunkers . . . the police forces! . . . and
Radio London! . . . the whole works! . . . he knew, and he
could tell by looking at me that I knew . . . a time comes
when there are no secrets . . . the only secrets are made up by
the police . . . I'd come to talk about our room, could he
kindly send a small detachment of police? I couldn't receive my
patients . . . my bed was occupied . . . the whole hotel was
overrun . . . the disorder was appalling! . . . I gave him the
details about the nut and his nurse . . .

Brinon was rather somber in nature and expression . . . secretive . . . kind of a cave animal (as X put it) . . . in his
office he'd practically given up answering questions . . . he
wasn't stupid . . . I always had the impression that he knew
perfectly well it was all a masquerade, that it was only a question of days . . .

"Oh, you know, a crazy doctor . . . he's not the only one
. . . we know that out of twelve French doctors, supposedly
French, supposedly refugees, ten are insane . . . really insane,
escaped from asylums . . . in addition, listen carefully, Doctor, Berlin is sending us, you can be expecting his visit, a certain 'Privat-Professor' Vernier, 'Director of the French Health
Services' . . . I happen to know, no surprise to me, my wife
told me on the phone, that this Vernier is a Czech . . . and
that he's been a German spy for the last seventeen years! first in
Rouen . . . then in Annemasse . . . then on the *Journal Offi-*

ciel . . . here's his picture! . . . here are his fingerprints! . . . as of today, he's your superior, Doctor! your superior! orders from Berlin! . . . if anybody's molesting you in your room take your complaints upstairs . . . the floor above you . . . to Raumnitz. You've been treating him . . . you know him! . . . see if he wants to take action! as far as I'm concerned, the Siegmaringen police, you know . . . all these police forces . . . bah!"

Brinon didn't want to get mixed up in anything any more . . . scabies . . . chancres . . . my tubercular women . . . the kids in Cissen that they were killing with carrots . . . or my screwball surgeon . . . he seemed to get a kick out of doing nothing . . .

"Ah yes, Doctor, one thing . . . I've got news for you! you've been condemned to death by the 'Plauen Committee!' Here's your sentence! . . ."

He reaches into the blotter and takes out a "notice" . . . same format, same wording as all the ones I'd received in Montmartre . . . same grounds . . . "traitor, in the pay of . . . , pornographer . . . Jew-baiter . . ." but instead of being in the pay of the Boches . . . it was the "Intelligence Service" . . . if there's anything really boring, it's these ferocious accusations . . . worse crap than love stories! . . . I can still remember later on, in prison in Denmark . . . I got them through in the French Embassy . . . or in the Scandinavian papers . . . they didn't knock themselves out! . . . all perfectly simple: "the unspeakable monster and traitor! . . . whom no words can describe! . . . my pen fails me! . . ." Always the same monstrous crimes: selling this and that . . . the whole Maginot Line! . . . the troops' underdrawers! . . . their shit! plus the generals! the whole fleet, the Toulon roadstead! the channel of Brest! buoys and mines! . . . auctioning off our Country! . . . Ferocious "*collabos*" or vicious purging "Fifis" . . . same difference . . . take it from me . . . London, Montmartre, Vichy, Brazzaville . . . all shady bastards! Bloodhound and Co.! . . . super-Nazi of the New Europe or London or Picpus Committee! watch your step! all looking for a chance to make meatballs out of you!

This way of slipping out from under . . . of leaving you

high and dry! . . . what's the matter with me? . . . I was telling you that Brinon had no desire to get mixed up in this business with the screwball . . . why didn't I go see Raumnitz?
. . . that didn't appeal to me very much . . . but after all
. . . with the state our room must be in! . . . first I'd go see
Madame Mitre . . . call for Lili . . . I've got to tell you
about Madame Mitre's apartment . . . it was worth it . . . a
collection of big and little pieces of furniture, console tables,
stands, carved wood, torsades, gewgaws, Gorgons, chimeras
. . . An auctioneer's dream . . . they'd have driven every
antique dealer on the left Bank nuts! and nothing phony! all
perfect Second Empire! . . . stained-glass windows, canopies!
settees with ottomans! . . . circular sofas with green plants! a
bathtub of chiseled copper with rococo foliage . . . a dressing
table, also rococo, with a flounce, room enough to hide twenty
hussars . . . tables, monuments of sculpture . . . angry dra-
gons! and Muses! all the Muses! the Princes in their time had
looted the whole rue de Provence, the rue Lafayette, and the
rue Saint-Honoré . . . you might still find collections like that
in the Empress' apartments in Compiègne . . . at Victor
Hugo's place in Guernsey . . . or at Epinay for the lady with
the Camellias . . . maybe . . . Lili and Madame Mitre were
sitting there in style . . . Lili was happy in this "Imperatrice"
setting . . . all women . . . I couldn't find fault with her . . .
the *Löwen,* our corridor, our bed, and now in addition the
lunatic . . . it was a lot for a woman to take . . . even a
brave one like Lili . . . from Madame Mitre's windows you
could see all Siegmaringen . . . all the roofs of the town . . .
and the forest . . . you get to understand Castle life . . . the
view from up there . . . the detachment of the nobles . . .
the great beauty of not being serfs . . . we were serfs! . . .
or worse! . . . I tell Madame Mitre about the hotel, our troubles with our room, and the pay-off . . . this lunatic surgeon!
oh, she understands that I should complain . . . but! . . .
but! . . . "There's nothing the Ambassador can do anymore,
Doctor! . . . or the police! . . . He didn't tell you everything,
Doctor . . . you know how discreet he is . . . believe me,
you don't know the whole story . . . eight bishops in Fulda!

. . . they claim to be French, and they demand to come here, to the Castle! . . . three astronomers in Potsdam . . . claim to be French! eleven 'Sisters of the Poor' in Munich! . . . six false admirals in Diehl . . . who want to come here too! . . . yesterday a whole convent of Hindu nuns, allegedly from the Comptoirs* . . . with fifty little Cashmere girls, supposedly raped and about to give birth . . . and we've got to find room for them here . . . little girls . . . or at the *Löwen* . . . or in Cissen! . . . plus three persecuted Mongols!"

Yes, definitely, that was a lot of people . . .

"You're not persecuted, are you, Doctor?"

"Ah, yes, Madame Mitre, very much so!"

"And what of the Ambassador, Doctor? And Abetz, Doctor! If you only knew! the denunciations! . . . How many would you say?"

"Oh, I don't know . . . a good many!"

"Yesterday three hundred! . . . of Laval! of ourselves! . . ."

"I can imagine."

"Three reports yesterday. Guess about what."

"Everybody."

"Not just everybody! about Corpechot! . . . and one report from Berlin! . . . that he had been seen in Berlin!"

"Oh, Madame, that's a lie! Corpechot never leaves the Danube! . . . he's guarding it, that's his mission! . . . he's not the man to desert his post! I vouch for him!"

"Even so, we have to answer! . . . the Chancellery! Would you care to write a few lines for me?"

"Oh yes, Madame Mitre . . . right away . . . I'll tell them that Corpechot doesn't go A.W.O.L., certainly not!"

"Ah, my dear doctor . . ."

"Lili, we must go now. Say good-bye to Madame Mitre . . . Bébert! Bébert!"

Bébert, that's the word that makes her get up . . . "Bébert" means that we'll stop by at the *Landrat's* for his scraps . . . the *Landrat* was at the other end of the main street . . . I'll tell you about it . . . first what a *Landrat* is . . . a kind of an official, somewhere between a mayor and a sub-prefect . . . I take care of his cook . . . dyspepsia . . . very good family, good bourgeoisie from the old days . . . I also had a tenant of the *Landrat's* . . . ninety-six years old . . . my oldest patient . . . how witty she was! what refinement! what a memory! Christine de Pisan! Louise Labé . . . Marceline! She recited everything, everything! She recited just the way I like it:

> *Alone I have remained!*
> *Alone I am!*

How true!

Even sweating and feverish as I was, I had no reason to think that this chill I'd caught on the riverfront, this attack, would go on for months . . . go lay an egg! I shook . . . ridiculous! . . . worse and worse . . . I was wringing wet, the whole bed was full of it . . . But even so I applied myself to writing . . . as best I could . . . I'm not the type to discuss working conditions . . . hell no! . . . that kind of stuff is from after 1900 . . . "Must I do it, mama?" . . . Either you were born a lazy pimp . . . or a worker! One or the other! . . . Me there shaking the bed . . . how about getting to work all the same! . . .

"Good Lord, let's hope it isn't somebody coming!"

Noises nearby . . . the dogs too . . . *arrgh! arrgh!* . . . it's an obsession as you get older . . . to be left alone, absolutely alone! . . . Christ! . . . Lili's talking to somebody . . . the door is closed but I can hear . . . I listen . . . something about Madame Niçois . . . a neighbor woman . . . Madame Niçois seems to be cold . . . she's been complaining . . . "What can I do?" the neighbor woman asks . . . I sing out:

"An ambulance! Versailles! the hospital! Telephone, Lili! Telephone! . . ."

The door opens . . . Lili and the neighbor woman come in . . . which is exactly what I didn't want . . . I bury myself under the blankets . . . under the mountain of overcoats . . . I don't remember how many overcoats! I'm poor in everything, but Christ! not in overcoats! That's what people who see our misery send us . . . they keep sending them . . . overcoats! they always have too many . . . oh, not overcoats you could wear, absolutely threadbare! you can't go out in them, but in bed with a fever you're very glad to have them! really not too many . . . low-cost central heating . . . we have so much trouble with ours that runs on gas . . . it ruins us! . . .

Lili and the neighbor woman leave . . . I didn't say anything . . . not a word . . . let them telephone . . . Versailles . . . the ambulance . . . no, I won't bother Tailhefer . . . she won't be badly off in Versailles, the hospital is very well heated . . . she'll be better off than at home . . . and maybe . . . I think it over . . . after my telling her about ghosts, about those bozos from *La Publique,* she didn't want to stay there any more . . . you're always on tenterhooks with your patients . . . did you say too much? or not enough?

I'm always beating my brains out, thinking up things to say . . . for my patients . . . for Achille! . . . 900 . . . 1,000 pages . . . or for Gertrut . . . one's as big a crook as the other . . . I'd like to see them skin each other alive right before my eyes! knife each other in all directions! chop each other into skunk stew! . . . but hell's fire! . . . cowardly cutthroats don't cut! . . . Loukoum less than anybody! that empty vagina! . . . in all this world and the next you won't find a more voracious gang of sharks! . . . false teeth . . . nylon fins! . . . and limousines as big as a house . . . all glutted on scribblers' blood! the quarts they've pumped out of me! I know what I'm saying!

Or don't I? Hell! . . .

This thing with the neighbor woman upset me . . . worse than *La Publique* . . . the ambulance . . . I've lost you again . . . you and the thread! Let's see now . . . we were in Siegmaringen . . . one memory . . . another . . . I've got it! . . . another memory cropping up . . . of Le Havre . . . Le Havre . . . I've got it! . . . I was substituting for a colleague, Malouvier . . . yes, yes, that's it . . . a patient in Montivilliers on the National Highway . . . I can still see that patient . . . and his cancer of the rectum . . . I was still mighty active, ardent, devoted . . . at that time . . . I ran myself ragged . . . I answered every call! . . . this cancer patient, two three times a day! . . . morphine and dressing . . . I was a whole clinic all by myself . . . but they took him away from me . . . not because I wasn't taking good care of him . . . no . . . because he was going mad . . . the family couldn't

control him, he was bashing into everything . . . the cupboard
. . . the window . . . breaking everything . . . said I was
preventing him from going to work . . . accusing me! his conscience was killing him . . . because he knew it was all over!
that he'd never go to the factory again! . . . the cops would
come for him, they were already there! he saw them coming in
the window! to take him to prison! for not working! he hadn't
stopped in sixty years! never! never missed a day at the floating
docks in Honfleur! not one day! "Help! help!" I did my best
. . . my soothing words and my 100 milligrams of morphine
. . . he'd never missed a day! . . . they'd had to take him
away . . . cancer isn't the whole story . . . the big thing is
conscience about your work! well, that is, not for people like
Brottin . . . or Gertrut . . . who wait . . . just wait . . .
for the work to pour in! . . . I'm here to prove it . . . like
Paraz* . . . the sick worker . . . they wait for the work to
come in! . . . fever or no fever! . . . "How you coming,
clown?. . . how many pages?"

Raumnitz was always there about five o'clock . . . you could almost count on it . . . from five to seven . . . then he went out to the Castle . . . or some place else . . . this wasn't his only headquarters . . . he saw people all over . . . every hour of the day and night . . . ten or twelve different places . . . at the *Löwen* it was from five to seven . . . room 26, directly over ours . . . all cops are like that, they've got dozens of offices, places to see people . . . same with politicians . . . and ambassadors . . . that's why you always get a funny feeling in certain streets of any capital . . . Mayfair, Monceau, Riverside . . . full of shady houses and people . . . no rundown furnished houses and apartments . . . even there in Siegmaringen, Raumnitz's secret quarters, take it from me! nothing like our dive! I knew his wing of the Castle, two floors! all full of flowers . . . azaleas, hydrangeas, narcissus . . . and those roses! . . . I'll bet you the Kremlin is full of roses in January . . . there in the Castle, with a whole wing to himself, two floors, Raumnitz had an army of flunkeys, chambermaids, cooks and laundresses, maybe he was even better off than Pétain! . . . more luxurious! . . . and he had other places in town . . . not only for himself . . . for his wife, his daughter and his mastiffs . . . you wouldn't find better in East End or Long Beach . . . if you're looking for magic, go ask the police . . . if they say no, they're lying, they've got plenty . . . if tomorrow Paris is ground to powder by the G, Z . . . or Y-bomb . . . there'll still be plenty of those neat little lovenests three hundred feet underground, with every comfort, bidet, azaleas, wine cellars, cigars this big, foam-rubber sofas, belonging to the police . . . this police and that police . . . and the police will always be around . . . subject of food supply, you should have seen those stocks of food cards between the flower pots . . . enough to feed all Siegmaringen! . . . Raumnitz, the missus, and their daughter . . . had too much of everything . . . but they never offered us one slice of bread! one crust! one ticket! . . . it was a point of honor with them . . . for us, nothing!

He didn't despise my medical ability, I treated him, bad case of aortitis . . . my fees? double zero! . . . his point of honor! right now, coming back from Brinon's, I wanted him to send some of his cops to throw out the lunatic and the nurse . . . for a starter!

I say to Lili: come! . . . first we've got to get through the landing! . . . even more people than before! . . . people from the *Bären,* even noisier . . . young people, the terror of Frucht, who expected them to demolish his hotel, his restaurant, his crapper . . . much wilder than our crowd at the *Löwen* . . . first the *Stam* down below, the beer . . . and whish, upstairs to piss, and diarrhea! smash the door and the bolts, and pour into the toilet . . . six or ten at a time . . . smash the bowl . . . the chain! take away the seat! . . . victory! . . . victory! by main force! another piss-together in the vestibule, on the stairs! . . . the deluge! . . . but hold your hats! just then . . . in the middle of the piss . . . two German girls peel . . . and go into position! . . . frantic! . . . sniffing! their skirts up like this! . . . and let her go! and all the young folks around them! stamping! mad with joy! clapping! . . . egging them on! . . . and pissing in unison! . . . two really good-looking girls . . . in a clinch . . . refugees from Dresden . . . the "city of artists" . . . all the actresses came from Dresden . . . the haven . . . the refuge of the arts! . . . these two, real swingers . . . were supposedly opera singers . . . outside the crapper and in front of Frucht and in front of everybody! . . . and the mob on the landing shouting hurrah! . . . "hurrah, Fräulein!" A brunette and a redhead . . . an orgy, really not the place for it . . . clinching right in the middle of the pond . . . I could see there wasn't a chance of opening the door . . . our door, No. 11 . . . I don't know how many people there were around my bed . . . around the nut with his patient under him . . . the rest of them were just as batty . . . egging him on! . . . "Atta boy! Atta boy! cut his ear off!" . . .

My presence of mind is famous! I didn't waste time . . . "Come, Lili, come!"

And don't forget that in the sky, high up in the clouds and lower down over the rooftops, the merry-go-round was still going on . . . God's perpetual thunder, Fortresses passing over! . . . London . . . Augsburg . . . Munich . . . grazing our windows with their wing tips . . . hurricanes of motors . . . deafening! you couldn't hear a thing! . . . not even the howling in the corridor! . . .

They were packed in all right, the whole *Bären* yelling for the girls to skin each other alive . . . and in our joint for the surgeon to cut the guy's ear off! . . .

You can imagine with that bedlam the trouble we had . . . Lili and I . . getting to the next floor! we shove! we push through! Christ! we made it! . . . the stairs . . . No. 28! I knock! Ah, it's Aisha! Frau Aisha von Raumnitz . . . she opens . . . they're married, really married . . . I'll explain . . . she opens . . . Aisha Raumnitz doesn't speak any more German than Lili . . . three words . . . she was brought up in Beirut . . . she's from around there, I'll tell you about it . . . right now I want to see her husband . . . I'm in luck, he's there . . . he's lying down in his dressing gown . . .

"Well, Doctor? Well?"

"Brinon has sent me to ask you . . ."

"I know . . . I know . . ." he cuts me short . . . "you've got a lunatic in your place . . . and the whole corridor full of lunatics! . . . Aisha! . . . Aisha! . . . You attend to this!"

No hesitation . . . He hands her a bundle of keys . . .

"Take the dogs!"

The two mastiffs! . . . he beckons to them . . . one leap and they're at his wife's feet . . . well, at her boots! . . . she's wearing boots . . . red leather . . . makes you think of an Oriental horsewoman, the way she keeps tapping on her boots . . . and an enormous yellow whip . . .

"Let's go, Doctor!" . . .

I've only got to follow her . . . with her I know that everything will be all right . . . the mastiffs know, too . . . they
start growling and show their fangs . . . enormous! . . . they
keep growling . . . they don't bite . . . they follow at Madame's heels . . . they're ready to rip anybody she says apart
. . . that's all! . . . admirably trained animals . . . and
powerful! Buffaloes! . . . muzzles, chests, haunches! the force
of the impact and you're out flat! . . . before you can open
your mouth! . . . Not to mention their fangs . . . you and
your carotids, one mouthful! . . . Aisha and her mastiffs, people move aside! . . . Real respect! . . . no questions . . .
Aisha doesn't say anything either . . . she moves rather lan-
guidly . . . swaying at the hips . . . not fast . . . the stinkers all pull their pants up . . . the loudmouth pissers . . .
they all flow down toward the street . . . the brunette and
the redhead too, they pull themselves together . . . and step
on it . . . orgasm or no orgasm! . . . the nymphos break . . .
they stop yelling! . . . nobody is yelling about anything anymore . . . not even the torture of needing to shit . . . In my
room, No. 11, the second they catch sight of Aisha, panic . . .
frenzy! they knock us over to get out quicker! and they climb
over each other to get out first! . . . ah, the surgeon and the
nurse and the garage man and his ear! . . . the way they
bounced off my bed! straightening, running! hell bent! . . .
now it's the surgeon that's yelling! he starts in! The one who
was under him, the refugee from Strasbourg, isn't yelling any
more . . . the nurse takes away the boxes of cotton . . . they
all try to get through at once! oh, but that won't do . . . Aisha
has a good idea! . . . she's languid but precise! "Stop! stop!"
she says to the three of them . . . they should stay right where
they are! nut, nurse, and victim! all three of them! right there!
nose to the wall! . . . she shows them! on their feet, flat
against the wall! . . . the mastiffs growl at their asses . . .
those fangs, I've told you . . . "And don't move" . . . they
don't move . . . the whole landing is clear and the long corridor and my room . . . not a soul . . . vacuum! . . . ah, the
pissers who couldn't hold it in! and the two opera singers! . . .
all those lunatics! abracadabra! a charm! . . . but that's not

all! Aisha had her idea . . . *Komm!* suddenly she's talking to them in German . . . to the three with their nose to the wall . . . they should come and follow her! . . . tag along! I want to see . . . Way at the other end of the lobby a little passage and then two steps . . . No. 36! . . . the door to 36 . . . *creak! creak!* . . . she opens . . . she motions to the nut to go in first, then the nurse, then the man from Strasbourg . . . they hesitate . . . ah! Aisha doesn't care for hesitation . . . "let's go . . . let's go! . . ." They start rolling their eyes! . . . especially the garage man! . . . they're wondering whether to go in . . . they look at the dogs . . . they climb the two steps . . . Room 36 . . . I knew that room . . . well, I knew it a little . . . I'd gone there twice for Raumnitz, to see two fugitives who'd been brought back from God knows where . . . two old men . . . it was the only solid room in the whole *Löwen* . . . fortified . . . concrete walls, iron door, barred windows . . . and those bars weren't thin! I know my super-prisons . . . all the other rooms in the *Löwen* sort of swayed and wobbled, cracks, loose bricks . . . all falling apart! plaster, ceiling, beds, everything! There wasn't a single bed that had all four legs . . . three at the most! a lot of them only one! you can imagine, the vibration of the planes! Beyond repair! Herr Frucht had given up! and the tenants contributed to the wreckage . . . that was their only way of avenging themselves on the Boches, on Frucht, on the planes, and being there . . . the whole business! two, three, four of them would sit down in a chair . . . smash it good and proper . . . ten or fifteen on the bed. What a mess! especially the soldiers in transit, the reinforcements on their way to the Rhine front . . . those *Landsturm* boys . . . Christ! the world's champion looters! . . . but there was nothing left to loot! . . . everything was gone or pulverized! like my place on the rue Girardon! the exciting thing about passing through is the stealing! . . . there was nothing removable left . . . the whole *Löwen* was reeling under the London-Munich Armadas . . . the roaring . . . a thousand motors . . . tiles flying through the air . . . the whole street was full of the pieces . . . the ceilings, you can imagine! . . . oh, but not the ceilings of Room 36! the

only one in the *Löwen* that could take it! . . . I'd noticed this
cell . . . I've told you . . . absolutely perfect condition! . . .
I wasn't going to ask questions . . . what had become of the
two old men? or what they were going to do with these three?
the nut, the nurse, and the garage man . . . they were "fugitives" too . . . so were we, I suppose . . . anyway Aisha was
in charge of Room 36, opening, stowing, and closing . . .
what went on in there? . . . I couldn't ask Raumnitz . . .
rumors . . . it seems they shipped people out at night . . . a
truck came by on certain nights . . . so they said . . . I never
saw any truck, and I went out pretty often at all hours . . .
one thing was sure: for whole weeks No. 36 was empty . . .
and then all of a sudden jampacked . . . the legend, the
rumor was that nobody was ever supposed to see that truck
. . . that they chained them and piled them in . . . all these
so-called fugitives . . . and hauled them away to the East
. . . further than Posen . . . supposedly to some camp . . .
I couldn't very well ask Raumnitz what he sent them to Posen
for . . . or Aisha . . . anyway one sure thing, she'd cleared
out our joint in two seconds flat! . . . pure panic! . . . Aisha
had plenty of authority! with her mastiffs! and her whip! . . .

At least I had no more nuts on my bed! . . . oh, the patients
would come back . . . they'd gone, but they'd be back . . .
of course I'd have to clean up . . . or try to! . . .

I wanted Madame Raumnitz to take a look . . . to see what
I was up against . . .

"Look, Madame Raumnitz!"

"There's a war going on, Doctor."

We talk awhile . . . she liked to talk to us . . . they'd lived
in France, in Vincennes . . . we talk about Vincennes . . .
Lake Daumesnil . . . Saint-Fargeau . . . the Métro . . .

I thought the patients would come back . . . but they didn't
. . . or the toilet enthusiasts . . . I guess they all hightailed
it to the cellars, the caves . . . their favorite caves . . . or
under the Castle? . . . they were scared shitless! . . . the
R.A.F. was nothing compared to Aisha and Room 36! . . . I
know . . . Lili and Aisha are there on the landing, talking it
over . . . this, that, and the other thing . . . fine! But I've got
to go see Luther . . . Kurt Luther, the Kraut Army doctor
. . . a conference! it was time! . . . and after Luther the *Milice* . . . I've got three, four bed patients, too . . . flu . . .
Darnan is in Ulm, I won't see him . . . I'll see his son and
Bout de l'An . . . it's not so far, but all the same a good half
hour from door to door . . . in fits and starts! . . . I've told
you . . . it wasn't just the Armada . . . they're way up in the
sky . . . it's the low-flying Marauders . . . You've seen
them, I've told you about the outing, the way they'd framed us
in bullets all along the Danube . . . from Luther's to the *Milice* was along the Danube too . . . the *Milice* were in barracks, great big Adrians with triple-decker bunks . . . the military style since 1918 . . . but the Villa Luther, where I went
for the conference, was pretty-pretty . . . William II baroque . . .
About that outing, while I'm on the subject . . . if they
didn't hit Pétain or his string of ministers, it's definitely because
they didn't want to! nothing to it! . . . not a Kraut plane in
the air! . . . never! . . . not a single machine gun on the
ground! no defenses, period! A pushover for those Pirates of
the Air! to pepper any man, cow, dog, cat, at 300 m.p.h. aim!
fire! good-bye! . . . automatic! . . . a Mosquito! a Marauder!
. . . they never stopped, they were always there on top of us,

looping the loop! never a lull! . . . they came in relays . . . a burst! another burst! ricochets! . . . *bzing!* . . . the idea was to "keep 'em off the roads" . . . take Doriot, one look at his car, it was on show outside the *Prinzenbau* (our town hall) for more than a week while the investigation was going on . . . chiseled from end to end, riddled small, like lace! . . . they'd caught him on the road, him, his bodyguards, stenographers, and photographers . . . *ack-ack-ack!* on their way from Constance to a meeting of Party leaders on the other side of the Pzimflingen . . . oh, a very secret meeting . . . but not so secret that they hadn't picked him up . . . and shot him to pieces! . . . if they didn't come down on Pétain's outing, Pétain and his crowd, it's because they had different orders . . . the order was to get Doriot . . . no question! . . . I doubt if they had any orders about me, nothing special . . . I was "routine" . . . "keep 'em off the roads!" . . . the Boches and the English were the same! . . . "keep 'em off the roads!" Anything that moves: *ping!* . . . in a word, we weren't supposed to get off alive! the shuppos on the ground, the R.A.F. Marauders up top . . . fire! at us! But in spite of the shuppos whistling and yelling at her: *Komm! Komm!* and the ricochets from the sky, Lili always came out to join me . . . the danger appealed to her, I've got to admit . . . it didn't appeal to me . . . when I left the *Löwen,* I told her: "Stay here, Lili! Don't move! Tell the other patients I'll be right back! . . . stay with Madame Raumnitz . . . don't stay alone!"

I, ordinarily such a boor, was all gallantry . . .

"Madame Raumnitz, won't you please sit down? . . . Stay with Lili just a little while? I'm going to the *Milice* . . ."

Madame Raumnitz had her troubles, too . . .

"Yes, Doctor, yes, I'll stay . . . but if you see Hilda, please tell her to come home . . . quickly! . . . I've been waiting for her since last night . . ."

"Yes, Madame Raumnitz, certainly! Count on me!"

I had a good idea where Hilda von Raumnitz would be . . . and two, three little friends . . . the nymphettes of Siegmaringen . . . well-bred, well-fed girls of excellent military or diplomatic family . . . who had never wanted for anything . . .

naturally at that age, in that cold bracing air, their lollypops itched . . . that's the desperate age . . . from fourteen to seventeen . . . and these deluxe little dolls . . . sheltered and pampered . . . weren't the only ones . . . it was the same with the poor devils! . . . different pretexts, homesickness, the constant danger, the sleepless nights, the rutting males! . . . poor devils themselves . . . and ragged! and lustful! and so passionate! every clump of bushes! every street corner! fourteen to seventeen . . . the desperate age, especially for girls! . . . but the girls in this very particular place . . . homesickness, the constant danger, the rutting men on every sidewalk . . . weren't the only ones . . . same thing on the rue Bergère or the place Blanche! . . . for a cigarette . . . for two cents worth of blah blah . . . Heartbreak, idleness, and sex go together . . . and not only the kids . . . grown women and grandmothers! naturally they're most passionate . . . fire in their twats . . . at times when the page is turning . . . when History brings all the nuts together, opens its Epic Dance Halls! hats and heads in the whirlwind! panties overboard! when the Fifis lead their oxen to slaughter! and Corpechot is Master of the Danube! I knew I'd find Hilda and her crowd at the station . . . sure thing! teenage spylets, soldiers, ministers' daughters, and gatekeepers all in a heap . . . in the waiting rooms! the attraction of fresh meat and troop trains, plus the piano and the field kitchens, you can imagine the orgies! something a little hotter than the poor garrulous little jerkoffs at the Seventeen Magots and Neuilly! . . . hunger and phosphorus make people rut and sperm and surrender without looking! pure happiness! no more hunger, cancer or clap! . . . the station packed with eternity! . . . the planes crisscrossing overhead! . . . dropping thunder! and the whole waiting room and the buffet exchanging lice, scabies, syphilis, and love! females, pigtails, expectant mothers of all ages, grandmothers, soldiers! every army and every branch of service, from the fifty trains in the shunting station . . . the whole buffet singing in chorus! *Marleen! la! la! G-sharp!* . . . in three or four voices! passionately! and enlaced! . . . lying in the chairs! . . . three on the pianist's lap! three of my pregnant women! . . . and

naturally, to top it off, plenty of bread! Army bread! and full
mess kits! without tickets! you can imagine that the girls
weren't particular! . . . four field kitchens full of kettles between trains . . . help yourself on the platforms! the Siegmar
switching yards, munitions trains, really the most explosive spot
in all South Württemberg . . . Freiburg-Italy . . . three
switches and all these trains! gasoline, cartridges, bombs! . . .
enough to blow the whole countryside as far as Ulm . . . sky-
high . . . blow the planes out of the sky . . . Well, you can
see I had my work cut out for me, fighting for Hilda's virtue,
keep her from getting laid under a train . . . *"Love is a gypsy
child! . . ."* Okay . . . so you're sorry for me! . . . neverthe-
less, duty comes first . . . first Luther! . . . three, four con-
sultants . . . Boche . . . French . . . and then straight to
the *Milice* . . . right next door . . . There I see two, three
bed patients . . . two prescriptions and some urine analyses
. . . Don't ask me if I knew the pharmacist *Hofapotek* Hans
Richter! . . . if I didn't go for the medicines and the results of
the urine analyses myself, I could wait all year! . . . he sabo-
tages me! . . . maybe he's anti-Hitler . . . he's certainly anti-
French . . . And as usual I'm perfectly "regular" . . . I only
prescribe absolutely reliable medicines that have been in the
Codex for at least fifty years . . . here it's the Pharmacopia of
the *Reichsgesundheitsamt* . . . thirty-two prescriptions . . .
oh, an excellent selection, quite sufficient! *Reichsprecept!* . . .
I'll even say, I make no bones, that we ought to take a cue in
our wasteful! pretentious! idiotic France! . . . Conti, the
minister of public health who wrote that *Reichsprecept,* was
convicted in Nuremberg of genocide . . . witnessed, authenti-
cated . . . a kind of Truman . . . and hanged! (not Truman)
. . . all the same his *Reichsprecept* deserves to survive him
. . . at the lowest figure, rock-bottom minimum, we
(eternal France) would save three hundred billion a year . . .
and our patients would be a good deal better off! less hysterical, egotistical, and poisoned! . . . I know what I'm talking
about . . .

That's all very well! . . . but the *Milice?* . . . the barracks
come after the Danube dike . . . the enormous embankment

of stones, bricks, and trees that protects the road . . . I'll show you the *Milice*, three big Adrian barracks . . . and a little shack, the guardhouse! . . . the most imposing thing of all is the enormous tricolor flag at the top of its pole! . . . the *Milice* covered itself with glory on its retreat to Siegmaringen, through five or six armies of partisans . . . the retreat from Berg-op-Zoom to Biarritz wasn't the only one! . . . greatly overestimated! France has known plenty of retreats! every type and style! . . . in less than twenty years!

All right, I admit . . . my prescriptions may have been use-less . . . even the drugs from the *Reichsprecept* . . . proba-bly . . . *Apotek* Richter was out of everything! Not to mention his ill-will . . . As far as he was concerned the whole lot of us, *Miliciens*, bigshots from the Castle, embroidered generals, *"col-labos"* in rags, spying housemaids, and haughty ministresses, plus the sick and dying at the *Fidelis*, were abject filth . . . fit for the garbage pail! that was definitely Hans Richter's opinion! . . . same as the heroes of London, Brazzaville, and Mont-martre! "Hang the whole shooting match! . . ." When I abso-lutely wanted him to fill a prescription, I went there in person and made him find the stuff! . . . I didn't waste time . . . *"für den Sturmführer von Raumnitz!"* . . . no nonsense! he found it! . . . I took it . . . he believed me . . . or maybe he didn't . . . but he was afraid to take the chance . . . every time the same racket: *für den Sturmführer!* . . . straight to the solar plexus! . . . unfortunately, solar plexus or not, no morphine! or camphorated oil! and those were my prin-cipal weapons! . . . he really had nothing left! . . . he wasn't lying, I knew it because the young ladies told me . . . his assistants . . . young ladies are always glad to betray . . . all young ladies . . . for a little friendliness . . . take it from me . . . *marivaudage* is our amiable secret weapon! . . . America, Asia, Central Europe never had their Marivaux . . . look how heavy, how elephantine they are! those loutish manners! anyway, I knew through the young ladies and Mari-vaux that Richter was really out of morphine . . . I managed to get some anyway! responsible and devoted as I am! heart of gold! much thanks it got me! . . . morphine! . . . morphine!

. . . my head on the block! the worst stratagems! for the exercise of my art and the last resource of the dying! morphine! . . . morphine! . . . oh, not easily, I assure you! . . . through runners! . . . gangsters, the worst kind of pirates . . . between the Kraut and the Helvetian police! I'll tell you about them . . . and out of my own pocket . . . no two ways about it . . . I ruined myself in Germany on Swiss medicines alone . . . naturally I can't expect anything from de Gaulle, some indemnity or diploma, or from Monsieur Mollet . . . they agree with Herr Richter that it would have been a blessing if the Boches had hanged me . . . Achille has the same idea! . . . his motive is my magnificent works . . . the way they'll *boom!* the other publishers ditto! the least I could have done was to end in the big house, and even now they do everything in their power to make me turn on the gas . . . they see me wasting away . . . "how long do you think he'll last? . . . six months? . . . two years?" . . . They're worried . . . "Ah, he's out for publicity . . . well, why doesn't he get himself some? The coward! the stinker!" They see my book gushing up from the cellars when I'm dead! . . . happy days for Hachette!

Whoa there, Bessie! My mare's running away! . . . where am I taking you now? . . . I'm sidetracking you . . . I was coming away from Luther, then the *Milice* barracks . . . exactly! now it's time to get Hilda back to her mother . . . no more horsing around . . . she must be in the waiting room with her little friends . . . The times I'd chased them out of that buffet! . . . the lousy little delinquents! . . . lectured them that this was no place for them! nor the field kitchens! nor for the pregnant women either! . . . more frantic than all the rest! . . . food, mess kits, bread! "Make her come home! . . . spank her! Do anything you want, only make her come home! . . ." So you see, I was used to it. "Get the hell out of here!" It made them laugh to hear me curse and swear . . . they'd run away, they'd frisk and gallop . . . and two seconds later I'd find them in another huddle . . . *Lili Marleen*, men all around them, in the buffet or the doors of the artillery trains . . . they ran away again . . . I was the big bad wolf . . . I didn't

mind that . . . but her father? maybe he'd think I was in cahoots . . . that would be the end of our friendly . . . well,
almost friendly . . . relations . . . Oh, I've had lots of experience of these lousy rotten situations . . . these icebergs about
to capsize . . . God knows that the Germans are mean . . .
especially the *vons!* . . . unctuous, amiable, and ghastly!
. . . the station was part of my beat, the medical aspect, first-
aid station, refugees . . . naturally that took in the waiting
rooms and the prostitution! I was expected to keep things
under control! . . . with what equipment? . . . none! . . .
everything was missing! . . . sulphur for scabies . . . salvar-
san for syphilis . . . nothing! . . . condoms? . . . not a
trace! . . . a perpetual headache . . . and now Hilda! . . . I
felt like a damn fool! . . . I'm talking about the troops in transit, all those trains that come and go for so-called reasons . . .
there are no reasons . . . it's a tradition! . . . all countries at
war are the same, trains full of troops in transit, going somewhere . . . and coming back from somewhere else . . . the
dance of the switches! poetry! . . . flesh was made to be on
the move! the perpetual coming and going isn't just in the sky
. . . same on the rails, train after train . . . endless trains
. . . soldiers and soldiers . . . every branch of service, every
nation . . . and prisoners . . . barefoot, their feet hanging
out . . . sitting in the doors . . . hungry too! always hungry!
and horny! . . . and singing *Lili Marleen!* . . . Montene-
grins, Czechoslovakians, Vlasoff's army, Balto-Finns, soldiers of
the European ragout! . . . of twenty-seven armies . . . don't
let them stay in one place! let them sing! bump! travel! and
armored trains, cannon the size of a house, bristling giants!
. . . dinosaur cannon with two, three locomotives apiece . . .
And always more trains, one after the other . . . engineers,
artillery . . . and still more . . . whole armies! with their
hairy, bare feet sticking out! . . . yelling, demanding girls!
. . . they can't stand it any more! . . . it's coming up too
hard! . . . which gives you an idea of the traffic: upstairs the
Armadas, London-Munich-Vienna . . . downstairs the troop
and supply trains, armed meat, hardware, Frankfort, Saxony,
Italy via the Brenner . . . it would have been child's play for

them, one bomb, to blow up the whole station! . . . marma-
lade! . . . blow the whole mess to pieces! . . . no! . . . it
had to go on! the worst part of it was that all these trains stayed
there switching and shunting . . . right in the station! for
hours! . . . and whole nights! . . . under the sheds . . .
they'd pull out . . . and come back! the line was cut! . . .
the switches demolished! . . . had to start all over again!
more soldiers around the piano! . . . my unmarried mothers
on other laps! . . . the party went right on! the same bedlam
as at the *Löwen* on our landing, outside the crapper, but here
everybody was in uniform and barefoot . . . no time to put
shoes on, too much of a hurry to get out of those cars and kiss
my big-bellied beauties and join the chorus! and better things
to eat than our kohlrabi! . . . the joy of my little scuppers! big
mess kits full of sausage and potatoes! . . . real fat, real butter, all you could eat . . . ah, those field kitchens!

Every station in the world is like that when troop trains are
stalled . . . life on earth must have started in a railroad station
. . . with stalled troop trains . . . the girls come running
. . . of course with my Hilda bitch it was only her feverish
puberty, no need of mess kits . . . healthy teenagers . . . the
sex appeal of the waiting rooms! . . . the perverse joy of seeing so many males pouring in at once, all sweaty, hairy, stinking . . . by the carload! . . . and every last one of them with
a hard-on yelling *lieb! lieb!* . . . the miracle was that Hilda
and her gang of teasers weren't nabbed, stripped, and worse by
the S.A. guards! . . . the station police in charge of the platforms . . . all they knew how to do was swing rifle butts and
billies! big bruisers! twice a day they crumpled everybody in
sight . . . When things got out of hand . . . disorder around
the kitchens or around the piano, so many people on the tracks
that the trains couldn't pull out . . . they were the ones who
restored order . . . with their clubs! . . . any back talk? *ping*
with their Mausers! . . . portable cannons! quick medicine!
When Hilda and her little friends saw the S.A. . . . they cut
and ran . . . like does in the forest! . . . and came popping
out of the next tunnel! . . . I'll say this much for Hilda, in
different times she'd have been married . . . I know . . . she

was only sixteen . . . but all the same . . . I'm speaking as a medical man . . . suppose I were handing out marks from one to twenty . . . even looking hard, you won't find one first-rate girl in a thousand! I mean it! . . . vitality, muscles, lungs, nerves, charm . . . knees, ankles, thighs, grace! . . . I'm difficult, I admit it . . . the tastes of a Grand Duke, an Emir, a breeder of thoroughbreds! . . . okay! we all have our little weaknesses! . . . I wasn't always what I am, a poor crippled, persecuted wreck . . . But I can tell you this . . . the anemic, rachitic, cellulitic . . . ageless and soulless monsters men run after! . . . heavenly day! . . . with cocks aflame, ah yes, my dear! . . . are enough to make the most priapic gibbons cut their balls off with neurasthenic disgust! . . . definitely! . . . Ah, but getting back to Hilda Raumnitz, let's give her a mark . . . conservatively, she'd have rated sixteen out of twenty in our feminine dog show . . . I agree with Poincaré: "If you can't measure a natural phenomenon, it doesn't exist . . ." The same with ladies and their charms, most won't get four out of twenty . . . maximum . . . including beauty-prize winners . . . the esthetic mean . . . ten out of twenty . . . is rare! The knees, the ankles, the tits on them! . . . cushions of fat and flabby meat, slapped on to a few little bones at the last minute! . . . lopsided! . . . Hilda, the little bitch, was one of Nature's surprises . . . absolutely no defects! . . . a well-turned minx, full of spunk! . . . perfect? . . . well anyway sixteen out of twenty! . . . I'm speaking of all this as a veterinarian, a racist so to speak . . . the socio-Proustian terminology of the drawing rooms could easily turn me into a murderer more or less . . . I'm only handing out marks . . . nothing else . . . "Hike up your skirts! Now let's see? What mark?" . . . call it horticulture . . . I don't want to offend you: a flower! Let's try to appraise this flower! . . . the petals! the stem! and give it a mark! We wouldn't want to let Poincaré down! . . . Hilda was also remarkably gifted in bitchery (a secondary feminine characteristic)! . . . ash-blond hair . . . not phony ash-blond . . . the real thing . . . hanging down to her heels! . . . really a beautiful Boche animal . . . and fine knees, fine ankles . . . all very rare . . . rounded thighs,

tight muscular buttocks . . . face not exactly friendly-affec-
tionate . . . more like a Dürer, like her father . . . anyway
not the supercharged servant-girl type, beaming as she sells her
butter and eggs . . . that plunges you into a bastard cock-
softening gloom . . . her father, the Major, must have been
very good-looking . . . Aisha, her mother, was a blowsy oda-
lisque . . . but she had that certain charm . . . I'm very
much of a racist, I'm suspicious . . . and the future will bear
me out . . . of extravagant crossbreeds . . . but Hilda, I've
got to admit, had turned out all right! . . . But how was I
going to get that damn kid back to the *Löwen*? . . . I could
see the situation was serious! . . . she and her playful friends!
. . . elfin delinquents! the whole station was full of them!
. . . I could have asked for reinforcements, the military police! . . . I didn't like to . . . I was thinking of my pregnant
women around the piano and all over the benches . . . they
were only eating, they didn't give a damn about the rest! . . .
six months gone! eight months gone! . . . double and triple
appetites! sausages, *bier,* goulash! I had none to offer them
. . . The M.P.'s would knock them cold! Women from every
corner of France, every province! . . . Why had they left?
. . . Why had they come to Siegmaringen? . . . informers,
village stoolpigeons? . . . small-town whores? or simply factory girls, for the trip? . . . or their men in the L.V.F.? . . .
or engaged to Boches? . . . or post office drudges? Practically
all of them had provincial accents . . . North, Massif-Central,
Southwest . . . no use asking them questions, they always lied
. . . only one truth: their appetite . . . it wasn't the few
extra noodles I could get them or the kohlrabi dishwater twice
a week that would fill them up! all this bread and goulash was
their Providence! . . . I wasn't going to get them arrested
. . . Hell, no! . . . I had other things to worry about . . .
the scabies, crabs, fleas, lice, and clap they were all passing
back and forth! merrily merrily! the station was made to order!
. . . In the end I expected to see some new germ crop up
. . . a real epidemic . . . some cockeyed little treponema
that would thrive in disinfectants! there are times when everything becomes possible! . . . I knew my pregnant women! two

in a bed, thirty or forty to a dormitory, they exchanged everything they had . . . their street was at the upper end of town,
Schlachtgasse, the former School of Agriculture . . . There
again it was my job, my duty to check up . . . on the general
state of the ladies' health . . . see if the stinkers were scratching all right . . . I felt pretty silly without sulphur, without
mercury, without mess kits! . . . especially the mess kits! nothing but words! . . . I'd have liked to see Hamlet philosophize
those pregnant women! *To eat or not to eat!* . . . but to tell
the truth, I didn't often find them in, hardly ever! . . . in a
way I thanked heaven for the tropism of the station! . . . the
attraction of the army chow! . . . the attraction of the piano
too . . . Happy in the laps of the chorus . . . and *Lili Marleen!* three, four pregnant women to a man in positions that
weren't the least bit chaste! learning the best German . . .
from *Lili Marleen!* . . . all those soldiers had good voices
. . . not a false note . . . choruses in three, four voices . . .
the whole buffet and the platforms and the field kitchens . . .
"painless childbirth" . . . don't give them anything to eat except a mess kitful during delivery! my patients would gladly
have had their babies in the station! . . . In their School of
Agriculture I had nothing to offer but noodles! . . . neither
did Brinon! . . . nor Raumnitz! . . . nor Pétain! . . . you'll
never see soldiers, Kraut, Slovak, Franzose, Russian, Japanese,
or Hottentot, refuse a bowl of soup . . . that's the great thing
about armies! . . . as long as there were real casernes, you
could live off the guardroom . . . the minute reveille sounded,
you had all you needed at the door . . . the ragged and needy
lined up . . . that's gone and nothing to take its place . . .
those really fine customs . . . everything goes, and nothing to
take its place . . . nowadays hypocrisy rules . . . they send
the poor to eat paper, blanks, and rubber stamps . . . and
keep moving! more and more of a hurry! tanks! . . . *Nacht-
Nebel* kettles . . .

My chorus boys and unmarried mothers, pregnant women
and soldiers of every branch, all tenderly enlaced . . . the
concerts they treated me to! footsloggers and floozies, engineers
and Comitadjis . . . you'll never hear an ensemble like that

again! . . . you should have seen that buffet, perfect harmony!
and that piano! not a single discordant note! Maxim's and the
Folies-Bergère are *ersatz* by comparison, ham exhibitionism!
two bits a spin! centenarian Venuses! bewigged Romeos, croak-
ing Carusos . . . pitiful . . . nothing compared to what went
on in my buffet . . . twenty, thirty trains a day! . . . all Europe in uniform and turgescent . . . and the prisoners! . . .
from the East, the West, the North . . . Swiss border . . .
Bavaria . . . the Balkans . . .

To tell the truth, a continent without war is bored . . . as
soon as the bugles start up, it's a holiday! . . . total vacation!
and the blood lust! . . . and those endless trips! . . . armies
always on the move! . . . mixing and mingling and traveling
some more! until they disintegrate . . . convoys, locomotives, *panzer* trains! . . . armored cars, "male munitions,"
more and more! you can see that Hilda and her friends had
something to wag their tails about! . . . shipment after shipment of "bare feet" . . . fresh meat! . . . I forgot to tell you
about the horde of poor "female workers" . . . 200,000 French
women in Germany . . . flowing back from Berlin, from all
over, from every factory in the country . . . to Siegmaringen! . . . for Pétain to save them! . . . also to eat, naturally!
. . . the second they pulled in to the station, they jumped out
of the windows . . . you can figure the number of hungry
people around the kitchens! the crowd! worse than our lobby in
the *Löwen,* worse than the crapper! . . . they peed right on
the benches . . . and in the middle of the singing and on top
of the pianist! . . . "constraint kills happiness." I've never seen
a musical instrument so flooded as that station piano! . . . and
I've seen the pianos of London, mounted on handcarts . . .
they were fountains of urine too . . .

Oh, but something else . . . I forgot! . . . that shipment!
. . . three trains all jammed with stenographers, office man-
agers, generals in civvies . . . three trains full of the Margotton Mission . . . They kept pulling out and coming back!
bound for Constance . . . they'd get as far as the switch! a
whistle! here we go! and back again! . . . another siding! . . .
forbidden to leave the train! . . . they run for it! barefoot

too! . . . they're all over the place! . . . big crevices in their
feet! for two months they'd been zigzagging around Germany
. . . from bombed roadbeds to wrecked culverts! . . . nobody wanted them anywhere! even raggeder than we were!
their eyes popping out still further from what they'd seen and
gone through! ten times they'd caught fire! . . . they didn't remember in which zigzag . . . under what tunnel . . . in what
province . . . put their train back on the rails themselves . . .
mended the roadbed themselves! . . . nobody to help them!
. . . to them Siegmaringen was Lourdes! . . . Pétain,
Mecca! Miracle Terminus! their eyes bugged even worse! and
in every door . . . twenty, thirty faces! . . . they expected
Pétain in person . . . to serve them in person . . . the menu
that would make up for their sufferings! . . . pheasant, champagne, maraschino ice . . . cigars as big as bananas! . . . But
when they saw neither Pétain nor banquet, the lay of the land
and no Santa Claus, they flung themselves on the army loaves!
. . . the field kitchen and the mess kits . . . in voracious res-
ignation! . . . oh, they didn't want to get back in, to ride in a
train again! Straight into the melee, all over the platforms and
the buffet, to see who could cadge the most mess kits . . . and
the biggest! . . . and all in chorus . . . who could piss fur-
thest . . . and steadiest! pure joy! directors, stenographers,
and generals! . . . replete, belching, singing! . . . *Lili Marleen* . . . the song that really created a furor through all the
cyclones and destructions of nations . . . all the armies on
both sides . . . you can't deny it! you'll tell me that fifteen,
twenty songs were more rhythmic, dirtier! sure! . . . but on
both sides? . . . in Buchenwald, Key West and Saint-Malo!
. . . I've got you there! the world refrain! Incidentally those
men from Central Europe practically always had good voices
. . . Slovenians, Bulgaro-Czechs, Polacks . . . songs in three,
five voices! . . . same for the piano, even if it was the complete urinal . . . pretty near every time there were three, four
pianists ready . . . and not bad thumpers! . . . I know what
I'm talking about . . . and plain, simple boys . . . peasants,
common laborers . . . we in France, our art is the word, applesauce and bull shit . . . the heart isn't in it! . . . a singer
is kind of embarrassed, unhappy at being forced . . .

Hell, and my story! . . . I'm boring you again! . . . I'm
forgetting my pregnant women and my female workers from
the trains, and the S.A. order squad . . . and the Margotton
Mission! . . . These last were French all right! To the hilt!
The way they bitched that the Marshal wasn't there to meet
them! and hadn't even sent anybody! They were going to write
him a letter! and right away! But first to the kitchens! *primum!*
primum! . . . if France perishes, it won't be from Z . . . Q
. . . or H-bombs! . . . it will be from *primum,* fill your belly!
All the Conquerors will have to do is set up as many field kitchens as square yards on the Place de la Concorde, and wine
unlimited . . . the French will rally . . . they'll fall in love!
they'll surrender with enthusiasm . . . you won't know where
to put them!

Their train was whistling for the Margotton travelers to
come back and get in! . . . that they were shoving off! . . .
waste of time! . . . they lay down right on the tracks! under
the cars! let the train run them over! . . . sabotage! she
leaves? she stays? . . . the S.A. bellowing: *los! los!* the train
should pull out anyway! the engine drivers hesitate . . . the
grandmothers on the rails! . . . I haven't told you about those
old women, another sect . . . the "wards" of our town hall
. . . yes, yes! ours! the French town hall! This welfare bureau
had one function . . . to send them somewhere else to eat!
anywhere! the other end of Germany! . . . any train! . . . get
rid of them! Haphazard! . . . I saw the mayor with his big
map on the wall, all Germany, picking a destination for them,
any destination! . . . "Here . . . your billeting order!" . . .
Old women with sons someplace . . . L.V.F., Poland, Silesia,
Kriegsmarine . . . wherever they were sent, they were thrown
out! . . . from bombs to sidings they came back . . . you saw
them at the station . . . dressed like Boche troopers, in rags
taken off corpses . . . anything they found! . . . they'd already run away from France . . . refugees from Drôme,
Lozère, Guyenne . . . their houses had been burned and
looted clean! . . . I know from my own experience . . . they
came back to Pétain every time! . . . for ladies of a certain
age Pétain was France . . . my mother too, she died like that,
Pétain was France . . . they always came back on foot, bare-

foot, from some one-horse *Dorf* in Brandenburg, Saxony, Hanover, dressed like soldiers! . . . oh, they didn't want to have anything to do with our Town Hall! . . . No dice! "Hurry, hurry! Take the first train, grandma! Here's your ticket!" That had happened to them four times! . . . ten times! . . .

If they'd died en route, blown to pieces, nobody would have known . . . hell, no. How many died? . . . the ones who came back, the experienced grandmothers didn't want any more tickets . . . they just wanted to stay in the station! faithful to Pétain! And lie down on the tracks! With the ladies of the Mission! . . . the time had come to resist all threats, clubs and doubletalk . . . you had to laugh the way they got their way at the kitchens . . . nobody could take their place! . . . one mess kit . . . another . . . As soon as they saw me in the distance, they yelled for me to hurry . . . to examine them . . . tongue, liver, blood pressure . . . it was like being back in Clichy . . . and the heartburn! . . . I had to make them lie down and give them a good going-over . . . feel their stomachs, the exact spot! that heartburn! . . . at home in Voulzanon (Lot), Dr. Chemouin (whom I was expected to know) had prescribed a certain powder . . . they didn't remember what it was called . . . but it was really marvelous! . . . I was supposed to know that too . . .

"Oh yes, yes, Madame! I'll bring you some! Stay right where you are!"

I gave at least twenty consultations . . . on benches . . . on the roadbed . . . in the buffet . . . there it was harder, too much singing! . . . the old women weren't my only patients, soldiers and civilians too! . . . the piano never stopped . . . or *Lili Marleen* . . . or the trains outside . . . or in the air the roaring merry-go-round of Fortresses . . . London-Munich . . . Dresden . . . this worry about the Sky falling is a lot of Gallic affectation! . . . a time comes when nobody gives a damn! . . . the mess kit is God! . . . fuck the Sky! grandmothers in uniform! my pregnant women, too! . . . they looked cute! . . . the boots they devised, bundles of newspaper, scraps of felt tied around with strings and straw . . . they could stay outdoors for hours, even in the rain! the prisoners' specialty was gaiters! made out of old tires . . . In Cameroon I'd seen whole populations in shoes made out of tires . . . People get used to anything . . . all over the world . . . here . . . and there . . . I've seen people getting along fine without shoes . . . After the H . . . V . . . and Z-bomb you'll see what our geniuses can do! . . . the combined talents of Manhattan and Moscow! . . . the bomb is only a moment of anger, shoes are a permanent problem! My problem, though, was getting the Raumnitz kid home . . . I had to watch my step with her father! . . . it was all very perilous . . . The sky, never mind, I was used to that! . . . those squadrons practically on top of the station and the Castle . . . one move, one little flip of the finger, they could have turned us into a bonfire . . . us and the bridge and all the troop trains! . . . one bomb! . . . all the ammunition would have exploded! . . . we'd seen Ulm! . . . Ulm had taken them fifteen minutes! . . . but right then I wasn't worried about grand strategy, I was worried about getting Hilda back to her father! I'd called her twenty times! Hilda! I could keep on calling! better take the bull by the horns: the S.A.! . . . Everybody out on the road! clear the platforms, the buffet, the tracks! Then we'd see! But right away they start yelling! protesting! "S.A., get everybody out of here!" I've told you about the S.A. . . . all muscle, big hulking bruisers, and mean, faces like gorillas . . . and those "pocket-cannon" Mausers!

"*Franzose? Franzose?*" they ask me.

"*Nein . . . nein!* Obersturmführer von Raumnitz."

I told them not to shillyshally . . . don't worry, they didn't . . . first the buffet! "*Raus! raus!*" the pregnant lap-sitting women and their feeler-uppers! "*Raus! raus!*" . . . and the benchloads of tender interminglings! . . . they move along, but they curse and threaten! . . . in Hungarian . . . Bulgarian . . . and *Plattdeutsch!* . . . every branch of service . . . infantry . . . engineers, and the *Organisation Todt* . . . and the Yugoslavian prisoners . . . pissed-off! especially the refugee girls . . . with their legs in the air! . . . the Lithuanians, very blond, white . . . almost like silver! . . . I remember them well . . . they'd learned all the choruses of the troops

and railroad stations . . . in three, four voices! *la! la!* G-sharp!
it was one big tangle! and the refugees from Strasbourg! *Lili
Marleen!* Christ Almighty! the piano and the singing boost the
morale! the pissing! and the *Bier!* and the friendly laps! and the
big tits! . . . *la! la!* G-sharp and the Margotton Mission, stenographers and solemn directors meeting in doorways, swiping
bread and sausages from each other! kittenish! and the monocles! I could see trouble ahead! . . . the grandmothers lying
on the tracks, pretending not to know what was going on . . .
a hell of a mess and anyway you look at it it was my fault! for
alerting the S.A. I shouldn't have said anything! now it was a
pitched battle! clouts and haymakers! who was going to evacuate that buffet? . . . the S.A.? the girls? the soldiery? Ticklers
and benders! and how about the piano? . . . and the field
kitchen? . . . who was going to come out on top? . . . I could
see the shock coming, a blood bath! . . . inevitable! . . .
Marleen or not! . . . all I cared about was for Hilda to go
home! her father! . . . if his daughter was manhandled, I'd
never hear the end of it! . . . hell, was I to blame? . . . Brinon wouldn't put in a word for me, or Pétain . . . or Bucart or
Sabiani or anybody else! . . . It's my face . . . I'm always responsible! for everything! . . . it gives everybody a kick what
a sap I am! whatever happens, I catch it, everything falls on
me! a godsend! and everybody else gets off! . . . good deal,
this Ferdinand! . . . Oberführer von Raumnitz was really a
Boche to watch out for! I knew him like a book! I saw him two
three times a day . . .

Well anyway, the S.A. cleared the buffet and the platforms!
no more *Marleen!* . . . no more piano! . . . Arm in arm . . .
bureaucrats . . . grandmothers and soldiers . . . okay, if
they couldn't be left in peace . . . so long! they'd take their
party to town! . . . and the Kraut housewives from the village! who had only come to watch! . . . arm in arm . . . I
consoled myself . . . it's all right! I'd catch Hilda and her
friends! . . . the S.A. were doing all right . . . if nothing had
gone wrong! but all of sudden *bzing!* I said to myself: they've
fired! trouble, trouble! . . . it was the S.A., twelve of them,
who were separating the men from the women! . . . cutting

their party in half! you get the picture! sending the men back to
the station and the women into town! . . . well, naturally
smash! bang! the mess kits begin to fly! Ferdinand, I said to
myself, your goose is cooked! . . . I'd kept out of it . . . two
more shots! and complete silence! Who had fired? . . . oh, I
hadn't far to look . . . a Kraut on the ground! . . . I go over
. . . a whole crowd around him . . . one of the S.A. men
had fired . . . this guy had had it! . . . blood gushing from
the bullet hole in his back . . . in pulsations . . . and out of
his mouth, *glug glug* . . . a Kraut from the armored train . . .
they had camouflage uniforms . . . his chameleon skin was
soaked red . . . his blood pouring all over the street . . .
never knew what hit him! . . . shot in the back! . . . I go
up, feel his pulse, I auscultate . . . nothing! all over! Okay,
may as well go back . . . sure, but now they were talking
again! yapping all around us! . . . and not gently! In their
opinion the S.A. were the world's worst brutes! and this was the
end! worse cannibals than the Senegalese in Strasbourg! and a
damn good thing they were coming . . . the Senegalese from
Strasbourg and the Fifis from Vercors! They'd welcome them
with open arms! . . . they knew them, they'd had dealings
with them, they'd passed through their partisan country! And
they could compare! Hurrah for the Fifis! That's what the
crowd was yelling! Hurrah for the Russians! All I knew was
that the housewives, the pregnant women, and the soldiers had
gone mad . . . they were going to rush the S.A.! they were
going to charge! this time there'd be a massacre! not just one
victim! Well, I can tell you . . . absolutely historical . . . that
Laval saved the day! If he hadn't come along, the bullets
would have flown! . . . but luckily he was just going for a
stroll . . . with his wife! . . . never the same time as Pétain!
. . . along the Danube too, but the other bank . . . so he'd
come down toward the station . . . luckily! If not for Laval,
no survivors! He comes over . . . I can still see him . . . he
sees me, he sees the lay of the land . . .

"Is it all over, Doctor?"

"Yes, Monsieur le Président . . ."

He knew about these things, he'd had the same in Versailles, nothing bogus, for real, X-rays . . . the bullet still gave him pain . . . he was a good man . . . he hated violence, not for himself like me . . . my abjectness in that respect is really discouraging . . . I, who had called him every known name including Jew, and he knew it and he really had it in for me for calling him a kike far and wide, I can speak objectively . . . Laval was the born conciliator . . . and a patriot! and a pacifist! . . . I tend to see butchers all around me . . . but not him! No! No! . . . I'd been going to see him for months up on his floor of the Castle, he told me some wonderful stories about Roosevelt and Churchill and the Intelligence Service . . . What Laval wanted . . . he had no use for Hitler . . . was a hundred years of peace . . . well, if peace was what he wanted, he'd come at the right time . . . this Kraut lying there! . . . I filled him in . . .

"Monsieur le Président! You've got to do something! The S.A. are out of control! They're going to kill everybody!"

That was God's truth. The twelve of them were standing there . . . with their mausers aimed at us! First Laval wants to see for himself, he goes over to the dead man, under the eyes of the S.A. . . . he bends down, he takes off his hat, he salutes . . . the others around him salute, too . . . the crowd . . . the women cross themselves, the S.A. stand at attention.

"Is it all over, Doctor?"

"Yes, Monsieur le Président!"

Then he addressed the crowd.

"All right! Now go home! All of you! Follow the Doctor!"

He turns to me: "You're going back to the *Löwen*, Doctor?"

"Yes, Monsieur le Président! . . . and the ladies to their dormitory in the School of Agriculture! . . ."

"You'll escort them?"

"Yes, Monsieur le Président . . . and Hilda, the young lady there, I'm taking her back to her father."

"Who's her father?"

"Major von Raumnitz . . ."

"Von Raumnitz . . . good! good! . . ."

Seeing Laval and his wife talking friendly with everybody, not the least bit proud, cooled the crowd off! . . . they stopped looking at the killers . . . and the dead man! Laval and his wife were the attraction now . . . They took the opportunity to question him . . . would it be over soon? . . . were the Germans going to win? or lose? . . . he must know! . . . he must know everything! . . . but they didn't leave him time to answer . . . they answered for him! . . . it was the Forum around Laval . . . the Stock Exchange! around Laval and Madame! Everybody shouting! Everybody was right! He hadn't understood this! He hadn't understood that! He should admit! Why didn't he admit? Laval was stubborn too! man of the last word! . . . Chamber! Forum! Firing Squad! . . . the voters couldn't faze him! . . . and the best part of it for me was that all these orators . . . the unmarried mothers and Laval and Madame . . . were going back up to the *Löwen* . . . that nobody was going back to the station . . . that much gained! . . . they kept after Laval, they grabbed him by the sleeves, they latched on . . . he should admit he'd been wrong! they knew everything! all the ins and outs! . . . Laval who'd been a lawyer . . . and Premier . . . who'd always been right! he found his masters, he was forced to listen to these people who were tugging at his sleeves, stepping on his feet ten at a time! . . . forcing him to pay serious attention! nothing like Aubervilliers or the Chamber!

The only thing that interested me was that they were coming away from the station.

Laval, who thought he was the great orator, hadn't found one contradictor . . . he'd found a hundred . . . unmarried mothers . . . housewives . . . female workers and refugees from Strasbourg . . . Lozère . . . and Deux-Sèvres . . . who knew a damn sight more than he did . . . and he should just listen! . . . if this had been in the Chamber, he'd have been voted down! So help me, I saw Laval coming back from the station under a barrage of advice . . . all he could say was: "Yes . . . yes . . ." from the station to the *Löwen* . . . snowed under by the talk . . . no violence! . . . no blows! only political passion and solid arguments! as long as they're headed for town is the way I looked at it! and don't change their minds! and start in the other direction! . . . but that was

Laval's genius! . . . he maneuvered them with "yes . . . yes
. . . yes" . . . he led the arguers . . . they wanted him to go
on listening! . . . he really saved the day! . . . not only for
me, for everybody else in the station, getting them out of there!
. . . the S.A. were in position . . . skin of our teeth if they
didn't fire . . . lay everybody out! it was Laval's doing if they
didn't fire! letting them all shout at him, fasten onto his cuffs!
pretending to be floored by their arguments until they were all
back at the *Löwen,* the *Stam,* the *Bier* and the crapper . . .
man, did they run for the tables! more *Stams!* more mess kits!
men and women! Herr Frucht blocked the door, he wouldn't
let the pregnant women in, they should go and eat where they
belonged! Up on the *Schlachtgasse!* another rebellion! negotia-
tions! Finally they agreed to evacuate, to clear out of the doorway with a kilo of synthetic honey apiece! . . . pregnant
women go for sweets! . . . anyway the crowd broke up . . .
they left Laval flat . . . Laval and his wife . . . he just had
time to say to me:

"Doctor, you'll come and see me, won't you?"

They went back home to the Castle . . . me, Hilda and her
playmates, and Lili . . . we went straight to Raumnitz's . . .
Aisha was waiting for us . . .

"The Major has gone out . . . with his dogs . . . he's at the
station . . ."

Not a word about my bringing her daughter home . . . not
a word to her either . . . a very unfriendly reception for my
money . . . but von Raumnitz at the station! . . . investigat-
ing the incident no doubt . . . he knew what had happened
. . . it was his job to know right away . . . to know everything! especially after the business in the Bois de Vincennes
. . . the mutiny . . . I'll tell you about it.

A time finally comes when this perpetual roaring, fire-spitting merry-go-round, the rat-tat-tatting of the Fortresses on the rooftops . . . all that idiotic grumbling thunder . . . gets you down . . . that's all there is to it! . . . it gives you the blues . . . the deep dumps . . . people are supposed to get neurasthenic for lack of distraction . . . under the R.A.F. merry-go-round you don't have a moment to think! . . . siren! . . . whistles! . . . and more machine-gun bullets! . . . another wave of Mosquitoes! . . . all that traffic from up above the clouds . . . looping-the-loop! . . . all the way down to the road . . . twisting and turning and coming back! . . . and never stopping . . . makes you want to go home . . . but you haven't got a home . . . ah, *not to be! be!* you're cornered by destiny . . . caught in a vise! . . . you're not through laughing . . . floundering and protesting! . . . you don't know where you're at . . . *not to be*, hell! you're really cooked! well anyway, one way or another . . . forced laughter . . . out of the wrong side of my face! I'll get on with my story . . . if I can . . . As far as I'm concerned, I don't have to tell you . . . my age . . . the biggest crime! . . . I'd much sooner be forgotten, croak in my corner, than knock myself out telling you about people, lunatics, women, and more or less . . . mostly less . . . credible happenings . . . the business with *La Publique* was enough, it seems to me . . . why, for your benefit, should I go roaming around those practically unmentionable regions . . . this place . . . that place . . . why? . . . but if you're caught in the vise . . . cornered by destiny . . . it's not so easy to wriggle out! . . .

All in all! . . . no bones . . . I'd better tell you things exactly as they were! . . . of course the malignant public will find a way to profane it all . . . screw it all up . . . stuff it with horrible lies! . . . in the end I'll look like a very shady character . . . even to myself! . . . an ectoplasmic gossip . . . a ghost come back from one place or another who doesn't even know what attitude to take . . . what words to say! When fate grabs hold of you, all you can do is confess . . . I see such people . . . people in my own situation, completely bewildered . . . balled up and stammering! . . . and they boast, so help me! sad sacks! all tied up in knots! . . . when you're caught in the vise . . . when you've been humiliated to the bone . . . to the marrow . . . there's nothing to do but confess . . . and don't be slow about it! your time is really counted! "Build at my age!" . . . Tell stories! hell! the young are all pimply idiotic feebleminded droolers . . . okay! . . . the "Incarnators of Youth!" Sure! Because they're not "cooked" . . . the old? oozing senility, full of inconceivable hatred and horror for everything that happens! and is going to happen! . . . because they're too cooked and worn out! . . . green wormy camemberts, running and stinking, put'em in the frigidaire quick! . . . in the pantry! in the boneyard! . . . consequently you haven't much chance of placing your poor old corny effects with this one and that one . . . old fogeys? . . . teenagers? . . . Bile . . . camomile . . . poison . . . marshmallow . . . nobody wants it . . . nobody . . . no place! What I'm doing . . . it's the circumstances . . . my obligations . . . the animals and Lili . . .

Achille? . . . Gertrut? . . . who cares? . . . both the same rope! . . . and let'em dangle! . . . and their cliques! . . . but first my money! . . . which one? . . . what do I care! . . . just don't let them get away without paying me! . . . after that? . . . hell! . . . higher! . . . shorter! . . . I'll go have a look at their tongues! . . . which is thicker! . . . which hangs out further! . . . lazy no-good bastards! . . . but don't let them die without forking over! . . . nobody ever gave up the soul . . . stinkers like that never had any souls . . . with pending debts . . .

My imprecations don't advance my beautiful book very much! my little fusses and troubles! and you don't give a shit either! I can say that again . . . so let's get back to the *Löwen* . . . I left you on the landing . . . Madame Aisha von Raumnitz . . . I'd brought back her daughter, the young and beautiful Hilda . . . it may come as a surprise to you . . . but I'm speaking as a clinician, embryologist, and racist . . . that this marriage of such an out-and-out nobleman, a Dürer in build and nature, and this Aisha, all Trebizond . . . Beirut! . . . sinuous, dark, lascivious, bovine . . . no Dürer about her! . . . should have produced so beautiful a child! . . . oh, cross-breeding is full of peril . . . risks . . . little Hilda was part exotic bitch . . . Beirut . . . Trebizond . . . but that mop of ash-blond hair! . . . light blue eyes, fairies of the north . . . Major von Raumnitz had had to marry her . . . so it seems . . . he had dishonored her, so to speak, somewhere . . . in Beirut . . . or Trebizond . . . he was on a mission in those parts . . . the ports of the Levant are perilous for captains "on mission" . . . Aisha had succumbed . . . so it seems . . . so it seems . . . If he hadn't married her and brought her back to Germany with him, she would have gone the way of fate and custom! . . . no question! those eunuch executioners in the employ of the Jealous Males of the Near East . . . the harems didn't vote in those days . . . it was a narrow squeak for Aisha! . . . This case wasn't so very unusual, the seduced Levantine married by a European nobleman the day before she was supposed to be hanged . . . in Baden-Baden, and later on the way across Germany, we'd run into a lot of Near Eastern women of the Aisha type, Sino-Armenian, Mongolo-Smyrnan, who'd become Landgravins . . . or Countesses . . . military attachés aren't only terrible skirt chasers . . . difficulties make them feverish! . . . they overturn Koran, Harems, Castes, and Cloisters! . . . the Devil in uniform! . . . they smash everything!

To give you an idea of the consequences . . . at my mother's on the rue Marsolier, there were these characters that came to see me, offering me enormous sums, real fortunes, if only I'd show a little more understanding for the intentions, the workings, the advantages, the profound motivations of the New Europe! . . . those tempters who came to see me at my mother's were also hybrids like Aisha, products of Prusso-Armenian unions . . . shady characters! . . . same as our own diabolical hybrids, ready for anything, Laval, Mendès . . . or their cousin: Nasser! . . . I questioned them, as long as I had them handy . . . oh, those messengers weren't any run-of-the-mill mongrels! and they didn't offend the eye! I'm speaking as an embryologist . . . really A-1 specimens, morally and physically . . . Colonels, and very well situated . . . operetta colonels! . . . Asiatic black hair . . . ebony cowlick like Laval . . . swarthy skin like Laval . . . alert, intelligent hybrids, and anxious, too . . . they had good reason to be anxious, those alert hybrid colonels . . . the look in their eyes . . . like Laval, but younger . . . they could perfectly well have been deputies . . . in Vitry or Trebizond . . . anywhere . . . taken Laval's place in Aubervilliers . . . or Nasser's in Cairo . . . If hybrids frighten me, I've got my reasons . . . or taken the place of Trotsky in Moscow! . . . these anxious hybrids are rootless and ready! . . . taken the place of Perón or Franco! . . . great future ahead of them! Spears in London, for instance! . . . and Mendès-France over here! . . . they get what they want! Disraeli . . . Latzareff . . . Raynaud . . . Hitler, semi-everything, image of Brandenburg, bastard Caesar, semi-painter, semi-ham actor, credulous stupid sly, semi-queen, and champion bungler! . . . he had his little stroke of genius, collecting all the hybrids, surrounding himself with them, appointing them this and that . . . colonel . . . general, minister and privy-councillor! with the result that you ran into a lot of swarthy skins where you least expected them . . .

No, you didn't ask me for all these details . . . I know . . . I should get back to my story . . . I only wanted you to understand that von Raumnitz wasn't so much of a racist! his marriage proves it! . . . but the consequences! . . . given to understand that he'd married wrong! . . . greaser! . . . after the trouble in Paris he'd turned into a vicious bastard! change of heart! . . . a total one hundred percent Boche! . . . you could expect anything! . . . yes, yes, the consequences! . . .

Hell! . . . where's my head? . . . the outrage was in Vincennes, not Paris! he and Madame occupied a very large, very rich house belonging to a very rich Jew who was traveling for his health . . . a sumptuous mansion on the edge of the Bois, crammed full of lacquered furniture and knick-knacks from China . . . Palace-museum-department store . . . the Raumnitzes were really doing all right! . . . the occupation could last a century! . . . but bingo! the "night of the Wehrmacht!" . . . Raumnitz was asleep, Madame, too . . . you've heard about it? . . . when the mutinous soldiers climbed over the wall . . . they pulled von Raumnitz out of bed and spanked him! . . . *biml! bam!* . . . tied! ten soldiers! . . . his ass all red! . . . I'm only telling you what everybody knows about, the Stupnagel plot . . . "operation balcony-spanking" . . . the best part of it was that Hermann von Raumnitz just happened to be the big boss *Oberbefehlssupercop* of the northern and eastern suburbs and Joinville! . . . and the whole Bois! . . . and Saint-Mandé! and the Marne! so you can imagine that getting him out of the sack like that and his wife too and spanking them! their asses all purple! . . . stuck in his craw . . . the kind of outrage he wasn't ever going to forgive! besides, he'd been demoted . . . broken to major! . . . you can imagine if he was waiting for us . . . the 1,142 . . . under his absolute boot! . . . what a sweet humor he was in! . . . wise guys! what were we cooking up?

I've shown you the station with all its bawling and singing . . . and the way nobody stopped at anything! . . . not even downstairs in the kitchen . . . pissing in the *Stam!* . . . it had been known to happen! . . . well, you wouldn't catch him napping this time, not the *Obersturmführer!* oh no, he had his eye on everything that went on . . . everywhere . . . and everybody! Raumnitz . . . and Aisha ditto . . . in her boots, with her big whip! . . . they weren't going to be caught with their pants down! . . . they were both on the *qui-vive!* . . .

Well anyway, I'd brought their daughter back to the *Löwen* in good condition . . . they might have thanked me, I thought . . . I had another think coming . . . what could you expect of sullen, shifty, spanked, and outraged hateful bastards like that! . . . all the same, a friendly word wouldn't have given

them a sore throat . . . "We have you to thank, Doctor . . ."
My foot! They thought they were still the conquerors! No reason to use kid gloves! . . . that's what the stinking Boches are
like . . . same with the English! . . . their horrible inborn
nature! . . . contemptuous conquerors! once and for all!
spanked or not! and on that subject, don't worry! I'd better
keep my trap shut! . . . one word out of me . . . and believe
me that word was itching to come out! . . . either to Raumnitz the spanked or his undulous mama! his houri with boots
and whip! . . . her mastiffs! . . . and her room 36! . . . her
room? . . . I know what I mean! . . . I go down to our floor!
. . . kind of invaded again! . . . the whole landing! . . .
Raumnitz must have given permission! his cops had let them
up again . . . he had the crapper opened . . . but there was
no more seat! they did it straight in the hole! okay! not so much
mess! it didn't overflow so bad . . . onto the landing! . . .
Good! Frucht would have less mopping to do! I'd just reached
our door, No. 11 . . . I hear a racket from downstairs . . .
"Clear the way! Clear the way!" like they're carrying something heavy . . . the crapper crowd go down to look . . .
they block the passage . . . *los! los!* oh oh! the bundle is a
man! . . . a big bundle! . . . the cops hoisting him up! . . .
there, that does it! . . . he's tied! . . . chained in fact! and
what chains! . . . from his neck to his ankles! he won't get
away! . . . say! I know that face! . . . it's Commissioner Papillon! he's so swollen I almost didn't recognize him! . . .
blown up to twice . . . three times his size! like the soldiers'
feet in the station! the Krauts sure gave him a going over! . . .
I haven't told you, I knew this Papillon! . . . special Commissioner of the Castle Guard of Honor . . . Specially attached to Pétain . . . Fool stunt! One look at him and I understood! It takes me quite a while to understand . . . I like to
understand very thoroughly . . . I'm of the Ribot* school
. . . "We see only what we look at, and only look at what is
already in our minds"—Special Commissioner Papillon was
constantly in my mind . . . had been for months! ever since he
had said to me: "How about it, Doctor? Let's go!" I can say this
much for myself: I turned him down flat . . . "Commissioner,

you can't win! It's a trap! . . . they'll bring you back in a jelly!
stay right here in the Castle!" No use! he had to have it his
way . . . and here was the jelly . . . he wasn't the only one
with the idea of crossing into Switzerland! . . . all 1,142 had
it . . . everybody in Siegmaringen thought wouldn't it be
lovely to escape to Basel by way of Schaffhausen! . . . but the
border! that was the rub! Special Commissioner Papillon had
sure got himself nabbed . . . and brought back in style! . . .
a "runner" was supposed to take him across! . . . runners in
our part of the country were perfectly normal and natural . . .
for cigarettes, morphine, flashlight batteries! . . . but for
yourself in person it was stepping into the meshes of the cops!
all kinds of cops, Kraut, Franzose, and Swiss! . . . well, Papillon had found out! I'd told him! Especially a "State Police" official like him, no virgin! far from it! well, the Krauts had won!
brought him back trussed and chained and deposited him on
the landing . . . *bump!* outside the crapper . . . to give people the idea . . . what crossing into Switzerland was like! . . .
I didn't need any details . . . they'd brought a hundred back
like him . . . that border was a deathtrap! . . . fifteen miles
on each side . . . same setup for centuries! *no-man's land puzzle!* the frontier guards . . . French, Swiss or Kraut . . . blast
you on sight! fire! . . . Fifis, S.A., or William Tells! . . . open
season! . . . anybody who set foot . . . secretly . . . openly
. . . *bzing!* bull's-eye! finished! day or night! . . . target!
searchlight! "Hey, you! Tourist, stop where you are!" felled,
tied, and taken away! five seconds flat the classical scenario
. . . left for dead or . . . depending on the orders from Berlin and Berne . . . brought back to Krautland like Commissioner Papillon, lying there in his chains on exhibition . . . for
everybody to look . . . and get the idea . . .

    If the Swiss won? . . . heads or tails! . . . then the guy was
shipped to Basel . . . by slow freight . . . And after that,
God knows where! . . . mostly handed over to the Fifis! La-
Chaux-de-Fond-Fresnes! don't believe what the papers say
about total wars! . . . no such thing! . . . atomic or not! . . .
no war can beat the police . . . they never go so deep! the
police need those no-man's lands . . . the threads between

cops and cops, always good neighbors, friendly and professional . . . in the worst fanatical cyclones . . . "Please,
please! Do take this little rabbit!" The cops have their own kind
of order . . . they maintain it . . . no use going on about
peace . . . there's always a certain kind of peace! . . . even
"total" wars are mere incidents! Commissioner Papillon? . . .
a pushover! . . . stopped! wrapped! and back where he came
from! . . . they could just as well have stuffed him! walking in
his sleep! not a peep out of him! . . . strolling along in complete innocence . . . he should have taken a look at his "runner" . . . any runner in fact, the faces on them! one squint at
their features, you're murdered in advance! . . . the look in
their eyes, those slanting profiles . . . I've seen whole prisons
full of degenerates, "congenital convicts," "Lombroso types,"
real museum pieces! but the characters in that Bocho-Helvetian
no-man's land . . . backwoods types, Cro-Magnon men, real
laboratory studies, highly instructive in a sense . . . "quater-
narians" . . . you wouldn't have been surprised to catch them
eating people . . . and naturally hand-in-glove with the police!
all police! . . . contraband, sure . . . anything you needed!
. . . all these degenerate, "recessive" types are stoolies and
runners . . . in Cameroon the Pygmies between Paouins and
Mabillas . . . or on the Boulevard Barbès the little men that
run minors and snow, the "Vice Squads" . . . or in Blooms-
bury, London, opium and abortions, Whitehall 1212 . . .

Anyway, as I was telling you, the way they'd taken him for
the count and hog-tied him . . . he was very quiet in his
chains! You'll tell me that a Commissioner . . . a "special"
Commissioner at that . . . isn't exactly a choir boy . . . falling into a trap like that! even a very ingenious trap! oh, oh, he
must know a thing or two about those things! it's his job! he
had only to take a look at the mugs on those "border runners"!
Those faces! . . . the treachery, the villainy, the degeneracy,
the stigmata! . . . regular carnival masks! . . . nature goes to
the trouble of putting masks like that on people! and it doesn't
wise you up . . . that's your hard luck! . . . provocateurs!
. . . talking big, bragging, and then all of a sudden humble,
crawling . . . chameleons, snakes, vipers . . . that's what

they were! . . . they molted before your eyes . . . Oh, of
course, you find the same type in the jails . . . or police line-
ups, or pretty near . . . all those Bocho-Helvetian runners
must have been on furlough from some place . . . the prisons
of the frontier zone . . . Swiss . . . Savoyard . . . Bavarian
. . . or deserters . . . in Siegmaringen we had ten, twelve
regular runners . . . they disappeared . . . they turned up
again . . . on furlough . . . that was the story . . . furlough
was Constance, a week in Constance! . . . the only quiet city
in all Germany, the only city that was never bombed, that was
always lighted like in peacetime, the stores all open and the
restaurants . . . Stock Exchange going strong, all foreign cur-
rencies and stocks! . . . Switzerland, France, Lausanne, and
the undergrounds . . . not to mention the food supply! all you
wanted from East and West! jam, chocolate, canned goods,
caviar! . . . genuine caviar from Rostov! . . . I'm not making
it up! . . . parachuted, believe it or not, by an R.A.F. squad-
ron along with the Reuters dispatches, the news of the week
. . . New York, Moscow, London . . . and the Café de la
Paix with its very sumptuous terrace on the lake front . . . to
give you an idea that it was worth the trip, an enchanted city,
very tempting . . . Commissioner Papillon knew . . . that's
where he went . . . and not alone! . . . not alone! with the
touching Clotilde! . . . the ill-fated Clotilde! . . . a very very
sweet, gentle child . . . child? . . . well, a young lady . . .
she'd been an announcer for Radio-Paris! the "Rose des Vents"
program . . . the crimes on her record! the monstrosities she'd
read! the horrors she'd sung into that mike! . . . one in particular! the payoff! . . . "De Gaulle king of traitors! *poom!*
poom! poom!" it's easy to see why she cleared out! besides, she
was in love! yes, she too! . . . she'd plighted her troth to the
Great Destroyer of Carthage*! . . . searched for him through a
thousand perils and found him! All the way from the Porte
Maillot to Constance, looking for her Great Destroyer! a miracle of love! But she hadn't picked the right time to drop in on
Hérold . . . not at all . . . Hérold Carthage wanted only one
thing . . . to be alone, all alone! here she'd gone through partisans, Fifis, the Senegalese army, and Strasbourg! the whole

works! and all he wanted was to be alone! all alone! didn't want
anything else! fed up! his Clotilde could go fly a kite! . . .
desolate Clotilde! . . . and plunked her back in the train! . . .
he'd join her again some day! . . . some day! . . . and he
ships her off! he ships her to us . . . just a note to Sabiani . . .
Sabiani's joint was the most heartrending in the whole town,
P.P.F. headquarters . . . the biggest accumulation of crow
bait . . . the big office, the back office and the two show
cases! there are witnesses, they'll tell you . . . worse than
the *Fidelis!* in both showcases, the sick and dying of all
ages, babies, grandmothers . . . and over them those solemn
signs . . . not the least bit encouraging . . . the only political messages I've ever seen that really said what they
meant . . . such as we'll probably never see again! not even
in the Chinese prison camps! "Never forget, always bear
in mind, that the Party owes you nothing, that you owe
the Party everything!" That's what the moribund worshipers of
Doriot were expected to realize! no mince-mince! old Roman!
no election flimflam! . . . it's a very exceptional moment when
political parties put their cards on the table, say what they
mean and stop gilding the pill to tickle the mob! the sick and
dying at P.P.F. headquarters, coughing up their guts and lungs,
were a permanent deterrent! . . . no more recruiting! everything in its time and place! . . . the idea was to scare people
away . . . They'd thrown Clotilde out . . . wouldn't even let
her die in the showcase! . . . "get back to the station, you no-
good whore! stinking bitch! the crust! . . ." asking for her
Hérold! . . . he'd said he'd be there . . . he'd promised! the
station? the station? she'd just come from there! After they'd
thrown her out of the "croakarium," she'd gone back down the
Avenue . . . I've shown you . . . where the riot was . . .
back to the station platform . . . sitting on a bench, poor
cunning little thing, all alone, high and dry . . . and hundreds
like her . . . forlorn, on every bench . . . fired from factories
. . . grandmothers . . . I've told you about the grandmothers, they were mostly interested in raising hell, charging
the locomotives, lying down on the tracks . . . no shame! The
young ones were more refined . . . Clotilde wept copiously

but softly, very pathetic . . . Commissioner Papillon just happened to pass by, "station duty" . . . one look at Clotilde, immediate sympathy . . . Plenty of other young women in as much distress as Clotilde, on every bench . . . but Clotilde . . . one two three! no eyes for anybody but Clotilde . . . his heart: *boom boom!* protest or not, she had to eat out of his mess kit . . . before they'd exchanged three words . . . four words . . . he'd sworn everlasting love! . . . he'd lay down his life! . . . and Papillon was no little fly-by-night, no softsoap artist, oh no! . . . four words and they'd already sworn never, ne-ver to believe in anything but the power of their love, their tenderness and the sublimity of their souls! . . . which shows you . . . I'm giving it to you straight . . . that foul embraces, wallowing bodies, impure amalgams weren't the whole story on those platforms and under those tunnels . . . Papillon and Clotilde . . . the living proof . . . sentiments that Héloïse, Laura, or Beatrice would have been very proud of . . . and in those nightmarish conditions! . . . bombs hanging in mid-air! . . . sirens, whistles that walked off with your ears! . . . the bumping and thumping of twenty-five troop trains! . . . the howling from the kitchens . . . soldiers, grandmothers, working girls all over the place . . . and naturally *Lili Marleen* and the forte piano in the waiting room . . . Papillon's job was to make the grandmothers let the trains pull out . . . to keep the S.A. from stepping in . . . to make them get up off the tracks! . . . Papillon was no slouch! it was thanks to him that the trains always left . . . mostly always . . . in spite of the bigger and bigger crowd of grandmothers . . . right under the locomotives! . . . well, the second he saw Clotilde, no eyes . . . no thought for anything else . . . to bring her happiness and right away! . . . not in twenty years! . . . console her for all her sorrows . . . give her a new life! . . . not in twenty years! . . . this minute! . . . Switzerland, a real life! Constance! . . . life, fairyland! Siegmaringen was death! Constance! Life! . . . Basel . . . Berne! . . . and they'd made up their minds! The first runner that came their way! right this minute, let's go! . . . and what a reception! . . . expected! . . . sleepwalkers of love . . . reception committee! . . . deep in their happiness! . . . going ahead without looking! . . . in a dream! . . . heading for a big poplar! . . . the seventh poplar: Switzerland! . . . but the sixth poplar . . . oh oh, twenty Boche bulls! with dogs and chains! . . . five seconds flat! . . . nabbed, tied, loaded, and shipped back . . . I saw him lying there on his side . . . a chained sausage . . . chained from his neck to his heels . . . he writhed and convulsed a little . . . not much . . . the floor was dry . . . the sewer had been cleaned up . . . they'd put him there right outside the crapper so everybody could take a good look and get the idea . . . Reminded me of Houdini . . . Houdini at the Olympia . . . I always get these childhood memories . . . the way he burst his chains . . . and much fancier chains, padlocks, and links! and much more complicated! . . . Papillon lying there . . . his convulsions were much too feeble to burst anything . . . definitely! on exhibition . . . lying there full length outside the crapper . . . the people climbed the stairs, they came in from the street . . . nobody spoke to him . . . they whispered to each other, they whispered some more . . . always the same thing: "Look what they've done to him!" black and blue and green and red! . . . I don't have to tell you that everybody knew Commissioner Papillon! They'd known him since Vichy! . . . Pétain's Special Commissioner! . . . Clotilde was known, too . . . from Radio-Paris and the railroad station . . . "Where did it happen?" She kept repeating between sobs, "Poplars, poplars!" He lying there trussed and tied, his nose bleeding on the linoleum . . . he was sleeping . . . yes, sleeping! . . . the chains on his hands should have been loosened . . . his wrists were pinned behind his back . . . with chains and a padlock . . . I know, it's been done to me! . . . later on they chained my wrists behind my back the same way . . . I was even taken on a tour that way in a caged bus . . . across the whole of Copenhagen from the Venstre to the Politiigaard to ask me if it was true that I'd committed this crime . . . or that crime? . . . But then, looking at Papillon outside the toilet, I didn't know . . . I can see Achille, Maurice, Loukoum, Montherlant, Aragon, Madeleine, Duhamel and other political hotheads . . . they don't know either! it would do them a hell of a lot of good! . . . they wouldn't be giving any more cocktail parties! . . . they'd just lie there quiet in the shit . . . and behave themselves! and get down to brass tacks! . . . the meaning of words and things! oh, it was bound to happen to me too! . . . you know what's going to happen if you only keep your eyes halfway open . . . there on the landing with his nose on the linoleum, there was only one thing to do . . . study the lesson! padlock? . . . sure there was a padlock! . . . but you needed the key! . . . nobody had the key! . . . Discussions were going on, but in an undertone . . . what we should do, or shouldn't . . . no violent arguments like at the station! . . . more like church . . . mostly there was sympathy for Clotilde . . . "the poor little thing! . . . the poor little thing! . . ." him not so much! . . . he'd got her into it! . . . all his fault! . . . thoughtless! . . . impulsive! . . . that's how the ladies felt! . . . she was deserving of sympathy, him not so much! . . . if it hadn't been for him, she wouldn't have gone! . . . the damn fool! . . . that dangerous sausage! . . . in the first place a cop! . . . monkey around the Swiss border? . . . Good God! . . . he must have known . . . after all . . . wouldn't you think so? . . . that hornets' nest! . . . only a dumb cop! . . . you only have to look at him! . . . The reckless blundering blockhead! . . . naturally he got caught! . . . the blockhead! . . . "the poor dear thing!" she was the poor thing! They were only sorry for her! the poor dear thing kept moaning "by the poplars! . . . by the poplars!" . . . the frail and tender victim! . . . the rubdown by the poplars was no surprise to me . . . or to Marion either! . . . he'd been there himself, at the exact same spot . . . reconnoitering the poplars and the brook that marked the border was a very risky business . . . he'd done it one Sunday . . . on Sunday the police, the S.A., Swiss and underground, eat and drink enormously and sleep . . . you've got a chance of passing unnoticed . . . although? . . . although? . . . the dogs? he'd gone . . . with the map . . . a pencil sketch . . . showing exactly where the famous border brook flowed . . . between the sixth and seventh tree . . . he hadn't met a soul! . . . real luck! . . . "I could have crossed if I'd wanted to!" . . . it wouldn't have done him any good, he was too well known in Switzerland . . . but he'd seen the spot . . . the exact same spot where the runner had led Papillon and Clotilde! . . . but with them it was different, a setup! . . . reception committee between the sixth and seventh trees! . . .

I don't have to tell you we had maps of that Baden-Swiss border . . . there were whole trunkfuls in the Castle library! heaps! mountains of albums . . . you could spend whole weeks following some little brook from century to century . . . new twists and turns . . . dams, litigation, disputes . . . disputes that were still going on! . . . inheritances that were never settled! . . . what had become of this little furrow? . . . was it the border? or wasn't it? . . . between the fifth and sixth tree? . . . ever since the first monastery . . . from the very first Hohenzollern and Co. rackets . . . down to the very last war . . . whole bundles of sketches of hamlets, borderlines, and swamps! . . . Württemberg, Baden, Switzerland! . . . and encroachments and landgrabbing and torts . . . a farm, a patch of ground, a stable, a ford . . . taking into account the hundred thousand cases of abduction and rape, the murders, divorces, Diets and Councils . . . centuries and centuries of "Princes' pleasure," marriages of reason, migrations of peoples and kingdoms, crusades, more rape! and more torts! . . . stuff like at my place on the rue Girardon . . . millions and millions of times worse! just to give you an idea that with all the documents, maps, tracings in that library you couldn't tell what was which! . . . compass in hand, you'd go wrong! . . . you had to be a frontier cop to know where that damned brook really went! and where you were! the way they'd twisted and changed it . . . widened it here . . . narrowed it there . . . it was unrecognizable! like Papillon's face! from one border post to the next you'd be lost! . . . and besides, I forgot to tell you, six centuries of religious gangsterism! . . . monastery against monastery! Catholic to Luther and back again! "I'll drain your little millstream! . . . I'll cut down your poplar! Tree of Satan!" . . . the result was a total puzzle, brook, loops, detours, you couldn't find a damn thing! a setup for the police . . . on this side . . . on that side . . . thirteen centuries of

phony thickets, phony hedges, phony scarecrows! . . . on
Sunday, as I've said, you had a slight chance of not being seen
. . . of getting through and taking a look . . . but on weekdays you were cooked! no two ways! even before the second
plane tree! . . . trussed! . . . and cured! . . . by the Krauts,
the Swiss or the partisans! . . . You didn't worry your head
about the brook! you were a sleepwalker, that's all! . . . a
sleepwalker in fairyland! . . . lovely, lovely! . . . picking
bunches of azaleas, blueberries, Saint-John's-wort, fairy flowers! . . . and cyclamen! . . . Marion had gone picking . . .
and reconnoitering . . . and he'd come back! . . . wonder
of wonders! . . . it was a Sunday . . . safe and sound! anyway I've always had the idea that he'd been seen and photo-
graphed! even if it was Sunday and the cops and customs
guards at dinner . . . even so! . . . even so! . . . even on
Sunday there are lookouts . . . you never know where . . .
on top of a plane tree? . . . in the middle of a haystack? . . .
a photoelectric cell . . . every clod of ground was full of little
gadgets, mines and contacts! no doubt about it! . . . *tick! vrrr!*
. . . all the approaches to Wichflingen . . . the lake . . . I
couldn't really imagine that Marion hadn't been seen regardless . . . not the least bit sure! . . . I made it, he said to me.
Okay, but I'll never go back! . . . every day we had proposi-
tions to run us across to Switzerland . . . and cheap . . . two
thousand marks! . . . enticing! . . . in addition they'd promise
and swear that the Fifis would be waiting to kill us with kindness! . . . a spread! and a "Certificate of the Resistance" . . .
and maps! and everything! . . . that Switzerland was more
"Red Cross" than ever! the Gestapo understanding, perfectly
willing! . . . at Schaffhausen, Payot and Gentizon would
bring Petitpierre* to meet us and Swiss passports for everybody . . . valid and in order! all we had to do was follow the
guide! report at the border! nothing to worry about! splendid
offers! Papillon there, out flat on the linoleum, I could see what
they'd done for him! . . . Lili and Clotilde sponged him off,
bandaged his head, gave him water . . . he was thirsty, asking
to drink . . . that was a good sign . . . but the people around
him were afraid to come too close . . . they'd come up to see

him from the restaurant, from the street . . . they went back down again . . .

All of a sudden I hear *"nun! nun!"* Raumnitz! . . . that was his voice: *"Nun! nun!"* it's him all right! he looks at Papillon . . . he looks at the people, the circle around him . . . they'd stopped talking . . . *nun! nun!* . . . that's all he said . . . he feels the chains . . . *nun! nun!* . . . and away he goes! . . . he goes upstairs to his place, the floor above, with his dogs . . . he must have just come back from the station . . . he's on his landing, over our room . . . he stops, he leans over the banister . . . "Doctor! Doctor!" he calls me . . .

"Would you mind? In a little while? . . . if you've got a moment . . ."

"Certainly, Major! . . . Certainly!"

Laval, I've got to see him too . . . and the *Landrat* too . . . and Christ Almighty, the *Fidelis!* . . . thirty forty bad cases at the *Fidelis!* . . . plus Madame Bonnard, aged ninety-six . . . and three . . . four . . . five . . . six calls at the other end of town! . . . Should I go? Or shouldn't I? . . . the *Landrat* was also for Bébert! . . . the chicken bones for Bébert! . . . I beg all I can at the *Landrat's,* I'm popular in the kitchen . . . I show the cook Bébert, she's delighted . . . she's crazy about him, I take him out of his bag . . . he's the boss in the kitchen . . . we leave with plenty of bones! . . . and more than bones! . . . there's meat on them! . . . Lili and I eat some of it . . . believe me, that *Landrat* wanted for nothing . . . no reducing diet! . . . I knew, I saw his kitchen . . . every day they bring him two three four pieces of game . . . and good stuff! . . . I saw it! . . . deer, woodcock, fat hens . . . the Black Forest is full of game . . . and the foresters were under him . . . *Landrat* and Master of the Hunt! . . . he was as well fed as Pétain . . . as de Gaulle in London . . . as the Kommandantur in Paris . . . tomorrow the Kommandatura! . . . as Roosevelt on his yacht! . . . as Franco in Madrid! . . . as "Tito-the-Smiling-Sideboard!" . . . So that was the first stop! . . . Bébert in his bag! back to the hotel! . . . and away we go! . . . ah, but first to kiss the old lady's hand . . .

"Au revoir, Madame Bonnard! au revoir!"

And out I go . . . I'll go see Raumnitz when I come back . . . he must want to speak to me about the station . . . maybe about Papillon too . . . certainly in fact . . .

Just as I expected . . . the people hadn't gone at all . . . our
landing was choked with *Landsturm* troops and civilians from
the trains, from the railroad station, refugees from Strasbourg,
so they said . . . the arguments! screaming at each other . . .
about what they'd seen and not seen! . . . Leclerc's army!
. . . the Senegalese with their chop-chops! . . . the details!
. . . we slackers in Siegmaringen couldn't have any idea! . . .
any inkling! . . . trouble was their private property! and nobody could tell them different . . . survivors of the most horrible massacres! . . . they occupied the stairs and the landing
and the crapper door . . . another invasion! . . . they came
up to piss three . . . four . . . ten at a time! . . . they
stopped next to Papillon . . . they looked at him . . . lying
there on his side chained, with his face all bruised and swollen
. . . as if he'd drowned! . . . they formed a circle around
him . . . they would have liked to talk to him, ask him what he
was doing . . . Clotilde, on her knees beside him, told them
the whole story . . . in sobs and snatches, as best she could!
the awful ambush! the poplar . . . the twelfth? . . . the thirteenth? . . . crying so hard she lost count . . . and the little
brook . . . The refugees from Strasbourg told her off . . .
they were in no humor for her sob stories! applesauce! stupid,
infantile, inept! . . . they'd really seen something! . . . they'd
been through real horrors! . . . they had a right to talk! nobody could tell them! . . . who was this Papillon anyway in
the first place? . . . a cop! a bull! a stoolie? . . . and this girl?
this weeping willow? what whore house was she from? . . .
the more Clotilde told them, the more plaintive and pitiful
. . . exhausted from weeping . . . the poplar! . . . the seventh? . . . the twelfth? . . . she didn't remember! . . . the

more she got on their nerves! . . . they were really sore! . . .
they hadn't escaped from Strasbourg . . . a miracle! . . .
and the chop-chop Senegalese to listen to the sob stories of
this floozie down there on her knees! hell no! they had a right
to holler! . . . after what they'd seen and gone through! . . .
rivers of blood! . . . not trickles! . . . nothing you could
hold in a handkerchief! . . . mass decapitations! hangings!
whole avenues of trees! . . . whole strings and circles of stiffs!
this sniveling bitch hadn't seen a damn thing! . . . and we
hadn't either! . . . slackers! yellow-bellies! . . . we hadn't
seen the Senegalese in Strasbourg or the Fifis that gouge out
your eyes! we hadn't seen a thing! . . . and we were driving
them nuts with our know-it-all airs! . . . they started talking
louder and louder, screaming and shouting about the blood-
bath in *their* Strasbourg! . . . more and more outraged that
this slut Clotilde, the nerve of her! . . . the cry-baby . . .
hell, she hadn't the faintest idea! . . . or the rest of us, idiots!
lazy buttercups! a little trip to Strasbourg! that's what she
needed! . . . teach her to appreciate the Swiss border! . . .
hamadonna! . . . they'd show her the Fifis . . . with her
twelfth . . . thirteenth tree! . . . hell, they'd find the right one
. . . the branch to hang her from! . . . their asses bled for
her . . . listening to that bullshit . . . wait till Leclerc gets
here with his army! . . . she'd see a real ambush! . . . they'd
cut her guts out . . . blubbering asshole! made you sick to listen! . . . intolerable! "boo-hoo! shut up!" The coons would cut
her tongue out! cutting out tongues was their specialty! . . .
and her cop boyfriend at the same time! . . . then she'd stop
complaining! . . . she hadn't seen a thing! . . . sniveling
phony, cop's moll . . . scissorbill! . . . the whole landing
agreed that she was a provocateur, stool-pigeon, and cop's
moll! and it was high time the coons came and scalped her! and
cut off her clit! then she'd shut up! and the best was still to
come! the rest of us too! . . . when they'd put our cocks in our
mouths . . . we wouldn't talk so much! . . . and this guy
chained on the floor! . . . Special Commissioner? . . . bullshit! . . . he'd tied himself up! chained himself . . . obvious!
cop's dodge! it wouldn't go down with them! the survivors of

Strasbourg! real gilt-edged horrors! . . . They ought to step on her! strangle her on the spot! . . . with her bull! . . . this hysterical whore with her song and dance about borders, ambushes, and kiss my ass! . . . the slut! if she and her cop had been in Strasbourg, you wouldn't hear them complaining . . . suffering ass peddler!

Just to give you an idea of their attitude . . . the new crowd on the landing! . . . really mean, unpleasant! . . . I could see the temperature rising! . . . they were going to thrash her themselves! right away! . . . especially the women, who were really worn out . . . they really had something to complain about . . . "puddles of blood this big! . . . am I right, Hector? Am I right, Léon?" . . . and children's heads cut off! . . . little angels! you couldn't count the heads! chop-chops this big! . . . they showed us remarkable lengths! . . . chop-chops! widths! axes! . . . "Am I right, Hector? . . . am I right, Léon?! Just listen to that slut! Do 'em good . . . and her flatfoot too! Give her something to cry about!" Clotilde was perfectly willing to be slapped, right then and there! she held out her face, her cheek, she wasn't afraid! but the refugees from Strasbourg, survivors of the worst massacres, hadn't come here to the Black Forest, to Siegmaringen and Pétain, for scenes like this . . . oh no! and say, what about Pétain? . . . and his gang! . . . some cathouse! . . . look at it! "Am I right, Hector?" . . . married women, respectable and all, with children . . . they had a few things to say! . . . they'd lost everything in Strasbourg! . . . but they had their dignity! . . . escaped from the horrible massacre! . . . why didn't we listen to them? . . . instead of listening to this filthy police floozie! and besides she was blocking the door . . . to the toilet! and more and more people were coming up . . . from the restaurant and the street . . . The situation is really going sour when . . . up comes a bishop . . . so help me, I'm not making it up . . . up the stairs . . . a bishop in a purple cassock, enormous hat, pectoral cross . . . and still climbing the stairs, blesses everybody . . . he turns around to bless the people in the street . . . and bless them some more . . . and the whole landing! . . . not very old as bishops go . . . pepper and salt,

goatee, not very fat either, more the ascetic type, discreet
omentum . . . oh, but shifty looking! . . . taking everything
in . . . right, left, front, back . . . all the while crossing himself and mumbling "in the name of the Father" . . . but the
effect was terrific . . . instantaneous . . . They were so exasperated with Clotilde's plaints and sighs I was expecting them
to strip her mother-naked! . . . but instantly, silence! they
stopped calling her names! . . . "bitch! mud-hen! liar!" . . .
this benedictioning bishop . . . well, he looked like a bishop
. . . they start wondering . . . where he came from? . . .
where he was going? to the crapper? and the blessings keep
coming . . . I wasn't nonplussed, I just get to thinking:
Maybe he's come to see me? . . . maybe he's disguised . . .
maybe he's a patient? . . . no, no! he comes up, makes a sign
that he wants to talk to me . . . Where's he know me from?

"Doctor, I am the Bishop of Albi!"

And then he whispers in my ear:

"The occult bishop!"

He looks around to make sure nobody can hear him:

"The Catharist bishop!"

So that's it . . . I try not to look surprised . . . perfectly
natural . . .

"Oh yes, of course!"

He has more to tell me: "Persecuted since 1929!"

I don't let him into our room, he's fine right here on the landing . . . he talks and he keeps right on blessing . . . over and
over . . .

"I am at the *Fidelis*, Doctor! the nurses are splendid! . . .
you know them! . . . I'm very comfortable at the *Fidelis*!
Yes, but comfort isn't everything! Is it, Doctor?"

"Oh no, certainly not, Monsignor."

"I need a pass for our Synod in Fulda! . . . you've heard
about it?"

"Oh yes, Monsignor!"

"There will be three of us . . . myself from France! . . .
and two others bishops from Albania! . . . ah, we haven't
seen the last of our troubles, Doctor!"

"I can imagine, Monsignor!"

"Neither have you, my son!"

He seizes my head, oh, very gently, he kisses me on the forehead . . . and then he blesses me . . .

"We are all of us persecuted, my son! . . . my children! . . ."

He addresses the whole crowd:

"Remember, all of you! . . . the Albigenses! God's martyrs! down on your knees! . . . down on your knees!"

The women comply . . . the men remain standing . . .

"Ah, but I forgot, Doctor . . . Monsieur de Raumnitz's office?"

"Next floor, Monsignor!"

Whatever he was, one thing is sure . . . he prevented a massacre! . . . those women were furies, I could see them tearing Clotilde limb from limb . . . and now all of a sudden they were looking at her tenderly . . . crossing themselves! countercrossing! weeping with emotion and sympathy! for Clotilde and Lili and the cop! . . . and for myself . . . we all hugged and kissed . . . communion! . . .

"*Nun! Nun!*"

Raumnitz's voice! that stopped everything! he leans over the bannister . . . he's fed up . . . this riot in the corridor! It had better stop.

"Aisha!"

Aisha and the mastiffs come down . . . that took the starch out of them . . . everybody moves aside . . . she motions to the men: they should pick up Papillon! and take him away! this way . . . she shakes her whip . . . back there . . . let's go! . . . they pick him up . . . chains and all . . . the whole bundle . . . heave ho! they take him away . . . The bishop looks on . . . still blessing . . . all of a sudden: "You're not a Catharist?" he takes advantage of the hubbub to ask me so nobody could hear . . . his name? he didn't tell me . . . I don't know . . . Monsignor what? . . . "No . . . no . . ." I bellow. "Not a Catharist!" so everybody can hear me! in spite of the racket! the whole landing! It was a reflex . . . self-defense! instantaneous! the reflex of self-defense! divine grace! animal instinct! I was too much detested by everybody, the butt of too many calumnies! and now this one? this phony persecuted

bishop calling me a Catharist! . . . Article 75 was enough
. . . Catharist? Catharist? . . . no thank you! This character
must be an extra-special provocateur! . . . fishing! . . . he
won't catch me! I shout some more! I want Raumnitz and
Aisha to hear me! "Not a Catharist! Not a Catharist! . . ."

Self-defense!

You won't catch me in a sucker trap so quick! Catharist, Al-
bigensian, Archbishop! Take me by surprise? . . . holy blazes,
no! . . . luckily the people carry him away! the bishop-arch-
bishop and his blessings . . . the whole mob on the landing
and Aisha and the mastiffs! the Commissioner in his chains
. . . and Clotilde in tears! . . . they all pour into the little
corridor leading to the rear . . . but then an incident! . . .
I'm just telling you what happened! Clotilde lets out a scream!
she turns . . . Clotilde so frail and tearful! and rushes the
brutes from Strasbourg! they send her back against the wall!
. . . so violently that she practically flattens out! oh, but she
bounces back! she attacks again! . . . the frail and weeping
Clotilde! she grabs Papillon by the end of his chain and she
won't let go! she freezes on to it! she grabs him by the head
. . . she kisses him! kisses him! the crowd carried them away,
drives them to the back . . . the door in back! . . .

Aisha's there already . . . she's waiting for them . . . she
and her mastiffs . . . she's outside the door, Room 36 . . . I
know, I know! . . . my phony doctor's there already . . . and
his nurse . . . I think so anyway . . . and the patient, too
. . . the one who was on my bed that he was just going to
operate, the big garage man from Strasbourg . . . and a lot
more that I never saw again . . . I think . . . I think . . .
I'm not so sure . . . why not take the opportunity and give a
look? . . . Room 36? . . . I've got my doubts . . . They
must be pretty cramped . . . I had a chance to go in now . . .
Papillon, Clotilde, the bishop . . . and all the pall-bearers
and their women pour in! . . . Aisha lets them pour . . . I
could let them push me in . . . Aisha stays by the door with
her mastiffs . . . she looks at me to see if I'm going in . . .
she'd let me . . . "oh, no, sister! no!" I'm pretty curious, but
not that bad . . . hell, I've fallen for enough shenanigans and

sucker traps! . . . I'm through! fatass Aisha! jiggly croup, snake charmer! . . . no soap! . . . get this through your stack! . . . I'm blazing mad! . . . hatred to the bone! . . . I'd impale you alive. See? you date-and-olive tart! I can see her at that door in 1900! . . . the snake charmer! . . . red crocodile boots and big sparklers! and the whip! Aisha, you bitch, I'd impale you! No, I won't go into Room 36! her Room 36! I drop everything and blow! I've got a few things to do! my duty! the patients waiting for me in Room 11 . . . yes, they come first . . . but then? the station? . . . the Castle? . . . first the station . . . more trains must have pulled in . . . down the Avenue again . . . from doorway to doorway . . . sidewalk to sidewalk . . . dangerous . . . not only the little bursts of machine-gun fire . . . also the talking machines that grab hold of you and won't let go . . . every time I leave the *Löwen* to see this one . . . or that one . . . it never fails . . . you run into some lunatic that stops you short . . . every doorway . . . every street corner . . . wants to know what you think . . . how things are going . . . and not some other time! right away! and frankly! the whole truth! a slap on the back . . . enough to throw your shoulder out of joint! a hand-shake that makes you reel and stagger! . . . "Ah, why, there's our dear doctor!" my, what a pleasant surprise! . . . what re-joicing! . . . ah, but watch your step . . . supercareful! . . . extra caution! this is the time for spontaneous, dynamic, opti-mistic answers! absolute conviction! the man who's asking you your opinion isn't any ordinary rank-and-file stool-pigeon! don't stutter! don't mince! give him the works! . . . "The Germans are winning, victory is in the bag . . . the New Europe is here to stay! . . . the secret army has destroyed everything in Lon-don . . . absolutely *kaputt* . . . Von Paulus is in Moscow but they won't announce it until the winter's over! . . . Rommel is in Cairo! . . . it will all be announced at the same time! . . . the Americans are suing for peace . . . we . . . you and I on the sidewalk . . . are practically home again! parading on the Champs-Elysées! . . . only a question of trains, transporta-tion! . . . not enough trains! . . . matter of weeks! return trip via Rethondes and Saint-Denis!"

The idea is to seem well informed! he scratches while he's talking to you . . . he's got the scabies! . . . oh, but don't talk to him about scabies . . . especially not scabies . . . only about the return through the Arch of Triumph! . . . our apotheosis! to revive the flame! . . . and de Gaulle in London and his clique and Roosevelt and Stalin, washed up! . . . tamed for ever! all of them, with rings in their noses! . . . and locked up in the zoo at Vincennes! once and for all! for life! especially don't show a quarter tenth of a doubt! Just say that "Rommel isn't so sure of taking the Canal . . . Suez is perfectly capable of holding out" . . . your goose is cooked . . . you'll never be seen again! . . . how many people have disappeared that way . . . just showing a little skepticism with those men in doorways? . . . Plenty! . . . and never seen again . . .

Naturally it was a good deal safer to stay home . . . but not so easy . . . not so easy . . .

Good Lord, how nice it would be to keep all this to myself!
. . . never to say another word, never to write anything
again, to be left completely alone . . . to go somewhere by the
seashore to die . . . not the Côte d'Azur . . . the real sea, the
ocean . . . I'd never talk to anybody again, absolutely at
peace, forgotten . . . but look here, Toto, how about the
grub? . . . trumpets and bass drum! . . . get up on those
ropes, you old clown! keep moving! . . . higher! . . . higher!
. . . the public is waiting for you! and they only want one
thing: for you to break your neck!

Achille sent word yesterday, what was the holdup? . . .
lecherous old goo-goo eyes, he never wrote a book . . . his
head never ached! . . . hell no! Loukoum, his flunkey, came to
see me, why was I so rude? . . . and so lazy? his dear, revered
Achille had spent fabulous sums on publicity of every kind,
cocktail parties, busses with flags and streamers, striptease
shows for the critics, enormous front page ads in the most hateful papers, the papers that were most venomously anti-me an-
nouncing the advent! that I'd finished my white elephant! and
here I hadn't given them a thing! . . . ah, Loukoum raises his
arm to high heaven! . . . I'm even stupider and lazier than last
year! he wouldn't dare to tell Achille! . . . the poor old man
. . . such a blow! . . . he simply wouldn't dare! . . . they're
so considerate of each other! . . . even of Gertrut with his sky-
blue monocle! . . . I'm the spoilsport, the cynical, foul-
mouthed, malignant calamity clown . . .

Doesn't it mean anything to me that Achille has to go to
Dax . . . and come back by way of Aix and Enghien? that he's
not as young as he used to be! that he'll be a hundred in July
. . . and doesn't want to leave until this business is settled

228

. . . all my manuscripts in his cellar! that he's already given up Marienbad on account of me! . . . and Evian! . . . that he's so lacerated by the sums he's put into this, invested in my glory! . . . he can hardly drag himself out to the Luxembourg . . . to the Champs-Elysées . . . that even the puppet show doesn't amuse him any more! . . . or the little train in the Bois . . . and I don't give a damn! . . . no conscience! . . . my white elephant ought to be in the dog pound!

"Loukoum! Loukoum! there's a taxi! Quick!"

He's surprised, but he gets up . . . he follows me . . . the garden . . . the sidewalk . . .

"Driver! driver! Take Monsieur to Lourdes! To Lourdes, driver! Quick! Quick!"

Ah, he came to shake me out of my apathy! I'll cure him! Lourdes or not! all three! all four of them can go to Lourdes! I wouldn't want them to be bored . . . I've got better things to do! I was telling you about Siegmaringen, the landing . . .

After Papillon and Clotilde and the Catharist bishop and the
phony doctor and his victim and the massacre at the station, it
seemed reasonable to suppose that this was enough . . . for
the time being . . . that we were entitled to a little peace and
quiet . . . to a few less Strasbourgeois, that mob of troublemakers . . . all kinds! . . . lunatics, bigmouths, females, im-
personators, phony thises and phony thats . . . Not at all . . .
more and more kept coming . . . from the restaurant, from
the street . . . from all over! they blocked the stairs, complete
bottleneck . . . if you tried to buck the current, you'd be
crushed, rolled thin! . . . because they were ripping mad in
addition, they wanted everything and right away! to eat, to
sleep, to drink, to piss! . . . and they were all yelling! riproar-
ing creeps! they wanted to piss, drink and eat in our room! . . .
I give it a try . . . "let me through!" "No! No! No! Cocksucker! stinker! . . . bloodthirsty bastard! . . . Come ahead!
We're waiting!" That was the way they felt about me . . . my
prestige! . . . It hasn't increased much since . . . my prestige! . . . but this was an emergency . . . I had to go to the
Castle . . . never mind, I'd go later! and Raumnitz? . . . the
floor above . . . so instead of going down I went up . . .
Room 28 . . . *knock knock!* . . . *herein!* . . . he's lying
down . . . smoking . . .

"I've forbidden you to smoke, Major!"

I light right into him! . . . it makes him laugh when I forbid
him this and that . . . but it's the only way . . . doormat, and
they walk all over you . . .

"Undress, Major! your injection!"

Almost every day I inject his 2 c.c.s . . . oh, he needs them!
. . . indispensable! . . . fatigue . . . a false move . . .

something very nasty could happen . . . there, stretched out naked on his bed, he looked exactly like what he was . . . an exhausted former athlete . . . swollen ankles . . . I auscultate . . . his heart . . . the heart never lies . . . if you listen, it tells you the whole story . . .

"Well, Doctor?"

"Oh, I've told you . . . five drops in a quarter of a glass of water for five days . . . and camphorated oil, your injection . . . and rest! no more fatigue! . . . and no more smoking! . . . especially no smoking!"

Raumnitz, I've got to admit, wasn't a bad sort . . . the kind of Boche you've got to take as he is . . . and considering where he comes from . . . I've lived with that brand of Boches in North Prussia-Brandenburg . . . I was there as a kid, nine years old . . . and later I was interned there . . . I don't think much of the country . . . a sandy plain, poor soil with huge forests all around! . . . potato, hog, and mercenary country . . . and the storms on those plains! . . . Christ! people around here can't imagine . . . and those forests of sequoias . . . can't imagine them either . . . the height of those giants! more than four hundred feet! . . . What about Africa? you'll say . . . oh, it's not the same! . . . no sequoias! . . . and I know . . . I've been to a lot of places . . . great big ones . . . and tiny little ones . . . I know the Prussia of the von Raumnitzes . . . no tourist country! . . . dismal little lakes, still more funereal forests . . . just like Raumnitz . . . where he comes from . . . a Prussian-double-dealing country nobleman, cruel, sinister, and swinish . . . but with his good sides too . . . a certain grandeur . . . the Grail, Teutonic Knight side . . . I'm a good hand at making people laugh, but that business in Vincennes, you can imagine, that spanking . . . had thrown him once and for all into such a brooding hatred that I had quite a time keeping him from flying off the handle and drilling me! . . . I could see it coming . . . right here and now! . . . especially in view of the spot I had to work on . . . the ridiculousness of his behind . . . I was always asking him if it still hurt . . . here? . . . and there? . . . it didn't look as if they'd only spanked him . . . they must have hit him with rifle butts! I could see the marks, the bruises . . . I put in the needle right next to them . . . I made him lie on his side . . . ah, they hadn't used kid gloves! . . . it reminded me of those certificates . . . "I, the undersigned etc. . . . to having observed etc. . . . bruises and abrasions resulting from blows . . . the beatings which Madame Pellefroid claims to have incurred . . . on the . . . , the . . . , the . . . etc. . . ." Sartrouville . . . Clichy . . . Bezons . . . I tried that one on him too! "beating which he claims to have incurred . . . etc." . . . a risky gag! . . .

"But he committed suicide, Doctor! the swine! the coward! Stupnagel! I knew him like a book! . . . I could have had him hanged a dozen times! do you hear? . . . do you believe me? . . . Stupnagel! a dozen times! . . . and everybody in the Castle too! that's right! . . . a dozen times! And everybody in Siegmaringen! a dozen times! traitors? Yes, traitors, every last one of them! I know them all. And Pétain! you believe me, don't you, Doctor?"

"Certainly, Major! Certainly! I'm sure you are excellently informed . . . but calm yourself, Major! calm yourself! . . . think of your heart!"

Mostly I was thinking that if his rage brought on a stroke when I was there it wouldn't look very good for me . . .

"And how about the railroad station? . . . You've been there? . . ."

I wanted to put him onto a different subject . . .

"Yes, I've seen the station . . . I don't think you realize, Doctor . . . in those little riots . . . trumped up! the whole thing was trumped up! . . . bullets tend to go astray . . . take care of yourself Doctor . . . don't go roaming around the streets so much . . ."

"Thank you, Major!"

I didn't want him to tell me any more . . . Brinon or he or the Devil's grandmother . . . people always regret their confidences . . . especially in rough times . . . confidences are for drawing rooms, for quiet conversational, digestive, somnolescent times . . . but here, with maniacs all over the place and the air full of Armadas . . . it was playing with thunder . . .

no time for analyses! oh no! the slightest spark . . . the slightest milligram . . . you wouldn't know what would hit you!

Raumnitz, as I've told you, had been a doughty athlete . . . none of your powdered pansy gentry! oh no! an Olympic athlete! Olympic swimming champion of Germany . . . there, all naked on his bed, I could see what was left of the Olympics . . . muscles reduced and flabby . . . the frame still presentable . . . very presentable . . . the face too . . . those Dürer features . . . features etched by Dürer . . . hard face, not at all unpleasant . . . I've told you . . . he must have been handsome . . . Boche eyes and expression . . . same look as his mastiffs . . . not bad eyes, but fixed . . . haughty you might say . . . you seldom see a face with something in it, most faces are mass produced . . .

"Are you going to the *Fidelis*, Doctor?"

"Oh yes, Major! Oh, certainly!"

The *Fidelis* didn't send me . . . I had my reasons . . . I'll explain . . .

"I'd like you to read a letter . . ."

"Later . . . later if you don't mind, Major . . . I won't be a minute . . ."

"You'll be back?"

"Oh, certainly . . . I hope so at least . . ."

"Watch out for Brinon! don't believe Laval! . . . don't believe Pétain! don't believe Rochas! * . . . don't believe Marion!"

"I don't have to believe them, Major . . . I don't worry my head about them . . . or you either . . . or myself . . ."

"All the same, read this letter!"

He really wants me to . . . I look at the signature first . . . Boisnières . . . I know this Boisnières, his job is guarding the nursing mothers at the *Fidelis* . . . the nursery . . . to prevent goings-on . . . misbehavior . . . between the mothers and the shamuses at the *Fidelis* . . . at least three hundred cops . . . four dormitories, two whole floors of the *Fidelis* . . . cops from every province of France, nothing whatever to do! escapees from every Préfecture . . . Boisnières, known as

Neuneuil, is the "nursery guard" . . . confidential police . . .
"don't let anyone in" . . . Neuneuil and his cards! . . . yes,
he's got a card file: three thousand names! the apple of his
eye . . . the Fifis took the other eye when he was fighting the
underground! gives you an idea how confidential he was! . . .
I didn't want to read his letter, I didn't have time . . . I knew
Boisnières-Neuneuil . . . I knew he was denouncing something again . . . or somebody . . . maybe me? . . . I know
him! a pest! . . . one-eyed, scabies and boils, and a very eager
beaver . . .

"Denouncing somebody again?"

"Yes, Doctor . . . yes . . . me!"

"To whom?"

"To Chancellor Hitler."

"Say, that's an idea!"

"Says he saw me going out in my car! Yes, me! To fish for
trout instead of keeping tabs on the French . . . I deny nothing, Doctor! It's a fact! I'm guilty! Neuneuil is right! But don't
you want to read his letter?"

"You've told me everything, Major . . . the essential . . ."

"No, not the essential! . . . your compatriot Neuneuil has
discovered something worse, much worse . . . he says . . .
his idea! . . . that I'm sabotaging the *Luftwaffe!* . . . that I
waste five gallons of '*benzin*' on my fishing expeditions . . .
and it's true! . . . absolutely true . . . I don't deny it! your
compatriot Neuneuil is perfectly right!"

"Oh, he's exaggerating, Major . . ."

"He's right to exaggerate!"

This is no time to contradict him . . . dialectics my ass!
birds of a feather! the whole lot of them! and their damned
Luftwaffe! . . . for all the good it does them! I wasn't going to
tell him that!

"Wait, Doctor . . . wait! I've sent for him!"

Making me read the letter . . . and not letting me go . . .
he wanted to show me Neuneuil!

"Please, Doctor! . . . Excuse me! . . . sit down!"

He puts on his pants . . . his boots . . . his jacket . . .

He goes to the door, he opens . . . he goes out to the bannister and leans over . . . he shouts . . .

"*Hier!* . . . Monsieur Boisnières! Isn't Monsieur Boisnières there?"

"Yes yes, Major! Here I am! I'm coming!"

He comes all right, there he is . . .

"Come in! . . . You are Boisnières, known as Neuneuil?"

"Yes, Major!"

"Then look me in the eye! Straight in the eye! . . . did you write this letter?"

"Yes, Major!"

"You admit it?"

"Yes, Major!"

"Whom did you mail it to?"

"You have the address, Major!"

Oh, not the least bit intimidated . . .

"I was only doing my duty, Major!"

"Well, Monsieur Boisnières, I'm going to do my duty! . . . alias Neuneuil! . . . look me straight in the eye! that's it . . . straight in the eye!"

Pow! . . . *Pow!* . . . two good hefty clouts that lift Neuneuil off his feet! . . . his bandage goes flying . . . torn off!

"Well, Monsieur Boisnières alias Neuneuil, that's my opinion! . . . moreover, I could have you punished a lot worse! . . . and you know it! . . . and I'm not . . . I could have punished you once and for all! miserable scum! . . . ah, so I waste gas? . . . ah, so I sabotage the *Luftwaffe?* . . . I won't waste a little bullet to shut you up, Monsieur Neuneuil! or a knotted rope! . . . you're not worth the rope! go! get the hell out of here! and don't let me see your face again! Never! If I ever see you here again, I'll have you drowned! You can go and visit the trout! Get out! Get out! On the double! To Berlin! Take your letter . . . Neuneuil! . . . don't lose it, Neuneuil! . . . You can read it to the Führer in person! to Berlin! on the double! Monsieur Neuneuil! *los! los!* and don't let me ever see your face again! never! . . . *los! los!* . . ."

He was really steamed up . . .

Neuneuil straightened his bandage . . .

"If I ever see you here again, you'll be shot! and drowned! . . . I'm telling you! There are plenty of grounds!"

That chewing-out had shaken Neuneuil . . . he was staggering . . . he put his bandage back on, but he made a bad job of it . . .

"Very well, Major! I have only to comply!"

He goes out, he closes the door behind him . . .

"Doctor, you've seen that man? . . . he has been in our employ for twenty-two years . . . a traitor for twenty-two years! . . . he betrays us! . . . he betrays you! . . . he denounces everybody to everybody! . . . he has betrayed England! Holland! Switzerland! Russia . . . he's worse than Father Gapon! worse than Laval, worse than Pétain! He denounces everything! everybody! I've saved his life twenty times, Doctor! Twenty times I've had orders to liquidate him . . . Neuneuil! I could have him shot on the spot! . . . He wrote to the English! . . . wanted them to kidnap Laval! . . . yes! . . . those are the people you listen to, Doctor! All traitors, Jews! plots in the Castle! . . . do you realize that?"

"I'm listening, Major! I'm all ears! . . . why yes, you're perfectly right . . ."

You can imagine, he could have told me I was a Mongol, I wasn't going to contradict him . . .

"Well, Doctor, just one thing . . . between you and me . . ."

He starts telling me the one thing . . . he stops . . . he starts up again . . . ah, here it comes . . .

"Maybe you know it, maybe you don't . . . I've had Ménétrel arrested . . . I could have them all arrested! . . . no! . . . the whole Castle! . . . but all the same . . . I ought to . . . they deserve it! . . . all of them, Doctor! and you too! . . . and Luchaire!* and your Jew Brinon! and all the rest of the Jews in the Castle! this Castle is a ghetto! . . . do you know that?"

"Certainly, Major. Of course I know it!"

"You don't seem to give a damn! But the Jews will get you!"

"You too, Major . . . they'll get you too!"

We were almost laughing . . . Such a whimsical future!

"Then would you please . . . would you kindly give me another injection? That charming man has fatigued me . . ."

"So I noticed, Major . . . so I noticed . . ."

"But don't murder me, Doctor! . . . not yet!"

We start laughing! . . . we're doubled up!

"Major, I wish to inform you that I don't murder anybody . . . neither here nor anywhere else! I've never let a single patient die! . . . however, in view of the circumstances . . . the conditions . . . as long as we're having this little talk . . . I should like to point out that these 2 c.c.s of camphorated oil that I'm going to inject were not procured from your *Hof* Richter *Apotek* . . . oh no! . . . Richter always tells me he hasn't got any! . . . you know everything, you must know that I get this camphorated oil from Switzerland! and that I pay a fortune for it! . . . I get it through a 'runner'! My own money! Not Adolf Hitler's! not the Reich's! . . . you who know everything . . . you know my room is full of gold . . . you'd love to seize it! like Leclerc's Senegalese! but you never will! because you know perfectly well that if you did there'd be no more camphorated oil for you! . . ."

"You mean I should be grateful to you, Doctor? Is that it?"

"You certainly should be, Major!"

"Very well, Doctor, you have all my gratitude! *stimmt!* but in that case I've got a little something to ask of you! It means a lot to me! you who like certificates so much . . . I want you to attest the behavior of this Boisnières! . . . that you witnessed it, that I should have shot him! and didn't! that he positively defied me! Did he or didn't he? . . ."

"Yes, yes, Major! it's a fact . . . but lie down . . . and strip again! your pants . . . just your pants . . ."

I give him another shot . . . in the buttock . . . and I pick up my equipment . . . ampuls . . . cotton . . . syringe . . . we hear voices outside . . . arguing . . . down below . . . on our landing again . . . always on our landing . . . they're starting up again . . .

"Where can my wife be?"

"Just don't move, Major! your injection! . . . stay right where you are . . . at least five minutes . . . I'll go see . . ."

I open the door . . . Neuneuil is there . . . haranguing the crowd . . . over the bannister . . . he hasn't even gone downstairs . . . everybody on the landing . . . our landing . . .

they're giving him the needle . . . the cracks come thick and fast! . . . they'd heard everything . . . the clouts! . . . and the names Raumnitz had called him! ho ho Neuneuil! . . . wise guy! his puss! . . . his bandage! . . . sure took a flier! . . .

"Whyn't you go back? ladyfinger! flannelmouth! . . . go on in! . . . spank him! . . . spank him! . . . he's used to it! . . . take his pants down! . . . eunuch! . . ."

Plenty of encouragement! . . . but oh no, he didn't want to go back! he wanted everybody to listen to him! . . . first . . . but neither the crowd downstairs, nor the crowd upstairs, wanted to listen . . . nobody wanted to listen . . . so Neuneuil starts going down . . . one step . . . two steps . . . he comes down to them . . ."Let me through . . . I'm going to the doctor's . . ." Lili is in our room . . . No. 11 . . . she lets him in . . . she hands him his box, he'd left it there . . . his card file . . . all Siegmaringen on cards . . . and they start hollering some more . . . on the landing! . . . calling him a cocksucking eunuch because he won't go up and slug Raumnitz! the brute! the *Obercopführer!* all he cares about is his card file! he doesn't give a hoot about the rest! . . . "Listen to me, the whole lot of you . . . bunch of punks! . . . get this! . . . I'm Neuneuil! And I shit on all of you! . . . I'm Neuneuil! . . . stinkers! motherfuckers! My message to you is shit! the whole lot of you! these hardships magnify me! I'll come back from Berlin stronger than ever . . . and more formidable!"

"Boo! Boo! flatfoot! . . . go get yourself buggered . . . in Berlin! Slug! . . . Garbage pail! . . ."

The whole landing was yelling . . . but they let him through . . . him and his card file . . . clutched tight . . . he shows it to them! he thumps on it! . . . "Yes, this is my card file! . . . you stupid bastards! . . . and everybody in Siegmaringen is in it! . . . nitwits! . . . I'll entertain them in Berlin! . . . I, Neuneuil! fishing for trout! Ha!"

He looks back, up toward the landing . . . he shakes his fist at Raumnitz! . . . he defies him! . . . the *Obercopführer!* . . . and those characters who'd been advising him to go spank him . . . all of a sudden . . . *zip!* . . . they change

their minds . . . the fun's over . . . they let Neuneuil leave
. . . the hysterical stupid bigmouth! . . . he could wear out
Raumnitz's patience! a guy like that is a menace! He had no
trouble getting down the stairs . . . they let him through all
right! . . . like they'd let the cholera through! they let him
split with his card file! . . . nobody holds him back, nobody!
the crowd melts away . . . not a peep . . . they all go down
to the *Stam* . . . the Strasbourgeois, the *Volkssturm*, the
housewives . . . a minute ago bedlam outside our door . . .
people for me, people for the crapper . . . Suddenly a vacuum! All of a sudden they couldn't even stand the sight of Neuneuil! . . . nobody left on the landing but me . . . he calls me
from downstairs . . . to come down . . . he wanted to speak
to me . . . I go down . . .

"What do you say, Doctor? You saw them! . . . they've got
the green shits, the whole lot of them! . . . and that stinker up
there, Doctor! . . . the brute! the stupid bastard! fishing for
trout! he's liquidated me! Okay! He's shipping me out . . .
he'll see me again! . . . ah, he thinks he's getting rid of me!
you'll see me again too, Doctor! I embrace you!"

He was in tears . . . he really shoves off . . . not in the direction of the station . . . or in the opposite direction . . .
the *Fidelis* . . . oh no! . . . the road that goes up the hill
. . . the road to Berlin . . . to the right as you leave the
hotel, then left . . . *Herzoggasse* . . . the little alley . . . I
motion to the *schuppo* at the door . . . that it's okay . . . he
should let him go . . . the *schuppo* had wanted to turn him
back . . . *nein! nein!* . . . that he's going to Berlin for Raumnitz! . . . on foot! . . . that it's absolutely secret! Hush!
Hush! I motion him to tell the other *schuppo* . . . the one
across the street . . . top secret! . . . and I talk to the
schuppo . . . "*Raumnitz befehl!* . . . *gut! gut!* . . ." . . . it's
okay! they let Neuneuil pass . . . he shoves off . . . very
chipper, I've got to admit . . . at a good clip, with his card file
under his arm . . . "Good luck, Doctor!" . . . He's all alone
on the road . . . he disappears not far away . . . behind the
trees . . . the trees right after the *Prinzenbau* . . . the road
uphill . . .

Hell, I didn't want to go out . . . but I had to . . . not the same day but the next . . . to get the scraps for Bébert . . . and while I was at the *Landrat's,* drop in on Madame Bonnard . . . I've told you about her, my aged patient, ninety-six years old, very frail and delicate, very sick . . . what charm! what distinction! what a memory! Legouvé by heart! all his poetry! . . . all Musset . . . all Marivaux . . . it was pleasant in her room, I stayed to listen to her, I kept her company, she charmed me . . . I admired her . . . I've got to admit, I haven't admired women much in spite of my skirt-chasing life . . . but there I was appreciative . . . I don't know if Arletty will affect me the same way later on . . . maybe . . . the great feminine mystery has nothing to do with ass . . . The Baudeloque and Tarnier clinics, all the maternity hospitals in the world, are chock-full of feminine mysteries . . . that spawn, bleed, confess, and scream! no mystery at all! the real feminine mystery is a different wavelength much more subtle than "cunts and loving hearts" . . . a kind of background music . . . not so easy to tune in on . . . Madame Bonnard, the only patient I ever lost, had those fine lacy waves . . . how well she recited Du Bellay . . . Charles d'Orléans . . . Louise Labé . . . with her I almost came to understand certain waves . . . my novels would be entirely different . . . she's gone . . .

Getting back to our *Löwen* . . . after Neuneuil's departure we had a practically quiet week . . . only three air-raid alarms . . . and two emergencies at the *Fidelis* . . . not bad . . . but it was starting to get cold . . . October 1944 . . . so they dreamed up a magnificent idea at the castle . . . farsighted . . . "firewood commandos" . . . it consisted of sending volunteers to pick up sticks, dead wood, and stumps and bring it all back in enormous bundles . . . the volunteers were all in harness . . . hauling the stuff back! on the double! let's go! . . . men and women, young and old! all in harness! and singing! Volunteers? a manner of speaking . . . willing . . . not willing? Same difference . . . all in harness . . . the Firewood Commandos . . . raise the morale of the hesitant . . . "Strength through Joy!" . . . the great Fourth Reich is dead with all its people and houses and Beethoven too! "Strength through Joy" chorus! Symphonic nation! Christ! Your Frenchman isn't very symphonic, those joyous "all out for brushwood" commandos made them more skeptical than ever . . . they'd hide under their beds . . . especially because the place they were taken to was in the middle of the Black Forest right near Cissen, the camp where they sent our babies . . . that was the site picked for the voluntary labors of the forest commandos . . . the pioneer brushwood collectors . . .

Their civilian occupation didn't matter . . . what counted was their good will . . . they should bring back all the wood, the whole forest, every dead twig, for the winter . . . that's all we'd have! the town halls . . . Boche and French . . . had warned us! no fuel allotment . . . we shouldn't expect any . . .

Hell, there was still a war going on . . . no time to argue . . . a wood-burning truck waited for the volunteers outside the town hall (*Prinzenbau*) . . . at a rather early hour, six-fifteen . . . it took them out . . . not back . . . had to get back by their own resources . . . sportsmen autonomous . . . harnessed to tree trunks . . . the Volga . . . Buchenwald . . . the Great Wall of China . . . Nasser and the Pyramids . . . the same racket! swift kicks in the ass are nothing new! . . . a job of work! and in cadence! . . . and no goldbricking! . . . *heave ho!* Volga barges, Pyramids! *heave! ho!* The "volunteers" were expected to report at six-fifteen . . . outside our town hall (the *Prinzenbau*) . . .

"Ah, Céline! . . . Céline! . . . my dear Céline! . . . you're
the man I've been looking for! . . ."

At last I had a chance to go out . . . nobody on the landing
. . . everybody in the restaurant . . .

"Ah, Céline! . . . Céline!"

I said to myself: the nut's coming up here! . . . and not
alone . . . with a lady . . . a young lady . . . they've come
up to see me . . . I let them in . . .

"Céline . . . Céline . . . I need you . . . I've just come
from Brinon's . . . he's given his okay . . . you'll do the scenario . . . naturally I'll do the dialogue! . . . it's in the bag
. . . I've just seen Laval, he's all for it! I'm the producer and
director, see? are you with us? . . . we're getting a camera
from Leipzig! . . . the Russians have given their okay, ah,
Céline, that authorization from the Russians, you can't imagine! But I've finally got it!"

He beats his breast . . . his pocket . . . where he keeps his
billfold . . . with the authorization . . .

"I'll do it all myself . . . the cutting . . . the dialogue . . .
everything! . . . the trouble we've had . . . Leipzig, imagine! . . . Leipzig! but you'll be quick about your scenario!
very quick, Céline! I've got to see Laval again tomorrow! it's
got to be ready! he's given his okay . . ."

The lady . . . his wife no doubt . . . didn't say a word
. . . she lets him talk . . . he talks all right . . . the vehe-
mence! the flow! he can't keep still! . . . one foot! . . . the
other foot . . . he marks time . . . and revolves! . . . and
gesticulates! . . . the passion, the frenzy! . . . as if he were
selling something! . . . ah, suddenly he stops short . . . he
realizes . . .

"Oh, forgive me . . . forgive me . . . forgive me, Céline . . . I'd forgotten my wife! . . . our star! . . . she's going to be our star . . . let me introduce you . . . Odette Clarisse . . ."

"Bonjour, Madame!"

I hadn't really looked at her . . . but her hat! not a bad little dip . . . panama with flowers . . . and a veil! . . . can you imagine? a veil? . . . at that moment in history? . . . in Germany at that time!

"Odette will be our star . . . it's settled . . . Brinon is agreed."

"Oh, splendid, splendid!"

"Odette, say hello to Madame Céline!"

Not a bad little number . . . I take a better look . . . she's dressed like a star . . . a star of the period, half-Marlene, half-Arletty . . . close-fitting skirt . . . the smile, too . . . a star! sure thing! that smile! . . . half-pixie, half-"I am going to commit suicide" . . . it was certainly the right time to end it all . . . but there was still a mystery . . . how had he come by a flowery hat with a veil, alligator shoes, handbag ditto, and sheer silk stockings in a Germany on fire? . . . that must have been quite an undertaking! outfitting this cutie! . . . when in all Germany right then you couldn't find a hairpin! . . . where had he come by all that? . . . and how had he brought his star here from Dresden? . . . and not only the girl . . . the way they were both spiffed out! . . . him in corduroy riding breeches, turtleneck sweater, leather puttees, shoes with triple soles! really a mystery! . . . and brushed and polished! . . . spotless . . . both of them . . . ready for the cameras . . . I knew him from the *Fidelis;* I'd treated him for sinus trouble . . . and here he was, completely cured! health! vitality! . . . tops! . . . Raoul . . . that was his name . . . Raoul Orphize . . . he'd gone to Dresden . . . the Mecca of the arts, meanwhile burned down . . . 200,000 dead . . . they'd left Dresden for Munich . . . and then Leipzig . . . and then back again to Dresden . . . Dresden in ashes! and now he was going to make a movie in Siegmaringen . . . oh, he'd thought it all out . . . the sequences, the rhythm! . . . I had only to follow his ideas, his cine-technic construction . . . "daily life in Siegmaringen" . . . Brinon at work . . . the printing press and editorial office of the newspaper *La France,* the editors at work . . . "Radio-Siegmar" broadcasting; the studio, the technicians . . . the *Milice* drilling! . . . and myself with patients! Pétain, his outing! . . . children playing! . . . and fathers and mothers playing too, playing bowls! joy forever! good humor! *Kraft durch Freude!* everywhere and always! Joy!

"I hear you've been depressed, Céline . . . is that true?"

"Of course not! Not at all! Good gracious! not depressed! even keel, that's the word! . . . my profession! . . . serious! . . . perhaps a little overworked! . . . but no more! . . . no more, Orphize!"

I don't want him to go blabbing all over the place . . . Orphize looks very much like a cop to me—if he wants to know . . . I won't tell him . . . people with high morale always scare me in the first place . . . and in the second place the way he's dressed? . . . where's he come from? . . . with all that stuff? brand new! . . . that jacket? breeches, puttees, shoes with triple soles? he was in rags like the rest of us at the *Fidelis* . . . and all that vim and vigor and that "ensemble" of hers? . . . the little plaid skirt, the embroidered blouse . . . where'd all that stuff come from? . . . made me think . . . memories . . . of the market in Chatou in 1900 . . . the little girls with their mothers . . .

"Where does all that elegance come from, Orphize?"

I couldn't help asking him.

"By parachute, Céline!"

Wise guy! . . . I didn't insist . . .

"Then I can count on you, Céline? it's okay with Brinon . . . the scenario tomorrow morning? . . . I'll see Le Vigan . . . I'll see Luchaire . . . I'll give them their parts . . . your wife will have a part, too! . . . oh, a splendid part! . . . by your side . . . as a nurse! . . . ah, and as a dancer too! you get the picture? . . . okay? . . . I can count on you?"

"Yes, yes . . . certainly! but where are you going to shoot?"

"In the street, of course! . . . in the street!"

I wasn't going to tell him that the street wasn't a very healthy place . . . more on the mean side . . . bullets flying . . . He was too hopped up to tell him that . . .

"Ah, but wait! the main thing! I need a visa . . . from von Raumnitz . . . I don't know this von Raumnitz . . . where does he hang out? . . . a mere formality . . . a rubber stamp . . ."

"Upstairs . . . right above us . . . next landing . . . Room 28! Just knock! . . . You'll find him . . ."

"Is this Raumnitz in a good humor?"

"So so . . . you may find him a little tired . . ."

"My word! You're all falling apart around here! I'll put Raumnitz in my picture too! . . . your Raumnitz! definitely! . . . and that morale of yours? that morale? I'll have you smiling yet, Céline! Come, come! I need you, Céline! . . . But not with that Ash Wednesday face! . . . the picture is going to be shown in France! Do you realize? in France! . . . more than a hundred theaters! . . . your mother, your daughter, your friends . . . they'll all see it! . . . a real attraction! and your friends! . . . you have friends in France, Céline . . . many more than you think! . . . you didn't know? . . . who admire you . . . who love you! . . . who are waiting for you! . . . crowds of friends! . . . don't be depressed, Céline . . . pull yourself together . . . all France hasn't gone Jewish! you can't imagine how they detest the Gaullists in France! you didn't know? my, oh, my! and how they love Pétain! . . . you've no idea! . . . more than Clemenceau! . . . you'll write an article for me in *La France*? . . . how about it?"

"Certainly, certainly, Orphize!"

I can't stop him.

"Just as they told me . . . 'Céline's morale is really shot . . .' That's what they told me . . . come along now! you're not going to back down on your principles . . . my word! . . . I'll be going upstairs now . . . back in a minute . . . you'll wait for me? . . . Room 28, you say?"

"Yes, yes, his name is on the door: Raumnitz!"

"Come along, Odette . . ."

He doesn't wait . . . he tugs Odette by the arm . . . and up the stairs! *knock knock* . . . *herein!* And there they go . . .

I don't surprise easily, but there . . . I've got to admit . . . Orphize, Odette . . . the veil, the alligator handbag, the triple soles! . . . and coming from Leipzig! . . . from Dresden! . . . especially as I knew a thing or two about Dresden . . . I'd seen the Consul from Dresden a week before . . . the last consul of the Vichy government . . . he'd told me all about it . . . the tactic of total squashing and frying in phosphorus . . . American invention! . . . really perfected! the last "new look" before the A-bomb . . . first the suburbs, the periphery . . . with liquid sulphur and avalanches of torpedoes . . . then general roasting . . . the whole center! Act II! . . . churches, parks, museums . . . no survivors wanted! . . .

They talk about fires in mines . . . illustrations and interviews! . . . they weep, they jerk off about the poor miners . . . those treacherous fires and explosions! . . . shit! . . . and poor Budapest, the ferocity of the Russian tanks! . . . they never say a word . . . and they're wrong! . . . about how their brethren were roasted alive in Germany beneath the spreading wings of democracy . . . one doesn't speak of such things, it's embarrassing! . . . the victims? . . . they shouldn't have been there, that's all! . . . well, this last Vichy consul owed his life . . . he'd passed right through the flames . . . to a pound of coffee . . . all that was left of the Consulate . . . he had his coffee under his arm . . . no card file . . . the firemen were out in front of the Consulate . . . just getting ready to leave . . . playing it double or quits! . . . the center of Dresden through bombs, sulphur, and tornadoes of fire . . . for a place where the bombs weren't falling . . . the hills outside the city . . . a mad dash! . . . the fire engine, the firemen, him, and the coffee . . . the idea wasn't to put out any fires, but to avoid being burned alive! the Dresden firemen had picked him up for his coffee! they hoisted him up and tied him to the fire engine . . . the top of the ladder! . . . a *heave* and a *ho!* . . . him and his coffee through the rivers of fire!

That's why I had my doubts . . . Orphize and his wife coming from Dresden . . . dressed fit to kill, war paint and la-di-da . . . plus the veil . . . food for thought . . . and wanting to put me in their picture . . . me! . . . and Le Vigan!

and Luchaire! . . . and his daughter Corinne . . . and Lili!
. . . and Bébert! . . . so our friends in France would get a
good look at us . . . and not forget us . . . He was going to
show it in Switzerland . . . and then in Montmartre! . . . his
breathtaking picture . . . "daily life in Siegmaringen" . . .
Corinne Luchaire wasn't there, she was in a sanatorium in
Saint-Blasien . . . oh, but don't worry! she'd come! no trouble
there! it was okay with her father! and Laval! and Brinon! and
Pétain . . . to give our admirers their money's worth! . . .

All that was food for thought . . . he was upstairs with
Raumnitz . . .

Somebody's coming down . . . "it must be them!" and so it
was . . . Aisha, too, and the mastiffs . . . he calls out to me
on his way down . . . "Céline! Céline! . . . I'm going with
Madame Raumnitz! to look at their camera! I won't be long!
just a minute! . . . I'll be right back . . . you'll wait for me?"

"Yes . . . yes . . . certainly!" I promise . . .

All three of them pass by our door . . . He's as chipper as
ever . . . full of dash . . . she not quite so lively . . . she
gives him her arm . . . she takes little short steps . . . eyes
downcast . . . I forgot to tell you! her eyes were made up
. . . long false eyelashes, Musidora . . . and even tiny paillettes! false lashes, paillettes in her eyebrows . . . the works!
. . . makes you think of *Sunset Boulevard* . . . I've seen
Sunset Boulevard . . . oh, years ago . . . I saw the three of
them moving along . . . talking about boulevards! down the
corridor and still further! . . . Aisha led the way . . . they
had only to follow . . . follow her . . . couldn't go wrong
. . . this way! . . . this way! Aisha, her whip, her mastiffs!
. . . this way! . . . it wasn't up to me to say anything . . .
"Don't look at them," I tell Lili! "Go back in!" I go in with
her . . . it's no time to know certain things . . . to talk about
them in the Castle . . . or to the *Milice* . . . or at the *Fidelis*
. . . if Raumnitz mentions it to me, I'll tell him I didn't see
anything . . .

Two . . . three minutes, not a sound . . . nothing . . .
and then steps . . . Aisha . . . we hear her coming back
. . . *knock! knock!* . . . she's at the door . . .

"Is everything all right?" she asks us . . .

"Oh, fine, Madame Raumnitz. My compliments, Madame!"
I make my voice kind of gay, young . . . glad to see her
. . . the social graces . . . some people appreciate the amen-
ities . . . she often knocks at our door like that and asks how
we're getting along . . . are we all right? . . . I always say
yes . . . sure thing! . . . just fine! . . .

All these little episodes . . . adventures . . . had prevented me from going out . . . you've noticed? . . . for two days . . . all the places I had to go . . . not only my patients at the *Fidelis* . . . the other end of town and the *Milice* . . . and then back to Luther's, this consultation . . . naturally somebody must be consulting in my place! . . . one more phony doctor . . . some impostor! . . . my office at Luther's was the rendezvous of the quacks . . . from all over Germany they landed at Luther's, and at "my hours" . . . my own consultation hours! . . . with their nurses . . . I was a kind of magnet . . . magnet for nuts . . . and if by any chance they took it into their heads to "operate," I could really see trouble ahead! . . . oh, if they only "prescribed" . . . they couldn't do much harm! *Hof* Richter was out of everything . . . But those bastards always wanted to operate! anything, any way, hernia, otitis, warts, cysts! . . . they all wanted to slice . . . they wanted to be surgeons! . . . it's an interesting fact, even in normal times, that the screwball bone-setters, chiropracters, faith-healers, fakirs etc. are never satisfied to dish out advice, pills, phials, good-luck charms, or caramels . . . oh no! . . . they've got to have Grand Opera! . . . the real thing! . . . they've got to see people bleeding . . . throbbing . . . oh, I won't go as far as Daudet,* but it seems pretty obvious . . . that surgery, even the most legal and official kind . . . has a good deal of the Roman Circus about it! . . . human sacrifice à la Tartuffe! . . . and the victims want more and more! absolutely masochistic! They want everything cut off or out . . . nose, bosom, ovaries . . . and the surgeons make hay! precision butchers, watchmakers! . . . your son's going into it? . . . has he got the real assassin's instinct? . . . innate? . . .

the old Anthropithecus inside him? is he a born trepanner, brain ladler, Cro-Magnon? . . . good! . . . good! . . . excellent! a cave man? splendid! tell him to sign up! He's got what it takes! . . . surgery's his cookie! he's got the makings of a great surgeon! . . . the ladies, so pinheaded, so sadistic, will swoon at the mere sight of his hands . . . "oh, what hands! . . . what hands!" . . . they'll go crazy! they'll get down on their knees and beg him to take everything! and not wait! their money! their dowry! their uterus! their essential! their tits! disembowel them completely! . . . turn their peritoneum inside out . . . clean them like rabbits! their guts . . . their organs! several pounds, a whole trayful! . . . oh wonderful, darling assassin! . . . "high priest of my heart!" Landru, Pétiot, the Academy!

Aztec idols? small time! clotted blood, grimaces! . . . Hottentot gourmands deprived of missionaries? . . . don't make me laugh! . . . Sade, the divine marquis? . . . kid stuff! any operating room . . . that's where you'll really see Great Art! . . . Real high priests! . . . and the vivisectionees, delighted! seventh heaven! . . . the animals in La Villette or Chicago are afraid! they have an instinct for what's going to happen . . . the Great Surgeon's dear patients get themselves butchered with delight . . .

My screwballs, these phony doctors at Luther's, certainly couldn't expect to be smothered in gold pieces . . . maybe ten marks . . . twenty marks a shot . . . my worry was that instead of sticking to harmless advice . . . they'd start cutting! . . . they all had the itch . . . every one of them . . . and I'd get the blame! for allowing this . . . or that! . . . I'd warned Brinon! But hell! warnings . . . I'm all in agreement with Louis XVI! "The good has gout, evil has wings!" . . . I could talk myself blue in the face . . . they'd always put the blame on me! . . . for the screwballs' massacres . . . "look at the books he's written!" . . . I'm not telling you anything new, my books have done me more harm than anything else! . . . in Clichy! . . . Bezons! . . . Denmark! . . . here! . . . you write? . . . you're sunk . . . Tropmann's "never confess" is a halfway precaution . . . "never write!" . . . that's the big thing!

If Landru had written, he wouldn't have had time to turn around, let alone pickle a baker's dozen of chicks! . . . he'd have had all Gambais on his neck! he'd have been sunk! . . . "Look at the books he's written!"

I could see it coming in Siegmaringen . . . "evil has wings!" . . . I knew I was cooked . . . one way or another . . . everybody agreed . . . in London, Rome, and Dakar . . . that I deserved to be put in cold mud for *Bagatelles* and ten times more here in Siegmaringen on the Danube! the haven of the 1,142! . . . if I was still alive and wriggling . . . it could only mean that I was playing a double game! that I was a Fifi? . . . or an agent of world Jewry . . . in any case I was washed up . . . "look at the books he's written!" . . . Besides, the 1,142 were counting on their little bonanza . . . that I'd pay for them all! . . . that everything would come out fine . . . thanks to me! they were all dreaming of slippers and firesides . . . thanks to me! . . . for me the Chinese tortures! . . . "look at the books he's written" . . . not for them! not them! . . . they were immune, sitting pretty, charmed . . . my job was to expiate for them all! . . . "look at the books he's written!" . . . I'd appease Moloch! that was the general opinion! . . . I couldn't beat the rap! . . . from the lowest bedridden shitass bum in the *Fidelis* to the most-high Laval in the Castle, it was a certainty . . . "ah, Céline, you don't like the Jews!" Those were the words that reassured them . . . I'd be hanged!

Definitely! . . . but not them! not them . . . oh, dear them! . . . "look at the books he's written!" you can't imagine the agonies of terror that I relieved with *Bagatelles!* just the right thing, just what was wanted of me! . . . the scapegoat book . . . on my throat the knife! . . . I'd be dismembered! not them! . . . no, not them! them so frail and sensitive! no, never! . . . all 1,142 of them . . . not a single anti-Jew left! . . . not one! . . . no more than Morand, Montherlant, Maurois, Latzareff, Laval, or Brinon! . . . the only one left was me . . . the providential goat! . . . I'd saved everybody with *Bagatelles!* the 1,142 warrantees! . . . same as on the other side I saved Morand, Achille, Maurois, Montherlant, and Tartre . . . I was the providential hero sucker! . . . I . . . I . . . not just

France . . . the whole world . . . enemies, allies . . . every-body . . . out for my blood! . . . plenty of blood! . . . they've dreamed up a new myth! . . . disembowel the goat . . . do we? . . . don't we? . . . the priests are ready!

Griping again . . . leaving you high and dry . . . Finally I was able to go out . . . "good-bye, Lili!" I take Bébert, his bag . . . you know, kind of a game bag with breathing holes . . . we're down at the bottom of the stairs . . . naturally the peo-ple in the restaurant see me . . . the *Stam* eaters, the whole beer hall, and the shuppo outside, guarding the door . . . I tell him I'm going to the Castle . . . oh oh! here comes some-body . . . they throw themselves on my neck! . . . Monsieur and Madame Delaunys! . . . effusions! I didn't recognize them . . . ah, Doctor! . . . Doctor! . . . so thin! . . . they'd just come out of the *Stam* . . . I'd had them both as patients . . . where had they been? . . . really all skin and bone! . . . "Where have you been?" "In Cissen, Doctor! . . . in the Camp . . . we were in the firewood brigade!" oh, I understood . . . gathering brushwood . . . "winter through joy!" . . . I could see it hadn't been a vacation! firewood brigade! . . . oh, plenty of good will! . . . but short rations . . . two mess kits a day . . . kohlrabi and carrots! . . . sleeping on straw in a tent . . . one tent for twelve to fifteen families . . . they hadn't put on weight, I could see that! . . . even Frucht's restaurant was better . . . oh, it was the same old *Stam* . . . but at Frucht's there were no blackjacks . . . while at Cissen, Christ! . . . to a pulp! . . . the brushwood squad leaders kept warm by beating them! . . . and no love pats! . . . the real *schlag!* . . . bruises, bumps, blisters! they'd really been warmed over . . . nothing was left of their clothes . . . covered with rags . . . knotted together, tied with string . . . shaped into boots, a jacket, a dress . . . odds and ends they'd picked up . . . swiped all over . . . from other families . . . other brushwood teams . . . it wasn't their profession . . . any of them . . . and they weren't the right age either . . . people from before the other war . . . they looked bad, even him with his wig and "Nubian" moustache . . . made you think of an oldtime barber's window . . . She'd given singing lessons on

the rue Tiquetonne . . . he was a violinist . . . really a settled harmonious couple . . . no variety honeymoon! married
thirty-five years! . . . all the good will in the world . . . devoted to their pupils! . . . devoted to the New Europe! . . .
same sincerity! no calculation! they'd come out for Europe
right away! no thought of gain! . . . not at all . . . he'd
played the violin (second fiddle) in the big orchestra at the
Grand Palais . . . New Europe Exposition, Common Market,
etc. . . . she'd sung for Madame Abetz at the Embassy . . .
what soirées! what guests! to give you an idea whether they
were in deep! . . . and whether they had received those death
"notices" and little coffins! . . . and a good stiff load of Article
75 . . . that Morand never got . . . or Montherlant! or Maurois! . . . these people were honest, serious! . . . skin of their
teeth! . . . their place had been sacked, completely wrecked!
all their belongings taken, moved! clearance! . . . like me on
the rue Norvins . . . that made us neighbors . . . well, practically . . . I didn't take it lightly, though . . . but they . . .
well, almost . . . no bitterness, no grudge . . . just grieved!
. . . especially at being beaten for not collecting enough
wood . . . they didn't deserve to be beaten . . . and called
lazy old bastards . . . it was the "lazy old" that didn't go
down! . . . "We lazy, Doctor? a whole life of conscientious
hard work . . . not a moment's idleness! You know us, Doctor!"

She had tears in her eyes . . . the ultimate insult! They lazy!
. . . "First prize at the conservatory! both of us!" . . . sobs
. . . "you know, I've told you, we met at the Concerts Touche
. . . laziness at the Concerts Touche?! . . . you knew Monsieur Touche, Doctor, didn't you? you know the kind of man,
the artist he was! . . . and the hard work! . . . a new program every week! . . . and no oompa-oompa! no café music!
You did know Monsieur Touche?" . . . "Oh yes, of course,
Madame Delaunys!" . . . The way they'd been beaten . . .
and not with daisies . . . I could see the marks . . .
thrashed for being lazy! . . . she really couldn't understand
. . . it was too much! . . . them! . . . and her husband on
the head! . . . "Look!" It was true . . . two places . . . big

patches of scalp gone . . . torn off! . . . hit really hard! . . .
oh, but not discouraged! far from it! you couldn't get him
down! . . . oh no, the future! he was a man of the future! his
sufferings in Cissen had brought it out! overcome his fears!
"Yes, Doctor!" a project! . . . and come to think of it, maybe I
could help him with his project . . . if I was willing? . . . my
influence with Brinon? . . . "Concert master!" . . . a word
from Brinon would do it! . . . "concert master" where? I didn't
get it . . . if I were willing? . . . yes . . . yes . . . un-
doubtedly the time in Cissen had been unpleasant, the blows,
the insults, but here was an opportunity to make up for it! . . .
concert master! . . . all his life, with Touche and elsewhere, he
had been on the verge of promotion to concert master . . .
never come through . . . for one reason or another . . . he
wasn't vain or forward, but he had the qualifications! . . .
"What do you think of it, Doctor? Here, now, in Siegmaringen!
. . ." he pointed out somebody in the restaurant, over
there . . .

"Do you see Monsieur Langouvé?"

I saw him . . . he was there . . .

"He's all for it!"

Monsieur Langouvé was there at a little table . . . at the
Stam . . . Monsieur Langouvé . . . the conductor of the Siegmaringen orchestra . . .

"Monsieur Langouvé has noticed my performance as second
fiddle . . . 'We owe you the position of concert master' . . .
his opinion! . . . imagine, Doctor . . . I'm only mentioning it
to you! . . . I don't go in for intrigue! . . . you know that!
. . . I'm not a climber . . . a careerist! perish the thought!
. . . but here, under the circumstances, I need the approval
of the Castle, and a word from you . . . you could . . .
couldn't you, Doctor? . . . or if you can't, I'll never mention
it again . . . but you've always been so good to us, so kind!
so encouraging! But I'm really being bold! I'm taking liberties!"

I could see Monsieur Langouvé, the orchestra conductor, at
his little table in the *Stam.* The soul of courtesy! worse than
Delaunys! . . . delicate, precious, he expressed himself like a
violin . . . in caressing waves! like Debussy's *Nuages* . . .

Of course I wanted to help them . . . Delaunys and his wife
. . . but how was I going to introduce them to Brinon? . . .

"They're putting on a celebration soon . . ."

"Where, Monsieur Delaunys?"

"Why, certainly . . . so I've heard . . . at the Castle! . . .
Monsieur Langouvé is already rehearsing the chorus! . . .
they're celebrating the retaking of the Ardennes!"

"Hmm . . . you don't say so . . ."

"Yes . . . yes! . . . all the ambassadors! . . a big celebration! . . ."

"Ah! . . . Ah?"

"Monsieur Langouvé . . ."

He's deep in a kind of revery . . . he's dreaming . . . he
sees . . . his wife doesn't see . . .

"Hector . . . really?"

She speaks up . . . she hadn't heard . . . I watch him
closely . . . yes, there is a glazed look in his eyes . . . could
they have knocked him a little silly in the brushwood brigade?
. . . hit him a little too hard? . . . could be . . . I wondered
. . . I asked his wife . . .

"Oh, they hit us so terribly, Doctor! . . . and the things they
called us!"

It was the "lazy" that stuck in her craw . . . that kept her in
tears . . . but him? I couldn't help wondering . . .

"Hard on the head?"

"Very hard!"

She started sobbing again . . . the one thing in his mind
was the Celebration . . . the Celebration for his benefit! . . .
and "Concert master" . . . the "Retaking of the Ardennes!"

"Then you will, Doctor? Concert master? You will? I only
hope that Monsieur de Brinon . . ."

"Why, of course, Monsieur Delaunys . . . Consider yourself
concert master . . ."

I gesture to his wife that it was all settled . . . she should
stop wailing! . . . he certainly seemed strange . . . ragged,
disheveled, that glazed look, yet in spite of everything a certain
dignity . . . in his tied-up, molded rags . . . the bad part was
his discolored moustache, faded from "Nubian" to tallow . . .

and his torn wig . . . it wasn't only his scalp that had suffered! . . . they'd dusted the whole man! . . .

"Oh, strictly a chamber orchestra . . . you get the idea, Doctor? . . . but what splendid works! . . . you'll hear Mozart! . . . Debussy! . . . Fauré! . . . oh, I knew Fauré well! . . . we weren't the first to play his music . . . but almost! . . . almost! . . . am I right, sweetheart?"

"Oh yes! . . . oh yes!"

"And Florent Schmidt too! . . . without boasting, I can say that we played all the young composers on the Boulevard de Strasbourg! . . . Did you know Monsieur Hass, Doctor? our pianist? . . . another First Prize!"

"Of course, Monsieur Delaunys!"

"Monsieur Touche was the soul of kindness! you know that, Doctor! . . . he wanted me to be concert master! . . . in 1900! . . . even then! . . . of course I declined! . . . I declined! . . . I was too young . . . I refused Monsieur Touche but with Monsieur Langouvé, yes, I accept! . . . I've made up my mind . . . I can't wait any longer! . . . the opportunity presents itself? I'll take it! not that I haven't always wanted it! . . . yes, I admit it! . . . but would you have expected me to rush? never! calculation? certainly not! . . . but the question of maturity, Doctor? . . . I wasn't mature, but now I am! you'll hear me! ah, Doctor, Madame Céline will be on the program too! she'll dance! she will, won't she? . . . we've taken the liberty! . . . an old dance . . . a chaconne . . . and two other dances . . . romantic . . . we'll accompany her! . . . you'll let her?"

His wife looked at me, to see what I was thinking . . . I motioned her not to say anything . . . that it was his head . . . his head . . . he really did seem to have a glazed look, but his words weren't those of a lunatic . . . only maybe a little surprising . . . this Celebration at the Castle! . . .

But one thing was sure . . . I could see that if he went up to Raumnitz and started talking about the Ardennes and the Celebration and the concert, Aisha would escort him out . . . he'd join the others . . . it couldn't fail! . . . he wasn't a bad sort . . . maybe the best way, as long as I was going, would be to take them to the Castle and try to find them a place to sleep . . . see if Brinon would take them in . . . anyway, I could try . . . maybe Madame Mitre could do something . . . Maybe they could use musicians in the Castle . . . because here at the *Löwen* they'd end up in Room 36 . . . without a doubt! . . . upstairs and down in two seconds flat! . . .

Madame Mitre would understand . . . a good deal better than Brinon . . .

Retaking of the Ardennes . . . Celebration of Rundstedt's Triumph? . . . where had he got that? . . . from Monsieur Langouvé? . . . the conductor? . . . Langouvé was a little touched, but not that bad . . . or in Cissen? . . . the brushwood commando? . . . they hadn't just clouted his noodle, they'd started a jamboree in it! . . . celebrations! . . . apotheosis!

I motion his wife to come along, they should follow me . . . I motion to Lili, too . . . "You'll start rehearsing," I tell her . . .

The main thing, when people have a screw loose, is not to thwart them . . . act as if everything were perfectly natural . . . no opposition! . . . same with animals! . . . no surprises! . . . everything is just fine . . . perfectly natural . . . same with incisions, injections, scalpels . . . "perfectly natural" . . . oh, but watch your step! . . . a quarter of a milligram too much or too little . . . and all hell breaks loose! . . . the Devil and his cauldron! . . . the emotions boil over! the patient jumps off the operating table with his belly wide open, dragging his guts . . . carrying everything away . . . scalpels, mask, balloon flask, compresses! . . . wide open! . . . and all your fault! . . . same in your love life: how often you see your lovesick little sweetheart turn into a homicidal maniac! "Sexfiend, rapist, monster!" You can't get over it! so docile, and now this arrogant rage! . . . a touch too heavy somewhere! . . . never mind . . .

Suppose you're a king . . . your people eat, drink, go to church, and leave you alone . . . all of a sudden fireworks on all sides! . . . they knock over your Bastille . . . and wipe out your regime! . . . Pont-Neuf, Grand Army, and all! you've said one little word too many! all it takes to break that "perfectly natural" charm! . . .

Without boasting, I can say that I watched my step . . . not a faux pas! I led them away as if it were the most natural thing in the world . . . Delaunys, his wife and Lili . . . we left the *Löwen* in plain sight of the shuppo . . . *Raumnitz befehl!* hush hush! . . . he salutes . . . okay! . . . direct to the Castle! we take the elevator . . . first Madame Mitre . . . actually she's the one that counts . . . I explain the case . . . the two of them are at the door, waiting for me . . . Madame Mitre understands right away . . . "You know how it is, Doctor, the Ambassador right now!"

It was always "the Ambassador right now" for one reason or another! This was a particularly bad time, his wife née Ulmann had just phoned from Constance that he should do this . . . do that . . . oh, Madame née Ulmann was a power! the story was that she was opposed to her husband's policies . . . pure hokum, according to Pellepoix* who knew them well, they bickered for the gallery, but they both belonged to the "Great Conspiracy!" . . . possible . . . but in the end one thing is sure, he was drilled, she wasn't . . .

I've told you, Brinon was always perfectly regular with me . . . not cordial, no! . . . but regular . . . he might have been put out with me for not having "superb morale," for not writing in *La France* that Boche victory was around the corner . . . for speaking very freely . . . not playing the game . . . what game was he playing? I never found out! . . . the fact remains that he never asked me any questions . . . he could have . . . I was a doctor and that's that! . . . oh, I practiced all right! I knew every passage, every blind alley and attic in that Hohenzollern fortress! bringing the good word to this one and that one . . . Subject of politics, Brinon left me alone . . . that's unusual! . . . mostly the bigshots in the double game aren't satisfied unless you wave your arms and really get yourself hooked . . . occasionally we exchanged a few words on the subject of letters from Berlin, from the Chancellery . . . mentioning medicine . . . and things I had said at one time or another . . .

"What do you think, Monsieur de Brinon?"

"Nothing . . . I'm reading you the letters from Berlin . . . that's all . . ."

As Bonnard said, Brinon was a cave animal . . . gloomy and secretive . . . you couldn't get anything out of him . . . all the same, six months before the end, I went to see him about some ointment . . . sulphur and mercury . . . "Oh, Doctor, come along, in six months it will all be over" . . . I didn't ask him which way . . . he never said anything about anything.

Anyway, with my raggedy Delaunys, it wasn't exactly the right time . . .

"What do you want of the Ambassador, Doctor?"

"To let them stay in the Castle, because if they go back to the *Löwen* you know von Raumnitz? . . . ."

Of course she knew him . . . and his little ways . . . I didn't go into details . . . neither did she . . . she knew all about it . . .

I dive right in . . . bull by the horns . . .

"I'll take them up to the music room . . . they'll behave . . . I vouch for them . . . they'll rehearse . . . I'll bed them down . . . they won't move . . . they'll sleep up there . . . Lili will bring them their *Stam* . . . Lili dances up there . . . I'll tell the servants, I'll tell Bridoux, I'll tell everybody it's for the big Celebration . . . all right? . . ."

Madame Mitre hadn't heard . . .

"What big celebration?"

"Oh, it's his idea . . . the banquet for the 'Retaking of the Ardennes!' "

Madame Mitre doesn't get it . . . she looks at me . . . have I gone off my rocker too?

"No, Madame Mitre . . . no . . . that's the pretext! . . . My mind's all right, but he believes in this Celebration! he's dead sure . . . and sure that he'll be promoted to concert master . . . it's his dream . . . Monsieur Langouvé has promised him . . . . you understand?"

She begins to catch on . . .

"But listen to me, Madame Mitre . . . if I take them back to the *Löwen* . . ."

Oh, she understands that . . .

"You know how they were treated in Cissen? beaten to a pulp . . . so you see . . . he isn't quite right . . . concussion! . . . at his age! . . . just take a look at his head! . . ."

"Oh, Doctor, I believe you . . . very well, I'll tell Monsieur de Brinon there's an orchestra rehearsing . . . for a benefit performance . . ."

"Fine . . . certainly . . . thank you, Madame Mitre! . . . hardly anybody goes up there . . . nobody but Bridoux . . . and the servants . . . it's too cold . . . if anybody asks, I'll say: it's the retaking of the Ardennes . . . the big celebration . . . good-by, Madame Mitre . . ."

So I climb my people up to the seventh floor, Delaunys, his wife, Lili . . . Delaunys and his wife are scratching even worse than we are . . . they'd reinforced their scabies out there . . . I've seen plenty of scabies, but the insects they brought back from the camp and the brush! . . . real flesh plows! . . . galloping scabies! . . . in addition to their bruises and blotches, they were living Chinese puzzles, checkerboards of scabies . . .

"Haven't you any ointment, Doctor?"

"No, but we'll have some soon, Madame!"

I comfort her . . . I don't want them to stop scratching, to stand still and think . . . the idea was to keep them moving . . . get them up those stairs . . . We made it! . . . here we are! the spacious concert hall . . . "Hall of Neptune" they called it . . .

"Oh, very nice! oh, splendid!"

They keep exclaiming . . . he's delighted . . .

"And excellent acoustics, I hope?"

"Admirable, Monsieur Delaunys!"

Indeed, the Hohenzollern princes hadn't stinted . . . the hall was a good six hundred feet long, all draped in pink and gray brocade . . . and down there on the stage at the end the porphyry statue of Neptune . . . brandishing his trident! . . . terrific! . . . standing in an enormous shell . . . alabaster and granite! . . .

I've got it! . . . the idea came to me instantly!

"How about it, Delaunys? . . . Monsieur de Brinon has

given his permission . . . you won't have to go out . . . you'll
sleep in the shell! . . . over there! both of you! . . . you see?
. . . no need to go out! . . . they'd pick you up and send you
to Cissen! . . . they'd take you back! . . . I'll bring you
blankets! . . . nobody'll see you! . . . you'll be a lot better off
than at the *Fidelis!* . . ."

They were only too glad to believe me . . .

"Certainly, Doctor! Certainly!"

"And you'll bring us some ointment?"

"Oh yes, Madame . . . tomorrow morning!"

So that's the story . . .

Just then Bridoux comes through! . . . General Bridoux in
his boots and spurs! . . . resplendent! . . . he crossed the
hall from end to end at lunchtime . . . to the ministers'
table . . . one two! one! two! . . . every day at the stroke of
noon! and every day at the stroke of noon he made the same
observation . . . "Get out of here!" He couldn't stand seeing
Lili dance in this hall! so closed-in! . . . not brutal but author-
itarian! . . . outside she had the terraces! and what terraces!
. . . the air, the view of the whole valley! . . . Minister of
War and cavalry general! . . . "Get out of here!" . . .

As for him, he had escaped from Berlin . . . "Get out of
here!" from the Russians . . . later escaped from the Val de
Grâce from the Fifis . . . "Get out of here!" . . . and ended
up in Madrid . . . "Get out of here!" . . . That's life in a nutshell . . .

One thing anyway, I had found a place for the Delaunys
. . . they spent about a month in Neptune's shell . . . Lili
brought them their *Stam* . . . they slept in blankets she
brought from the *Löwen* . . . they got along fine with Bridoux
. . . they went out on the terraces to please him . . . Later on
things happened . . . a lot of things . . . I'll tell you.

I leave Lili at work . . . rehearsing her dances with the De-launys, her pieces for the Celebration . . . it's no joke any more . . . all "perfectly natural"! . . . chaconnes, passe-pieds, rigadoons! . . . after a while we got very serious about it . . . don't tip the kettle . . . don't let the devils out! the "Retaking of the Ardennes"? Certainly! all the ambassadors will be there! . . . of course! the triumph of Rundstedt's army? Oh la la! triumph is putting it mildly!

As for ambassadors, only one . . . the Japanese . . . and a single consul, the Italian . . . maybe in a pinch the one from Vichy . . . who'd escaped from Dresden? . . . and the Ger-man Ambassador? Hoffmann? . . . accredited to Brinon . . . Otto Abetz* still gave little "surprise parties" now and then . . . oh, all very harmless and innocent . . . Without pre-judging the future but taking the past into account, the Chancel-lery of the Greater Reich had worked out a certain mode of existence for the French in Siegmaringen, neither absolutely fictitious nor absolutely real . . . a fictitious status, half way between quarantine and operetta, elaborated by Monsieur Sixte, our great legal expert at the Foreign Ministry in Berlin, who had drawn on every possible precedent: the Revocation of the Edicts, the Palatinate, the Huguenots, the War of the Span-ish Succession . . . finally we were granted the "conditional, exceptional, and precarious" status of "refugees in a French en-clave" . . . Visible marks of our status were our stamps (por-trait of Pétain), his *Milice* in uniform, and our unfurled flag on high! and our clarion reveille! . . . but our "exceptional en-clave" was itself an enclave in Prusso-Baden territory . . . and watch yourself! this territory itself was an enclave in South Württemberg! Just to give you an idea . . . The total unity of

Germany dates from Hitler and not so very unified at that! for instance: there were trains going from Germany to Switzerland that crossed the border ten times, the same one, in fifteen minutes . . . *länder*, loops, hamlets, riverbeds . . . hell . . . I go on and on . . .

One way or another, we were short on ambassadors for this celebration . . . make do with Japan? . . . of course we could invite Abetz . . . as ambassador of what? . . . Abetz went around in a wood-burning car . . . you were always running into him . . . three hundred yards: breakdown . . . another three hundred yards: another breakdown! . . . his big noggin slashed and battered! . . . bubbling with ideas, all of them wrong . . . everybody in Paris knew Abetz, I didn't know him very well . . . no sympathy . . . really nothing to say to each other . . . practically any time you saw him he was surrounded by "clients" . . . courtiers . . . courtier-clients from every Court! . . . the same ones or their brothers! you can drop in on Mendès . . . Churchill, Nasser, or Khrushchev . . . always the same people or their brothers! Versailles, Kremlin, Vel d'Hiv, Auction Rooms . . . Laval! de Gaulle! . . . you'll see . . . gray eminences, punks, shady characters, Academists or Third Estate, pluri-sexuals, rigorists or proxenetists, eaters of hosts or piddle-bread, you'll find them forever sybilline, reborn from century to century! . . . that's the continuity of Power! . . . you're looking for some little poison? . . . some document? . . . that big chandelier? . . . or that little dressing table? . . . that rolypoly groom? . . . yours! . . . one wink, and it's fixed! . . . On his return from Clichy (Dagobert's court) Agobert, bishop of Lyons, already (632) complained that the Court was a sink! a den of thieves and whores! . . . Agobert of Lyons! . . . he should come back in 3060 . . . thieves and whores! he'll find the same! Don't doubt it . . . Groom-Eminences and Court hookers!

I'm taking you away from Siegmaringen . . . my head's a puzzle! . . . I was telling you about the street in Siegmaringen . . . shuppos . . . but not just shuppos! . . . soldiers of every rank and branch of service . . . chucked out of the station . . . the wounded of disbanded regiments . . . units of Swa-

bian, Magyar, Saxon divisions cut to pieces in Russia . . .
cadres from God knows where . . . officers of Balkan armies
looking for their generals . . . flummoxed . . . same as you
could see right here during the big Schelde-Bayonne "shellac
steeplechase" . . . addled colonels . . . Soubises without lanterns* . . . you saw them outside shop windows staring in, as
if they were looking for somebody inside . . . pretending . . .
Abetz in his woodburner stopped every three hundred yards
. . . he couldn't have failed to notice that Adolf's army was in
a very bad way . . . Abetz never spoke to me . . . I saw him
go by, he didn't see me . . . if his car had broken down, he
looked in some other direction . . . okay! . . . and then one
morning he stopped me . . .

"Doctor, please . . . would you come to the Castle tomorrow evening? . . . dinner with me and Hoffmann? nothing
formal! just ourselves . . ."

"Certainly, Monsieur Abetz!"

I was in no position to hem and haw . . . at the appointed
hour, eight o'clock, I was in the Castle . . . Abetz's dining
room . . . a maître d'hôtel takes me somewhere else, the other
wing, the other end of the Castle . . . corridors! . . . corridors! . . . "never be where you're supposed to be! . . ." another little dining room . . . there could always be a bomb
under the table! especially since the attempt on Hitler's life!
. . . precautions! well, here we are! the other little dining
room . . . attractive . . . porcelain knick-knacks all over
. . . Dresden . . . statuettes, vases . . . menu's less attractive! . . . I see, it's on my account . . . the "special Spartan
menu!" I see, I see! . . . they knew about my malicious
tongue, my evil mind! Hoffmann and Abetz wouldn't touch this
menu, they'd wait till I was gone! They'd heard the stories that
were going around among the villeins, about the delicacies
they piled in . . . the Ministers, *Botschafters* and Generals . . .
behind their thick walls! the feasts! morning! noon! and night!
legs of lamb! hams! caviar! soufflés! . . . and the cellars full
of champagne! . . . I could see they were showing me the
perfect Spartan menu! . . . No need for me to open my
mouth! . . . Abetz had his monologue all ready . . . the story

of his "resistance" . . . the way he'd taken the swastika flag
down from his embassy on the rue de Lille! . . . oh, the rue
de Lille was a bad street for them! . . . I thought, I listened, I
didn't say a word . . . rue de Lille, the same street as René!
. . . René-the-Racist! René stayed put! . . . they were
sacked, booted out! . . . I know René! . . . he tore up eight
orders not to prosecute me . . .

There at the table I looked at Abetz, he was playing with his
napkin . . . well-fed, clean-shaven . . . he'd eat again when I
left . . . and not exactly what they were serving me! radishes
without butter, porridge without milk! . . . he was perorating
for me to listen and repeat . . . that's what he'd invited me
for! . . . they serve us a slice of sausage, one slice each . . .
in that case, hell, let's have some fun at least! . . . I dive
in . . .

"What will you do, Monsieur Abetz, when Leclerc's army
gets here? right here in Siegmaringen! . . . in the Castle?"

My question doesn't faze them . . . neither Hoffmann nor
him, they'd thought about it . . .

"We have men in the Black Forest, Monsieur Céline! utterly
devoted! our Brown underground! . . . got away from your
Fifis on the rue de Lille! . . . it'll be ten times easier here!
. . . a bad moment, that's all! but you'll come with us, Céline!"

"Oh, certainly, Monsieur Abetz!"

As long as this was a diplomatic lunch, I had to say my piece
. . . it was on my stomach . . . even worse than the radishes!

"See here, Monsieur Abetz, see here! . . . there's a slight
difference! . . . which you pretend not to see! . . . you,
Abetz . . . even one hundred percent defeated, crushed, occupied by forty-nine victor powers . . . by God, the Devil, and
the Apostles . . . you'll still be the loyal, dutiful German,
honor and fatherland! defeated but legitimate! while a damn
fool like me will always be a stinking filthy traitor, fit to be
hanged! . . . a disgrace to my brothers and the Fifis! . . .
first tree! . . . you'll admit there's a difference, Monsieur
Abetz?"

"Oh, you're exaggerating, Céline! you always exaggerate! about everything! victory is in the palm of our hands, Céline! . . . the secret weapon! . . . you've heard? . . . no? . . . but let's suppose Céline, let's look at it from your point of view! . . . defeatism! all right, we're defeated! there! if that's what you want! . . . some vestige of National Socialism will always remain! our ideas will regain their vigor! . . . their full vigor! . . . we have sowed, Céline! sowed! sowed blood! . . . ideas! . . . love!"

The sound of his voice made him ecstatic . . .

"Not at all, Abetz! not at all! . . . you'll see! . . . History is written by the victors! . . . your History will be a dilly!"

The flunkey passes the radishes around again . . . gives me another slice of sausage . . .

"All the same, Monsieur Céline . . . listen to me! . . . I know France . . . you know, everybody knows . . . that I taught drawing in France . . . and not only in Paris . . . in the North . . . in the East . . . and in Provence . . . I did thousands of portraits . . . men and women! Frenchmen! . . . Frenchwomen! . . . and on the faces of those French men and women . . . of the common people! . . . mark my words, Céline . . . I've seen an expression . . . an honest, beautiful expression . . . of really sincere . . . really profound . . . friendship! not only for me! for Germany! a very real affection, Céline! . . . for Europe! . . . that's what you must try to understand, Céline!"

Comfort makes people soft in the head, that's how I felt about it . . . they were both beaming! . . . Hoffmann too, across the table . . . it wasn't the libations! nothing but water on the table . . . it was words . . . words! I really had no answer . . . now it was the *Stam* . . . still the *Stam* . . . but a special *Stam* with real carrots, real turnips and, I think, real butter . . .

"Yes, Monsieur l'Ambassadeur!"

Abetz wasn't the barbarian type . . . no . . . nothing to be afraid of like Raumnitz! . . . he hadn't been spanked! . . . not yet! . . . but even so . . . even so . . . better not go too far . . . I'd said enough . . . the affection of the French peo-

ple? Okay . . . "Shoot the works, kid!" I heartily approve . . .
"Oh, you're right, Abetz!"

That does it! I've started him up again! I'm in for it! . . . the
New Europe! and his pet project, his great work as soon as we
return to Paris, the super-colossal bronze statue of Charlemagne at the end of the Avenue de la Défense!

"You see, Céline? . . . the Aachen-La Défense axis!"

"Of course I see, Monsieur Abetz! I was born at the Rampe
du Pont!"

"Then you see!"

I could see Charlemagne and his valiant knights . . . Goebbels as Roland . . .

"Oh, you're so right!"

"You see! You see! two thousand years of history . . ."

"Magnificent! magnificent!"

Hoffmann was of the same opinion! Abetz's idea really appealed to him! the great symbolization that all Europe was
waiting for! Charlemagne surrounded by all his valiant knights
on the Place de la Défense!

I watched Abetz's enthusiasm, telling us how it would be
. . . his enormous statuary composition . . . his cheeks were
on fire! . . . not from liquor! . . . nothing but mineral water,
I've told you . . . pure enthusiasm! . . . he stood up to de-
claim at his ease and mime Charlemagne and his valiant
knights! . . . his knights: Rundstedt . . . Roland . . . Darnand! . . . I said to myself: this is enough! . . . he's going to
wear himself out . . . I'll slip out quietly . . . enough is
enough! . . . just then a flunkey whispers in his ear . . . what
is it? . . . somebody's here! . . . Monsieur de Chateaubriant!
. . . Alphonse°! . . . he wishes to speak to the Ambassador!

"Show him in! Show him in!"

Alphonse de Chateaubriant! . . . the flunkey leads the way
. . . here he comes . . . he's limping . . . He comes in . . .
at our last meeting in Baden-Baden he didn't limp so badly, I
think . . . at the Hotel Brenner . . . he had the same dog, a
really fine spaniel . . . he was dressed the same . . . like a
character in his novel . . . ever since his film *Monsieur de
Lourdines* . . . he'd been dressing the same . . . his protago-

nist . . . flowing brown cape, hunting boots . . . oh, but . . . yes! . . . the Tyrolian hat is new . . . with a little feather! in one hand he holds the spaniel's leash, in the other an ice-ax! . . . where was he going in that rig? . . . he told us right away . . . oh, I forgot: his bush! . . . the beard he'd grown since Baden-Baden! . . . a Druid's beard! . . . a mere draw-ing-room beard in Baden-Baden . . . now it was thick, gray, and shaggy . . . enveloping . . . you couldn't see his face any more . . . only the eyes . . .

"My dear Abetz! My dear Céline!"

Same voice as in Baden-Baden . . . warm! . . . urgently affectionate!

"Forgive me . . . I just got here . . . I tried desperately to notify you, my dear Abetz . . . unfortunately . . ."

"Come, come, Chateaubriant . . . consider this your home!"

"You are too kind, dear Abetz! we had a home!" He heaves an enormous sigh . . . "Yes, it's true . . . our chalet has been occupied!"

"Ah? . . . really?"

"Yes, I have fled! . . . They've come!"

"Who are 'they?' "

I ask him for the laugh! . . .

"Leclerc's army! . . . use your head, Céline. Oh, but not at all downcast, my dear Céline! I've seen them! . . . I've seen the Blacks! . . . Very well! . . . Blacks? the ultimate provo-cation? total war? so be it! Am I right, Abetz?"

"Certainly! certainly, Alphonse!"

Alphonse was only pausing for applause . . . he starts up again . . .

"Try to understand, Céline! just as I've written: victory will go to the most highly tempered soul! . . . the spirituality of steel! . . . we have that quality of soul, haven't we, Abetz?"

"Oh certainly, Chateaubriant!"

Abetz wasn't going to contradict him!

"The soul! the soul, that's our weapon . . . I have the bomb . . . I will have!"

Hell! I want to know all about this . . .

"What bomb, Alphonse?"

"Listen carefully, Céline! a few true and tried companions!
. . . we've chosen the place! . . . oh, I've been through worse
trials!"

He ponders . . . three enormously deep sighs . . . and he
continues . . .

"An absolutely inaccessible valley, very narrow, a bowl you
might say, between three mountain peaks . . . in the middle
of the Tyrol . . . and there, there, Céline! . . . we shall iso-
late ourselves! . . . you catch my meaning? . . . and we shall
concentrate! . . . we shall perfect our bomb!"

Hoffmann doesn't quite get it . . .

"This bomb . . . what are you going to make it out of?"

"Oh, my dear Hoffmann . . . not a bomb of steel! or dynamite! . . . a thousand times no! . . . a bomb of concentra-
tion! of faith, Hoffmann!"

"And then?"

"A message . . . a stupendous moral bomb! . . . don't you
see, Abetz? . . . how else did the Christian religion triumph? a
stupendous moral bomb! . . . don't you see, Céline? . . . am
I right?"

"Oh certainly! certainly!"

We were all entirely of his opinion.

That's what the stick and the little hat and his Tyrolian commando were for.

Plain as day!

As far as Abetz was concerned, victory, with or without a
bomb, would take care of itself . . . as long as he had his
monument! his gigantic, stupendous Charlemagne! his Aachen-
Courbevoie axis! his hobby!

"You see, Chateaubriant . . . You see the place I mean?"

"Oh, perfectly!"

"You wouldn't put it anywhere else?"

"Oh, certainly not, my dear Abetz! perfect!"

"Then I can count on you? for an ode! . . . you will be our
Bard of Honor! an Ode to Europe!"

They understood each other perfectly . . . complete agreement! . . . the Victory celebration on the Place de la Défense, delegations from all over Europe around the enormous

statue, ten times bigger, wider, taller than "Liberty" in New York! really something! the Bard of Honor and his beard!

Just then, I don't know why, they stopped being in agreement . . . Chateaubriant thought it over . . . Abetz, too . . . Hoffmann, too . . . I didn't breathe a word . . . Chateaubriant broke the silence . . . he's got an idea! . . .

"Don't you think, my dear Abetz, that for such an event the Berlin Opera? the Paris Opera? both orchestras?"

"Certainly, certainly, my good friend."

"The Ride of the Valkyries! that's the music! . . . there's no other!"

We agreed again! completely! the Ride of the Valkyries!

But then he starts whistling! the Valkyrie! . . . out of tune! . . . he hums it . . . still more out of tune! . . . he mimes the trumpet with his ice-ax! all the way up to the chandelier . . . as if he were blowing! . . . blowing like mad! . . . Abetz ventures a word . . .

"Chateaubriant! Chateaubriant! Please . . . allow me . . . the trumpet only on the C, the final C . . . not on the G . . . the trombones play the G! no trumpets . . . no trumpet, Chateaubriant!"

"What? No trumpet?"

Suddenly I see a disconcerted man . . . just like that! . . . his ax falls from his hands . . . in half a second his face has changed completely . . . that remark! . . . he's haggard! . . . it's too much . . . he'd been in full flight! . . . he looks at Abetz . . . he looks at the table . . . he grabs a saucer . . . and *Whing!* he flings it! . . . and another! . . . and a plate! . . . and a platter! . . . like at a country fair! he's really steamed up! it all breaks against the shelves of crockery on the other side of the room! smithereens . . . and *bam!* . . . *crash!* and it keeps on coming! more wreckage! . . . an apoplectic fit! . . . the nerve of this Abetz punk telling him his Valkyrie wasn't right! the arrogance of that upstart! He wanted a victory celebration, did he! . . . *crash! bang!* ballistics and clay pipes! he'd show them! beside himself with rage! Abetz and Hoffmann duck on the other side . . . under the table! under the tablecloth! *clatter! smash!* dishes crashing all around them! that china really took some punishment! . . . He's unrecognizable in this fit! bristling! . . . his hair and his bush bristling with rage! disparaging remarks about his trumpet! . . . there must have been bad blood between them to begin with! definitely! . . . I'd heard there was trouble about the rent for their chalet in the Black Forest . . . that Abetz didn't want to pay it any more . . . or maybe his wife, Suzanne . . . trumpet, Valkyries, and Charlemagne weren't the real reason for his wild outbreak . . . it was something else, more serious . . . well, in a way . . . anyway here was Alphonse, always so polite, so well-bred, turned into a Valkyrie himself! . . . everything went! the whole room! . . . all the knick-knacks! an emotional volcano! madness! if Myrta, his dog, hadn't suddenly got so scared and started barking so loud! for all she was worth! Myrta, Alphonse's spaniel . . . *bow wow!* and she runs away! Alphonse calls her . . . she's far away! he runs after her . . . he dashes down the stairs . . . "Myrta! Myrta!" Abetz and Hoffmann yell after him: "Chateaubriant! Chateaubriant!" . . . you can imagine, I take the opportunity to clear out! I made a dash! I don't take the elevator! . . . it's pitch dark outside the Castle . . . air-raid warning! . . . there's always an air-raid warning! . . . I find Alphonse on the sidewalk . . . his Myrta hadn't gone far! she's very glad to be out of there! she makes a big fuss over her dear master! I can't see the dear master, it's too dark . . . but he speaks to me, his voice is still choked . . . with emotion! anger! . . . that crockery bombardment! . . . He'd certainly broken a lot of dishes! . . . he, always so precious, ceremonious, well-mannered . . . all of a sudden I saw him! a total barbarian!

"Well, Chateaubriant? Well?"

"Oh, Céline! My dear Céline!"

The old warmth was back again.

He clutches my hands, he squeezes them . . . he's in need of affection.

"Nothing at all . . . a mere trifle!"

"Do you think so, Céline? Do you really think so?"

"Come come! a little joke!"

"You think so, Céline?"

"Certainly . . . forget it!"

"But even so . . . how many plates do you think?"

It wasn't only plates he'd broken . . . all the china and soup bowls! very thorough! He hadn't seen himself in action: a regular maelstrom! *boom! bang!* against the shelves across the room, the rest of the china! the worst of it was that those things were marvels, complete sets, period Dresden! . . . they'd taken it from Gabold's, the fourth floor . . . all in Dresden . . . marquetry and fine porcelain . . . all pure Meissen . . .

"You know, Céline, I'm going to sleep at the *Bären*, I won't go back to the Castle . . . they've reserved a room for me . . . but they can keep it . . . I'll sleep at the *Bären* . . . We're leaving at dawn . . . all my men are at the *Bären*, my whole 'commando'" . . .

"Oh, certainly, Chateaubriant . . ."

His "men" were the moralists, the men who were supposed to manufacture the bomb . . . anyway that's what I thought . . .

"But Céline, would you? would you be so kind? I'd never find my way alone . . . the *Bären* . . . would you guide me? . . ."

Of course I would . . . I could find my way blindfolded anywhere in Siegmaringen . . . I never got lost . . . not in the darkest alley . . .

"This way, my friend! this way!"

Oh, but there was still his *rucksack!* his knapsack! his matériel . . . his crap! it weighed a ton! . . . quite a supply of something! . . . he had to pass it over his big cape . . . or under! we tried . . . he couldn't make it . . . too heavy, too big! . . . we decided to carry it between us, we'd each take a strap . . . but very slowly, I couldn't go fast . . . neither could he . . . he used his ice-ax for a cane . . . that way he could manage . . . I told you he limped pretty badly . . . three of the collaborators had the same limp . . . a "distinguished limp" so to speak . . . Lesdain,* Bernard Faye,* and himself . . . none of them from war wounds, all "temporary deferment" . . . they even had their nickname . . . "the hobble brothers!" . . . to show you how malicious people can be! so the two of us start off, each with his strap . . . very

slowly . . . we rest, we start up again every ten, twenty steps
. . . some cargo! . . . we laugh about it! even he laughs!
. . . we stagger . . . his matériel! he expects to get to the
Tyrol with that? *Halt!* somebody up ahead of us! . . . I can't
see this somebody . . . he flashes a beam in our eyes . . . a
flashlight . . . he sees us! . . . must be a Boche! . . . it's a
Boche policeman . . . "Where are you going?" we're not supposed to be out . . . he must know me . . . "to the *Bären*," I
answer, "to the *Bären* . . . he's sick . . . *krank* . . ."

"*Nur gut. Nur gut! gehe!*"

We were all right . . . but Alphonse starts protesting! nobody had asked him anything . . . he stands up to the cop, his
big bush in the flashlight beam . . . "*Kraft ist nicht alles!*" he
shouts in his face! "force isn't everything" . . . I can see he's
going to get himself pulled in! no! . . . the cop doesn't get sore
. . . he even takes hold of the two straps, the famous *rucksack*,
a feather for him! . . . he carries it . . . he escorts us . . .
fine, we follow him . . . Chateaubriant and myself . . . it
doesn't take us long to the *Bären* . . . we hear the Danube
. . . the Danube breaking against the arches! . . . ah, the
noisy, angry little river! . . . here we are! . . . the cop knocks
. . . three knocks . . . another three knocks . . . somebody
opens . . . there we are . . . "*gute Nacht!*" I leave Chateaubriant in the doorway . . . with his dog . . . the policeman
puts the knapsack down . . .

"Good-by, my dear Céline!"

I never saw dear Alphonse again . . . I took the shuppo
back to the *Löwen* with me . . . to get them to open the door
. . . that crummy Frucht would have been only too glad to
leave me outside . . . always have the police on your side
. . . one of the things you learn in the mazes of life . . .

I was supposed to go to Laval's and I took you to Abetz's
. . . that little dinner . . . forgive me! . . . another little
digression . . . I'm always digressing . . . old age? . . . too
full of memories? . . . I don't know . . . I'll know later . . .
or other people will know . . . about oneself it's hard to tell
. . . Anyway, to pick up where we left off . . . we were leaving the music room . . . I was supposed to go see Laval . . .
I'd wanted to go for the last three days . . . since the skir-
mish at the station . . . when really it was his doing if it
hadn't ended in a general massacre . . . only one dead! . . . I
really had to go and congratulate him . . . and not discreetly!
loud and clear! it's no good treading lightly with politicians!
heavy does it! massive! . . . same as with dames! . . . politicians are debutantes as long as they live . . . admiration! . . .
admiration! votes! You don't tell a young lady she's nice . . .
no, you talk to her like Mariano: "Der's nobod lika you in alla
woil!" that's the least she'll stand for . . . same with your poli-
tician! . . . besides I had a purpose . . . that he shouldn't raise
a stink about the Delaunys . . . Brinon wasn't the only power
in the Castle . . . I'd prepared my little spiel . . . at last I
was on my way . . . from the music room to Laval's, one floor
. . . only one flight . . . I've explained . . . I've told you
what it was like . . . his setting, his office, his apartment, his
floor . . . all First Empire . . . perfect First Empire! . . .
you won't find anything better in Malmaison . . . or I'd even
say as good . . . we know the terrible drawbacks of First
Empire, that buttock-gouging style . . . absolutely impossible to sit down! . . . chairs, armchairs, divans! . . . reso-
lutely "peach pit" . . . chairs for colonels, marshals! . . .
barely time to listen and take off! . . . to fly from victory to

victory! no connection with "Capuan delights!" but I was so tired, so much insomnia to catch up on, that I made myself very comfortable on the peach pits . . . I took a very nice rest . . . Naturally I started in with my compliment . . . How splendid he had been! Laval of Auvergne and the Maghreb and Alfortville! the incomparable! the attenuator-conciliator for whom London, New York, and Moscow envied us! . . . once I'd said my little piece, there was nothing left for me to do but nod, wag my head amiably . . . no need to talk . . . it was very comfortable at Laval's . . . he babbled all by himself . . . he didn't ask anything of me . . . except to listen, that was enough! . . . he was doing the talking . . . and he really threw himself into it! . . . he pleaded! . . . this . . . that . . . and then his case! . . . his Cause! . . . you could only nod, he "incarnated" France much too much to leave him time to listen . . . compliments or no compliments! I'd come to tell him that it was thanks to him the massacre had been nipped in the bud . . . that if not for him there would have been a hecatomb! . . . the sincere truth! . . . he didn't give a shit! all he wanted was for me to listen . . . he tolerated me as a listener! . . . not as a commentator! so I stowed my compliments . . . I sit down with my bag on my lap, my instruments, and Bébert on my lap, too, in his game bag . . . I knew his plea . . . he'd dished it out to me ten . . . twenty times . . . "that under the present conditions . . . the weakness of Europe . . . only one way of straightening everything out": his Franco-German policy! . . . *his!* . . . without his collaboration no use trying . . . there wouldn't be any History! or any Europe! that he knew Russia . . . etc. . . . . etc. . . . . I could nod and wag away . . . this would go on for an hour . . . at least . . . I knew all the variants, the mock objections, the impassioned appeals . . . he felt as if he were already buried! . . . in his family vault! . . . in Chateldon! . . . yes, but first . . . first! he'd demolish them all! all of them! . . . they wouldn't down him so easy! . . . he'd crush them first! . . . first . . . all of them! . . . all those jealous . . . envious deserters! all of his grotesque, slanderous detractors! yes! because he, Laval, he and nobody else, had France in his blood! . . .

and all those idiotic midgets would have to admit that he had it in his pocket . . . and America, too . . . yes, America! . . . he could wind it around his finger . . . immense America! in the first place through his son-in-law! . . . and through his daughter, who was an American . . . and through Senator Taft, Roosevelt's Great Elector! . . .

"Ah, the High Court! . . . listen to me, Doctor!"

He made the High Court crawl on its belly! absolutely! . . . I tried to interrupt him just a little . . . give him a breathing spell . . . hopeless! . . . the way he was launched, not a chance of mentioning Delaunys . . .

Best way would be to let him talk . . . and slip out . . . I had plenty of things to do . . . the *Landrat* for Bébert's left-overs . . . then my patients at the *Milice* . . . then the hospital . . . then see Letrou . . . and then the *Fidelis* . . . even so I tried to interrupt him . . . a few words about my practice, my little troubles . . . maybe he could give me a little advice? . . . he knew more about it than I did . . . naturally! . . . he knew more than everybody . . . about everything . . . that greasy Arab with his ebony cowlick, nothing was missing but the fez . . . he was the real Abdullah of the Third Republic, who talks to everybody in the train, who knows better than anybody what they ought to do and don't . . . who knows more than the farmer about planting his alfalfa and clover, more than the notary about those little inheritance pettifog-geries, more than the photographer about those first com-munion pictures, more than the post office clerk about short-changing you on stamps, more than the hairdresser about permanent waves, more than election workers about ways of taking opposition posters down, more than the police about putting on handcuffs, and much more than the housewife about wiping the baby's ass . . .

You had a good rest listening as long as you watched your expression . . . He kept an eye on you . . . if you didn't seem quite convinced . . . he took another windup . . . he floored you for the count!

Ah, Mornet* and Co. wouldn't listen to him . . . they pre-ferred to shoot him! . . . big mistake! . . . he had something

to say . . . I know . . . I heard him ten times . . . twenty
times . . .

"You can take it from me . . . I had the choice . . . they
offered me the moon and the stars, Doctor . . . De Gaulle
went looking for them . . . I made them wait! . . . the Russians too!"

I couldn't go on wagging the whole time . . .

"What did they offer you, Monsieur le Président?"

I had to seem to be paying attention.

"Anything I wanted! the whole Press!"

"Ah! Ah!"

That's all I said . . . no more . . . I knew the listener's role
. . . he was pleased with me . . . not a bad listener . . .
and especially . . . because I don't smoke . . . being a non-
smoker, he wouldn't have to offer me any . . . he could show
me all his packages, two big drawers full of Lucky Strikes . . .
you bummed a cigarette off him, he wouldn't see you again!
. . . never! . . . or even a light! . . . a match!

"The English offered you all that, Monsieur le Président?"

"Absolutely . . . they begged me, Doctor!"

"Ah! . . . ah!" Amazement!

"I can even give you a name! . . . it won't mean anything
to you! . . . an embassy name . . . Mendle! he offered to
buy me twenty-five newspapers! and as many in the provinces!"

"Certainly, Monsieur le Président! . . . I believe you! . . .
I believe you! . . ."

"I'm going to have a little fun, Doctor! . . . you hear? . . .
very well! Strike me down, I'll say to them! Strike! Strike hard!
don't miss me the way you did in Versailles! . . . don't tremble! go right ahead! . . . but I'm warning you! . . . I've
warned you! . . . you will be assassinating France!"

"Bravo, Monsieur le Président!"

The least I could do was show a little enthusiasm . . .

"Ah, you agree with me?"

"Completely, Monsieur le Président!"

He had me where he wanted me . . . straight to the gut!

"You agree with a Jew?"

Here we go! That word! The word Jew! . . . naturally he was going to bring it up! the stinker, he'd been biding his time!

He takes the offensive . . .

"You did call me a Jew, didn't you, Doctor? Yes, I know, you weren't the only one . . . There was also *Je suis partout!*"*

"Not in so many words, Monsieur le Président! . . . they didn't call you that in so many words! but I did, Monsieur le Président!"

"Ah, I like that! Right to my face!"

He bursts out laughing . . . he's not a bad sort . . . but he didn't take me by surprise, I knew what was going to happen . . . inevitable! . . .

"But you wrote the same thing yourself!"

"Oh, that was for my constituents . . . in Aubervilliers!"

"I know! I know, Monsieur le Président!"

Something else on his mind . . .

"But you, Doctor, why are you here? . . . why are you in Siegmaringen? . . . they tell me you complain a good deal . . ."

Who did he think he was fooling?

"If I'm here, Monsieur le Président, it's entirely thanks to you! you absolutely refused to send me anywhere else! You could have! Absolutely!"

I'm beginning to get sore! hell! his air of innocence! I know what I'm saying! . . . it would suit that scowling Arab for me to pay for the whole gang! to take the rap for all those lousy three-timing connivers! to foot the bill! and as long as we're talking frankly . . . and he's fooling around putting me on trial . . . it's my turn to bring up a few unpleasant truths! . . . I'm not dozing any more! . . .

"You found a spot for Morand! you found a spot for Maurois! . . . and Fontenoy!* you found a spot for Fontenoy! . . . you found a spot for your daughter!"

"That's enough! That's enough, Céline!"

He stops me . . . I had a dozen more . . . a hundred!

"You found a spot for Brisson . . . Robert! you found a spot for Morand! I was right there . . . in his house!"

I don't pull any punches . . . I've got a memory like an elephant . . . people always think they can con me, my dumb look . . .

He has to have the last word . . .

"Then you know what people say about you?"

"Me? . . . I'm of no interest! . . . better talk about the big news . . . would you care to hear some really interesting news, Monsieur Le Président?"

"Where did you get it?"

"In the street! . . . really hot! . . . and very convenient for you . . ."

"Spit it out! Quick!"

"Well . . . the story is that the Russians are going to fight the Americans! there you are, Monsieur le Président! . . ."

"That's what they're saying in Siegmaringen?"

"Absolutely!"

He thinks it over . . .

"The Russians fight the Americans? That's absolutely stupid and inept, Doctor! Have you stopped to think?"

"No . . . but that's what they're saying!"

"But that would mean chaos, Doctor! . . . chaos! do you know what chaos is?"

"Quite well, Monsieur le Président!"

"You've never been in politics?"

"Oh, so little . . . and really I'm so incompetent . . ."

"Then you can't understand! you don't know what chaos is!"

"I've some little idea . . ."

"No! . . . you don't know! I'll tell you! Chaos, Doctor, is a Julius Caesar in every village! . . . and twelve Brutuses to a county!"

"I believe you, Monsieur le Président!"

I won't let him have his last word!

"But I'm not Caesar, and you could perfectly well have found a spot for me . . . like Morand, Jardin, and the rest of them! . . . I wasn't asking you for much . . . I wasn't asking for an Embassy! . . . you didn't do a thing! . . . I wasn't Brutus either! . . . you'd have handed me over to the Fifis if I hadn't come to Germany!"

I stick to my guns! . . . I know my stuff . . . absolutely sin-

cerely right! . . . I'm the rightest man in Europe! and the least
appreciated! I've got fifty Nobel prizes coming to me!

"No, Monsieur le Président, I wouldn't be here!"

I want him to know!

He picks up his phone.

"I'm calling Bichelonne, I want him to hear you! . . . I want
a witness! everybody's curious to know what you think! now
everybody will know! . . . and not just me! . . . that I lured
you into a trap here . . . an ambush?"

"Exactly, Monsieur le Président!"

He's got Bichelonne on the phone . . .

"Do you know what Céline has been telling me? . . . he
says I'm a crook, a no-good, a traitor, and a Jew!"

"Not all that! you're exaggerating, Monsieur le Président!"

"No, Céline! . . . that's what you think! and you're entitled
to your opinions! . . ."

He keeps on at the telephone . . . he talks . . . not about
me any more . . . one thing and another . . . I watch him
while he's talking . . . I see him on the slant, in profile . . .
oh, I had the right idea! . . . if I wanted to compare him to
somebody . . . I can still see him . . . somebody from now
. . . I'd put him between Nasser and Mendès . . . the profile, the smile, the complexion, the Asiatic hair . . . one thing
is sure! underneath the banter, he can't stand my guts . . . he
was exactly in tune with present-day France, pure and sure,*
and pro-flunkarino . . . they shouldn't have drilled him, he
was worth at least ten Mendèses!

"Come on over!"

He insists . . . Bichelonne isn't in the mood . . . he needs
coaxing . . .

"He's coming!"

And there he is . . . not the Afro-Asiatic type . . . oh no,
not he! he was the big blond type . . . his head was really
enormous! A giant spermatozoid! . . . all head! . . . Bonnard
is the same . . . the giant spermatozoid type . . . giant tad-
poles . . . one more millimeter they'd be on exhibit . . . in a
jar! . . . oh, it's Bichelonne all right! . . . but say . . . I can
hardly recognize him . . . so drawn and pale . . . a sad state

. . . trembling . . . that's why he hadn't wanted to come . . .
Laval doesn't give him time to recover . . . He starts right in
. . . He wants Bichelonne to listen! he's too upset, he doesn't
hear a thing . . .

"What are you trembling about, Bichelonne?"

Good reason . . . plenty good reason . . . he tells us . . .
he's stammering with emotion! . . . they've broken a windowpane on him! . . . one of the windows in his room! . . .
Laval has had ten broken! . . . he tells us all about it . . .
he's kidding Bichelonne . . . nothing to tremble about! . . .
but Bichelonne isn't joking . . . not at all! . . . he wants to
know who? . . . how? . . . why? . . . a stone? . . . a bullet?
. . . a plane? . . . propeller blast? . . . a cyclone? that's
what kills him, not knowing who? . . . how? . . . why? . . .
Bichelonne is no canary . . . not at all, but here all of a sudden he's panicked . . . not knowing why? and how? . . .
flummoxed! . . . the planes come so near his window! . . .
they practically graze it! . . . but maybe a bullet from the
street? . . . maybe? . . . he hasn't found any! . . . he's
looked all night! . . . meticulously! . . . the ceiling . . . the
walls . . . nothing! . . . naturally he doesn't give a shit about
what the President wants him to know! that I called him this!
and that! he doesn't listen! his windowpane! his windowpane!
. . . how? who? . . . that's what interests him! . . . Laval is
wasting his breath . . . Bichelonne paces the whole length of
the immense First Empire desk! . . . his hands clasped behind
his back . . . thinking . . . thinking hard! . . . his problem!
. . . Laval starts all over again: I've accused him of this . . .
and that! . . . he gilds the lily! . . . I've called him a contemptible swine for saving Morand, Jardin,* Guérard!* and a
hundred others! a thousand others! and deliberately sacrificing
me! . . . a private racial grudge! . . . so the niggers of Leclerc's army would find me here! and chop me into small pieces!
. . . absolutely premeditated!

I wasn't going to interrupt him! he was in full swing!

"Bravo, Monsieur le Président!"

Plea for the prosecution! I applaud! . . . He's prosecuting
himself! . . . before another High Court! . . . the High

Court of the imagination! . . . like the other . . . Both museums! . . .

"Bravo, Monsieur le Président!"

He's turned me into the Supreme High Court! . . . Bichelonne doesn't listen, not interested . . . he paces, he mutters
. . . suddenly he fires a question at Laval!

"What do you think?"

He doesn't give a damn about what I've said . . . or not
said! . . . his problem is his window! he goes on pacing . . .
limping . . . not the "distinguished limp" in his case . . . a
real claudication! . . . a fracture that hasn't knit right . . . in
fact he wants to have it fixed, to be operated before our return
to France! . . . operated right here in Germany! . . . by
Gebhardt! . . . I know Gebhardt well . . . another character! A fraud, I'd thought at first . . . not at all! . . . he'd been
a general on the Russian front for six months . . . in command
of a *panzer* team . . . and for six months he'd been chief surgeon of the enormous S.S. hospital in Hohenlychen, East
Prussia . . . you'd have taken him for a charlatan, too . . . a
clown! . . . I was mistaken . . . I sent a friend of mine . . .
extremely anti-Boche . . . to watch him operate . . . this
S.S. surgeon Gebhardt was very skillful! . . . nuts? . . . definitely! in his super-hospital in Hohenlychen there were six
thousand surgery patients, a city, four times the size of Bichat!
. . . he staged football games with one-legged teams . . .
war cripples . . . he was cracked like the supermen of the
Renaissance . . . he excelled in two, three rackets . . . tank
warfare, surgery . . . ah yes, and singing! . . . I heard him at
the piano . . . very amusing . . . he improvised . . . there
I'm a good judge . . . during the Hitler period the Boches
came close to developing a race of Renaissance men . . . this
Gebhardt was one of them! . . . Bichelonne was another . . .
in a different way . . . he was a Polytechnician! . . . There
hadn't been a genius like him since Arago . . . what impressed
me was his memory! . . . prodigious! . . . in the Vichy government he'd been in charge of the railroads . . . making
them run come hell or high water! a labor of Hercules! . . .
every line, switch, timetable, and detour in his head! . . . to
the minute! . . . to the second! . . . with all the culverts,

tracks, and stations that were blown up every night! It was no joke! and patching! and mending! and rerouting! and getting her moving again! . . . and two seconds later more dynamite . . . someplace else! The Fifis wouldn't let him sleep! Europe will never recover from that dynamiting mania! hysterics and pie crust! everything sky-high! . . . the habit has sunk in! . . . it'll take the atom bomb to make the place normal and livable again! and now this business with the windowpane . . . stone? bullet? propeller? Bichelonne couldn't take it . . . his nerves were on edge from Vichy . . . and now this windowpane was too much! . . . from the street? . . . from the air? . . . I understood . . . his nerves were shot . . .

It wasn't only his nerves they had wrecked! . . . his leg, too! . . . he'd been riding in a car . . . a little bomb! *plump!* happy landing, your Excellency! . . . he'd been on his way to the Ministry of Information . . . three fractures that hadn't knit right, they'd have to break his leg again to get it straight . . . and he wanted it done right away, in Germany! he didn't want to go back to Paris in this condition! he knew Gebhardt slightly . . . he was dead set on going up there to Hohen-lychen . . . Gebhardt had offered . . . it didn't sound very good to me. . . . I hadn't much faith in Gebhardt . . . he was sold on him . . . okay . . . he had the faith . . . okay . . . but this situation! . . . my goodness! he kept mumbling instead of listening to Laval . . . pacing the whole length of the big First Empire desk . . . mumbling the pros . . . and the cons . . . a bullet? . . . a propeller tip? . . . sunk in his meditations . . . he was pretty funny with his enormous head . . . but Laval wasn't amused! . . . in fact he was getting good and sick of him! . . . he hadn't sent for him to pace and mumble about a windowpane . . . he wanted him to listen! "Look at that! . . . are you looking, Doctor? . . . he's not listening! . . . his windowpane! . . . all he cares about is his windowpane! . . ."

Laval calls me to witness . . .

It couldn't go on like that! Laval knew the way . . . the one way to shake him out of his meditations: to ask him a stickler! no matter what! . . . put a different bee in his bonnet!

"Tell me, Bichelonne . . . I'd appreciate it . . . I used to know . . . I've forgotten . . . I need it for a little paper I'm doing . . . the capital of Honduras?"

Bichelonne pulls up sharp . . . now he's listening . . . he's not mumbling any more . . . he's going to answer . . .

"Tegucigalpa, Monsieur le Président!"

"No, no! I'm sorry, Bichelonne . . . British Honduras?"

"Belize, Monsieur le Président!"

"Area, Bichelonne?"

"21,000 square kilometers . . ."

"Principal products?"

"Mahogany . . . resin . . ."

"Fine! Thank you, Bichelonne!"

Bichelonne gets back to his window . . . pacing and limping again . . . but he's a little less preoccupied . . . Belize has done him good . . .

"Tell me, Bichelonne, as long as I've got you here . . . I need your help again . . . I used to know all those things! . . . I've forgotten! . . . tungsten, Bichelonne? . . . Rochat is always talking about it . . . he took some away with him . . ."

"Atomic weight 183.9 . . . density 19.3 . . ."

Once he'd got that off his chest, Bichelonne sat down . . . He's tired of pacing . . . he massages his leg . . . Laval sees his chance . . . he goes to the mirror, smoothes his cowlick . . . he straightens his tie . . . he's going to give us some more High Court! . . . ah, not so fast! not so fast! . . . I've got a few words to say too! always listening to other people . . . a little wave of pride comes over me! . . . not very bright of me! . . . I thought I'd shut them up once and for all! I was quick to regret it! I still regret it! I seldom let myself go . . . but I'd been listening to them too long! . . .

"Here," I said. "Take a look at this!"

I put my cyanide down on the table in front of them . . . on Laval's desk . . . my little phial . . . out of my pocket! . . . as long as they're talking about rare metals! . . . I've always got my cyanide on me! . . . ever since Sartrouville . . . here, they can see it . . . and the red label . . . they both look . . .

I was always being asked for cyanide . . . I always said I didn't have any . . . oh, they're not bashful . . . not these two . . . they're arguing already which one gets it! . . . it's all right with me . . . I've still got three phials . . . sealed the same way . . . same cyanide . . . the trouble is that they'll blab . . . sure to! . . . and I'd never mentioned it to anybody . . .

"Can I have it? Can I have it?"

Both of them . . . oh, they're not joking any more!

"Share it!"

Let them work it out between themselves . . . Then I change my mind . . .

"No . . . don't fight . . . I'll give you each one! Once it's open, you know, once it catches the humidity, it's no good!"

"But when? . . . but when?"

Ah, now they're beginning to take me seriously! I take another phial out of another pocket . . . and still another out of my lining! I don't tell them the whole story, my hems are full of little packets . . . I don't want to be caught without it . . . okay! . . . I can see they respect me now . . . they've stopped talking . . . but they're happy . . . they'll talk again . . . nothing good!

"What can I do for you, Doctor?"

"Monsieur le Président, if you'll kindly listen to me . . . in the first place don't open the phial . . . in the second place don't tell anybody . . ."

"Yes . . . that goes without saying! but yourself? . . . you must have some little wish?"

I get another little idea! I'd always refused everything! everything! . . . but the way things are . . . what difference does it make?

"Well, Monsieur le Président, you could appoint me governor of Saint-Pierre and Miquelon . . ."

No point in pussyfooting!

"Granted! . . . it's a promise! . . . you'll make a note of it, Bichelonne?"

"Certainly, Monsieur le Président!"

Laval has a little question though . . .

"Who gave you that idea, Doctor?"

"Just like that, Monsieur le Président! the beauties of Saint-Pierre and Miquelon! . . ."

I tell him about them . . . not from hearsay . . . I'd been there . . . at that time it took twenty-five days from Bordeaux to Saint-Pierre . . . on the very frail *Celtique* . . . Saint-Pierre was still a fishing port . . . I know Langlade and Miquelon well . . . I know the road well . . . the only road from one end of the island to the other . . . the road and the memorial "milestone" . . . the road cut out of solid rock by the sailors of the *Iphigénie* . . . I'm not making it up . . . real memory, a real road! . . . and not only the sailors of the *Iphigénie!* convicts too! . . . they had a penal colony on Saint-Pierre . . . which left a memorial, too! . . .

"You ought to see it, Monsieur le Président! in the middle of the Atlantic Ocean!"

The main thing: I was appointed Governor . . . I'm still Governor! . . .

Appointing me governor, archbishop, or road mender didn't improve things any . . . bad to worse! . . . the reality was the hallucinated mob from Strasbourg, the triple reservists of the *Landsturm*, the fugitives from Vlasoff's army, the bombed-out refugees from Berlin, the horror-stricken demented from Lithuania, and the defenestrated from Koenigsberg, the "free workers" from all over, shipment after shipment, Tartar ladies in evening dress, opera singers from Dresden . . . all camping in holes and ditches around the Castle . . . or on the banks of the Danube . . . in addition to the terrified fugitives from France, Toulouse, Carcassonne, and Bois-Colombes, hunted by the Underground . . . and the families of the *Miliciens*, and the new recruits of the N.S.K.K.,* who were supposed to drive to Denmark for butter . . . plus Corpechot's ardent recruits, who were waiting to be shipped aboard the Danube flotilla . . . plus a lot of phony Swiss who claimed to be pro-German . . . all in tribes, with children of every age . . . enormous bundles, dishes, cooking utensils, pieces of stoves, and nothing to eat . . . Siegmaringen was a kind of port for the derelicts of Europe . . . the whole town . . . the castle, the moats, the streets, the station . . . was full of them . . . every variety of costume, rags and camouflage, people from all over, every conceivable lingo . . . the sidewalks, the waterfront, the shops . . . all overflowing . . . One place that was picturesque was Sabiani's P.P.F. headquarters . . . the P.P.F., the biggest of the "parties of the future" . . . I've already told you: Doriot in person never came to Siegmaringen . . . neither did Hérold, his mouthpiece! . . . nor Sicard . . . Sabiani ran this Party office . . . it had two showcases . . . both full of sick people in the worst possible shape . . . dying of hunger, old age, tuberculo-

287

sis, and the cold . . . and cancer! . . . and all scratching like mad! . . . naturally! . . . in one window camp chairs, in the other steamer chairs . . . for a good two months I saw a P.P.F. grandmother dying with her grandson in her lap . . . without moving, in a steamer chair, spitting her lungs out! . . . the office was full of the dying, too . . . all over the benches . . . along the walls . . . or even stretched out on the floor . . . or in piles . . . Sabiani himself stayed in the back room . . . he took applications, handed out membership cards, which he signed and stamped . . . he had "full powers" . . . France was a hairsbreadth from going P.P.F. . . . if Hitler hadn't been so dumb! Sabiani drew a big crowd . . . everybody joined . . . everybody that looked in the windows . . . a way of coming in and sitting down . . . the P.P.F.* was certainly the recruitingest party . . . the showcases and the benches did it . . . if he'd dished out something to eat in addition, the slightest mess kit, he'd have recruited the whole town, including the Boches . . . soldiers and civilians! . . . a time comes in the course of events when only one thing counts: to sit down and eat . . . ah, there's something else: stamps! . . . I forgot to tell you! . . . hunting for stamps, collecting! . . . every post office I'd seen all over Germany . . . not only in Siegmaringen but in the biggest cities and the smallest holes . . . was always full of customers, all at the "collectors' windows" . . . lines and lines, collecting Hitler stamps, all prices! . . . from one pfennig to fifty marks! . . . If I were Nasser for instance, or Franco, or Salazar, and I wanted to see where I stood . . . if I really wanted to know what people thought of me . . . I wouldn't ask my police! . . . hell, no! . . . I'd go to the post office in person and look at the lines waiting for my stamps . . . your people are collectors? . . . the jig's up! . . . there must be millions of Adolf Hitler collections in Germany! . . . they started years in advance! at the very first damn foolishness . . . Dunkirk . . . they started collecting! diviners, magicians? don't waste your time! . . . the stamp's the thing . . . tells you the whole story ten years in advance! . . . they're collecting? they know what they're doing! In our post office . . . in addition to Hitler we had Pétain . . . his stamps!

. . . two complete collections! you should have seen our post office! almost as many people as at Sabiani's! French and Boche collectors! I've got to admit, though, that there's something worse than stamps, worse than liquor, worse than butter, worse than soup! cigarettes! . . . cigarettes are the real winners! . . . anywhere . . . under really implacable conditions . . . I've seen it under fire and I've seen it in the prison infirmary, the last and ultimate human preoccupation is smoking! . . . which proves, you won't tell me different, that man is first a dreamer! a born dreamer! *primum vivere?* it's not true! . . . *primum* blow bubbles! . . . the long and the short! . . . dreams at any price! . . . before food, wine, and tail! not a shadow! men kick off for a lot of reasons, but without a cigarette they can't do it! . . . take a man with his back to the wall or on the steps of guillotine . . . he can't he can't! . . . he's got to smoke first . . . I was in the dream department, too, at the P.P.F. office . . . the ones who were in too much pain . . . I dropped in and gave them a portion of dream . . . 2 c.c.s . . . I made them dream! . . . oh, I was very sparing with my 2 c.c. ampuls . . . there was plenty of demand! . . . though Sabiani, give the Devil his due, didn't kid anybody, he gave them the lowdown . . . it was written on big signs, in great big red letters . . . "Party member, never forget that you owe the Party everything and that the Party owes you nothing!" He didn't gild the pill! . . . that didn't keep anybody away . . . in fact, more and more kept coming to join, to sit down, and to conk out under the signs . . . and outside the windows more and more people collected to watch the grandfathers dying . . . "look! look! he's shitting right there!" They tell us about the Asiatic crowds, the Brahames, and Bocudos! Hell! I'll make the whole of Europe Asiatic overnight! card-carrying members! political fanatics! . . . five, six corpses in every garbage can! famine and reproduction! . . . the future belongs to the yellow race! . . . and their good old ways!

Speaking of Sabiani's joint, the Castle pulled a mean trick on me about that time . . . a really crummy dodge! . . . a plot to get rid of Luchaire . . . for once they decided I was the perfect doctor . . . the ministers got together . . . they wanted me to certify TB, dangerously contagious . . . to be evacuated immediately! . . . don't worry, I refused! . . . I never go along in that kind of business . . . especially as putting two and two together I wasn't so sure they weren't out for my guts . . . to get me evacuated! . . . like Ménétrel! . . . oh, a time comes when that's all people think about! doing away with you! . . . it's a disease! everybody gets it! . . . you've done this! . . . you've done that! . . . *bam!*

Ah yes, another one . . . more foul play at the Castle! . . . one of the ministers' daughters was knocked up! the parents wanted her to get married! and quick! the young man was right there . . . a sheik . . . he was willing . . . but the hitch! . . . the Boche mayor of Siegmaringen insisted on having the consent of the parents! . . . in writing! the sheik's parents were in France, in Bagnoles-les-Bains! . . . how was it possible to get their consent? . . . no use applying to the Senegalese in Strasbourg! or the F.T.P.* in Annemasse! . . . the Burgermeister was a stubborn bastard, adamant! . . . They start working on Lili . . . I could see what was coming! the mother in tears . . . her whole face running with lipstick . . . she comes up to the *Löwen* and implores Lili . . . the scandal would kill her . . . she'd drown herself in the Danube . . . the desperate mother! . . . to make me do something! in short and to the point, get me to do an abortion! . . . think it over! . . . I can see one more little joke on the horizon: Céline the abortionist! . . . first gently, then firmly, I sent her packing! . . . I'm still cashing in on the hatred! I was sunk either way! . . . that hatred is still pursuing me twenty years later! . . . I'm still getting poked in the kidneys for that abortion I refused to perform . . . I can tell by certain rumors . . . here and there . . . In these little human interest stories connected with great historical upheavals, the exoduses, the general panics, it's always the practitioners . . . the masseurs, chiropodists, abortionists . . . that aren't to be found . . . the adulterers and "tender whisperers" always find each other . . . a dime a dozen! but the family chiropractor! . . . that's where you run into trouble! the lady in tears! . . . people fornicate as they breathe . . . but the chiropractor? the abortion-

ist? Watch your step! all the tender whispering you want, but
where's that abortion coming from? . . . It's hard to get animals to reproduce in a zoo, but people, even condemned to
death, even hunted by Leclerc's army, with the woods full of
Fifis and the whole R.A.F. on top of them thundering day and
night, don't lose their desire to squirt! . . . not in the least!
. . . I certainly wasn't going to worry my head in addition
about all those little discharges, tabes, soft chancres! hell, no!
. . . all that could wait till they were back in France, one way
or another! . . . in the first place, what was I going to treat
them with? I didn't have anything . . . advise them to stop
screwing! Never give advice! let them scratch, fuck and gouge
each other, let them stew in their own juice and rot! . . . the
more the better! . . . one little piece of advice and people
never forgive you! . . . take France! . . . I've told her over
and over again the condition she'd be in one of these days! and
look how she's treated me! . . . the state she's reduced me to!
me! the only one who diagnosed her right! . . . and the stu-
pidest disastrous assholes, so proud! crowing on top of the
manure pile . . . this ghastly ruin! In Siegmaringen, I've got to
admit, I began to go easy: After being a victim for thirty-five
years I began to catch on! *alas! alas!* too late, I'd spilled it all!
. . . the one thing they want of you is to impale you! Darnand's commandos or Fifis, Restif's killers or Leclerc's coons!
. . . your opinions are of no interest to anybody except the
perpetual debaters . . . "Who bought you? how much did you
get? . . ." . . . doddering old fool! naturally! stinking old bastard! . . . oh, I knew all that . . . Mostly I stopped bestir-
ring myself except for emergency cases . . . but they were all
"emergencies"! . . . gripers, provocateurs, and stoolpigeons,
but very sick at the same time! . . . lovely patients! . . .

Enough of that! Pithecanthropus has got a new myth! you'll
see if the blood gushes! if the cutlasses are ready or not! . . .
hell! twelve hundred billion quarts of alcohol make you close
your eyes to a lot of things!

But here's another gooseberry! . . . on the fourth floor, over
the Raumnitzes, in No. 91, I was taking care of Monsieur Miller
from Marseille, a tubercular bed patient, bad hemoptysis . . .

luckily I had a little "retropituitin" . . . it hadn't fallen from heaven . . . hidden in my pocket since Bezons . . . I did what I could . . . day and night . . . This Monsieur Miller, so it seemed, held a very high position in the *Sureté* in Marseille . . . okay! . . . I didn't want to know any more . . . anyway Herr Frucht griped something terrible about his occupying a bed at the *Löwen* . . . said he'd infect the hotel with his coughing and spitting . . . His crapper overflowed all over the stairs! . . . and my patient was the menace! a lot of phony pretexts! . . . his room would be uninhabitable! . . . I should have him sent back to Germany! . . . but this Monsieur Miller of Marseille wasn't the least bit dangerous! . . . those people were scheming something else! . . . I could see it was another plot, like with Luchaire . . . I was perfectly willing for Monsieur Miller of Marseille to move out . . . but where could I put him with his TB? I went to see the lady doctor, a Boche, *"führerin"* of everything connected with tuberculosis . . . Dr. Kleindienst . . . she was really anti-French! . . . she told me off! . . . No surprise . . . she'd always refused me everything! I'd gone to see her a hundred times for my working women with pneumothoraxes . . . there were plenty of them . . . Frenchwomen working in the factories . . . for a quarter pound of butter . . . a pound of sugar . . . *no! no!* . . . and I knew perfectly well that she sent anybody she pleased . . . much lighter cases, whole families from the Castle . . . to the big sanatorium at Saint-Blasien in the Black Forest . . . "send him back to France" was her only advice . . . The S.S. Sanatorium at Saint-Blasien wasn't for my patients! . . . I could see the plot coming . . . petitions all over the hotel and the restaurant, to send this Miller home to Marseille . . . and me with him! . . . to throw us both out! all three of us, Lili and Bébert! or ship us to a camp! . . . I saw it coming! . . . Cissen! . . . oh, they were certainly thinking about it! all four! . . . Le Vigan too! . . . I seem to be exaggerating a little . . . not at all! not at all! . . . I wasn't sure of Brinon! . . . and not at all sure of the Raumnitzes . . . and in spite of the cyanide not the least bit sure of Laval . . . or Bichelonne . . .

Even so the days passed . . . and the nights . . . it was getting really cold . . . Marion comes to see us . . . he tells me that Bichelonne has pulled out . . . suddenly, just like that, without a word . . . without telling me anything . . . gone away to get himself operated up there in Prussia . . . okay! I tell him about the Miller business and my troubles with Kleindienst . . . I tell him it's a plot . . . he thinks so too, he agrees . . . Marion . . . the Minister of Information . . . isn't optimistic . . . he had a shit-colored outlook . . .

I've told you a good deal about Herr Frucht and his troubles
with his toilet . . . but there was a Mrs. Frucht too . . . Frau
Frucht, on our landing, Room 15 . . . No. 15 was more than a
room! . . . a regular apartment with bathroom, dining room,
smoking room . . . I haven't told you about it . . . or about
Frau Frucht . . . I took care of her . . . well, I gave her injections . . . menopause trouble . . . I got them from Basel
. . . through "runners" . . . but even so Frau Frucht didn't
like us! . . . not at all! . . . any more than her Julius! . . .
repulsive *Franzosen!* . . . we were contaminating her hotel,
etc. . . . why couldn't we go somewhere else? . . . which
didn't prevent her from having herself entertained by the
bodyguards from the Castle . . . who were very, very French!
. . . three, four bodyguards per minister . . . which made
quite a crowd, and those boys had good appetites . . . for
lunch and dinner . . . *Franzosen*, athletes, and such lechers!
. . . who weren't bashful and really piled it in! . . . and it
ended in some jamboree! . . . a real Vrench orgy! The lady of
the *Löwen* kept open board for the bodyguards . . . all the
Rhine wine they wanted, schnapps . . . even absinthe! . . .
better than at Pétain's . . . Frau Frucht was having a burning, writhing menopause, hot flashes and torments of the ass!
. . . I think the husband was in on it, he'd take a peek between two sessions at the crapper . . . two shithouse tantrums! . . . the perfect Boche! . . . Anywhere you go, you'll
find people who manage to enjoy themselves . . . if tomorrow
the earth turns into ashes and plaster . . . a cosmos of protons
. . . in some hole in the mountains you'll still find a batch of
haggard lunatics buggering and sucking each other, swilling
and piling it in . . . deluge and *partouze!* . . . that's what it

was like at the *Löwen,* I've got to admit it . . . and what's
more, only two steps from our door . . . on the same landing
. . . I knew all about it . . . I never mentioned it to anybody
. . . not even to Lili . . . oh, I never talked about Room 36
either! . . . you don't talk about things like that! . . . Frau
Frucht never went out by way of our landing . . . she went
down to her restaurant by her own winding stairway, from her
bed to the kitchen . . . nobody entered her room except the
bodyguards . . . her muscular friends, her masseurs . . . all
bodyguards are masseurs, they sure massaged that lady! . . . I
could see the marks of their massages, the palms, the fingers!
. . . she was mottled with massages! . . . with her, her maids
were on the receiving end . . . she had her own way of
massaging them, *à la schlag!* maids and cooks! . . . she'd ask
them up to No. 15 for a lecture! *boom! boom!* . . . old and
young! . . . for never cleaning the stairs properly! . . . for
breaking dishes in the restaurant! . . . *crack! smack!* on the
ass!   on the back! . . . they didn't like it? . . . repeat performance! . . . "lift up your skirts! . . . higher! . . . higher!
. . ." . . . old or young! . . . nothing light about her touch!
. . . Frau Frucht had a whip, too . . . like Frau Raumnitz!
. . . as I saw later, in prison . . . the whip is a natural for
dealing with maids, society women, and prisoners . . . they've
all got a screw loose! . . . straighten them out, cure their complexes, there's only one way! I saw them coming out of Room
15 in tears and hysterics . . . they'd been straightened out
. . . you think you ought to interfere? . . . how do you
know the flagellees don't like it? . . . that getting themselves
whipped isn't a vice with them? . . . one way or another, it
was vice all right! . . . I knew . . . I didn't talk about it . . .
The Frucht apartment, as long as we're there, was as fluffy
. . . cushions, settees, furs, overstuffed velvet easy chairs . . .
as our hovel was sordid . . . and talk about incense and per-
fumes! . . . Frau Frucht was always spraying her bed, the
hangings, and chairs . . . a bottle of lavender . . . another!
heliotrope, jasmine! made you think of the *Chabanais!** . . .
maybe you never knew the *Chabanais* . . . but a *Chabanais*
crossed with Paillard's! . . . ass and stomach! . . . enormous

orgies! . . . the whole works! the mixture of smells! . . . jasmine and rich food . . . leg of lamb, chicken, pheasant *au vin* . . . hit you on the landing . . . the door across from ours, next to the crapper . . . sent you reeling! Frau Frucht was just right for her boudoir, all ruffles and flounces and luxury . . . you could easily see her in a whorehouse . . . the build, the eyes, the tits! The whole picture! . . . and those wrappers, all lace and cabbage-bow ribbons! and those pale pink and green kimonos! . . . and whole cupboards full of silk stockings and garters! . . . menopause or no menopause, Frau Frucht was going strong! . . . the thrashings she gave the maids, plus my hormone injections, plus the bodyguards kept her in a state of prickling desire! . . . I played it dumb . . . I didn't see a thing . . . she gave us little extras . . . Lili and Bébert and me . . . a small platter of noodles now and then . . . who cared about the rest? . . . oh, she wasn't the generous type! Messalina if you will, but also a ruthless hashhouse operator! . . . she took it as a pretext for whipping her maids when they swiped her *Stamgericht* for their mothers or husbands . . . or worse . . . when they took it to the station! . . . I repeat, it was only a pretext . . . any pretext to whip! . . . and make them bellow! . . . *Striptease?* Don't make me laugh! Whipping shows are the thing! You'd fill the Opera a little fuller than for *Faust* or *Meistersinger!* . . . any pretext for vice will do! but she was worth knowing . . . not only her boudoir apartment, the tomato herself . . . that face! made you think of the Place Blanche and the worst pickups in the Bois . . . I'm talking about the old days when there were still real whores, talented creatures, really passionate, asses of flame . . . before the automobile . . . yes, her body, and I can claim to be very particular, was still on the up and up . . . the minute I came into her room, she lay down for her injection, she took off everything, kimono, silk stockings, she wanted me to palpate, to give her a thorough examination . . . *intus et exit* . . . her skin wasn't bad for a woman of her age . . . her muscles were still in good shape, no cellulitis, no muscular atrophy . . . she must have been a peasant, used to heavy work, spading and plowing . . . the breasts still very firm . . .

but the face! . . . Boulevard Rochechouart under the Métro
tracks . . . pulpy, gluttonous mouth, maybe even worse than
Loukoum! . . . a mouth that could have swallowed the sidewalk, the urinal and all the customers, plus their organs and the
bread crusts! . . . her eyes? . . . glowing coals! . . . the fire
of live volcanoes . . . dangerous! . . . I gave her her injection . . . oh, but I was on deck! . . . I was sure her old man
was watching . . . I didn't know where . . . too many draperies and hangings! but I knew! . . . I had to be affable too!
. . . she wasn't putting anything on for me . . . she was so
sultry by nature she couldn't have done any more . . . When
the injection was done and I'd put my syringe away . . . two
three words to be polite . . . she grabs me by the hand . . .
just like that, stark naked! . . . oh, it wasn't her nakedness
that interested me . . . it was her eyes, those coals! . . . not
to see if they're sexy or not! . . . it was the danger that made
me look at her eyes . . . is she going to rape me? . . . no!
. . . no! . . . that's a relief! . . . she wants to speak to me
up close! . . . closer! . . . she wants me to listen . . .
  "*Ihre Frau!* . . . *tanzerin!* . . . *Eh?* . . . *schön!* . . . beautiful! beautiful! *barizerin. ya? ya?* eh? *schöne beine!* beautiful
legs?"
  "Oh yes! . . . oh, yes!"
  Certainly . . . I won't deny it!
  "'*Sie! sie!* you? lend me? . . . *hier!* . . . *hier!* . . . *schlafen
mit!* . . . sleep with me! *willst du?* will you? will you?"
  She's not a volcano anymore . . . she's pure fire! . . . this
bitch is burning! . . . she wants it! . . . she wants Lili! . . .
  "*Gross ravioli willst du haben!* . . . *schön!* . . . *schön!* . . .*"
  She shows me the ravioli I'll get . . . an enormous platter of
ravioli! . . . gigantic!
  "Yes, yes! Frau Frucht! . . . I'll speak to her!"
  And then suddenly, my presence of mind, I grab her square
in the ass and kiss her! . . . *smack!* full in the ass! and on the
other cheek! *plop!* . . . that makes us intimate! we understand
each other!
  I'm not going to cross her . . . give her the idea that I won't
bring her Lili . . . we'd wake up in Cissen! . . . sure as shit!

... one way or another ... But there I get to thinking
... maybe this is a trap! ... perfectly possible! ... a plot
with her old man to get rid of us both! a little trick! the vice
squad! ... turn me in for a pimp! ... and Lili for an ad-
venturess who stops at nothing! ... in judging people's instincts I go by the eyes ... and the look in those eyes was
bad ... lesbian passion? ... don't make me laugh! ...
sure, la Frucht went in for vice! I'd seen others like her! thousands of them! sure she was horny ... that doesn't mean a
thing! her hatred was certainly stronger than her sex fever!
... maybe she'd have helped herself to Lili ... maybe
... and then the bounce! ... Cissen! ... the "monstrous
couple" ... the perverts of the *Löwen* ... I may be a little
rundown, but I think fast! ... plenty fast! ... luckily! ...
I was careful not to leave that room too fast! ... not to seem
to be in a hurry! ... I kiss her ass again, her thigh, her back,
her oyster ... *mff* ... *mff!* an all-around job! ... the
works! ... to seem like an accomplice, a real fan! make her
think I'm going to bring Lili *zu schlafen mit!* ... yes, yes, of
course! ... and I leave very slowly ... I don't say a word
... not a word to Lili ... or to anybody ... I clam up
... I'm beginning to think that if la Frucht goes that far she
has orders ... from the Castle? from the Raumnitzes? ...
or that she knows it's only a matter of hours before we're flat-
tened out like Ulm? ... that somebody's given her the word
... maybe Berlin? or via Switzerland? that they're going to
wind up the circus, the merry-go-round in the clouds, the R.A.F.
fantasia, the storms that nobody's afraid of any more ...
that we're going to see something! burnt to a crisp like Dresden! ... that our half hour has come? ... maybe tabasco
Frucht knows all that? so this is the time to indulge ... to
help herself! ... *tanzerin* ... *barizerin* ... maybe?

"The kitchen and the restaurant are full of soldiers!"

"What kind? . . . French? . . . Krauts?"

"Krauts with an officer!"

"But who? . . . which?"

"They're coming up!"

It's true, I open the door, I see them . . . they create order . . . order! . . . they clear the landing . . . and our room . . . and the toilet . . . everybody out, let's go! . . . down the stairs! nobody left on our floor . . . have they come to arrest me? . . . that's my first idea . . . I want to see that officer . . . ah, here he comes! . . . I know him! . . . I know him well! . . . it's their Oberarzt Franz Traub . . . head physician at their hospital . . . I know him all right . . . dressed . . . fit to kill! . . . dagger! swordbelt, tunic, Iron Cross! . . . gray pants, perfect crease . . . cream-colored gloves . . . dress uniform . . . just to see me? hmmm! . . . nobody left on the landing . . . all cleared . . . only his escort . . . well, two, three squads, armed . . . okay! . . . I wait for him to say something . . . he greets Lili, he takes off his cap, he bows . . . he shakes hands with me . . . I bring him into the room, I give him a chair . . . Bébert has the other . . . we have only two chairs . . . Bébert's great game is jumping from one chair to the other! . . . Bébert gives the occupant a dirty look . . . some nerve! That's his opinion! I look at them, Oberarzt Traub and Bébert . . . who's going to speak first? . . . as long as I'm the host, I start in . . . I apologize for the poor reception . . . our quarters . . . etc. . . . etc. . . . he answers in French: *"c'est la guerre!"* and a gesture meaning to think nothing of it . . . details! . . . he sweeps them away . . . introductory remarks . . . okay, okay! . . . but there's one idea he hasn't swept out of my head . . . has he come to arrest me? that's what I'm wondering . . . and this deployment of police outside our door? . . . that was how they operated when they arrested Ménétrel . . . a doctor and an escort . . . Ménétrel was a doctor too . . . this one, Traub, is the cold type of German . . . oh, of course he detests the French! . . . like all the Boches . . . no more, no less! We French are "special detestables" . . . entitled to be specially detested by every Boche in the village! . . . because we're here! and we shouldn't be! we're compromising them! . . . they all listen in on Bibici . . . all Siegmaringen! *dong! dong! dong!* Bibici tells them what to think! . . . of us and Pétain! . . . our names, our places and dates of birth, our crimes! four, five times a day! and we should all be strung up! . . . Pétain first! next the French troops in Siegmaringen! . . . three, four times a day they notified the real French! the ones we were expecting! the purest legions of the Underground! Brisson, Malraux, Robert Kemp,* the colonels in Leclerc's army . . . that we hoodlums represented exactly what the real France detested most! and that they, the good Germans, should assassinate us, and right away! that we were taking advantage of their kind hearts! . . . betraying them same as we had betrayed France! that we deserved no pity! . . . exactly the opinion of my pirates on the rue Norvins . . . who at that very moment were having the time of their lives wiping me out! . . . the Bibici is the organ of Fualdès* . . . it plays while they murder! . . . and the Boches fell for it! . . . four, five broadcasts a day! . . . they were waiting for Leclerc's army with open arms! ah, we filthy, mangy, lazy devourers of *Stam!* their *Stam!* we'd see if the Senegalese didn't make us vomit up their *Stam!* . . . and our guts! . . . and our blood! . . . the gutters would be full of it! the honor of Siegmaringen avenged! . . . and naturally Oberarzt Franz Traub tuned in on Bibici! . . . Our professional relations had always been correct, no more . . . he'd certainly get along better with the Fifis . . . he'd always refused me everything . . . like Kleindienst . . . sulphur ointment, mercury ointment, morphine . . . *Leider! Leider!* . . . he was about my own age . . . in his fifties

. . . I could stand on my head before he'd admit one of my patients to the hospital! He unloaded all my cases on the *Fidelis,* I'd find them all there plus his own! . . . He'd admitted Corinne Luchaire after a terrible fuss and only on condition that she'd stay just long enough for an X-ray . . . he was like all the rest . . . he didn't want the "liberators" to say he'd shown the slightest indulgence . . .

But why now this plush-horse visit? . . . creased pants and dagger! . . . with his swastika? and all this escort? the whole landing full of them . . . I didn't get it . . . finally he speaks up . . . he starts in . . .

"Colleague, I've come to ask you a favor . . ."

He speaks French without too much accent . . . he's crisp, succinct . . . he explains that he has a patient . . . a wounded German soldier . . . who's had an operation . . . he'd like me to come and see him . . . his wound . . . a shell had blown off his penis . . . that this wounded German soldier is a married man and he wants an artificial penis . . . that these artificial penises are on sale, but only in France! . . . only one manufacturer in all Europe! . . . that he, Traub, could apply to Geneva, to the Red Cross . . . but it would be much better if I were to write directly to Geneva . . . allegedly! . . . allegedly! . . . for a wounded prisoner! . . . because the Red Cross was Gaullist . . . the French prisoners were Gaullists! and I was another Gaullist! . . . Well?

"Certainly! Certainly!"

Certainly! . . . We had a little laugh . . . wasn't it funny! . . . would I? . . . of course I would! . . .

Ah, but something else . . . he had another reason for coming to see me! . . . this is more delicate . . . he hesitates . . .

"Well, you see, I have notified Monsieur de Brinon that I am obliged to bar the *Miliciens* from the hospital . . ."

Why? . . . because they defecated in the bathtubs! . . . and wrote all over the walls in shit! *"for Adolf!"* . . . Naturally Traub could understand that kind of thing! *c'est la guerre!* but the staff? . . . the nurses? . . .

"You understand, colleague, you do understand? it won't do! . . . I've notified Monsieur de Brinon . . ."

Oh, of course! . . . he had been perfectly right! . . .

"Then you agree with me, colleague?"

Something else coming up! . . . is he going to arrest me now? . . . make up his mind? . . . the Boches are so mealy-mouthed, they'd introduce you to the guillotine . . . "won't you cut your little cigar? . . . *lieber Herr!* . . . *bitte sehr!* . . . help yourself! . . . the matches are over there!" No . . . it's not the knife quite yet . . . he wants to talk to me about de Brinon . . . his prostate . . . "Monsieur de Brinon came to see me the other day . . . he has difficulty in urinating . . . he's in pain . . . of course we could operate! . . . but here? . . . here? . . ." Brinon had come to me for advice, too . . . same answer as Traub . . . "When you get back!" . . . how pleasant and practical it is to have a phrase that fixes every-thing . . . "When you get back!" we might as well be going back to the moon . . . ! what were we going back to anyway?

At that point Traub's expression changes . . . suddenly . . . before my eyes . . . he takes a different tone . . . he'd spoken rather lightly of de Brinon and the bathtub . . . now all of a sudden he's talking very seriously . . . still about pros-tates . . . but this time it's his! . . . his own prostate! . . . "Aren't you a bit of a specialist?" . . . oh no! but I know some-thing about it . . . he's been having trouble . . . he urinates frequently like Brinon . . . "how many times at night?" I ask him . . . "and in the daytime?" . . . "five . . . six times . . ."

"Would you examine me?"

"Certainly . . . please remove your trousers . . ."

He stands up, he goes to the door, he says three words to the sentries . . . I can see that Lili's presence embarrasses him . . . Lili goes to the door, too . . . "see that nobody comes in" . . . now he can take his pants off . . . there's only the two of us . . . and Bébert . . . but he's a man, too . . . he relaxes . . . he gets confidential . . . he unloads . . . he con-fesses . . . he's got plenty on his mind . . . plenty! . . . his hospital is a hell! . . . a battle, a free-for-all between the de-partments! the doctors, surgeons, and nuns! . . . they all hate each other, they accuse, they denounce! . . . worse than with us! . . . to see who could get who arrested! for every-

thing! . . . plots! buggery! Black marketing! He confided in
me, he had to get it off his chest . . . it was no surprise to
me . . . go lift up the cover of the Kremlin . . . the House of
Lords . . . the *Figaro* . . . or *l'Humanité* . . . any cover
. . . salons . . . political parties, Castles . . . populaces . . .
backstages . . . monasteries . . . hospitals . . . you'll be all
worn out the way they denounce each other, get each other
arrested, garrote each other, drive spikes under each other's
nails . . .

"You won't speak of all this? . . . you promise, colleague?"

"Professional secrecy!"

The tears came to his eyes . . . those people in the hospital!
. . . he was sobbing! . . . worse than the people in the Castle!

"You won't mention it to a soul?"

I swear! . . . I double-swear! . . . not a word! . . . he
wouldn't ask for advice at the hospital . . . no, never! . . .
but he could trust me? . . . *ya! ya! ya!* . . . he tells me the
whole story . . . he'd been to Tübingen, he'd consulted a specialist, a *Professor* . . . at the university . . . in the Professor's opinion his prostate was quite operable . . . sufficiently
enlarged . . . but he, Traub, didn't consider himself operable at
all! . . . not at all! . . . in fact he was scared shitless of being
operated . . . and admitted it . . . yelled it in fact! . . .
really afraid! . . . especially under the circumstances! so what
about me? what did I think?

"The prostate, my dear colleague, you know as well as I, is
subject to inflammation . . . we can wait . . . it will calm
down . . . naturally surgeons always want to operate . . .
eighty percent of men over fifty are prostatic . . . we don't
operate them all! certainly not! . . . they piss on their heels
now and then . . . what of it? what difference? they'll die a
natural death! . . . they only smell of urine a little . . . is that
anything to worry about? you'll be careful, Traub, that's all!
you'll watch yourself . . . no liquor . . . no beer . . . no
spices . . . no sexual intercourse . . . and in ten years you'll
go back to see your specialist again . . . you'll come and tell
me what he thinks . . . and whether he's been operated . . ."

My comforting words did him a world of good . . . with his hard, hatchet Boche face, he looked at me almost affectionately . . . absolutely! . . . the nectar of my words! . . .

"Would you examine me, my dear colleague?"

"Why, certainly!"

I slip on my rubber finger . . . smear it with vaseline . . . he takes his pants off . . . his gray pants with the fine crease . . . he kneels down on my cot . . . he doesn't remove his tunic or his sword belt or his dagger . . . I palpate . . . yes . . . it's a fact! . . . his prostate is considerably enlarged . . . in fact it seems rather hard . . .

"Oh, all that can wait . . . with a very strict diet . . . your prostate will take care of itself . . ."

"Excellent! . . . excellent, my dear colleague! . . . but my diet?"

"Noodles! . . . just noodles! . . . nothing else!"

It's all right with him! he adjusts his pants . . . his sword belt, his revolver . . .

"Oh yes, my dear colleague . . . oh yes!"

"Come back and see me in a month! . . . we'll see if it's better . . ."

Now I'm the boss! . . . very honestly, without deluding him, I'll be easier in my mind from month to month . . . I'd been worried . . . why all these men on the landing? this escort? . . . and all armed . . . I was on the point of asking him . . . I never found out . . . maybe everything he told me was hokum? . . . but the prostate at least . . . I could be sure of that . . . Well, finally he gets up and leaves . . . ah, one word more! . . .

"You'll drop in at the hospital tomorrow, colleague?"

"Yes, yes, certainly!"

"Splendid! To see about that penis!"

He whispers in my ear . . .

"Sulphur ointment! A jar! . . . you'll take it?"

"Oh, certainly! Oh, many thanks!"

"And a little coffee . . . you'll take it?"

Would I take it! . . . he shows me a small bag . . .

"Oh yes, thank you!"

He's spoiling us . . .

"Discretion! . . . secrecy, you understand?"

"The tomb . . . the tomb, colleague!"

He opens the door . . . a word to the sergeant . . . the men all come to attention! Assembly! They go down . . . Kraut colleague Traub goes last! they all leave! . . . what had they come for? . . . I never really found out . . . to arrest me? . . . maybe not . . . one thing anyway, Traub came back to see me . . . I kept him on noodles and water for seven months . . . and then he stopped coming . . . I never heard from him again! . . . there must have been some reason for all that! . . . I never found out! . . . but I made the best of it . . . a day is a day! . . . one day is a big thing sometimes . . . and we had some coffee . . . oh, not very much . . . and some sulphur ointment . . . not very much of that either . . .

Two . . . three days more . . . oh, not quiet days! . . . more and more people in the streets . . . by road and by train . . . they kept coming! from Strasbourg and the North . . . from the East and the Baltic countries . . . not just for Pétain! . . . to get through to Switzerland . . . but they stayed right there, camping as best they could . . . piling up in doorways and hallways . . . all kinds! . . . men, women, children . . . soldiers on the run, every branch of service . . . you can imagine if Corpechot was recruiting! he promises them everything, signs them up, slips on an armband! . . . and he's got one more sailor! . . . for what boat? what flotilla? we'll see! . . . Lots of activity in the sky! . . . Mosquitoes and Marauders come! and dive! and go! . . . they could make hash out of us any time they wanted! one little bomb! . . . no, they only seem to be taking pictures . . . "have your picture taken in front, profile and hind view by the R.A.F.!" . . . they had nothing to worry about! . . . not a single Kraut plane in the air! . . . or on the ground! . . . never . . . or the slightest sign of A.A.! . . . their whole Defense was hot air! Goering's paunch! all they're good for is making our life impossible! the whole lot of them! . . . as I was saying—two, three more days . . . and three nights . . . shaking, quaking nights! propellers, more propellers! passing, passing again! whole fleets of "Fortresses!" . . . enough to pulverize the whole country as far as Ulm . . . they graze . . . they knock a roof off . . . two roofs . . . that's all . . . tiles! I guess we weren't worth a bomb . . .

Somebody's coming . . . *knock knock!* . . . it's Marion! . . . he's come to see us . . . I remark on the ruckus in the sky . . . he hasn't forgotten us, he's brought us his rolls and some scraps for Bébert . . . we laugh about the state of

affairs, how idiotic it's all getting! the stupidity of our waiting
around like this! what are we waiting for? . . . and I ask him
what's going on at the Castle . . . he gives me the news . . .
Brinon won't see anybody any more . . . or Gabold . . . or
Rochas either . . . they're putting on airs! . . . they weren't
that way a year ago . . . here as always, the airs come too
late! like "visions of the future" . . . always too late! . . . *we
are always dam' wise after the event!* (talking about England, I
might as well trot out my Berlitz) . . . we talk about the ministers' table . . . Bridoux takes everybody's helping, it seems
the others aren't eating any more, or hardly, except Nero, who's
still eating well . . . very well! . . . Nero's a kind of Juanovici who's always trailing around after Laval . . . working up
his "business," so it seems . . . gossip . . . but Marion does
tell me one thing . . . I expected it . . . no, I didn't expect
it! . . . Bichelonne is dead . . . died up there at Gebhardt's
in Hohenlychen . . . during the operation . . . well, there's
nothing to say! . . . he'd wanted to go . . . of course he
could have waited "till he got back" like everybody else! . . .
perfectly well! . . . they haven't announced his death yet
. . . they'll announce it later . . . those are the orders . . .
"don't offend the Germans" . . . okay . .

"It seems you have some cyanide, old man?"

Laval has told him . . . must have! . . . probably Bichelonne too before leaving? . . . it's no crime . . . but now
they'd all be asking me . . . and I had only two phials left
. . . damn!

Now he suggests that instead of staying in our room we go
down to the pastry shop, he wants to introduce me to somebody . . . sure! . . . I don't think much of that pastry shop,
but I can't say no to Marion . . . we go down, myself, Lili,
Bébert . . . To tell the truth . . . no hysteria! . . . we expected the whole place to explode from one minute to the next
. . . or go up in smoke! phosphorus or shrapnel! . . . nothing left . . . The Kleindienst pastry shop was right next door
. . . this Kleindienst was the doctor's sister . . . you know
. . . Dr. Kleindienst, the one who refused me everything . . .
the pastry sister didn't refuse, but she hadn't much to offer

. . . that awful *ersatz* . . . petit-fours that break your teeth
. . . toasted coconut and manioc . . . cookies for crocodiles!
to drink, *ersatz* coffee, crushed clover . . . if it were even chic-
ory! . . . well, you don't go there for the pastry, but to sit
down . . . not very comfortably, but anyway . . . and there
are plenty of people! . . . When the crowd is finished looking
at the dead and dying at the P.P.F., both showcases . . . and
the Castle . . . the flag being raised! the flagpole, the *Milice!*
. . . there's nothing left but the Kleindienst . . . to flop
down, ten or fifteen to a little yellow table . . . flopped in a
ring like that, they look like a wreath around the table . . .
what's Marion brought us here for? . . . we were just as comfortable in our room . . . I don't care for this place at all . . .
I see enough people . . . Marion isn't crazy, he must have a
good reason . . . he tells me why on the stairs . . . he wants
me to meet Restif . . . Horace Restif . . . Restif calls himself
Palmalade . . . I think . . . or something else . . . they all
have these monickers . . . I don't know Restif . . . or his
men . . . Marion sees them, he gives them lectures on History
and Philosophy . . . Restif and his men are off by themselves
in a farmhouse . . . nobody goes to see them . . . they live in
isolation . . . a special "team". . . in charge, so it seems, of
the great Z-Day executions . . . the minute we get back to
France . . . the great "purge". . . the final accounting! . . .
the "Triumph of the Pure," canton by canton! . . . all the
people who sold out to England, America, Russia! . . . you
can imagine the lists! . . . the "enemies of Europe!". . . grist
for the mill and meat for the chopper! They'd counted a hundred and fifty thousand traitors! all to be liquidated in three
months! . . . the hounds of London . . . and Brazzaville
. . . and Moscow! . . . Then there would be a new Europe!
absolutely brand new! a happy, thrice-happy continent! . . .
with one thing and another Restif had proved his mettle!
that's what counted! he could give lessons . . . in "special
techniques"! . . . he'd been an "activist" in several parties
. . . and several police forces . . . he was given credit for
Navachine* in the Bois de Boulogne . . . the Roselli brothers*
in the Métro . . . and plenty more! . . . his own . . . very

special technique . . . the carotids! . . . a little trick . . . his
man went down! quick from behind . . . with a big razor!
fsst! not a peep! both carotids! . . . two streams of blood! and
that was it! . . . fast and deep! one stroke! clean work! that's
what he taught them! *fsst!* . . . both carotids! the modern
coup du Père François! . . .

His team was separate . . . they lived by themselves, they
didn't mix much . . . when two members met in town, they
saluted and bounced to attention! . . . one shouted: *Ideal!*
and the other came back with *Serve 'em hot!.* . . . at their farm
they were always training . . . on pigs, or sheep . . . if they
didn't come to town much, it was because they didn't care to be
seen . . . the one thing they really went for was lectures . . .
and not on spicy subjects, the cavortings of the vamps . . .
oh, no! real History! real Philosophy! Marion had the enthusiasm, the gift, the extensive culture . . . he was highly es-
teemed on the Restif farm . . . never a word about the famous "technique"! never a word . . .

Nothing but Philosophy and Mystique and "selected readings . . ." very attentive audiences, never an interruption! the
students raise hell in their classrooms at the Collège de France
or the Lycée Louis le Grand . . . that's for virgins! . . . virgins young and old . . . carotid specialists are dignified . . .
especially Restif's men . . . Restif himself never opened his
mouth! he sat in the first row and listened . . . he admired
Marion . . . he whispered in his ear . . . he personally didn't
care about being admired . . . not in the least! . . . he
thought his little trick was practical and expeditious! . . . no
more, no less . . . same as I think my style is practical and
expeditious! no more, no less! . . . and you can't tell me different! it is simple and expeditious! . . . but nothing more! . . .
I don't blow it up into a mountain! if I had something to live
on, if I weren't driven, I'd keep it to myself! . . . that's right!
. . . I don't care about being admired! . . . I haven't got the
temperament of a star! or a starlet! Restif thought his system,
his "Père François, special" was superior to any other! . . . but
he wasn't stuck up about it! . . . superior to the guillotine; no
more, no less! . . . if you mentioned the Rosellis or Navachine

to him, he blushed and went away . . . it was you he wanted
to listen to . . . your stories, your own story! he and Marion
got along fine . . .

So, as I was telling you, we were at the Kleindienst . . .
Lili, Bébert, Marion and me . . . *ersatz* pastry . . . at the
next table the party "hopefuls". . . the ardent élites of the
P.P.F. and the R.N.P., Bucard . . . they were really sounding
off! the whole pastry shop could hear them! the total reshaping
of Europe! . . . the things they were going to do . . . when
they got back! . . . when they got back! the great Purge! . . .
France was going to see something! The Message of France!
. . . staggering reforms! revolution? you can say that again!
. . . Pétain? . . . a disastrous cacochymic paranoiac! . . .
throw him out! throw him out! . . . maybe they'd take Bucard, the "hero of the infantry" . . . maybe! . . . or Darnand,
another "hero of the infantry" . . . maybe! . . . but only as
second to Déat! . . . no more! Déat was their man! . . . he
had this! . . . he had that! really the only valid idol! a giant of
political thought! Doriot? a demagogue and crypto-Commie!
. . . cross him off! he'd turn Commie again! . . . couldn't
help it! . . . Laval, naturally, was through, he'd been too stupid too long! he'd go back to his Cheteldon! . . . Brinon?
Brinon? ditto! . . . a jockey! . . . a jockey and a Jew! . . .
no question! . . . and whom would they take on the other
side? De Gaulle? . . . ha ha! thinks he's Napoleon! the cadet's
dream! . . . cop, lousy provocateur! . . . couldn't hold a
candle to Clemenceau! seemed to take pride in his height! and
Maginot? even taller! cross off de Gaulle! . . . whose real
name was van de Walle! . . . a foreigner, de Gaulle van de
Walle! they knew everything at those little tables! and a passion, a warmth that I've never seen since . . . a style, a national fervor . . . a kind of spirit! . . . it's gone! . . . it was
only after the Purge that the Defeat became really evident . . .
the total Collapse . . . the new myth . . . Bullshit is king
. . . the beards are gone too, that Athenian-sheik cut . . . effervescent political youth . . . budding deputies . . . sure
they talked a lot of hot air! . . . but what do we see around us
now? . . . hordes of natives ashamed to be themselves . . .

and still more nauseating "sub-sub-whites! . . . Eurasians, Euroabdullas, 'Eur'" everything under the sun . . . as long as they can get themselves accepted as somebody's toadies! . . . and drink! . . . and get themselves taken into a herd! degraded, putrid, washed up! . . . disappear under somebody else's skin! . . . not theirs! oh, not theirs! . . . so naturally they get kicked! and kicked some more!

I don't see the sheiks anywhere nowadays . . . any more than you'll see Louis XVI again on the Place de la Concorde . . . The Chinese won't go looking for the emplacement of the guillotine . . .

Let's get back to my pastry shop . . . Restif was there with us, attentive, discreet . . . there was nothing special about him . . . I've known a lot of assassins, I've seen them close up, very close . . . in the place where the bluff falls off, in prison . . . no phony bigmouths . . . the real article, third . . . tenth offenders . . . they had something if you watched them closely day and night . . . in the big house . . . there was something funny about them . . . but Restif, not at all! . . . not the slightest tic . . . but even so! even so! later . . . I saw him flip his wig . . . I'll tell you about it . . . an attack! a real wild beast! but there, talking to us at the Kleindienst, absolutely dignified and normal . . . the others, at the next table, the "hopes" . . . they weren't at all dignified, really effervescent! scandalous! the clash of the "programs"! their reshaping of Europe! . . . what should . . . and shouldn't be done! ferocious sectarians! neo-Bucards! . . . neo P.P.F! . . . neo-Commies! neo-everything! the new men, the superforce that all France was waiting for! . . . the élite of Siegmaringen! their first duty: the pure! inflexible! Fourth Republic! the whole world should sit up and take notice! the Intransigent Fourth Republic! . . . and they'd all appointed themselves ministers! right then and there! they were already in Versailles! proclamation in Versailles! Hitler gets hanged, that goes without saying! and his Goering with him, the enormous porcine traitor who'd sold the sky to the English! . . . all you had to do was look up! . . . Goebbels? impaled! that criminal Quasimodo! he wouldn't tell any more lies! Those were the real fanatics, the gilt-edged malcontents, who had really cruel reasons, ready to sign up! . . . beards, ferocious vocabularies . . . who really had something to complain about! . . . all of them with Article 75 on their ass! . . . you can't do anything serious except with people who are starving . . . take the Chinese! . . . three weeks in Touraine, I'll give them back to you, I'll pick them up with a spoon . . . they'll all be getting complexes . . . the indomitable Chinese! "Should I take Gide standing? . . . or his grandmother lying down?" Marion had had his reasons for taking us down to the Kleindienst . . . Restif couldn't very well show himself in the *Löwen* . . . there were already enough jokers coming to see me . . . supposedly to consult me . . . and Room 36? . . . and the Raumnitzes right on top of us? Yes, it was better like this . . . We talk about this and that . . . and then all of a sudden: cyanide! I might have expected it! . . . Laval must have blabbed . . . Bichelonne too probably . . . by this time everybody must know, all Siegmaringen . . . that I had tons of it . . . everybody would come around asking! ah, and another piece of news! . . . from the Castle, too! . . . that Laval had appointed me Governor! they didn't know exactly of what . . . but somewhere! which reminded me . . . I had no proof . . . with Bichelonne dead I had no witness . . . Laval could deny it . . . I wouldn't put it past him . . . we laugh . . . even Restif, not easily amused, finds me amusing as Governor . . . I explain: Governor of the Islands! . . .

I ask Marion politely what we've come down here to the Kleindienst for. "We're going to see the train . . . aren't we, Restif?" and they tell me what it's all about! . . . the train that's going to take them to Hohenlychen for Bichelonne's funeral . . . the official delegation, six ministers, plus Restif, and two other delegates . . . who? . . . probably Marion and Gabold . . . but careful now! the train is tucked away in the middle of the forest on the other side of the Danube . . . nobody must know! or see it! it's hidden . . . buried under a heap of branches! invisible from the air! . . . an engine is coming from Berlin to pick them up . . . an "extra-special" train, two cars . . . they'd be notified when the engine came

. . . any minute now! . . . Hohenlychen isn't exactly around
the corner . . . 750 miles . . . the other end of Germany,
from South to North East . . . I've told you about Gebhardt
and his S.S. Hospital, 6000 beds . . . but how had Bichelonne
died? . . . nobody knew . . . well, up there they'd find out!
. . . find out? . . . really? . . . Marion didn't think so . . .
the Boches could tell them anything they pleased . . . I think
it over . . . I've got my own ideas . . . it was Gebhardt who
had operated . . . I didn't like Gebhardt . . . anyway, while
they were waiting for their train . . . well, the engine . . .
we'd go take a look at this "special train". . . only Restif
knows where it is . . . under which branches . . . after the
big bridge . . . perfectly camouflaged, so it seems . . . but
Restif hasn't any faith in the camouflage or the branches . . .
it'll be spotted in any case, he explains . . . because they've
got nothing but coke to fire her with! . . . all their engines are
running on coke! you can spot them with your eyes closed! you
can see them coming all the way from Russia! enormous trails
of cinders! . . . which explained the perpetual circus of planes
over the tunnels . . . the entrances, the exits . . . *boom!* bull's
eye! . . . sitting ducks! on the way out of the Eiffel Mountains
there's a permanent merry-go-round, at least thirty of them!
. . . the trains come and ask for it, practically . . . perfect
targets! practically on purpose . . . we found out later . . .
Restif knew . . . he knew a hell of a lot . . . but it was no
time to ask him questions . . . to ask him why and how . . .
he was guiding us, that's all . . . Lili, Marion, myself, and
Bébert . . . we were going to see this special train . . . that
was supposedly hidden . . . Long detours . . . here we are
finally at the big five-span, three-track bridge . . . we cross
. . . we dive into the forest . . . there, I've got to admit,
where he was taking us, those zigzagging paths . . . we'd
have got lost . . . it was so dark . . . they seemed to have
felled the biggest pine trees . . . it was a kind of vault overhead . . . and down below an impossible tangle . . . cut
branches, intertwined . . . we follow the roadbed . . . the
rails too . . . but all these trees across the tracks! . . . felled
Christmas trees! . . . we come to an even bigger pile of

branches . . . with a crowd of people around it . . . Restif
knew . . . that was the place . . . the train was underneath
. . . the buried train . . . total camouflage! . . . but this
mob! . . . they'd found the secret train all right! people from
the *Löwen,* from the town, soldiers and civilians, an army! and
chewing the fat! in every language! . . . worse than the Kleindienst! . . . soldiers in camouflage and without camouflage
. . . French and Boche refugees . . . everything! . . . even
my dying patients from the *Fidelis,* who were supposed to be
in bed . . . were there, having the time of their lives! . . .
families of *Ost* workers . . . deported from the Ukraine
. . . with ten, twelve kids! . . . all playing in the branches . . .
jumping and squealing, and swinging all over the place
. . . The mystery train! . . . and the shuppos! and the S.A.
. . . and Admiral Corpechot in person! . . . all commenting
with authority! they knew everything! all there was to know
about this train . . . Hitler's "special"? . . . no! . . . for Pétain? . . . for Admiral Corpechot? . . . for Stalin? . . . to
bring de Gaulle from London? . . . they climb in to look . . .
they turn everything upside down! chairs, cushions, easy chairs!
real luxury! . . . parents and kids and cops . . . I knew they
hid in the woods at night, but I'd never have thought this many
. . . They beat it to the forest for fear of being burned in
their hovels . . . hit by bombs! . . . but such a mob!
scared that it would be our turn soon! a bonfire like Ulm! why
not? it had been announced often enough! . . . even some of
the sick and dying from the showcases! . . . and the pianists
from the buffet . . .

They kept climbing in and out of the cars . . . the two cars
. . . everybody with a lighted candle! as if they wanted to
start a fire! even the brats! clusters of brats! enough to set fire to
the whole forest! they want to see everything! the kitchen car
and the crapper! the mosaic crapper! they all had to go in and
touch everything! a midnight forest party . . . a snakedance by
torchlight! . . . they had to touch everything! "Is all this for
Hitler? or for Leclerc? or for the Senegalese?" Plenty of laughs!
. . . guffaws! explosions! it had been worth coming!

Restif knew better . . . this train was a special, very special train which William II had ordered, but it had never been used . . . specially ordered for the Shah of Persia . . . who had come on an official visit in August 1914 . . . it had never been delivered . . .

You can't conceive of the luxury! A mixture of all the elegance of Wilhelminian Germany, Persia, and Turkey! . . . brocades, tapestries, hangings, braided cord! . . . worse than Laval's apartment! . . . divans, sofas, embossed leather ottomans! and the carpets! the thickest they could find! . . . super-Bukhara! . . . super-India! . . . curtains that weighed a ton, to cut off drafts! . . . oh, they hadn't stinted! lamps and fixtures in the "Lalique Métro" * style, "Barisian" monuments that took up half the car . . . the Shah would certainly have been happy! . . . they couldn't have put any more in! . . . I remember, I said to Marion: "I don't know if you'll get there, but at least you'll be comfortable." Restif is the practical kind. Carpets and window curtains are all very well, but what about the kitchen? . . . he wants us to go see . . . in the other car . . . That kitchen was certainly well equipped . . . everything you need . . . stoves and kettles! . . . but where's the coal? . . . no coal! This kitchen won't work with coke!

"Don't worry, Monsieur Marion! . . . I'll get you two dozen chickens, I'll have them cooked at the *Löwen* . . . we'll take them '*à la gelée.*'"

That was the simplest way . . . and he'd get his chickens! . . . he wasn't boasting! Marion isn't worried . . . they never refuse Restif anything on the farms . . . and free, gratis! . . . they refuse us . . . they even refuse Pétain everything . . . even for the Raumnitzes they haven't got any . . . but for Restif they've got plenty . . . it's his charm . . .

Naturally the locomotive from Berlin never came . . . an accident, so it seems, between Erfurt and Eisenach . . . the whole roadbed blown to pieces . . . and in another place . . . around Cassel . . . the engine itself! that made for delay . . . the Delegation could wait! . . . the enthusiasm was gone . . . this didn't look so good! . . . after a lot of talk they finally admitted that there wouldn't be any locomotive from Berlin . . . the two cars would be towed by a "wildcat" engine from right here in Siegmaringen . . . except it would go very slowly, it would be a long trip! . . . more whispering, discussions . . . who'd go . . . and who wouldn't . . . a ferocious debate between the Castle, Raumnitz, and Brinon . . . about who would be delegated to the funeral . . . antipathies! . . . who would be sick, down with the grippe, exempt? . . . rheumatism? . . . too sensitive to the cold? . . . in the end they found seven in relatively good health . . . and more or less persuaded them . . . ministers, active or "on ice" . . . I won't name them here . . . it might hurt them . . . yes, yes, even now, twenty years after! . . . partisan hatreds are a business proposition! . . . and never forget it! . . . people made careers for themselves in the Purge, burying collaborators . . . people who were pure shit got to be great big avengers . . . bigshots . . . with enormous privileges! . . . so naturally they'll go on "resisting" to their last breath! . . . until their last granddaughter is nicely married! the collaborators' worst bad luck was having been such a windfall for the rottenest horde of stinking good-for-nothings . . . just tell me, what would Vermersh,* Triolette, or Madeleine Jacob be good for faced with a milling machine? or a sheet of paper? or a broom? . . . hyenas! get back to your kennel! catastrophes like that!

windfalls! not once in a century! a surprise orgy for the pin-brained hatchet girls! they're in no hurry to give up being the Most-High-and-Mighty Paladins of the supercolossal reverse-parade of 1939! . . . I'm not going to give them anything to work on! oh no! I'll wait until the Most-High-and-Mighty Seneschals of the supersensational whammy of 1939 are six feet under . . . I won't give them anything to work on! I'll wait until they're all out of commission . . . it won't be long! . . . a time comes . . . the age curve . . . when it goes very fast! I collect death notices . . . I know! . . . the "Great Assembly"! executioners and victims! . . . anyway, Marion was a member of this delegation to the funeral . . . I've told you . . . Marion and Restif . . . Horace Restif was supposed to represent the "Special Teams" . . . he'd be the "Quartermaster" too, in charge of the kitchen . . . and the chickens! he'd roasted the chickens at the *Löwen* as promised . . . but with all the shilly-shallying and waiting for the engine, they'd been eaten . . . yes, wing by wing . . . there wasn't anything left on the day set for departure . . . a bad start! . . . all they'd got from the Castle in the way of provisions was two little packages per minister! little packages of sandwiches! jealousy! and from the hotels? Balloon juice! . . . the trip was expected to take three days and three nights, from Siegmaringen up to Prussia . . . talking about clothing, I may as well tell you, they were wearing the same as when they'd left Vichy, light topcoats, suede shoes . . . not at all the right thing for below zero . . . in Siegmaringen in November it wasn't so bad, but going north they wouldn't be happy . . . they found out! . . . not happy at all! especially when it came to sleeping! when they'd finished their sandwiches, when there was nothing left, there was an awful lot of stamping and foot rubbing . . . the trip wasn't over and they were still going north . . . and the thermometer getting lower and lower . . . and it was beginning to snow . . . first a few flakes . . . then blizzards! . . . especially after Nuremberg! thick! like cotton! . . . you couldn't see a thing! . . . neither the tracks, nor the roadbed, nor the stations . . . the sky and the horizon were all cotton! . . . we went through Magdeburg without seeing a thing . . . our train was supposed to go up by easy stages, avoid Berlin, detour through the suburbs . . . our luck that there was never an air patrol . . . that one of the Marauders didn't take us! . . . we must have been sighted! not a doubt! the old locomotive that was pulling us sent out streams and trails! flaming cinders! . . . especially on the upgrades . . . they couldn't miss us . . . we must have been visible from the moon! . . . there were reasons why they didn't see anything! must have been! . . . the explanations come later, when nobody's interested . . . when they don't mean anything . . . anyway, in that air-cooled car, not a windowpane, full of winds! and what winds! nobody could sleep . . . too cold and too shaken up! . . . especially after the Castle! instant bronchitis! . . . they were all coughing! . . . even with heat nobody could have slept, the springs must have been shot . . . "peach-pit suspension" . . . coming and going, stamping to get warm, the ministers were all bumping into each other! Jolts! . . . hell, earthquakes! you wouldn't catch them going to any more funerals! after two days and two nights, they were all in! and this was only one way! . . . the real fun was the return trip! but the northward run gave you the idea . . . Restif was ingenious, practical . . . he took his knife to the draperies! . . . *krrr! zip!* and there were plenty of them! rivers of silk, velvet and cotton . . . hanging, cascading all over the place . . . really a super de luxe car! and all the ministers started in! *krrr! zip!* like Restif! . . . floral designs, carpets, braid! . . . anything to get warm! . . . they disemboweled the car! . . . a battle! everybody made himself an overcoat . . . the real thing! . . . super-overcoats! thick, four layers! kind of cavalry coats! . . . but really good ones! . . . I know what I'm talking about . . . ours in the 14th were horrible imitation! . . . the slightest rain and they soaked up all the water, they crushed you under their weight! the coats the ministers made themselves, cut with a knife, four thicknesses, plus the Bukhara carpets, and gathered at the waist, may have looked silly, but never mind . . . they were all right! especially for sleeping in the little stations around Berlin . . . we were stalled for hours . . . here . . . and there . . . with the locomotive puffing . . . nobody came around to see how

we were getting along . . . nobody offered us anything . . .
not a *Stam* . . . not a sausage . . . maybe they didn't have
any themselves? . . . you never know with the Boches! . . .
we'd have had time to ask . . . but talk some more? . . . it
was getting really cold now . . . full in the north wind . . . it
was cold in Siegmaringen, but nothing like this! . . . and it
was only the beginning of November . . . We started off
again, bumping and jolting . . . it was getting really mean
. . . the snowflakes . . . like cotton, so help me, you couldn't
see the plain or the sky . . . the train was moving very
slowly . . . so slowly maybe it wasn't on the rails any more
. . . must have skidded . . . skidded off the rails? . . . ah,
at last, a station! . . . same thing, nobody comes out to see us
. . . we were floating forward as if in a mirage . . . all we
knew was we were going north . . . further and further north!
. . . Marion had his compass . . . Hohenlychen was north-
east . . . Marion had a map, too . . . after Berlin it was more
to the east . . . we weren't going to complain . . . the engineer didn't talk to us . . . we tried . . . he must have had orders, too . . . okay! . . . he could keep his orders . . . with
us it was *krrr! zip!* . . . another seat cover! and another! all
trying to see who could tear the most! . . . because it was getting colder and colder! a hole! *krrr!* at the top of the slipcover
. . . that gave you a quadruple cape . . . and tearing warms
you too . . . and *rip!* . . . and *rip* again! the window cov-
ers! . . . and plenty of them! ah, the Shah! Wilhelminian
ornamentals! . . . Turkish delights! Arabian bazaar! . . . another Bukhara! shit! we'll get even if they won't talk to us!
"damn Boches! . . . thugs! . . . vampires! . . . starvers! . . .
pricks!" that's what the funeral delegation were yelling,
absolutely unanimous! if they won't tell us anything . . . we'll
give them William I! II! III! and IV! in the snout! And where
are they taking us anyway? to the North Pole? . . . to Russia?
. . . not to Hohenlychen at all! bastards . . . perfectly capable . . . traitors to the bone . . . We rip up their whole car
shouting "Boches! Saxons! pigs!" We tore everything off, we
put it on! We really covered ourselves! ah, the stuffing! Let's
have the stuffing! they're not giving us anything to eat, they're

starving us on purpose! the bumping is on purpose too! At least
we can smash their car! all their folderols!

And then Restif discovers a treasure! . . . a vein! . . . a
hiding place! he rummages all over . . . from under the big
sofa he brings out one . . . two . . . twenty pieces of violet
muslin . . . Parma violet! it must have been to hang on the
nightmare ornaments . . . garlands . . . all across the car
. . . big flounces! . . . suddenly I get to thinking . . . this
Parma violet color? . . . it rings a bell! . . . a "throwback"
. . . ah, I've got it . . . I know a thing or two about Germany . . . more than I want to! . . . this Parma muslin . . .
right! . . . Diepholz, Hanover . . . Diepholz, the *Volks-
schule!* . . . 1906! . . . they'd sent me there to learn Boche!
. . . come in handy in business! . . . Hell! ah, Diepholz,
Hanover! . . . sweet memories! . . . even then they were vicious mean! maybe worse than in '44 . . . the clouts they gave
me in Diepholz, Hanover! in 1906! . . . *Sedantag! Kaisertag!*
the same savages as in 1914 . . . the same as I faced in Poelcapelle,* Flanders! which reminds me that Madeleine wasn't
there! in Capelle, Flanders! or Vermersh! or even de Gaulle!
standing up against the Germans really takes men! nor Malraux,
the idol of the youth! and they don't leave many of them intact!
take me for instance!

Getting back to that muslin! . . . they had the stuff hanging
over all their china closets, lamps and balconies in Diepholz,
Hanover! no wonder I remember! with the other school kids, all
over the streets, across the streets! the same muslin . . . Parma
violet . . . the *Kaiserin's* birthday, her color . . . I was the
only *franzose* in Diepholz, Hanover . . . you can imagine if
they put me through the mill . . . if they made me hang muslin! I remembered well! . . . Kaiserin Augusta! . . .

This treasure he'd unearthed! miles of muslin! all the ministers want some! secretaries of state, excellencies pounce on the
bolts of Parma violet . . . unroll it all, wind themselves dresses
and turbans out of it! they think they look better . . . more
dignified in half-mourning . . . but there's not enough muslin
to go around . . . especially five, six layers from head to foot!
only the ministers! . . . they're pleased with their little num-

ber! . . . they billow and smooth . . . they gather in the
waist with upholstery braid . . . the whole car is full of it . . .
all the draperies . . . *krrr! rip!* . . . are they going to get out
like this . . . in Parma violet gowns? . . . if they ever arrive!
. . . our calliope starts going even slower . . . *choo! choo!*
from jolt to jolt . . . I said to myself, something's happening
. . . you could see the roadbed, you could see the tracks . . .
we must be getting somewhere . . . are we in Russia? I ask
somebody . . . half joking . . . it's perfectly possible . . .
maybe they've sent us to Russia . . . handed us over to the
Red Army? with the Boches everything is possible, you've got
to know them! the whole car is yelling, ready for the Russians!
tovaritsh! tovaritsh! "they won't be any worse than the Germans!" that's the unanimous opinion . . . Franco-Russian alli-
ance? . . . why not? good deal! . . . let's go! especially
swathed in Parma violet! . . . it'll put the Russians' eye out!
. . . with them maybe we'll eat? . . . the Russians eat! . . .
in fact they eat like elephants! . . . some of our passengers
know all about it! . . . borscht, red cabbage, etc! salt pork!
they know what we'll get! it's all right with me! . . . so I fill
them in, I inform the Delegation that I'm the author of the first
Communist novel ever written, that they'll never write another!
never! . . . they haven't got the guts! . . . and we'll announce it to the Russians! . . . to clinch it: translated by Aragon and his wife! they mustn't land like nobodies . . . they
should tell them who they are . . . and who's with them! . . .
it's not enough to talk about borscht! maybe do a *danse triste?*
with sobs? . . . a little "downcast impromptu"? . . . won't
look bad in Parma violet! I'm full of ideas, but I can't make
them laugh . . . me and my gags . . . they want to eat! . . .
they want to see those mess kits . . . Chinese, Turkish, Russian! . . . so long as it's chow! and would we find the L.V.F.?
Possible . . . maybe they'll take us to the L.V.F. . . . why
not? . . . we speculate . . . and their field kitchen! *canard
aux navets!* . . . yum yum! . . . and heaps of meatballs! all
you can eat! possible! possible! wouldn't that be a good one?
but *brrt!* the train vibrates, comes to a stop . . . yes . . .
completely! and *tzimm! BAM! boom!* a band! . . . an anvil

chorus! . . . on top of the embankment . . . Russians? . . .
no! . . . Boche soldiers! . . . the *Horst Wessel Lied!* Boches
all right! . . . way on top of the snow bank! serenading us
. . . it's really for us . . . Krauts! genuine Krauts! . . . not
the L.V.F., not Russians! it's not even a station, we've stopped
in the middle of the steppe . . . is it Hohenlychen? . . .
nobody knows! . . . where's the hospital? . . . we don't see
it, we don't see a thing . . . all we see is the embankment,
the band on top, and the Boches . . . the Boches in high
boots . . . their leader has a beard, he waves his baton . . .
the *Horst Wessel Lied* again . . . and again . . . they must
be expecting us to climb up . . . the leader motions to us . . .
ah, it's not so easy! . . . especially in the pumps we've got on!
never mind, we help each other up, we ascend . . . here we
are! . . . oh, they've thought of everything! . . . a suitcase
full of *butterbrot!* . . . it doesn't last long! . . . three shakes
and it's all gone! nothing left! . . . they're still playing their
Horst Wessel . . . we haven't got any boots . . . looks like
they're going to lead us . . . we'll follow . . . but here comes
a handsome young officer . . . he salutes us . . . from up top
next to the band . . . has he brought us something to eat?
. . . he requests us to line up . . . first "Justice"! . . . he
must be the protocol officer . . . I've told you about the protocol . . . "Justice" first! . . . "Justice" represents Pétain . . .
after Justice, the band . . . and then the rest of the Delegation . . . but in strict order! . . . oh, but they've changed
their tune! . . . it's not the *Horst Wessel* any more, it's the
Marseillaise! . . . We start out . . . we skid . . . especially
"Justice"! . . . we put "Justice" back on his feet! . . . it's slippery as hell! . . . gales and gales! . . . the wind of the Urals
six months out of twelve! . . . you've got to feel it to know
. . . then you understand all the retreats! . . . all the disas-
ters in Russia! nobody can take it! Napoleon's a little boy, Hitler a delirious straw in the wind! really that plain is no place to
be! if we didn't have the Vosges and the rampart of the Ar-
gonne, we'd have the same gale! . . . you get to understand
the conquerors of the East, their hordes are maddened, drunk
with the cold . . . they should stay home and croak! why send

us up there? that's what I'd like to know! . . . it takes the politicians of today, who've never taken off from the Gare de l'Est, to miragine what goes on in those places! . . . the taxis of the Marne and blah-blah! . . . why don't they go see?

I won't tell you the names of the ministers behind the band . . . or the other people's either . . . Marion, okay, you know him . . . he's at the tail end . . . that's his place in the protocol, the last born of the ministries . . . we're nine in all . . . too damn slippery, we're really pooped . . . the officer puts us back together, arm in arm . . . and we start off again . . . where can that hospital be? . . . we can't see it! . . . you can't see anything in this snow! . . . even clutching each other this way we keep on slipping, we're not getting anywhere! . . . it's frozen like a skating rink . . . it's all right for them, for the band, they've got hobnailed boots! they can play the *Marseillaise!* with us it's a miracle we don't fly away and break our necks . . . the whole lot of us . . . and never get up . . . and every bone . . . naturally there were protests! . . . slower! slower! *langsam!* they don't hear us, if anything they go faster! Where are they taking us? ah, there's something after all . . . up there . . . it must be! . . . in the snow . . . something in the distance! . . . a flag! . . . I see it! . . . an enormous flag! . . . that must be for us! "wave wave grand flag!" . . . tricolor, blue, white, red, in front of a kind of shed . . . that's where they're taking us, must be! . . . not to the hospital at all . . . the officer makes a sign: halt! . . . the music stops, too . . . okay! . . . the officer comes over and starts telling us something . . . okay . . . we listen . . . he speaks French . . . "It grieves me to inform you that Monsieur Bichelonne is dead . . . he died ten days ago . . . at the hospital . . ." he points out the hospital . . . too far for us! we can't even see it . . . through the snow! . . . he tells us they've been expecting us for ten days! we're too late! . . . Bichelonne is in his box . . . here under the shed? . . . nothing remains but to pay the last honors . . . would one of us like to speak? . . . nobody feels like it! . . . too cold, too much snow, we're shivering too hard . . . Even in this getup, all swaddled in muslin, carpets, double curtains, puffed and stuffed, our teeth are chattering like knitting needles! speaking is out of the question! it's wonder enough that we got this far! I'm getting to understand the Great Retreats better and better . . . that they lie down in their own horses' bellies! fresh-opened and warm! in their guts! horrors! that's easy to say! we haven't got any horses, only this military band! and they start up again! . . . the *Marseillaise!* looks like we have to go over to the shed to pay the last honors . . . are we the honors? . . . who'd pay us any honors if we crack our skulls on this ice? nobody! . . . not a soul! . . . but as long as we're here by some miracle, I'd like to see Gebhardt at least! . . . he oper-ated on him . . . he's not here, I don't see him, he hasn't come . . . too many operations, so it seems . . . I wonder if they're all so successful! I guess he doesn't exactly want to see us . . . nobody wants to see us . . . and no mess kits! Noth-ing! all they've got for us is a wreath! a wreath apiece, ivy and immortelles! . . . holding together, we struggle up to the shed . . . is this where he is, under this shed? . . . we lay our im-mortelles on the coffin . . . is Bichelonne in it? . . . no confi-dence in the Germans . . . you never know . . . anyway it's a fine coffin! Bichelonne doesn't have to account to anybody any-more! . . . with us it's different, it's not over yet! . . . we've got a bit of explaining to do! we've got to account to everybody . . . even to my pillagers! . . . I'm always talking about my-self! . . . It was easy for Hamlet to philosophize about skulls! . . . he had his "security"! We certainly didn't!

The protocol officer sees that we don't want to say any thing . . .

"*Nun, messieurs!* the ceremony is ended! You may return, Messieurs!"

Oh, the flag . . . we were forgetting the flag! . . . we were supposed to take it back to the Marshal . . . the musicians rip it out of the ice . . . with a great deal of difficulty! . . . they hand it to us! . . . plenty heavy, I assure you! . . . the wind rushes into it! we grab hold of the pole seven . . . eight . . . ten of us . . . it carries us away! . . . we sail with the gusts . . . we and the band! . . . luckily the wind is blowing from east to west . . . in the direction of our car . . . assuming it's

still there! . . . the Delegation rolls and pitches! . . . ministers and musicians together . . . hanging on to the flag . . .
bam! . . . we're all reeling! we crumple! we lie down! . . .
ah, but then the wind starts up again! . . . everybody up,
let's go! but the flag isn't vertical any more, oh, no! now it's flat,
horizontal! everybody on the pole, but lengthwise! . . . we
discovered the gimmick! . . . the band follows us! . . . they're
still playing their *Marseillaise* . . . we're still slipping, but
not so much . . . the whole thing is finding the gimmick!
we're not skidding any more . . . the officer follows us . . .
we get to the top of the embankment . . . right next to
our car . . . was he glad to get us into that train! we didn't
need to be asked twice . . . we'd paid those last honors! . . .
but how were we going to stow this enormous flag? . . . it's
as long as the car! . . . luckily there's no glass in the windows!
. . . it barely fits . . . lengthwise along the sofa . . . and a
little on the slant . . . but what about the engine? . . . is it
still here? how are they going to turn it around? . . . is she
going to push instead of pulling? . . . I ask a Kraut . . . she'll
push us as far as Berlin . . . Berlin-Anhalt . . . then there'll
be a different engine . . . okay! . . . this old railroad man
fills me in . . . Berlin-Anhalt! . . . a little courtesy after all! it
won't kill them to be a little polite . . . so we take our places
. . . that is, we pile up . . . we're not in Berlin-Anhalt yet
. . . the officer salutes us from up on the bank . . . a big
sweeping salute! . . . his band plays the *Horst Wessel* again
. . . no more *Marseillaise* . . . come to think of it, everything's gone off fine . . . except for the chow . . . not a
crumb! . . . We're getting sore . . . "How about it? How
about it?" Restif yells at his nibs up on the bank . . . "Give us
something to eat! We're starving! . . . *fressen! fressen!*" . . .
the train was pulling out . . . the character up there, the officer with the saber, pretended not to hear us, he kept on salut-
ing! the whole car starts in *"butterbrot! butterbrot!"* Stupid up
there didn't give a shit . . . but he called out to us: "You'll get
some in Berlin!" Berlin my eye! he's sending us somewhere to
croak . . . that's what we're thinking . . . the general opinion . . . sure thing: *puff! puff!* . . . the locomotive is pushing

. . . the Shah's car was home ground to us! we'd swaddled ourselves in it! . . . all the curtains went! . . . and the carpets! we were something to look at! all those layers of muslin! . . . we were freezing anyway! even lying all together piled up on the floor! Funny, we're not jolting! . . . we seem to be sliding along . . . maybe we've gone off the track? maybe we're sliding over the frozen roadbed? . . . we've been moving at least three hours . . . this must be some suburb . . . ruins, rubble . . . some more rubble . . . maybe it's Berlin? . . . yes, you wouldn't think so . . . but there's a sign . . . and an arrow! . . . *Berlin!* and another . . . *Anhalt* . . . very slowly we pull in . . . sliding along . . . here we are . . . a platform . . . two . . . ten platforms . . . really an enormous station! . . . three . . . four times the size of the Gare d'Orsay . . . it's taken a lot of punishment . . . not a window . . . not a pane of glass . . . but plenty of tracks and switches, worse than Asnières! . . . and the mob on the platform! . . . especially women and children! jampacked! . . . the second our two cars stop, we're invaded! . . . we're smothered! submerged under women and brats! . . . a flood, they walk on us, they squash us . . . they pour in through every opening . . . and porters! here come the porters! they throw in crates on top of us! . . . I know those crates! . . . canned goods . . . is it for us? . . . *"Red Cross"* it says . . . *Red Cross* for us? and enormous bags of bread . . . *Red Cross* too . . . tons! enough to eat for a hundred and ten years! . . . the damn train can start moving, we'll put it away . . . bumps or no bumps, let's get moving! . . . hell, and all these women and brats! . . . we don't want to die in the Anhalt station! here we go! a whistle! Christ, we're moving! but those crates aren't for us, no dice! . . . right there in the station the brats have broken everything open . . . ten or twelve of them to a cover! real savages! . . . and the stuff they pull out! the things they eat right then and there! . . . buckets of jam! bread and jam! and not just the brats, the women too! some of them very old . . . but greedy! . . . and some pregnant women . . . okay . . . okay . . . the whole lot of them devouring . . . and not just jam . . . whole hams! . . . yes, hams! . . . we

see it all, it's all happening on top of us, square on top of us!
. . . What do they think we are? mattresses? . . . bundles?
. . . they don't give a damn! . . . neither do we! . . . we
catch what we can . . . when they don't want any more . . .
the bottom of the crates . . . the stuff is still good! . . . whole
strings of sausages! they let us eat, they're full . . . they
give up, they collapse . . . they sleep . . . fine! . . . that
gives us two, three hours of peace . . . the train jolts ι . . . but
not too much . . . where can we be going now? . . . but then
they wake up! first they start yacking! and then singing! in
chorus! how many can there be? . . . forty? . . . fifty? . . .
in three voices and in tune! and gay! . . . the children are
from Königsberg, the pregnant women from Danzig . . .
I've still got their tunes in my head . . . *tigelig!* . . . *ding!*
. . . *digdigeling!* . . . little bells . . . must be a Christmas
song . . . they must be rehearsing? . . . anyway, they're enjoying the trip . . . a trip full of jam and millions of oranges
and chocolate! everything! . . . but then they go too far, they
get difficult . . . they start stripping everything off us . . .
they want our blankets! they've got their own from the Red
Cross! damn brats! they want our frippery too! all our carpets
and muslins! that we've been to such pains . . . everything
we've got on . . . they tear us to pieces! we've got to defend
ourselves! terrible pirates these kids! . . . girls and boys! . . .
horrible little tearing baboons, worse than we are! they go for
our rivers of muslin! they take advantage of the jerks and jolts
to skin us! . . . ten at a time! and pull! and rip! . . . the ministers are sawing wood . . . they go for them! . . . they undress them! especially after the fifth day they got to be real
thugs! five days shut up, no chance to go out! five days and five
nights . . . and still they find parts of the car to wreck! ah,
the Shah's train! . . . vestiges of easy chairs! . . . and all
fighting and yelling at once! throwing everything they can
break off out the windows! or at us . . . the *Fraülein*, their
nurse, does the best she can! you can imagine! . . . name
of Ursula . . . she's not even speaking to the kids anymore . . . "Fraülein Ursula! Fraülein Ursula!" they want her to
watch how they're smashing everything . . . really every-

thing! . . . and they're proud of it! . . . she's stopped paying attention . . . she's given them everything there was in the crates . . . condensed milk, buckets of jam . . . she's stuffed the damn brats and us too! . . . plus what they've thrown out of the windows! naturally they've all got the shits! luckily the toilet works . . . but even so . . . there's shit all over the place! . . . that's another sport, shit all over the place! . . . the Fraülein tries to stop them, the brats won't listen . . . "*Kinder! Kinder!*" she does her damnedest, but it's no use! the kids are sick of their Fraülein! What they want is for her to stop the train and right away! they want to run around in the country! right outside the window! and bring them more jam! . . . more! more! and open more crates! . . ah, beer! . . . they want to drink beer too! . . . like the ministers . . . right out of the bottle! . . . they clink bottles! . . . *glug! glug!* . . . you can imagine the effect on the kids! . . . the beer knocks them for a loop . . . they're sleeping with the ministers right on the floor of the car . . . we've passed through a tunnel . . . Marion tells me, I hadn't noticed . . . sleeping as fast as the kids? . . . and I hadn't had anything to drink . . . I never drink . . . except my can of water . . . but Marion was right, we'd passed through a tunnel . . . Marion explains . . . the Eiffel Mountains . . . hadn't seen a thing! . . . there'd been bombs on the way out, so it seems . . . hadn't heard! . . . all the better! . . . we'd changed engines, we'd shunted back and forth . . . under the tunnel . . . all that while I was asleep? . . . all the better! . . . a knockout sleep! . . . the Fraülein was lying asleep too . . . she was out cold! . . . their little nap had really rested the brats! wilder than ever! devils multiplied by ten! . . . there they go depluming the ministers! . . . really enjoying themselves! . . . uniforms, braid and muslin, especially muslin . . . they start in again! they peel them bare! they make coats for themselves! and capes . . . the girls, too . . . gowns with trains! . . . a carnival! . . . the ministers defend themselves a little, the best they can, not much, they're afraid the brats will fly out the windows! all fighting and punching and yelling . . . all over the car! . . . the pregnant women are quiet at least, stretched out on the floor . . . rea-

sonable . . . but in their condition . . . shaken up! . . .
batted together! disgraceful! . . . I feel sorry for them . . .
puff! puff! puff! . . . we're moving anyway . . . I'm doing
the locomotive for you . . . these pregnant women were practically all "due" . . . well, at least in their eighth month . . . I
hope we'll get there first! I hope . . . a fine mess for me if one
of them starts spawning! . . .

How much longer will it be? if nothing goes wrong? I figure
. . . at this rate at least another two days . . . to Ulm . . .
but if they bomb the tracks? . . . and Ulm? . . . suppose
they make us get out in Ulm? . . . I wouldn't put it past them
. . . if they tell us this train isn't for us! we should hike to
Siegmaringen . . . the men on foot! that means us! that the
train is only for the kids and pregnant women! and not for
us! . . . thirty miles from Ulm to Siegmaringen! . . . I don't
see how we could make it . . . especially as it's getting colder
. . . not as cold as up there in Prussia, but even so . . . the
cold and the snow . . . especially after these kids, these damn
savages, had torn off practically all our clothes . . . our muslin
and carpets! . . . whole layers! . . . and even our thin suits!
. . . right off our backs . . . we're not naked, but down to
our underwear! that's what the kids had done! the Fraülein
couldn't say anything . . . our thin little shoes would never
hold out . . . we wouldn't have any feet left! . . . Oh, I was
really scared of Ulm! suppose it wasn't there any more? and no
station either? . . . wiped out! . . . it wouldn't be the first
time! of course there'd always be the S.S.! . . . and the S.A.!
. . . the S-cops! . . . those things always grow up again!
they grow on the worst ruins! cops! cops! cops! meanwhile
we're moving very slowly . . . *puff! puff!* I can easily see the
bulls coming: "*Raus! Raus!*"

Ah, I wasn't mistaken, this was it! . . . we were there! . . .
we were in the station . . . except there wasn't any station
. . . we stop . . . here we are! . . . this is it, a sign . . . but
no more Ulm! . . . the sign says ULM . . . and that's all!
. . . gutted sheds all around us . . . twisted scrap . . . the
houses are nothing but grimaces . . . big chunks of wall
. . . enormously off balance, waiting for you to pass under-

neath . . . the R.A.F. had come back . . . while we were up there . . . they'd wrecked the wreckage . . . okay! are we going to move? . . . is that the stationmaster? . . . big red cap . . . he's coming . . . he looks . . . he looks at us . . . he could tell us to get out . . . no! . . . everybody buttons up . . . even the brats . . . there's no more Ulm, no more station, but that's no help . . . if he stops the train . . . makes us get out . . . no, no! . . . a good guy! . . . "All aboard! . . . Siegmaringen! . . . Constance!" we start moving . . . we're bumping again . . . not a kid has escaped! . . . sheer luck! . . . they were afraid of the stationmaster! . . . I congratulate Ursula . . . "good stationmaster!" . . . we've only got two hours more to Siegmaringen . . . she's got three to Constance . . . she'll be in Constance at midnight . . . with her women and kids . . . one good thing anyway, Ulm is completely razed, they won't come back right away! . . . I hope! . . . there's a slight chance that they'll miss us! No more Ulm! . . . there won't be any peace in the world until all the cities are razed! I mean it! it's the cities that infuriate everybody, boiling tempers! no more music halls, no more bistros, no more movies, no more jealousies! no more hysterics! . . . everybody out in the fresh air! with his ass in the ice! hibernation! a cure for mad humanity! . . .

Anyway we're not there yet . . . we and our train! . . . our car jolts, jumps, and plunges back down like we were riding on cobblestones . . . they must have put on square wheels . . . at least it shows that we're still on the rails . . . if we were on the roadbed, we'd stop bumping . . . and anyway, hell! it can do as it pleases if only we get there! . . . the Fraulein asks me to come with her, to follow her . . . one of the women is in pain . . . . I look her over . . . yes, labor pains are setting in . . . she's no softy . . . not hysterical, she's not putting anything on . . a primapara . . . I examine her . . . but without gloves! . . . no place to wash my hands . . . I've never been so miserable and humiliated, "examining" without gloves! . . . and already dilated what's more! . . . the size of a fifty-centime piece . . . a primapara . . . she's good for four, five hours . . . right away I suggest that the way things are . . . she'd better get off in Siegmaringen . . . I'm equipped for it in Siegmaringen . . . a whole dormitory for maternity cases . . . she's a refugee from Memel . . . she'd join her friends later . . . in Constance . . . after she's had her baby . . . oh, it's all right with Ursula! . . . she'll be alone when we've left . . . all alone with her little hellions! now they're asleep, but they'll wake up at daybreak, and this childbirth in addition? "Oh yes! oh yes!" I should take her with us . . . I'd send her back to Constance! fine! the Delegation put in their two cents worth . . . all the ministers . . . we all agree! they all agree! . . . Restif too! . . . you'll say: but you couldn't see in the darkness! . . . not very well, I admit, but well enough . . . thanks to the little lamps we got from Switzerland, automatic with rollers . . . they ran by palm-power . . . not festive illumination . . . no . . . but when everything goes, no more current, no more powerhouse, these little lamps come in very handy! they hold up! a little generator right there in your fist! I'm telling you, in case you haven't thought of it . . . if one of these days you find yourself under myriatons of wreckage, an expiring, bellowing troglodyte . . . a mole! . . . "France . . . all France for a match . . . with Aquitaine thrown in!" nobody'll give you a match! Don't count on it! . . . my "fist lamp" will save your life!

In this train, it's a cinch . . . stepping over things in the jolts, disentangling yourself from all the bodies, trying not to squash the women and children . . . we'd have been sunk without those little lamps . . . The train was still moving . . . oh, very hesitantly! . . . *puff! puff!* but moving . . . we'd be there about midnight . . . we didn't hear any planes . . . we'd make it . . . Restif thought so too! . . . we'd make it . . . so did Fräulein Ursula . . . she'd been pretty nice . . . all things considered . . . she could certainly have had us put out anywhere, thrown us off . . . her first reaction had been pretty cool . . . almost hostile . . . then she'd got friendly, very friendly in fact . . . maybe a little flirtation between her and Restif and Marion? . . . I hadn't seen anything! . . . if we came through it was thanks to the Red Cross with its kids and pregnant women! . . . we had something to be grateful for! . . . without the kids and the pregnant women and the crates from Sweden, America, and Cuba we'd have starved! . . . as it was, the whole Delegation was sawing wood, jolts or no jolts, stuffed and intertwined, under the pregnant women, cozy and warm! . . . they had nothing but rags left, the kids had everything! but never mind, what they'd put away since Berlin-Anhalt! . . . at least fifty crates! of everything! . . . and nothing but the best! . . . the kids had taken all their clothes! . . . really plucked them bare! . . . muslins, satins, velvets, and their coats and pants! . . . they'd dolled themselves up the same way! . . . some party! . . . the devastation! . . . a cyclone! . . . fifty kids shut up in that box! if we'd arrived in the daytime, we'd have had to wait for nightfall, we couldn't have shown ourselves like that, especially the ministers! . . . but at midnight it didn't matter, there wouldn't be anybody at the station . . . but they'd have to give me a hand getting this lady to the School of Agriculture . . . I tell Restif, he understands . . . the school isn't a stone's throw . . . especially in the snow . . . this woman, as I've told you, was no weakling, but even so . . . I suggest that we carry her . . . she prefers to walk . . . it's almost a mile from the station to the School . . . she'll give me her arm . . . Restif the other arm . . . my expectant mothers are lodged in the School of Agriculture . . .

The train is pulling into Siegmaringen . . . I say to Restif . . . this is all very well, but we've got to wake them up . . . and another thing . . . they've got to make themselves useful before they go back to the Castle . . . they're going to help us from the station to the School . . . through the snow with this woman . . . she's in labor . . . she thinks she'll be able to walk . . . she won't . . . it's pretty near a mile . . . we'll have to carry her . . . they'll help us . . . they can go back to the Castle afterwards . . . plenty of time . . .

The train is moving slower and slower . . . ah, here we are! there's a bit of a moon . . . we won't need our lamps . . . I recognize the station . . . the platform . . . now we've got to get out without the brats starting to yell! and falling out of the train! . . . and my woman of Memel . . . get her down

gently . . . the kids aren't in the mood for yelling . . . they're
sound asleep . . . let them sleep! . . . don't wake them up!
. . . it's cold on the platform and deep snow! . . . it was almost mild when we left a week ago . . . here we are all of us
on the platform . . . except the brats who haven't moved . . .
oh, but our flag! . . . we'd forgotten it . . . the flag for
Pétain! . . . hell, it's rolled up! it's someplace! Restif goes
back to the car, he finds the flag . . . he pulls it out from
under the kids . . . it's not too badly torn . . . we roll it up
again . . . the ministers out there on the platform feel that they
haven't slept long enough . . . they don't know we've arrived
. . . luckily it's not very light yet . . . they practically
haven't any pants . . . the kids have peeled them! it's no time
to stand still! . . . I ask the S.A. man on duty to let us out . . .
I tell Restif . . . I remembered . . . that we wouldn't hold
the flag up in the air, but horizontal! and everybody on the
pole! . . . that'll hold us together climbing up to the *Löwen*
. . . all the ministers on the pole! and still uphill to the School
of Agriculture . . . quite a ways! we told them . . . they're
willing . . . they yawn, they stretch, they shiver . . . but let's
go! not as cold as Hohenlychen, but even so . . . not the
same boreal gale . . . but practically naked like that they've
got something to shiver about . . . Luckily Restif leads us
. . . he knows the way . . . I know the way too . . . my
parturient absolutely refuses to be carried . . . Restif and I
give her our arms . . . she complains, but not very much . . .
the moon goes behind the clouds . . . we work our palm
lamps . . . that's all you can hear . . . the little wheels
clicking . . . they've all got one . . . luckily! . . . we look
cute . . . like a glowing caterpillar in the snow . . . all those
little lamps . . . *zzz! zzz!* . . . in a string . . .

Ah, at last . . . the house, the School! . . . and here's my
dormitory for pregnant women! . . . oh, strictly a dormitory,
but not at all gloomy, not dark like the *Fidelis* . . . no furniture, just partitions and cots . . . but even so the pregnant
women were better off than outdoors or at the station . . . of
course they'll keep going to the station, it can't be helped . . .
but when we come in, they're present . . . every last one of

them . . . I'm surprised to find them all there . . . they see me . . . they're surprised, too! . . . they'd been sleeping . . . right away questions . . .

"Who's she? . . . where's she come from?"

"She's a woman just like you! . . . she's going to have her baby . . ."

"Where? where? . . . is she a Boche?"

"She's going to have her baby here . . . she doesn't speak French, be nice to her . . ."

"She's going to have it right now?"

"Yes . . . yes . . . she'll go to Constance afterwards! . . . she's a German from Memel . . . a poor thing . . . a refugee like you! . . ."

I look them in the eye, I tell them what to do.

"Where's Memel?"

"Up there . . ."

Hold her hands . . . very gently . . . say everything nice they know in German . . . not open the windows . . . tuck her in well . . . so she won't catch cold . . . they know . . . they know all about it . . . some of them are multiparas . . . I figure at least another three hours of labor . . . plenty of time to run down to the *Löwen* for my equipment . . . especially my gloves! I leave them three little roller lamps . . . they're delighted! what luck! they didn't have any . . . they wouldn't give them back! . . . little jokes! okay . . . I leave with Restif . . . the Delegation is waiting for me . . . "Gentlemen, I thank you . . ." they can go home to the Castle, it's all right with me . . . they know the streets . . . it's easy to find the way . . . Wohlnachtstrasse . . . and there's the Danube . . . another turn to the left, the drawbridge . . . oh, but they hold right on to the flag! the Marshal's present . . . in memory of Bichelonne! . . . their mission! . . . okay, okay . . . they know . . . I don't hold them back . . . little boys with bare hairy calves. . . there'll be bronchitis and grogs! . . . they've got everything they need . . . at the Castle! . . . not like me at the *Löwen* . . . God knows . . . I take a little shortcut . . . that town had no secrets for me . . . I'm there in half a second . . . the stairs . . . and there I am . . . I can

tell you that Lili was brave, but she was worried all the same
. . . I'd left without a word . . . mighty worried! . . . didn't
know what to think . . . I explain . . . she understands . . .
I'd had to go . . . why, of course! . . . and what about her?
what had happened? . . . in the last week . . . ten days . . .
oh, people had been looking for me from all over . . . everybody wanted to know where I was . . . what had become of
me . . . at the *Fidelis* . . . at the Castle . . . at the *Milice*
. . . at the hospital . . . and a lot of other places . . . five
. . . ten addresses . . . *Sondergasse* . . . *Bülowstrasse* . . .
. . . I could imagine . . . I'm no fly-by-night, I don't run out
on things . . . if I'd gone up there so suddenly, so far and so
fast, it was because I had a serious reason . . . I expected to
see Gebhardt up there, to catch him on the spot . . .

Everybody has his little secret . . . mine was to ask him to
send us to Denmark . . . of course he could have! . . . he
had hospitals up there, several sanatoria . . . in Jutland and
Fyn . . . I knew . . . Gebhardt didn't like me very much,
but all the same, he could have . . . a slight chance . . . our
chance! . . . I tell Lili . . . hadn't even been able to see him
. . . she understands . . . it was worth trying . . . I tell her
about our expedition . . . for the laughs . . . we laugh . . .
one more hope gone! she has a lot to tell me but I can't stay
. . . I've got Memel! . . . my little Memel . . . I tell her
about Memel . . . I've got to get back to the School . . . no
use getting there after the baby! she was just about due . . .
and all shook up! . . .

I've got to admit, it seemed like enough to me . . . seven . . .
eight hundred pages . . . I'd reread the whole thing . . .
and have it typed . . . and ship it out! . . . to Brottin or
Gertrut! . . . which one? . . . who cares? . . . to the highest
bidder! . . . birds of a feather! . . . to the one that's least
scared of what people are going to say! . . . let him have it!
. . . I've turned into a materialist? . . . hmm! . . . possible!
. . . but not really! . . . my jealous thieving looters are certainly a lot worse materialists than I am! . . . and in my condition, sick, crippled, old, and broke . . . it would take a great
big bank account . . . like Claudel, Thorez, Mauriac, Picasso
. . . to put a little wind in my sails . . . an account at the
Chase National . . . Like all real artists . . . wages or piece-
work . . . I'll always be miles behind Jimmy Higgins, laborer,
not to mention the crummiest bone-setter! . . . and that's why
I'm giving my fine work to the highest bidder! . . . eight hundred . . . twelve hundred pages! . . . hell! and double hell!
. . . the grocer doesn't give a shit! . . . or the coal man! and
they're the only people who count . . . austere and smiling
and serious! . . . the price is the price! . . . metronomes of
our existence! . . . Publishers? . . . much more to be feared!
same mentality, but monsters! . . . plus every known vice!
and to think you're totally dependent on them! . . . champion
two-timers! their rackets are organized with such precision
. . . so expertly tangled it would put you in the bughouse
. . . three straitjackets . . . to try and figure it out . . .
how they go about it . . . even a faint idea . . . from the
distance . . . You ingrate! you who owe them everything! . . .
and they never owe you anything! . . . their cars get bigger
and bigger . . . maybe they'll let you hang on behind in your

rags, with your tongue hanging out on the street! . . . out of
pure kindness of heart maybe they'll deign to throw you a
crust! . . . you're dying in the poorhouse? . . . splendid!
. . . that's the least of your duties! . . . you won't even get a
forget-me-not! . . . the orchids are for Miss Gash! . . . plati-
tudes, you'll say . . . here's another platitude! . . . I can see
the both of them hanging! and swinging in the breezes! swinging high and swinging low! Brottin and Morny! what a jig!
. . . frozen smiles and monocles! I listen to progressive, committed people, Communists, Anarchists, Cryptos, fellow travelers, Rotarians . . . they're all nitwits! . . . "anti-boss" is all
you need! . . . you've got him right there in front of you! you
know what you're talking about . . . ! Your Commie dialectifies, splutters, and charges windmills! . . . But Morny and
Brottin . . . exist! they exist! . . .

I'm not saying anything about my patients . . . I've stopped
talking about them . . . I stopped counting on them long ago
. . . they cost me money, that's all . . . if I weren't a doctor,
I'd stop heating . . . I'd spend the whole winter in bed . . . I
can't count on anybody or anything any more . . . lying in
bed, I'd think about my stupidity . . . always been a victim
. . . crusading for beans! . . . shit! . . . while other people
cleaned me out of everything . . . including my manuscripts
. . . and yes, thank you, they're doing fine! all my furniture to
the Flea Market! . . . every kind of injustice, I can say . . . I
haven't missed one! . . . prison, sickness, wounds, scurvy!
. . . plus the *Médaille Militaire!* . . . what about the resistants? you'll say . . . one of them jumped out of the window*
. . . Between 1914 and 1918 millions of people jumped out
of the window! did you make much? no! and Jeanne d'Arc? in
my bed I could think about the talents I had . . . that I
squandered! for swine! . . . the strings to my bow! . . . I
couldn't win! . . . if you're a real artist, it makes too many
people jealous! . . . if they murder you, it's only normal! . . .
I'm thinking of my apothecary jar on the rue Girardon . . .
the purifiers went up, so drunk with patriotic fervor they
couldn't help carting everything off to the Auction Rooms! . . .
my friends and relatives, uncles, cousins, nieces . . . pre-

ferred the Flea Market! . . . they would have impaled me too, that would have been real pleasure! practically everybody has forgotten me . . . not they! not they! . . . the people who've robbed you never forget you! . . . or the ones who copy from you either! . . . hell! . . . they owe you their life! . . . Do you expect Tartre to come clean? "I, plagiarist and paid stoolie, I confess! I am his asshole! . . ." Don't count on it! . . .

More of my rancor! . . . you'll forgive me for being a little soft in the head . . . but not if it gets so bad that I bore you . . . me and my three dots . . . a little discretion! . . . my supposedly original style! . . . all the real writers will tell you what to think of it! . . . and what Brottin thinks of it! . . . and Gertrut! but what does the grocer think of it? . . . that's what counts! . . . that gives me food for meditation! Hamlet of the carrots . . . I meditate up here in my garden . . . a splendid view . . . a really admirable situation if you've got the wherewithal . . . but if you're the nervous jittery type, anxious about everything! . . . everything and all the time! . . . about carrots . . . and taxes . . . and everything else . . . to hell with the view! . . . dreaming isn't for you! . . . shit on the panorama! . . . delinquent the pauper who dreams! . . .

All the same, Paris catches the eye . . . the whole of Paris down there . . . the loops of the Seine . . . Sacré-Coeur far in the distance . . . up close Billancourt . . . Suresnes with its hill . . . and Puteaux between the two . . . Puteaux, memories . . . the Sentier des Bergères . . . and Mont-Valérien, more memories . . . the Foch Hospital . . . come to think of it, why don't I put in an application? . . . I'd be all right at Mont-Valérien . . . I can see myself as governor . . . the governor of Mont-Valérien really has peace and quiet to work in! I can see his residence clearly with my spyglass, a really magnificent Greco-Romantic mansion . . . just what I need . . . that severe . . . military sumptuousness . . . with Doric columns . . . he gets the full benefit of the rising sun . . . and he's higher than we are, a good hundred and fifty feet . . . oh, don't feel sorry for the Governor of Mont-Valérien! . . . maybe we could get together . . . make an "exchange"? . . . wherever I go, I hear people talking about "exchanges" . . . "will exchange this for that . . ." maybe my qualifications will be contested . . . maybe they'll say I haven't got Saint Pierre and Miquelon . . . that Laval is dead . . . and Bichelonne left no word, nothing in writing! . . . that there's no record at the Ministry of Colonies, and that my say-so isn't enough! . . . but look how sick and anemic I am, I could certainly use some sun . . . I really need it! . . . seventy-five percent disability! . . . I have rights! . . . Clemenceau said so . . . and wouldn't that be friendly Justice! and the guy that's governor up there is certainly younger than I am . . . up there in his Greek temple, I'd finally have some peace and quiet . . . I could work at my ease, no more highway, no more cars, no more factories . . . the woods around the house . . . a little prison under my heel, for pests . . . the one Henry* committed suicide in . . . they're still arguing whether he really committed suicide . . . or if they didn't help him a little . . . take it from me . . . Mont-Valérien hasn't given up all its secrets! even with binoculars you can tell: all very enigmatic! . . . oh, you wouldn't catch me idle at Mont-Valérien . . . I'd make those cells talk! . . . and here, alas! alas! they don't leave me time to meditate! . . . harassed I am! . . . I wonder which would suit me better . . . Governor of Mont-Valérien? or Governor of Saint-Pierre? meditations . . . fat chance . . . especially these last few days . . . I've been really worried for the last few days . . . oh, nothing very serious . . . but . . . well, presentiments . . . actually a little more than presentiments . . . the postman told me . . . and a kid too . . . that Madame Niçois had come back . . . yes . . . that she's home . . . I didn't really believe it . . . that she's home from the hospital . . . back on the former Place Faidherbe . . . feeling fine . . . completely cured! . . . fine, so much the better! . . . I couldn't quite believe it, but if that's what they're saying . . . of course she might have let me know . . . maybe she doesn't want to see me any more? maybe she's taken another doctor? . . . zounds, she'd be perfectly right! . . . perfectly right! . . . I won't go so far as to say "good riddance" . . . but it would certainly suit me fine! . . . at a certain age, especially after certain hardships, you only want one thing: to be left alone! . . . or better still, you'd like people to think you're dead! in a recent poll on "what the young people think," they all thought I was dead . . . died in Greenland! not bad! . . . anyway, talking about Madame Niçois, I couldn't see myself traipsing down to the former Place Faidherbe, the riverfront, and climbing back home! twice a day!

Instead of hopping myself up imagining I'm Governor of Mont-Valérien . . . or of Saint-Pierre-Langlade over there . . . it would make a little more sense if I really asked the postman if Madame Niçois had really come home . . . he could find out in a second, he'd only have to go up and knock . . . she'd be there . . . or she wouldn't . . . anyway I was going to be alone again . . . Lili had to go to Paris . . . she never left me alone very long . . . of course she had to go now and then . . . errands . . . this and that for her pupils . . . especially her pupils . . . unbelievable the amount of slippers those pupils can wear out! . . . so Lili goes! . . . I stay home with the dogs . . . I can't claim to be really alone . . . the dogs keep me posted . . . they tell me the mailman's coming when he's still three miles away! or Lili's at the station . . . they know when she gets off the train . . . they never go wrong! I've always tried to find out how they knew . . . they know, that's all there is to it! . . . we knock our heads against the wall, we're mathematical idiots . . . Einstein wouldn't know if Lili was coming . . . or Newton either . . . or Pascal . . . all deaf, blind, and knuckleheaded . . . Flute knows too! my cat Flute . . . he'll go to meet Lili, he'll go down to the road . . . just like that, he knows . . . as soon as he starts moving, I'll listen . . . for the moment, nothing! . . . first his ears! . . . I'll know in plenty of time . . . a mile from the station at least! . . . it's all a matter of waves . . . dogs have waves, too . . . but not so subtle as Flute's . . . the birds' waves are even subtler than Flute's . . . ten miles away they register . . . they know! the birds are the kings of the waves! . . . especially titmice! . . . when I see them take flight . . . when Flute starts off . . . Lili will be practically in Bellevue . . . I'll tie up the dogs . . . because it's terrible if you let them gang up . . . your ears! . . . you can hear them in Grenelle! . . . but it's not time yet . . . I can still meditate awhile . . . that's how you know you're old, you never really sleep, but you're never really awake, you're always dozing . . . even when you're on tenterhooks, you doze . . . that's how it was, waiting for Lili . . . I must have been a little better than dozing, I didn't hear the dogs . . . and I didn't see Flute the cat take off . . . or the birds fly away . . . but now I hear something plainly! . . . coming out of my dream . . . a voice! a real voice! . . . it's Lili! . . . I listen hard! . . . yes, it's Lili! . . . oh, but she's not alone . . . two other voices! . . . the cats have come back! . . . there they are! . . . *purr! purr!* not exactly disinterested, to be sure . . . it's their day for liver! . . . they don't stir an inch from Lili! . . . welcome home! . . . *miow! miow!* but I heard three women's voices! I wasn't dreaming . . . my eyes aren't so good, but I'm not blind . . . I see Lili at the end of the garden, I recognize her perfectly . . . ah, and another lady! . . . and Madame Niçois! . . . yes, it's Madame Niçois! . . . they come up very slowly! . . . ah, here they are!

"See, Madame Niçois is much better . . . she came home two days ago . . . she wants to speak to you!"

"Oh, splendid! splendid! how are you, Madame Niçois?"

She comes closer . . . I can't see that she's so much better . . . it seems to me that she's even thinner . . . she's holding the other lady's arm . . . they've climbed all this way . . . I tell them to sit down on the other bench . . . Madame Niçois doesn't see any better than a month ago . . . she looks up in the air, over my head . . . not a thing! I can shout . . . she doesn't hear me . . . I'm curious to know what they did to her in Versailles? . . . the other one answers, the other lady, not the least bit embarrassed! ah, I can say without exaggeration that she was a talker! I don't know her, never seen her . . . where's she out of? . . . she tells me . . .

"We met in Versailles . . . in the cancer ward . . . yes, Doctor!"

In case I doubt her word, she tells me again . . . she repeats . . . she and Madame Niçois had got to be very good friends . . .

"I was there for a breast, see, Doctor?"

"Yes, yes, Madame . . ."

"They took it off . . . I don't think there was any point . . . no point at all . . . they just took it into their heads . . ."

Ah, how funny they were in Versailles! stupid! it made her laugh! Hee! hee! in stitches!

"If you could only have seen them, Doctor! Hee! Hee!"

She's having a convulsion! so idiotic those people at the hospital! . . . really hilarious . . . they'd thought she had cancer! hee! hee! hee!

"Can you imagine, Doctor? Can you imagine?"

Those people at the hospital! Really too funny! too funny! Hee! Hee!

"Oh, you're perfectly right, Madame! perfectly right!"

With Madame Niçois they'd seen what was what! oh, not a doubt! . . . she had cancer all right! . . . the galloping kind in fact . . . she hadn't long to live, poor woman!

"You think so too, don't you, Doctor?"

"Oh yes, certainly, Madame . . ."

She's hee-hee-heeing again . . . all of a sudden I strike her as just too funny . . . same as the other doctors . . . me too!

"I'm going to call you Dr. Stringbean! . . . it seems you haven't any patients left! hee! hee! hee! not a single patient! . . . Madame Niçois has told me! . . . not a one . . . hee! . . . hee! . . . all about it! . . ."

At the same time she smacks her thighs! . . . real clouts! *crack! smack!* and me too . . . and Madame Niçois! *crack! smack!* with all her might! really the life of the party!

I risk a question: "How old are you, Madame?"

"Same as her . . . seventy-two next month! but look at her, Doctor! the state she's in! . . . you've noticed, haven't you, Dr. Stringbean! hee! hee! hee! . . . and look at me! . . . feel my muscle! I've never felt so peppy! they thought I was the same as her! they wanted to take off both breasts! . . . see here, Dr. Stringbean! those people have cancer on the brain! all they can see is cancer! maniacs! luckily I stuck up for myself! I was right, wasn't I? Wasn't I right, Dr. Stringbean?"

Ah, how funny they were in that hospital! she gives me some more smacks! *biff! bang!* . . . and a few to Madame Niçois

. . . poor old thing with her cancer! she should have a little fun too! *bang!*

"Call me Madame Armandine! You will, Doctor?"

"Where do you live, Madame Armandine?"

"With her naturally! At her house! . . . We live together! . . . she's got a big place! You've been there . . ."

There's a nice little arrangement that promises plenty of good times . . . they're really close friends . . .

"The surgeon insisted: 'Take somebody with you . . . don't stay alone . . .' I live in Le Vésinet, you see . . . Le Vésinet is far . . . From Sèvres . . . with the buses . . . I can go to Paris whenever I feel like it! she doesn't need me the whole time . . ."

She's got her convulsions back . . . her hee-hee-hee's and wiggles! . . . and another clout for Madame Niçois!

I can see she's a little nervous . . . in fact she's definitely cracked . . . but she's got a kind of youthful vigor for seventy-two! cancer and all . . . and even a certain coquetry . . . that plaid skirt, for instance . . . pleated! and the blue on her eyebrows and eyelashes! . . . and her raincoat, more blue! . . . and the color of her eyes . . . china-blue . . . and makeup on her cheeks . . . pastel pink! . . . you get the picture? . . . and smiling like a doll . . . pert and comely . . . she only stops smiling long enough for her little spells of hee-hee! . . . sadness isn't in her line! Madame Niçois has got herself some companion, she won't be bored! though it doesn't seem to make her talk! she doesn't say a word! . . . I ask her how she's feeling . . . better? . . . no answer . . . of course there's the fatigue, the path, the hill . . . I look at her more closely . . . her face . . . one side looks very set . . . the right half . . . one corner of her mouth is down and won't come up . . . like Thorez! . . . oh, but Armandine answers for her . . . she knows all about it . . . she was in the next bed . . . they hadn't just treated Madame Niçois for her cancer . . . hee hee! hee! . . . she was there! she knows . . . hee! hee! hee! she had a stroke besides! . . . no kidding! . . . her whole side paralyzed! . . . Yes! hee! hee! . . . that's why she doesn't talk . . . a stroke! . . . Armandine talks

enough for two! . . . I don't think Madame Niçois is listening
to her . . .

"You see, she makes in her pants! . . . hee! hee! hee!"

She reassures me . . . she'll keep her clean!

"After all, we're living together! . . . cleanliness first! . . .
I'm used to old people! . . . You can set your mind at rest,
Doctor! . . ."

"Fine! . . . fine! . . . glad to hear it! but what about her
dressings?"

"You'll come and do them every day! . . . the surgeon insisted! and the applications! He said you'd know what to do!"

She saw I was a little hesitant . . .

"We made it up here . . . you can certainly come down to
see us, can't you, Doctor?"

"Certainly, Madame Armandine!"

"You won't have to do anything for me! . . . not a thing!
they couldn't get over it in Versailles the way I mended!
quicker than the young chickens! only a week! in one week, I
was all healed up! they couldn't get over it! hee! hee! look, you
can see for yourself! . . . and Madame can look too! your
wife! . . . they say she's a dancer! look!"

She gets up off the bench, she goes out into the middle of the
lawn . . . she lifts up her skirts . . . hoopla! . . . and her
petticoats! . . . and she bends back! she does a complete
backbend! as supple as can be! . . . and up goes one leg,
straight as a die! . . . like the Eiffel Tower! . . . actually you
can see the Eiffel Tower from our lawn . . . oh, way in the
distance . . . and almost always in the mist . . .

"Bravo! . . . bravo!"

We applaud . . . she stayed like that for a while . . . with
her leg in the air . . . and then she stands up . . . as supple as
can be! . . . and fixes herself . . . her eyelashes, her eyes,
beauty! . . . a pencil stroke on her eyelashes . . . she has
everything she needs in her schoolbag . . . a mirror, her powder, her rouge . . . and probably a lot of other little things
. . . a very big schoolbag! . . . Claudine at School! . . . I
wonder what Madame Armandine did in the world . . . I
won't ask her . . . she'll certainly tell me . . .

"I'll be down to see you tomorrow, Madame Armandine . . . tomorrow afternoon . . . after my consultation . . ."

"No, no! this evening! she needs it! . . . this evening, Doctor . . . hee! hee! hee! . . . Stringbean!"

She seems a little demanding to me . . .

"All right! all right! . . . I'll be there . . ."

She wasn't the kind of woman you could contradict . . .

GLOSSARY

2. VRENCHMEN. (*Vrounzais* in original). This coinage expresses Céline's contempt for real or alleged "furriners" who claim to be French although they allegedly can't speak the language properly.

2. PACHON. One of the standard French apparatuses for measuring blood pressure. Named after its inventor, Michel-Victor Pachon.

4. GRÉVIN. Waxworks museum on the Boulevard Montmarte in Paris, founded by Alfred Grévin (1827–1892).

5. ARTICLE 75. Article 75 of the French penal code, Book III, Title I, Chapter I, Section I, states that the crime of treason is punishable by death and lists the actions coming under this head: bearing arms against France, "intelligence in time of war with a foreign power or its agents, with a view to favoring the undertakings of that power against France," etc.

6. DREYFUS'S ROCK-PILE. *Le bagne Renault*, the Renault penal colony. The Renault factories, of which Pierre Dreyfus (born in 1907) has been the director since 1955. Before

the second world war, *"le bagne Renault"* was the standard term used for these factories in Communist propaganda.

6. GASTON'S ROCK-PILE. By extension, the Gallimard publishing house, directed by Gaston Gallimard. Founded in 1911
as the Éditions de la Nouvelle Revue Française, it is one
of the leading French publishing houses and has published much of the best modern French literature, including the later works of Céline. Gaston Gallimard may well
figure in the present work under a pseudonym.

8. PÉTIOT. Dr. Pétiot (1893–1946). Between 1942 and 1944
he murdered 27 persons, for the most part Jews, whom he
lured to his premises by promising to smuggle them out
of the occupied zone of France. He was tried, convicted
and executed in 1946.

8. ABBÉ PIERRE. Pseudonym of Henri Groues, born in 1912.
Entered the Church and took the name of Abbé Pierre in
1942. Founded the Association d'Emmaüs (1951), devoted
largely to building emergency housing for the homeless.

8. JUANOVICI. Joseph Joinovici or Joanovici, known as Monsieur Joseph. Rumanian Jew, came to France from Bessa-
rabia in 1925. Founded his own scrap-metal firm. In 1939
Joinovici Frères was a thriving concern. After the French
defeat, transferred nominal ownership of his business but
remained effectively in charge and supplied metal to
WIFO, a Berlin firm. Obtained forged records proving his
Aryan origin. Operated on black market, purchasing metal
for the Germans. Later confessed to having made 25 million francs under the Occupation. Member of the Bonny-
Laffont police group, working for the Germans. At the
same time worked for the Resistance, helped Jews, hid
American parachutists, and worked for Honneur et Police,
the Resistance group in the French police.

Well-known Resistants later testified in his favor. Responsible for the arrest of Bonny and Laffont after the
Liberation. He, too, was arrested but soon released. The
authorities decided again to arrest him. Fled to the American zone of Germany but gave himself up in 1947.
Tried in 1949, condemned to five years in prison, a fine of

600,000 F. and confiscation of his holdings to the amount of 50 million francs. Freed in 1951, placed under house arrest at Mende, whence he escaped to Israel.

After the French government opened proceedings against him for tax fraud in 1957, Israel refused him the status of immigrant and he was expelled in December, 1958. Imprisoned in Marseille. Tried, acquitted of tax fraud but held on two other charges. In 1961, condemned to two prison terms of one year each for issuing bad checks. Released in 1962, he died in Clichy in 1965 at the age of 63.

8. LATZAREF. Pierre Lazareff, French journalist born in 1907. Directed *Paris-Soir* from 1937 to 1940. During the war directed the French section of the War Information Office, first in New York, then in London. Now director of *France-Soir* and other publications.

9. BOILEAU, RACINE. One wonders what Boileau and Racine are doing here. The idea is that they were in some measure historians of Louis XIV, their feed bag.

10. GNÔME ET RHÔNE. This is an allusion to Paul Claudel (1868–1955), ambassador, poet and dramatist. He was a member of the board of the firm of Gnôme et Rhône, specialists in the manufacture of armaments.

10. DENOËL. Publisher in 1932 of Céline's first important work, *Journey to the End of the Night*. Assassinated in 1945. His body was found during the night of December 3, 1945, at the corner of the Boulevard des Invalides and the rue de Grenelle. He was killed while trying to repair his stalled car.

11. PURGES. The measures taken to cleanse the French administration of persons accused of collaborating with the German Occupation. Many professional groups also purged themselves, not always very equitably.

12. VAILLANT. Roger Vailland (1907–1965), French writer, author of *Drôle de Jeu* (1945), *la Loi* (1957), etc. Member of the Communist party, active in the Resistance.

14. "CROSSES." Possibly an allusion to traffic in Swiss gold coins.

15. RENAULT IN FRESNES. Louis Renault (1877–1944), the fa-

mous builder of automobiles and tanks, collaborated with the Germans. Imprisoned after the Liberation, he is believed to have died as a result of bad treatment incurred in Fresnes prison.

17. "FAMILY, WORK, COUNTRY." *"Travail, Famille, Patrie."* The Vichy regime substituted these words for the motto of the French Republic: "Liberty, Equality, Fraternity."

17. KRONPRINZESSSGADE. Céline's often capricious spelling of non-French words, especially names, has been followed throughout. It no doubt expresses contempt for all things foreign, but it also conveys the impression made by foreign languages on those who do not understand them.

19. ALTMAN. Georges Altman, left-wing journalist who, in 1932, expressed his enthusiasm for *Journey to the End of the Night,* but later condemned Céline's anti-Semitic writings.

19. TRIOLETTE. Elsa Triolet, writer, born in Moscow in 1896, wife of Louis Aragon and sister-in-law of Maiakovsky.

19. LARENGON. Louis Aragon, French writer born in 1897. Collaborated with André Breton in founding the Surrealist movement, which he abandoned when he joined the Communist party.

19. BOUGRAT. Dr. Pierre Bougrat (1890–1961). Accused in 1925 of assassinating a bill collector, whose body was found in a closet in Bougrat's house. Condemned to forced labor for life. Six months after his arrival in Guiana, he escaped to Venezuela, where he practiced medicine until his death in 1961.

20. LANDRU. Famous criminal. Arrested in 1919, accused of murdering ten women whom he had promised to marry and who disappeared after he had invited them to his villa in the environs of Paris. Guillotined in 1922.

33. LAVARÈDE AND HIS THREE SOUS. *Les Cinq Sous de Lavarède,* an entertaining adventure novel for children by Paul d'Ivoi, published in 1894.

42. FELLAGHAS. "Fellaghas," or road cutters, was the name given to the Algerian guerillas during the Algerian war.

44. L.V.F. Légion des Volontaires Français contre le Bolché-

visme. Founded in 1941 by Brinon and Doriot. Its purpose was to recruit French volunteers to fight for the Germans in Russia. It had little success.

45. RUE DE CHÂTEAUDUN. The French Communist party has its headquarters on the rue de Châteaudun in Paris.

47. CARBUCCIA. Horace de Carbuccia, French publisher born in 1891. Founder of the weekly *Gringoire* (1928–1944) of fascist tendency.

48. CHARTRON. Quarter of Bordeaux inhabited by high society (wine growers, wine merchants, shipbuilders, importers). Epithet applied to the Bordeaux bourgeoisie.

51. LOUISE MICHEL (1830–1905). French revolutionary. Active in the Commune (1871). Known as the "Red Virgin."

60. ARLETTE, SIMON. Accompanied by the screen actors Arletty and Michel Simon, Céline goes to the Radio Building to record selections from his works. Arletty reads two passages from *Death on the Installment Plan*, and Michel Simon reads the beginning of *Journey to the End of the Night*. In addition, Céline sings two of his own songs. (Pacific No. LDPS 199, 1957, issued in 1956 as Urania No. URLP 0003.)

61. JACOB. Madeleine Jacob, French journalist of the extreme left, specialized in court proceedings.

62. BOUSSAC. Marcel Boussac, French industrialist born in 1889. Director general of important textile and chemical firms. Breeder of race horses.

63. BÉCART. Marcel Bucard, born in 1895, referred to later by his right name. Active in several fascist movements. Active collaborationist during the Occupation. Spent some time in Sigmaringen. Condemned to death and executed in 1946.

63. FAGON. Guy-Crescent Fagon (1638–1718), chief physician to Louis XIV.

89. LE VIGAN. Robert Coquillaud, screen name Robert Le Vigan. Outstanding motion-picture actor (*Pépé-le-Moko, Quai des Brumes and Goupi-Mains rouges*). A friend of Céline, he collaborated under the Occupation. Spent several years in prison after the Liberation, went to Spain in

1950 and to the Argentine in 1951, where he played in several mediocre films and died.

110. BICHELONNE. Jean Bichelonne. First in his class at École Polytechnique. Minister for Industry and Commerce in several Vichy cabinets. Followed Pétain to Sigmaringen and died in Germany under mysterious circumstances in a hospital where he had been obliged by the SS to undergo an operation.

110. BRINON. Fernand de Brinon. Journalist. In 1933, published the first interview with Hitler to appear in France. President of the Comité France-Allemagne. In December 1940, Laval appointed him delegate general of the French government in the occupied territories, with the title of "Ambassadeur de France." Set up a "Government Commission for the Interests of French Subjects in Germany," which was disavowed by Pétain and Laval. Was condemned to death and executed.

110. DARNAN. Joseph Darnand, born in 1897. Started out as a cabinetmaker. After the first world war, leader of the Camelots du Roi, then joined the Croix-de-Feu and later Doriot's P.P.F. (Parti Populaire Français). Active in Deloncle's C.S.A.R. (the Cagoule). During the Occupation was a leader in the L.V.F. and in 1942 founded the Milice, a French police organization in the service of the Germans. In 1944, Secretary of State for the Interior in the Vichy government. A member of Brinon's "Government Commission" in Sigmaringen. Condemned to death and executed in 1945.

111. NORDLING. Raoul Nordling (1882–1962). Swedish diplomat, Swedish consul general in Paris from 1926 to 1959. His intervention with General von Choltitz in August 1944 is believed to have prevented the destruction of Paris.

113. SOUFFLOT. Germain Soufflot, French architect (1713–1780). Builder of the Panthéon in Paris, originally as a church dedicated to Saint Genevieve, but transformed by the Revolution into a monument to the great men of France. Many of the most illustrious men in France are buried there.

120. CARBOUGNIAT. A satirical deformation of the name Carbuccia, see above. In popular French, the word *"bougnat"* is applied to the coal dealers, for the most part natives of Auvergne, known for their greed.

122. LACRETELLE. Jacques de Lacretelle, born in 1888. French novelist, reputed for his psychological penetration. Elected to the Académie Française (1936).

128. JAVERT. A character in Victor Hugo's *Les Miserables.* The type of stern, incorruptible detective who tracks down his quarry, undeterred by any consideration of sentiment.

130. P.P.F. Parti Populaire Français. Founded by Jacques Doriot in 1936. One of the two main fascist parties during the Occupation.

131. ABEL BONNARD. French writer born in 1883. Elected to the Academy in 1932 and expelled in 1944. In 1940, minister of National Education in the Vichy government. Sentenced in 1960 to ten years of banishment.

131. SABIANI. Member of the leading committee of the P.P.F.

132. MILICE. Founded by Darnand in January 1942. A French police force collaborating with the Germans, it was responsible for any number of crimes. When it went to Germany with the retreating German army, it provided itself with a "treasury" by requisitioning bank funds. Disavowed by Pétain in August 1944.

133. DULLIN. Charles Dullin (1885–1949), actor and director, founder of the Théâtre de l'Atelier and of a well-known dramatic school which still bears his name.

134. TROPMAN. Famous nineteenth-century criminal.

134. DEIBLER. Official executioner between the two wars.

136. GABOLD. Minister of Justice in the Vichy government.

144. K-BREAD. *Kriegsbrot* (Wartime Bread).

149. LUCIEN DESCAVES (1861–1949). Novelist of the naturalist school. Member of the Académie Goncourt (1900).

150. CHARLOT [de Gaulle] SHOOTING BRASILLACH. Robert Brasillach (1909–1945). Journalist, disciple of Charles Maurras, contributor to *l'Action Française.* Became editor-in-chief of *Je suis partout* in 1938. Published novels. Taken prisoner in 1940. Freed in 1941 and resumed his editorship of

Je suis partout. Arrested in 1944. Condemned to death and shot on February 6, 1945. François Mauriac is said to have interceded with de Gaulle to obtain his pardon.

152. FIFIS. F.F.I., Forces Françaises de l'Intérieur. Name given in 1944 by the National Committee of Liberation to all the underground movements struggling against the German Occupation.

153. MARION. Paul Marion. Journalist, leading member of the P.P.F. since its founding in 1936. Resigned from the P.P.F. after Munich. Became Secretary of Information in the Vichy government in 1942. After the Liberation, condemned to ten years at forced labor.

154. CORPECHOT. Imaginary character, or conceivably Admiral Bléhaut.

155. ADER. Clement Ader (1841–1925). French engineer. "Father of aviation." In 1890 built *l'Éole,* a heavier-than-air craft aboard which he rose from the ground. In 1892, he flew two hundred meters aboard *l'Éole II.*

157. DELONCLE. Eugène Deloncle (1890–1943). Engineer. Joined *l'Action Française* in 1934, but soon broke with it to found the C.S.A.R. (Comité de l'Action Révolutionnaire), better known as the Cagoule. Convicted of complicity in a plot in 1937 and sentenced to a prison term. Freed at the beginning of the war, he founded, at the end of 1940, the M.S.R. (Mouvement Social Révolutionnaire). Merged the M.S.R. with Déat's R.N.P. (Rassemblement National Populaire), but the union was short-lived. After the Allied landing in Algeria, arrested by the Sicherheitsdienst because of his secret relations with Darlan. Murdered by the Gestapo.

157. NAVACHINE. Russian economist living in Paris. Mysteriously murdered in 1937. See below, note on Navachine and the Roselli Brothers.

157. BOUT DE L'AN. One of the chiefs of Darnand's Milice.

157. HEROLD PAQUI. Jean Hérold, alias Jean Hérold-Paquis (1912–1945). Journalist. Took part in the Spanish Civil War on the side of Franco. Appointed by Vichy government Delegate for Propaganda in the Hautes-Alpes department (1940). Beginning in 1942, daily news broad-

casts over Radio Paris. Joined the P.P.F. Fled to Baden-Baden and Landau. Directed the Radio-Patrie radio station. Escaped to Switzerland in 1945. Handed over to the French authorities, sentenced to death and executed.

157. DORIOT. Jacques Doriot (1895–1945). Metal worker. Joined Socialist party in 1918. Broke away from it with the Communist fraction at the congress of Tours. Delegate to the Third Congress of the Communist International. Expelled from party in 1934 and founded the P.P.F. (Parti Populaire Français), which moved rapidly toward fascism. Mobilized in 1939. After the defeat, resumed his activity in the P.P.F. Helped to found the L.V.F. and volunteered to fight on the Russian front. Sigmaringen in 1945. Founded, with Hitler's support, the Committee for French Liberation. Was killed on his way to a meeting with Déat, when his car was machine-gunned by an American plane.

157. DÉAT. Marcel Déat (1894–1955). Professor of philosophy, Socialist (1932), then Neo-Socialist deputy. Aviation Minister in 1936. Under the Occupation, founded the R.N.P., Rassemblement National Populaire. In Vichy government, Secretary of State for Labor and Foreign Affairs (1944). Condemned to death in absentia, he evaded arrest and died in Italy in 1955.

158. NOGUARÈS. Louis Noguères, president of the High Court of Justice, before which all the big trials of collaborationists were held after the Liberation.

159. BRIDOU. General Bridoux, Minister of war in the Vichy government.

167. GAZIER. Albert Gazier, born 1908. Trade unionist, Socialist deputy from the department of the Seine under the Fourth Republic, several times minister. Minister of Information under Pflimlin (1958), the last cabinet of the Fourth Republic. Now retired from political life.

168. SARTINE. Antoine de Sartine, comte d'Alby (1729–1801). Lieutenant general of police under Louis XV. He took measures to improve the street-cleaning and illumination of Paris.

171. COMPTOIRS. The *comptoirs* (trading posts) of India. The

five cities of India retained by France after the Treaty of Paris (1763): Pondichéry, Yanaon, Mahé, Karikal and Chandernagor. Were ceded to India by the Treaty of Delhi (1956).

175. PARAZ. Albert Paraz, writer born in 1899. Author of *Bitru, Le Roi tout nu, Le Gala des vaches,* etc.

208. RIBOT. Théodule Ribot (1839–1916). French psychologist of the associationist school.

211. GREAT DESTROYER OF CARTHAGE. (*Grand Pourfendeur de Carthage*) Jean Hérold-Paquis. He concluded his daily newcasts with the words: "Like Carthage, England will be destroyed."

217. PETITPIERRE. Perhaps Max Petitpierre, Swiss statesman, president of the Swiss Confederation in 1950, 1955 and 1960.

233. ROCHAS. Rochat. Intimate friend of Laval and Secretary of Foreign Affairs in the Vichy government.

236. LUCHAIRE and CORINNE LUCHAIRE. Jean Luchaire, French journalist (1901–1946). In 1927 he founded the weekly *Notre Temps,* which he directed until 1939, and in 1940 the evening daily *Les Nouveaux Temps.* In 1944 he called on the Germans to exterminate the Resistance. Commissioner of Information in Brinon's "Government Commission" in Sigmaringen. Fled to Italy in 1945 and was arrested. Condemned to death and executed. His daughter Corinne was a film actress. Sentenced to 10 years of "national degradation." Died shortly after of tuberculosis.

249. LÉON DAUDET. French writer (1867–1942), son of Alphonse Daudet. Notorious anti-Semite. Became a disciple of Maurras and founded with him in 1907 the royalist daily *l'Action Française.* Deputy from Paris from 1919 to 1924.

258. DARQUIER DE PELLEPOIX. Born 1898. Real name Darquier. De Pellepoix added after events of February 1934. Attacked Brinon for his Jewish wife. In 1942, appointed Commissioner General for Jewish Affairs in the Vichy government. A fanatical anti-Semite, he strictly observed the German directives with regard to the Jews, and derived

personal profit from the administration of confiscated Jewish property.

262. ABETZ. Otto Abetz (1903–1958). Starting out as a teacher of drawing, Abetz attended, beginning about 1930, meetings between young Frenchmen and Germans. Here he met Jean Luchaire. German Ambassador to Paris (1940). Hitler put him in charge of "Franco-German collaboration."

264. SOUBISE WITHOUT LANTERNS. Charles de Rohan, Prince de Soubise (1715–1787). Marshal of France. Defeated at Rossbach in 1757 by Frederick the Great. After this defeat, a caricature showed him wandering around in the night with a lantern, looking for his soldiers.

267. ALPHONSE. Alphonse de Chateaubriant (1877–1951). French writer. Goncourt Prize in 1911 for *Monsieur de Lourdines*. Visited Germany in 1935 and became enthusiastic over National Socialism. Member of the central committee of the L.V.F. In 1945, took refuge in the Austrian Tyrol, where he died.

272. LESDAIN. Jacques de Lesdain, extreme right-wing journalist, outspoken advocate of "collaboration." Director of *l'Illustration* during the Occupation.

272. BERNARD FAYE. Historian. Born in 1895. During the war, professor at the Collège de France. Appointed administrator of the Bibliothèque Nationale under the Occupation. Director of the anti-Masonic service of the Vichy government. In 1946, condemned to forced labor for life. Escaped to Switzerland in 1951. Given an instructorship at the Institut de lange française in Fribourg, but student protests forced him to resign.

276. MORNET. French magistrate. Prosecuting attorney of the High Court of Justice, acting at all the great anti-collaborationist trials after the Liberation (Pétain, Laval, etc).

278. JE SUIS PARTOUT. Extreme-right weekly published in Paris from 1933 to 1939 and from 1941 to 1944.

278. FONTENOY. Jean Fontenoy. Journalist. Former Communist. Member of P.P.F. Joined L.V.F., killed in street fighting in Berlin in 1945.

280. PURE AND SURE. Speaking at a Socialist party congress, Guy Mollet declared that the party must become "*pur et dur*" (pure and hard).

281. JARDIN. Jean Jardin. Laval's office manager. Sheltered endangered Resistance members in his home.

281. GUÉRARD. Jacques Guérard, secretary general of the Vichy government. Judged in absentia in 1947.

287. N.S.K.K. Nazionalsozialistisches Kraftfahrer-Korps. Association of National Socialist Truck Drivers.

288. P.P.F. Parti Populaire Français. Founded in June 1936 by Jacques Doriot and other Communist dissidents. In 1937 the party moved toward fascism, advocating an anti-Communist "front for freedom." Of all the French parties of the extreme right, the P.P.F. was closest to fascism in ideology and structure.

290. F.T.P. Francs Tireurs et Partisans. Under the Occupation, an underground resistance group under strong Communist influence. In 1944, incorporated with the F.F.I.

295. CHABANAIS. The most luxurious and perhaps the most celebrated of Paris brothels, on the rue Chabanais in the Opéra quarter. Like all other French brothels, closed in 1946.

300. ROBERT KEMP (1879–1959). Eminent French literary and dramatic critic. Drama critic on *Le Monde* from 1944 until the time of his death.

300. FUALDÈS (1751–1817). French magistrate assassinated in 1817. An accomplice of the assassins played the barrel organ outside the ill-famed hotel to which he had been lured, in order to drown out his cries. The incident was the theme of a mournful popular song.

308. NAVACHINE and the ROSELLI BROTHERS (see above). The murder of the Russian economist Navachine and of the Roselli Brothers, Italian anti-fascist refugees in France, was attributed to the Cagoule.

315. LALIQUE MÉTRO. The first entrances to the Paris Métro were not designed by René Lalique but by another modern-style artist, the architect Hector Guimard (1867–1934).

316. VERMERSH. Jeannette Vermeersch, born 1910. Textile worker. Communist deputy from the department of the Seine. Widow of Maurice Thorez, secretary of the French Communist party.

320. POELCAPELLE. Town in Flanders where Céline was severely wounded in the head and arm in November, 1914, receiving the médaille militaire for his heroism. As a result of this wound he was trepanned and accorded 75% invalid status.

337. ONE OF THEM JUMPED OUT OF THE WINDOW. Allusion to the death of Pierre Brossolette (1903–1944), a resistance member who jumped from the sixth story of a building used by the Gestapo in Paris to avoid talking under torture. Historian and Socialist deputy, Brossolette was an adviser to de Gaulle in London. He was several times parachuted into France.

339. HENRY. Hubert-Joseph Henry, French officer (1846–1898). Accused of having forged a letter, dated October 1896, from the Italian military attaché to his German counterpart, compromising Dreyfus. Arrested, he committed suicide in his cell at Mont-Valérien.

SELECTED DALKEY ARCHIVE PAPERBACKS

FOR A FULL LIST OF PUBLICATIONS, VISIT:
www.dalkeyarchive.com

SELECTED DALKEY ARCHIVE PAPERBACKS

FOR A FULL LIST OF PUBLICATIONS, VISIT:
www.dalkeyarchive.com

Printed in the USA
CPSIA information can be obtained
at www.ICGtesting.com
JSHW082150140824
68134JS00014B/153